FROM THE PAGES OF
THE METAMORPHOSES

My mind is bent to tell of bodies changed into new forms. O gods, for you yourselves have wrought the changes, breathe on these my undertakings, and bring down my song in unbroken strains from the world's very beginning even unto the present time.

(Book I; page 3)

Thus had Narcissus mocked her, thus had he mocked other nymphs of the waves or mountains; thus had he mocked the companies of men. At last one of these scorned youth, lifting up his hands to heaven, prayed: "So may he himself love, and not gain the thing he loves!" (Book III; page 55)

"Keep the marks of our death and always bear your fruit of a dark color, meet for mourning, as a memorial of our double death."

(Book IV; page 68)

At length, finding himself unequal in strength—for who would be a match in strength for Atlas?—he said: "Well, since so small a favor you will not grant to me, let me give you a gift"; and, himself turning his back, he held out from his left hand the ghastly Medusa-head. (Book IV; page 80)

At once her hair, touched by the poison, fell off, and with it both nose and ears; and the head shrank up; her whole body also was diminished; the slender fingers clung to her side as legs; the rest was belly. Still from this she ever spins a thread; and now, as a spider, she exercises her old-time weaver's art.

(Book VI; page 106)

"Ah, if I could, I should be more myself. But some strange power holds me down against my will. Desire persuades me one way, reason another. I see the better and approve it, but I follow the worse."

(Book VII; page 122)

The scorching rays of the nearer sun softened the fragrant wax which held his wings. The wax melted; his arms were bare as he beat them up and down, but, lacking wings, they took no hold on the air. His lips, calling to the last upon his father's name, were drowned in the dark blue sea. (Book VIII; page 149)

"Be brave against timorous creatures," she says; "but against bold creatures boldness is not safe. Do not be rash, dear boy, at my risk; and do not provoke those beasts which nature has well armed."

(Book X; page 200)

The mourning birds wept for you, Orpheus, the throng of beasts, the flinty rocks, and the trees which had so often gathered to your songs; yes, the trees shed their leaves as if so tearing their hair in grief for you. (Book XI; page 207)

"In these bodies of ours the heart is of more value than the hand; all our real living is in that." (Book XIII; page 252)

Scylla infests the right-hand coast, unresting Charybdis the left. The one sucks down and vomits forth again the ships she has caught; the other's uncanny waist is girt with ravening dogs. She has a virgin's face and, if all the tales of poets are not false, she was herself once a virgin. Many suitors sought her; but she scorned them all.

(Book XIII; page 261)

"So long as we fear worse fortunes, we lie open to wounds; but when the worst possible lot has fallen, then is fear beneath our feet and the utmost misfortune can bring us no further care."

(Book XIV; page 279)

"Our souls are deathless, and ever, when they have left their former seat, do they live in new abodes and dwell in the bodies that have received them." (Book XV; page 293)

THE METAMORPHOSES

OVID

Translated by Frank Justus Miller

*Edited with an Introduction and Notes
by Robert Squillace*

GEORGE STADE

CONSULTING EDITORIAL DIRECTOR

BARNES & NOBLE CLASSICS

NEW YORK

♫ℬ
Barnes & Noble Classics
New York

Published by Barnes & Noble Books
122 Fifth Avenue
New York, NY 10011

www.barnesandnoble.com/classics

Ovid's *Metamorphoses* is thought to have been completed around 8 A.D.
The present text is a revision of Frank Justus Miller's English translation that was
originally published in 1916 by G. P. Putnam's Sons. This edition's maps are taken
from *An Atlas of Antient Geography* by Samuel Butler,
published by Lea & Blanchard in 1851.

Published in 2005 by Barnes & Noble Classics with new Introduction, Notes,
Biography, Chronology, Note on the Translation, Who's Who, Inspired By,
Comments & Questions, and For Further Reading.

Introduction, Notes, A Note on the Translation,
Who's Who in *The Metamorphoses*, and For Further Reading
Copyright © 2005 by Robert Squillace.

Note on Ovid, The World of Ovid and *The Metamorphoses*,
Inspired by *The Metamorphoses*, and Comments & Questions
Copyright © 2005 by Barnes & Noble, Inc.

The Metamorphoses
ISBN-13: 978-1-59308-276-5
ISBN-10: 1-59308-276-2
LC Control Number 2004116679

Produced and published in conjunction with
Fine Creative Media, Inc.
322 Eighth Avenue
New York, NY 10001

Michael J. Fine, President and Publisher

Printed in the United States of America
QM
9   10   8

OVID

A master's master who influenced Chaucer, Milton, Dante, Shakespeare, Goethe, and countless others, the poet we call Ovid (his full name was Publius Ovidius Naso) was born in 43 B.C.E. in the town of Sulmo, 90 miles east of Rome. The Roman republic had recently fallen; the city marked the first anniversary of Caesar's assassination just days before Ovid's birth. By the time the future poet was twelve years old, Octavian had defeated Mark Antony and Cleopatra, and within another four years had assumed the title Augustus Caesar and become emperor of the entire Roman world.

Ovid grew up in a prosperous family who planned a traditional career in law or politics for their son, and educated him accordingly. With his natural brilliance and love of language, he excelled in the art of rhetoric. Private tutoring, followed by instruction in Rome and a grand tour of the Mediterranean, groomed him for a successful career as a judge; for a time he held some minor judicial posts but soon abandoned such work in order to write poetry.

His first work, *Amores* (*The Book of Love*), probably begun when he was still a young man, was published in 22 B.C.E.; Ovid's witty epigrams and tongue-in-cheek advice for lovers reveal his broad learning. A fertile creative period followed: *Heroides* (*Heroines*), the lost tragedy *Medea*, *Ars Amatoria* (*The Art of Love*), and *Fasti* (*Calendar*) all appeared between 15 B.C.E. and 8 C.E.

Ovid completed his masterpiece, the *Metamorphoses*, around 8 C.E., just before his life changed irrevocably. That same year the emperor Augustus, reputedly outraged by the explicitly erotic *Ars Amatoria* and an undisclosed political transgression, banished Rome's most celebrated poet to Tomis (now Constanta, Romania), near the Black Sea. Ovid spent his final ten years lonely and unhappy in the small inclement town. His last works—*Tristia* (*Sorrows*) and *Epistulae ex Ponto* (*Letters from the Black Sea*)—detail his unhappiness but show no diminution of his talent. Unable to secure a return to Rome, Ovid died in Tomis in 17 C.E.

TABLE OF CONTENTS

THE WORLD OF OVID AND THE
METAMORPHOSES

43–22 B.C.E.	In the town of Sulmo (now Sulmona), some 90 miles east of Rome, Publius Ovidius Naso, whom we know as Ovid, is born on March 20 in 43 B.C.E., shortly after the first anniversary of the murder of Julius Caesar. Ovid's prosperous family educates him with a private tutor, followed by instruction in Rome and abroad. He receives rigorous training in rhetoric, which gives him a foundation to study law or enter politics; his native gift for language makes him an excellent public speaker. Ovid's father wants him to play a role in public life; for a time he holds some minor judicial posts, but he soon turns away from such work in order to write poetry.
39–38	The poet Virgil, a generation older than Ovid, begins publication of his pastoral *Eclogues*.
c.35	A Roman copy is produced of the sculpture *Laocoön and His Sons* (now at the Vatican Museum; the original was lost c.150 B.C.E.) depicting a scene that later will be described in Virgil's *Aeneid*, in which Laocoon and his sons battle two large sea serpents.
31	Julius Caesar's grand-nephew and adopted son, Octavian, defeats Mark Antony and Cleopatra at the battle of Actium.
30	Horace publishes the *Epodes*, warnings and exhortations to the Roman people.
29	Virgil publishes the *Georgics*, four books on farming and rural life.
27	Octavian receives the title Augustus Caesar and becomes emperor.
23	The first three books of Horace's *Odes* appear.
22	Ovid publishes his first work, *Amores* (*The Book of Love*); written in couplets, it gives witty advice on conducting love affairs. (The dates of Ovid's works are uncertain, roughly

	determined from allusions to contemporary historical events.)
19	Virgil's *Aeneid* is published soon after the poet's death; the twelve-book epic recounts the journey by the Trojan hero Aeneas that ends in the founding of Rome.
15	Ovid publishes the first series of *Heroides* (*Heroines*), responses by the eminent women of mythology to events recounted in the ancient epics. Around this time he writes the dramatic tragedy *Medea*, which has been lost.
12–7	The third book of *Amores* is published, along with a reissue of books 1 and 2.
7	Horace dies. Augustus divides Rome into fourteen wards.
2 B.C.E.– **2 C.E**	Ovid publishes the satirical *Ars Amatoria* (*The Art of Love*), on the art of courtship and romantic intrigue, and *Remedia Amoris* (*The Remedies of Love*), advice on how to extricate oneself from a love affair. The erotic content of *Ars Amatoria* may be seen by the emperor Augustus as a challenge to moral reforms he advocates and thus may be one reason he will later send Ovid into exile. The second, expanded series of the *Heroides* is published.
8 C.E.	Ovid completes the seamless narrative of the *Metamorphoses* in fifteen volumes. He also finishes the *Fasti* (*Calendar*), which tells mythological, religious, and historical stories within the framework of the Roman calendar; only the first six books (January–June) survive.
8	Augustus exiles Ovid, Rome's most celebrated poet, to Tomis (now Constanta, Romania), near the Black Sea. In addition to the Emperor's displeasure with the sexual content of *Ars Amatoria*, Ovid may have been exiled because he committed a political indiscretion.
9–12	*Tristia* (*Sorrows*) expresses Ovid's bitter, mournful reaction to his exile.
13–16	His *Epistulae ex Ponto* (*Letters from the Black Sea*) continues the themes he developed in *Tristia*.
14	Augustus dies.
17	Ovid dies in Tomis, having never been allowed to return to Rome.

INTRODUCTION

Order, Power, and Poetry

That Publius Ovidius Naso (43 B.C.E.–17 C.E.), familiarly known as Ovid, wrote the epic *Metamorphoses* (8 C.E.) at all may be as surprising as anything in the poem itself, filled with miraculous transformations though it is; indeed, the work constitutes a startling metamorphosis of the epic genre itself. It came virtually from nowhere. Ovid's earlier work had dealt almost exclusively with love in the witty manner of Roman elegy, a genre devoted not primarily to remembrance of the dead, as in later eras, but to the expression of any intensely personal emotions, or even of political commentary. The titles of Ovid's elegiac books indicate their matter: *Amores* (first two books, 22–21 B.C.E., reissued with third book 12–7 B.C.E), *Ars Amatoria* (2 B.C.E–2 C.E.), *Remedia Amoris* (2 B.C.E.–2 C.E.)—in effect, *The Book of Love, The Art of Love,* and *The Remedies of Love.* Ovid had even written a poem about makeup, *Medicamina Faciei* (*Cosmetics for the Female Face*), which, alas, has been only partially preserved. None of these poems tell extended stories about mythic characters in the manner of epic. Before the *Metamorphoses,* in fact, Ovid's narrative output consisted of a single play, the lost tragedy *Medea* (probably written between the first and second publication of *Amores*), and a work belonging to the Hellenistic genre known as epyllion, the *Heroides* (15 B.C.E.; expanded 2 B.C.E–2 C.E.), a series of invented letters from mythic heroines to their absent lovers. The *Heroides* consists of short, intense, often very personal responses by such women as Penelope and Dido to incidents found in the epic tradition, but it assumes the reader's prior knowledge of these tales. The events to which the correspondent responds (in first person) are not even included in the text, let alone narrated in the lofty epic style. One can hardly take *Medea* or the *Heroides*, then, as harbingers of the *Metamorphoses*. Indeed, Ovid began the *Amores* with an image (borrowed from the third-century B.C.E. Hellenistic Greek poet Callimachus) in which Cupid intervenes to prevent the author from embarking on an epic poem. As Ovid tells it, the god of love steals the final metrical foot of the second line of his verse to lame any epic ambitions he might have: Epic poetry was written in hexameter lines (six feet per line), while elegies were composed in distichs (paired lines—in this case, a line six feet in length followed by a line of five feet). If a poet cannot reach the end of his second line in epic style, what promise of ever attempting the genre does he offer?

If the fact that Ovid composed an epic at all is surprising, that the epic he composed was like no other is not. Inspired by the structure of loosely linked tales pioneered in Callimachus' lost elegy *Aitia*—which, however, not only was written in elegiac distichs but, at four books, was hardly of epic length—Ovid rejects much of what had previously seemed the defining characteristics of the genre. Such foundational texts as the *Iliad*, the *Odyssey*, and the *Aeneid* unfold their narratives with utter chronological clarity, defining before and after, cause and consequence, in unmistakable terms. The stories may flash back and forward in time, but they can do so without producing the least confusion because the chronology of the events between which they move and the logic of their connection to each other is so firmly and explicitly established. There is never any doubt, for instance, that Ulysses (Odysseus to the Greeks) arrives on the island of Phaeacia after and as a result of his sojourn in the land of the dead. Ovid, by contrast, continually muddies the temporal relations between the various tales he recounts, with narrators who themselves belong to a vaguely defined past setting the tales they tell in an even more indefinite time that came before them. His transitions between tales flaunt the absence of any causal link; if a character comes to an end in Thrace, the next episode might begin with an unrelated character who happens to be passing through that province at more or less the same time. The previous landmarks of the epic genre scrupulously maintained narrative unity, so carefully marking the parameters of the story—what did and did not advance it toward the resolution of its central problem—that they could safely digress without threatening that narrative line. That is, no digression—whether Homer's long description of the shield Hephaestus forges for Achilles or Virgil's account of Nisus and Euryalus—could be mistaken for anything but a digression, rather than a serious division of narrative interest. But the *Metamorphoses* is all digression, with no one character, theme, or issue unifying the whole except the motif of transformation itself. Critics have some-times discerned a central issue in the poem, but it is rarely the same one that others have purported to find. Indeed, the absence of the sort of central character always found in previous epics, an individual on whose fate the tale concentrates its energies, virtually rules out narrative unity. The *Iliad* may not culminate in a resounding event—both the death of Achilles and the fall of Troy occur beyond the horizon of the poem's end—but the humanization of Achilles before Priam's grief mutes the brooding hero's rage, which the first line of the poem had identified as the work's theme. While some di-vinities reappear with relative frequency throughout the 250 stories that make up the *Metamorphoses*, no god or human provides any such sense of centrality.

Having somehow gotten itself written, the *Metamorphoses* might have flickered back out of existence almost at once; Ovid was exiled by the emperor Augustus from Rome to the Black Sea city of Tomis on what was then the fringe of the Roman empire in the very year his epic appeared. All the poet's works were banned from Roman public libraries, an important means of the distribution and preser-vation of manuscripts. Evidently, Ovid maintained sufficient popu-larity among private collectors for the majority of his poems to survive the Augustan sentence, but a close examination of the un-equal conflict between the poet and the emperor ultimately illumi-nates the nature of Ovid's challenge to the traditions of the epic genre, even though the events leading to the poet's exile are myste-rious. The reason for the banishment given by the emperor, who was rather strait-laced about other people's sexual lives, was that the *Ars Amatoria* encouraged (female) adultery. Few classicists lend this ex-planation much credence, though; after all, the poem had already been in circulation for at least six years before sentence was passed. In the works he wrote in exile (chiefly *Tristia* [*Sorrows*], which ap-peared between 9 and 12 C.E., and *Epistulae ex Ponto* [*Letters from Pontus* (*The Black Sea*)], 13–16 C.E.), Ovid mentions his offensive poetry as a factor in his exile, but he also hints somewhat obscurely that what he, at least, considered a minor political transgression resulted in a disproportionately harsh sentence that the emperor or his successor might one day reasonably commute. (It never happened; having pinned his hopes to the rise of the urbane Germanicus, Ovid gained little favor when hard-edged Tiberius wound up succeeding Augustus upon his death in 14 C.E.) His various descriptions of this political *error* ("mistake") or *peccatum* ("wrong"), like frosted glass, obscure all but the vague outline of the reality lying behind them. In any case, since the poet hoped openly for a revocation of his punishment, it is hard to gauge the degree of honesty with which he chose to couch his defense, particularly given how elusive and ambiguous his statements tend to be under even the best circumstances—when Ovid affects sincerity, he is often his most ironic.

It is unlikely that any evidence will ever be produced to establish what specific incidents, if any, prompted Augustus to banish his city's leading poet. But the fundamental opposition between their outlooks, regardless of how it manifested itself in action, is clear enough without recourse to any historical detective work. In particular, each envisioned the idea of order in an entirely different way, a disparity that parallels the manner in which Ovid reorganized the genre of epic in opposition to his poetic forebears. This distinction is not simple. To identify Augustus with repressive, totalitarian control and Ovid with anarchic subversion of all authority, poetic as well as political, would caricature their positions. Augustan order, though it concentrated a good deal of power in the hands of a single man, was a surprisingly informal affair, resting as much on recognition of the emperor's personal precedence as it did on any statutory definition of his precise governmental role. The senate, supreme governing body of the old Roman republic, continued to meet for generations, though its role and influence, in any case greatly restricted by the powers concentrated in the emperor's person, differed from one regime to the next. Augustus himself preferred to be addressed as *princeps* (roughly, first citizen) rather than *imperator* (emperor). Nor, contrary to the impression left by a number of Hollywood sword-and-sandal epics, did the empire curtail rights enjoyed by ordinary citizens under the republic; indeed, the imperial era saw a rapid extension of Roman citizenship to masses of non-Italian peoples, and a relative improvement in the still-miserable conditions of slave life (though such trends were not yet necessarily evident in Ovid's lifetime).

But the purpose of Augustan order, to mitigate or even suppress the danger personal desire poses to the smooth conduct of public life, sorts very ill with the themes of Ovidian poetry. The *Metamorphoses* in particular not only identifies desire as the sovereign power of the universe, but does so within the framework of a genre, epic, traditionally used to celebrate the triumph of "masculine" restraint over "feminine" desire; he thus implicitly challenges the imperial and epic visions simultaneously. Achilles, after all, achieves his moment of enlightened maturity in the final book of the *Iliad* when he relinquishes the wrath with which his passions—for Briseis, his war-prize, and for his companion/lover, Patroclus—fill his human breast; his Trojan rival, Hector, rejects the feminine even more explicitly, putting aside his wife's fear in order to give his life for his city. In Homer's other epic, Odysseus must keep himself in check and coolly plot the demise of the suitors who consume his household, hiding not only his feelings, but even his own identity. Indeed, Augustus had helped confirm for his own generation the value of heroic conquest over selfish passions by commissioning Virgil's *Aeneid*, the protagonist of which must abandon his lover (to her death) at the behest of the gods, the foundation of Rome itself depending on his compliance. Both Virgil and Augustus, after all, had endured the violent chaos of the Roman Civil Wars, which had ended when Ovid was still a child. The endorsement of masculine suppression of feeling was far more ambiguous in these earlier epics than ancient commentators tended to assume, but the mere fact they were capable of being mistaken for such celebrations of martial valor allowed them actually to be used to support the social dissemination of such values.

The *Metamorphoses*, which avoids narrating the heroic exploits even of those martial figures it does depict (Hercules, Theseus, Aeneas, and so forth), declares its suspicion of the power of restraint, and even of power itself, virtually from its beginning. Ovid's extremely influential vision of the Golden Age—Shakespeare echoes it in Gonzalo's famous speech about humanity's natural innocence in act 2, scene 1 of *The Tempest*, and Camões virtually quotes it as an old man's unheeded anti-imperial plea in the *Lusiads*—identifies human bliss with the absence of any structures of control: "There was no fear of punishment, no threatening words were to be read on brazen tablets; no suppliant throng gazed fearfully upon its judge's face; but without judges lived secure" (p. 5). Indeed, the exertion of power over the unwilling earth to make it bring forth crops, metals, and precious stones—the defining elements of civilization—is pictured as a kind of rape, the first of many images of enforced domination in a rape-haunted text. Moreover, Jupiter, to whom Augustus is compared on several occasions in an ostensibly flattering manner, has express responsibility for the introduction of seasonal change, tellingly imagined by Ovid not as the imposition of order for human benefit by a god devoted to humanity, as in the Bible's book of Genesis—"While the earth remaineth, seed-time and harvest, and cold and heat, and summer and winter, and day and night shall not cease" (8:22), God promises Noah after the flood—but as a draconian curtailing of the eternal summer that had theretofore blessed human beings. In the *Metamorphoses*, creation itself does not resume after Jupiter's vengeful flood by clear and orderly divine plan, but from the merciful endurance of primal chaos, of the disorderly union of opposites that endures even at the root of order: "For when moisture and heat unite, life is conceived, and from these two sources all living things spring. And, though fire and water are naturally at enmity, still heat and moisture produce all things, and this inharmonious harmony is fitted to the growth of life" (pp. 13–14). The first tale following the water's recession and the re-creation of humanity confirms the primacy of desire. Apollo, the god of rationality and daylight, foolishly boasts that the martial power of his arrows surpasses the gentle shafts of Cupid, only to be stricken by the son of Venus with an unquenchable lust for the horrified Daphne. His pursuit of her may not end in the literal rape that concludes so many other tales, but the outcome nonetheless suggests that power is actually exerted, not for public benefit or in self-restraint, but in order to forcibly dominate the desired object: The leaves of the laurel tree into which Daphne has been unwillingly transformed (she had prayed for escape through the loss of her beauty, but that beauty is all her transformation preserves) become symbols of conquest: "With you shall Roman generals wreathe their heads, when shouts of joy shall acclaim their triumph, and long processions climb the Capitol. You at Augustus' portals shall stand a trusty guardian, and keep watch over the civic crown of oak which hangs between" (p. 17). Gentler rebukes of the epic spirit also abound in the *Metamorphoses'* carnivalesque inversion of many of its own genre's conventions, as when Ovid parodies the epic list—a famous example is the litany of the Greek ships that sailed to reclaim Helen in the *Iliad*—by detailing the name, parentage, and illustrious feats of each of Actaeon's dogs. Perhaps the only narrative poet funnier than Ovid is Chaucer, and all clowns implicitly deride the sort of *dignitas* ("worth," "merit") and *auctoritas* ("responsibility," "power") on which Augustan order was founded.

Despite his exile from Rome in the year of his poem's publication—Ovid later insisted that the work had not been fully completed and that he had burned the original in despair, though this claim so closely mimes the fate of the genuinely unfinished *Aeneid* that one doubts Ovid's veracity—the *Metamorphoses* endured and even flourished. Indeed, its versions of the myths it recounts became their standard Western forms, largely due to their wide dispersal throughout Europe in, of all places, the monastic libraries of the Middle Ages, and their subsequent dissemination in printed form throughout the early modern or "Renaissance" years. Medieval commentators found ways to accommodate Ovid's appealing distrust of earthly power to Christian morality, often transcribing his epic along with interpretive commentary to guide the reader who might be confused by the poem's evident pagan sensuality; these manuscripts, known as the *Ovide moralisé* ("moralized Ovid"), spread the Ovidian stories across time and space to Dante and Chaucer. The resurgent classicism of following years embraced Ovid less as moralist than as poet; Shakespeare almost certainly learned the technique of his soliloquies from the interior monologues of the Latin poet, and images from the *Metamorphoses* stocked the canvases of innumerable artists, who could trust their patrons to recognize even what are now the epic's least familiar episodes. The vigor, humor, and invention of the poem, in fact, appealed to all audiences until the Romantic revolution in taste at the end of the eighteenth century, when the *Metamorphoses* began to fall into some neglect, its arbitrary and idiosyncratic transitions from tale to tale answering poorly to the Romantic demand for organic unity—once again, Ovid had run afoul of the demand for order. Romantic canons of aesthetic value informed critical judgments until very recently, so that the renewal of academic attention the poem received in the 1990s rivaled or exceeded any of the past century.

From today's perspective, Ovid stands almost precisely at the midpoint of literary history; the preservation of language in Egyptian hieroglyphics and Mesopotamian cuneiform began about as many centuries before his lifetime as he himself lived before the era of e-texts and digital printing. While the dating of past history was certainly less precise in Roman times than it is now, from his own vantage point Ovid could see that centuries of written tradition preceded him; indeed, an allusive engagement with previous poetry already marked his Hellenistic forebears. More than any of his other works, the *Metamorphoses* expresses Ovid's acute sense of the massive accumulation of history and legend, attempting as it does to "bring down [its] song in unbroken strains from the world's very beginning even unto the present time" (p. 3). Moreover, the poem is shaped to induce in its readers an experience of peering down vertiginous historical depths. Just as modern works on the history of Earth often note that the arrival of humanity on the planet would correspond, on a twenty-four-hour clock, to just a minute or two before midnight, so Ovid's poem sets foot on the mainland of Italy only in the fourteenth of its fifteen books; further, this epic of universal history reaches the events of Ovid's own lifetime just sixty lines before the end of its final book. Indeed, the poet's consciousness of time would be impossible had centuries of written records not been available to him. When, again in book XV, Ovid has the pre-Socratic philosopher Pythagoras base his perception of the eternal flux of existence on a myriad of such facts as the changing courses of rivers, the erosion of peninsulas into islands, and the gradual decline of once-mighty cities into barren plains, the poet assumes a world in which the permanence of writing makes it possible to know intimately the enormous distance between past and present by the comparison of what is to what texts say had once been.

In singing the tale of ceaseless change, of course, Ovid implicitly raises the question of his own relevance to readers of a later time. Over the nearly 2,000 years since the appearance of the *Metamorphoses*, the plan of the poem itself inspires one to ask whether the ceaseless flow of cultural change has left Ovid's magnum opus a bare and sterile field, fit only to furnish material for a kind of archaeological study of what poetry no longer is, to serve as a morgue of dead men's tales? Can a readership so distant from Augustan Rome embrace a work so dependent on its reader's intimacy with Greco-Roman myth—with the life of Hercules, the travels of the Argonauts, the course of the Trojan War, the adulteries of Jupiter, and many other stories far less familiar than these to a modern audience—that it often alludes only by the slightest gesture, the verbal equivalent of a raised eyebrow, to the main features of these tales, concentrating instead on the microscopic details of what even for Romans were generally their lesser-known episodes?

While the *Metamorphoses* may demand more work from a modern reader and more annotation from an editor than a self-contained narrative like the *Odyssey*, in other ways—compared to, say, Homer or Hesiod—Ovid stands almost in our midst. The authors of the Greek epics, like the anonymous creators of the Egyptian *Book of the Dead* or the ancient Near Eastern epic *Gilgamesh*, lived in a world where the transmission of stories occurred primarily by word of mouth, and such written texts as did exist primarily served the needs of public performance. Even for the playwrights and philosophers of the Athenian "golden age" of the fifth century B.C.E., the idea of reading a text to oneself was at best peculiar and at worst intellectually suspect—Plato in particular thought writing a poor alternative to speech, which sharpened the memory and allowed for a logical exchange of ideas, rather than the mere repetition of the writer's words in the reader's mouth. But Ovid was a writer in something much closer to the modern sense, composing and revising his works with an eye to their reception by a literate audience of private readers—indeed, Ovid is one of the earliest writers explicitly to imagine his work being read by women as well as men. Removing the distribution of stories from the public realm, in fact, made them far more available to women, who were often consigned to purely private lives (similarly, many centuries later the rise of the novel, the genre most devoted to the domestic realm, owes itself both to women readers and women writers). Indeed, Roman practices of book distribution are similar enough to ours that classicists commonly refer to the "publication" of works during this period. The subjects of the Roman empire did not purchase books from stores, but volumens (scrolls) or codices (unbound sheets) from professional copyists; or, more likely, they read them in libraries. Regardless, they consumed them privately, as we do now.

Being a writer rather than a storyteller and being all the more aware of the context of written discourse because it had developed in the very recent past, Ovid draws remarkably close to the present world in his central themes, concerns, and method of narration. We, too, live in a world where consciousness of ceaseless change is inescapable. Indeed, such a state of uncertainty has often been thought to define the modern condition. Everything old is new again; Ovid not only perceives the instability of all relations and structures (whether social or natural), he also recognizes that the widespread presence and preservation of the past tends to blur the distinction between past and present. Looking backward through contemporary eyes, we too cannot help imagining the past as a version of the present, however much clothes and customs may differ; even the most scrupulously accurate historical novel will necessarily be written in the language of its present readers. Conversely, the sort of culture an historical consciousness produces will perceive the present as the outcome of decisions, precedents, and circumstances hundreds or even thousands of years past. Fashion models, supposedly the most modish creatures, are frequently styled to allude to the look of Marilyn Monroe, of Louise Brooks, or even of Nefertiti, whose famous bust, found in an Egyptian tomb of around 1340 B.C.E., inspired a recent L'Oreal ad. In the same way, the *Metamorphoses* continually, often playfully, confuses past and present; even though Pythagoras lived before Sparta and Athens had attained the full heights of their power, Ovid has the philosopher speak of them from the perspective of Ovid himself, as cities long declined—though at the same time Pythagoras correctly cites Rome as a city still in its infancy. Further, the natural though unstated conclusion of his analysis of the rise and fall of empires is that Rome, too, will decline: The present is always itself passing into history. Indeed, Ovid tends to describe the most distant worlds of gods and humans in terms and images immediately familiar to his Roman contemporaries, dressing all time in the toga.

Further, though purporting to sing a universal history, Ovid rarely differentiates between myth and fact, and he leaves the precise chronology of his epic extremely vague. (Literal belief in the miraculous transformations Ovid narrates was hardly common in advanced Roman thought; in the *Metamorphoses* itself, Ovid winkingly allows Pythagoras to dismiss "shades and empty names, the stuff that poets manufacture, and their fabled sufferings of a world that never was" (p. 293). While one can, with tolerably close attention, discern the succession of large, loose gatherings of tales that form the work's limber spine—which are, in order, creation and its aftermath, the tragedies of the house of Cadmus, the triumphs of Perseus, human challenges to the gods, the journey of the Argonauts and the age of Minos, the songs of Orpheus, the Trojan saga, and the rise of Rome—within or attached to each section are tales whose relation to the overall time frame is completely unintelligible. Such tactics throw readers searching for conventional narrative coherence off their bearings, entangling them in story-threads the logical relation between which the author seems never to indicate; the *Metamorphoses* offers no sequential unfolding of a unified response to a clearly defined problem, no rising action, no climax. Works demanding such prolonged interpretive attention, works assuming so developed a historical consciousness, emerge only from an age of self-conscious literacy like Ovid's, like our own. Indeed, self-consciousness is one of the work's central concerns. Unlike any previous epic, Ovid's records at length the thoughts and emotions occurring inside its characters (especially the women, more associated by the ancients with interiors of every kind—womb, home, and mind). Usually, the drama of exterior events is secondary to this play of internal response. Reading a tale in the *Metamorphoses* may thus feel more like reading a modern psychologized novel than like reading Homer or Virgil.

Since Ovid's poem does not conform to the expectations created by epics, like Homer's, that arise directly from oral storytelling traditions, it is tempting to dismiss its epic aspirations altogether and regard it simply as a massive anthology of Greco-Roman myth. Such a reading, however, neglects both the frequent thematic interplay between tales, particularly within one of the loose narrative frameworks such as the Trojan War story, and the scrupulously respected requirement, apparently arbitrary and self-imposed though it may be, that every tale concern or conclude with a bodily transformation, a metamorphosis. The thematic interplay prevents the experience of reading the poem from becoming unpleasantly disorienting; even if the path one follows seems, like history itself, to lead in no particular direction, one's local surroundings at any point along it remain reassuringly coherent. The unity of subject matter, meanwhile, lends the work as a whole a depth of significance that no chance collection of tales could ever display.

A few examples should suffice to demonstrate the way Ovid attaches a group of tales like spokes to the hub of an implicit thematic center, giving sections of the poem a book or more in length the concentrated suggestiveness of a first-rate short story. Perhaps the most obvious such concatenation is the tale of Cadmus, the king and founder of Thebes, and his doomed grandchildren, Actaeon, Semele, and Pentheus, which is nearly coterminous with book III. Characteristically, the sequence most tellingly reveals its thematic coherence when its story line seems most digressive: In the midst of narrating the disasters of the Theban royal house, Ovid pauses for 171 lines to elaborate on the fate of Narcissus, whose only apparent connection to book III's central events is that the prophet Tiresias once foretold his doom, as he also would in the case of Pentheus. Ovid turns the youth's rejection of Echo in favor of his own reflection into a dazzling tragicomic commentary on the problematic nature of self and other. First, by carefully specifying the age of Narcissus as sixteen, Ovid associates the youth's peculiar fate with the dawning of a self-consciousness (amounting almost to self-obsession) that is a near-universal fact of adolescence; indeed, Ovid's Narcissus is the eternal adolescent, a figure more broadly parodied later in the poem's account of the Cyclops Polyphemus' attempt to make himself presentable enough to win the nymph Galatea (book XIII) by combing his hair (with a rake) and primping for the first time. The curse of self-love alights on Narcissus, in fact, from the mouth of a rejected male suitor, by the addition of whom to the traditional story Ovid suggests that what the youth spurns is not Echo per se (she is herself an image of another adolescent response to self-consciousness: a complete submergence of self in other), but any contact outside the circle of himself. For Ovid's Narcissus makes no mistake about the identity of his beloved; the poet boldly allows him to recognize unequivocally that he is besotted with his own reflection. Indeed, the youth's idea of love itself is pure reflectivity. What he adores so much about the image in the pool is not merely its beauty, but the manner in which it mimics his own actions and feelings, thus erasing any division between subject and object, self and other. How many teenagers, after all, have dreamed of a lover whose every feeling, impulse, and desire would mirror their own in a frictionless unity? Indeed, the often very young writers of the early nineteenth century's Romantic era would frequently dally with the theme of sibling incest, perceiving a sympathetic identity of mind as the definition of love.

That the blind prophet Tiresias should be the one to foretell the doom of Narcissus is more than a convenient way to link the tale of self-transfixed youth to the story of the demise of the Theban royal house (the inevitable doom of which, like that of the line of Atreus in Aeschylus' *Oresteia* or the heritage of Oedipus in Sophocles' plays, provides an image of inherent human limitations). By detailing the manner in which Tiresias received his prophetic gifts, Ovid establishes him as the precise opposite of Narcissus; while the youth cannot accept the advances of man or woman, the old seer has lived and made love as both. His transgendered experience—separating a pair of copulating snakes in the woods, he becomes a woman for seven years, only to be reconverted to masculinity when he repeats the action—allows Tiresias a unique knowledge of both self and other, particularly across the gulf of gender. Since he is literally a unique figure in this respect, he establishes by contrast the incapacity of the rest of sentient creation to know the other—indeed, Ovid himself, for all his interest in and sympathy toward women, proves unable to regard them in such tales as the transgendering of Hermaphroditus (book IV) and the transformation of Iphis (book IX) as anything but non-men; Ovid imagines womanliness as a simple negation or absence of masculine qualities rather than as a full-fledged state of being in itself. Nor do even Jupiter and Juno have any more intimate a knowledge of what it is like not to be themselves than any ordinary human, despite their divine talent for imposture, for changing themselves into outwardly other forms; they must ask Tiresias to tell them whether men or women have more pleasure in sex. His answer (women—a typically classical response, since submission to sexual desire was generally considered a weakness and women the weaker sex) seems less the point than the result of giving one at all: He is stricken blind (by Juno) and given the compensatory gift of prophecy (by Jupiter), which suggests that his prophetic power is essentially identical to his simultaneous knowledge of self and other, his loss of outward sight emphasizing his inner vision.

The tales of Actaeon, Semele, and Pentheus, while obviously connected by the fact that the three leading characters are first cousins and by the death each suffers for seeing what he or she ought not to have seen, draw into an even tighter thematic orbit because Ovid has inserted the examples of Tiresias and Narcissus at their center. Indeed, by raising the question of whether Diana's punishment of Actaeon was or was not just without providing an answer, Ovid encourages readers to look outside the tale itself in order to understand what significance the hunter's death might have. When we read about it in the context of the stories of Tiresias and Narcissus, it seems clear that, being torn apart for observing the naked body of the goddess of chastity and childbirth (the primary achievements for which women might uniquely receive credit in the ancient world), Actaeon provides another example of the unknowability (particularly the sexual unknowability) of the other (particularly the other gender). The point emerges even more clearly through Ovid's choice to pair Actaeon's story with that of Semele. Immolated when a disguised Juno tricks her into asking Jupiter, god of thunder and lightning, to make love to her in his full divinity as he does with Juno herself, Semele provides the female counterpart to Actaeon; that even the king of Olympus cannot revoke the favor he unthinkingly grants his human mistress before he has learned its nature suggests that the ruinous incapacity of males and females to know each other fully in matters of desire and bodily experience is written into the way of things, inalterable even by the world's ostensible master. Further, the tale of Pentheus at the end of book III acts as a bookend with that of Actaeon, both young men being torn apart by or at the behest of women associated with childbirth for the crime of looking into secrets forbidden to the male eye (Agave, in a Bacchic trance, tears her son Pentheus' head from its shoulders with her bare hands). At the same time, Ovid manipulates his sources to imply the equal guilt of resting too securely within the conventional role of one gender or the other. Unlike his namesake in the fifth-century play *The Bacchae*, by the Athenian Euripides, Ovid's Pentheus is not seduced by the god into trying to impersonate a woman in order to watch the sacred mysteries without detection; he charges fully armed up the hill on which the Maenads are celebrating their rites, ready to subdue them by the masculine sword. He thus reenacts the conflict between Cupid and Apollo at the beginning of the post-Flood world by asserting the primacy of masculine, military power over the natural force of feminine creation (as female power was conceived by the ancient world) only to discover his own frailty. Like Tiresias, like Cupid in Apollo's mocking words, his opponent Bacchus is an androgynous figure, child-like, feminine, and male all at once. In the end, neither Actaeon nor Pentheus nor Semele can observe the truth of the opposite sex from a position of safety; one cannot know the other without self-exposure. Beset by his own hounds, Actaeon wishes for the very sort of distanced perspective on himself that our inalterable occupation of our own lives and not of others makes impossible: "Well, indeed, might he wish to be absent, but he is here; and well might he wish to see, not to feel, the fierce doings of his own hounds" (p. 51). Bodies are transformed into different shapes in the *Metamorphoses*, but, as in the Pythagorean doctrine of the transmigration of souls expounded in book XV, no one's fundamental identity is ever altered. Ironically, in fact, Pentheus and Actaeon face dismemberment as the consequence of a surfeit of anonymity, of the very distance the role of exterior observer seemed to offer as a guarantee of safety: In the end, they cannot make their actual identities known to the very beings outside of themselves to whom they should be most familiar, faithful dogs and loving aunts and mother.

A subtler thematic web spreads itself from the tale of Caenis/Caeneus (book XII) around the whole Ovidian redaction of the Trojan War story. Though the destruction of Troy (and, in fact, ultimately most of its Greek conquerors as well) remained the central epic theme of the Greco-Roman world in Ovid's time, infused with fresh blood by Virgil's *Aeneid*, Ovid seems to pay it only glancing attention in his swift flight through time. That is, he appears to use the war only as a convenient backdrop against which to play out such incidents as the debate between Ulysses and Ajax over inheritance of Achilles' magnificent armor, which offers a witty narrative that seems to illuminate the conflict between physical and rhetorical power without touching the major issues of the war itself. The abduction of Helen and her ultimate fate, the death of Hector, the Trojan horse stratagem—none of the most familiar traditional episodes can be found in the pages of the *Metamorphoses*; Ovid narrates even the death of Achilles with such compression that it seems intended only to introduce the question of who will inherit the great warrior's arms.

But the *Metamorphoses* is a poem of indirection; the digressive story of Caenis/Caeneus illuminates all the issues of conquest, rape, and warfare that Ovid's sketchy narrative of the Trojan War itself seems to avoid. Nestor, king of the Greek city-state of Pylos and a full generation older than any other warrior before the gates of Troy, recalls the invulnerable Caeneus, ostensibly, as a simple parallel to what Achilles has just done and dispatches the similarly impenetrable Trojan warrior Cygnus by clubbing him savagely with his huge shield and then strangling him with his own helmet's chin strap. The gods can save this mortal child of Neptune from death only by transforming him into a swan. But the analog ultimately has much greater significance than the minor incident of Achilles' victory that evokes it; the tale of Caeneus metaphorically describes the whole ten-year war of which the Achillean defeat of Cygnus is just a moment. Caeneus, Nestor recalls, had begun life as a woman, Caenis. After being raped by Poseidon, Caenis requested invulnerability from any repetition of such humiliation; the god responded by transforming her into a man whom no weapon could penetrate. But at the wedding of Pirithoüs, friend of Theseus, drunken centaurs attempt to carry off the bride, and a vicious combat breaks out. Ovid's extremely graphic account of the violation of male bodies as they are pierced by weapons of every description makes it clear that putting on the magical garment of masculinity is no safeguard against violent penetration; warfare simply transfers the target of rape from the female body to the male. Indeed, the climactic assault that Caeneus makes upon a centaur opposing him (who, in fact, had struck futilely at the hero's loins) reads as a compensatory reenactment of his own earlier rape, an invasive penetration of a helpless body by a wounding phallic sword: "Clear to the hilt he drove his deadly sword in the other's side, and there in his vitals twisted and turned the buried weapon, inflicting wound within wound" (p. 238). That recent cases of the maltreatment of prisoners of war have similarly involved sexual humiliation provides horrible confirmation of the poem's continuing relevance. Further, the fact that the occasion for Caeneus' short-lived vengeance—he is soon buried by his irate foes under whole forests of uprooted trees, at best ambiguously escaping, like Cygnus, in the form of a bird, his human life unequivocally over—should be the centaurs' attempted abduction of a bride from her own wedding suggests a paradigmatic association between the violence of rape and of male warfare. Marriage, after all, is the most basic social tool for imposing order and control on sexual behavior; its violation by the half-human centaurs implies that to lack such control is to fall short of full humanity. Not having come armed to the wedding, most of the warriors on both sides ironically employ the products of civilization and peace—goblets, candelabrae, even an altar—to desecrate the bodies of those suddenly transformed, in a metamorphosis so terribly natural it may escape a reader's notice, from celebrants to combatants. To reinforce the contrast between the destructive sexualized aggression of warfare/rape and the possibility of mutual sexual pleasure, Ovid brilliantly weaves the interlude of Cyllarus and Hylonome into the midst of the mayhem. Though centaurs, this couple not only court each other in the most equal fashion, with no hint of the violent expressions of male (and sometimes even female) sexual desire so frequent in the poem, they take care of and honor their own bodies: "She smoothed her long locks with a comb, now twined rosemary, now violets or roses in her hair, and sometimes she wore white lilies. Twice each day she bathed her face in the brook that fell down from a wooded height by Pagasa, and twice dipped her body in the stream. Nor would she wear on shoulder or left side anything but becoming garments, skins of well-chosen beasts. They both felt equal love" (p. 236). Their mutuality is fixed in death, and for once the deadly wound is small, the description of bodily suffering muted.

Thus, Nestor's tale illuminates the assault on Troy by mirroring the same issues of gender and conquest. Not only does it connect itself to the Trojan saga by the parallel between Cygnus and Caeneus, the fates of both of whom, like the penetration of the divinely built walls of Troy itself, suggest that no invulnerability to violence can be obtained in the mortal world, but through the presence of Peleus, father of Achilles and uncle of Ajax, at the Lapith-Centaur battle; the whole struggle is just a generation removed from the launching of the thousand ships. And, of course, what begins the Lapith-Centaur conflict is the attempted abduction of Pirithoüs' bride, just as the abduction of Helen begins the Trojan War. Rather than narrating anew the familiar events of the war over Helen, Ovid suggests its essential character in the miniature reflection of the Lapith-Centaur war, the very diminution of scale of which suggests the ugly reality behind the heroic inflation of traditional epic. The horrific detail in which Ovid paints the murderous fighting, after all, clearly mimics the Homeric vision of combat in the *Iliad*, but the everyday implements used to conduct the wedding-hall struggle rob the victors of even the modicum of glory that attaches to their triumphs in Homer's poem. For all its heart-felt skepticism of the value of pursuing dominance and conquest, the *Iliad* does allow its heroes to face their social equals in fair duels undertaken with costly, magnificent weapons. As a literate Roman, in sum, Ovid knew not only his native Latin but also Greek, in which the verbs "to kill with a sword" and "to rape" are identical.

While a number of such narrative clusters as these lend the *Metamorphoses* a sense of local continuity, no one prevailing theme leads in an unbroken thread from beginning to end of this labyrinthine poem; only the fact of transformation itself is constant. Every critic seems to assess the poem's use of metamorphosis differently, but most point out that the sort of change Ovid depicts, far from being a riotous confusion of constantly shifted shapes and altered identities, is bound by a number of order-imposing rules: The metamorphoses all involve humans or lesser divinities such as nymphs (alas, no dog or horse becomes human in the pages of the epic, though one dog and its quarry are changed into statues so that the pursuit may go on forever), they are always permanent, and they all broadly follow pre-existing narrative traditions. Why should a work asserting perpetual change as the condition of existence both in its opening lines and in its longest episode—the account of the teachings of Pythagoras that sprawls across its final book—at the same time respect both the validity of old tales and the irreversibility of transformation? One solution is to regard these tales of metamorphosis as metaphors for the moments of transformation our own actual bodies undergo in the process of time—metaphors, that is, for the onset of desire around puberty (virtually no young children change forms in the *Metamorphoses*, while countless young lovers do), for the ordeal of pregnancy and childbirth, for the isolation and grief of old age, for the inalterable memories left behind after death. Thus, the epic embeds the fragments of a universal history of the individual life cycle in its account of the larger course of human events, an eternal repetition of age and youth played against the one-way flow of historical time, eddies in the river of time.

The story of Narcissus provides one obvious image of a stage of life frozen in art. Less obvious a metaphor for a universal phenomenon is the tale of Myrrha and Cinyras, one of the most striking instances of an apparently grotesque tale serving as a magnified analogy for far more ordinary developments in the human cycle of maturation. Myrrha falls in love with her father, and has the misfortune to realize her erotic dreams about him. In a post-Freudian world, it is hard not to regard her consciously expressed desires as a more explicit image of a normal unconscious phase in the passage toward a mature erotic life. But it does not take the psychological theory of the past century to find reason for reading Ovid's tale as metaphor. Significantly, Ovid puts Myrrha's tale, along with a number of others about seemingly obscure desires, into the mouth of Orpheus. This grieving poet—who loses his wife to a fatal snakebite on their wedding day, then reclaims her from the dead by his transcendent song, only to lose her again when he tries to look the miracle of his art's contrivance in the face—himself embodies the longing that eternally precedes fulfillment, the stage when we want but have not yet had. What's more, the tragedy that befalls Eurydice, dead on her wedding day, metaphorically expresses the condition of living in time, condensing years of normal life into a moment: The very process of physical maturation that leads to desire and mating inexorably ends in death and separation. The major transitions of life, it is commonly imagined, end with marriage, thus making every wedding a funeral as well; certainly, countless myths envisioned initiation into sexuality as death's equivalent, so linked were these points of the human life cycle in the ancient mind. Indeed, Orpheus concludes his song with the tale of Venus and Adonis, another example of youth plucked away at its ripest moment. Ritual mourning for the death of Adonis, in fact, related the human life cycle to the endlessly repeated seasonal death and birth of the land. These rites, common in pagan Rome, extended not only to Greek antecedents, but to Canaanite/Phoenician ceremonies that themselves derive from one of the first stories ever committed to writing, the Sumerian narrative of Inanna and Dumuzi, which precedes Ovid by at least 2,000 years.

We are thus prepared by the setting of Myrrha and Cinyras to read the desires it describes figuratively. And, in a typical piece of irony, Ovid has Orpheus introduce the tale with an elaborate warning that appears to distance it from ordinary experience but that in fact disconcertingly suggests that Myrrha's desire for her father might be an unspoken universal of human experience: "A horrible tale I have to tell. Far away be daughters, far away, fathers; or, if your minds find pleasure in my songs, do not give credence to this story, and believe that it never happened" (p. 194). After all, what danger could the tale have to fathers and daughters who hear it except to inspire imitation, and how could it inspire imitation if the desires it describes didn't exist in nascent form before it had been heard? Then, in his unfolding of the tale, the poet universalizes Myrrha's guilty desire in an even more revealing way, depicting it not merely as the product of natural (if normally repressed and unconscious) desire, but as a horrifying expression of sociocultural mores that operate in an only slightly less repulsive manner on an accepted, everyday basis. Myrrha, after all, recognizes her shame and is ready to die to avoid the tortures of her sinful yearning. But her old nurse concocts a plan for its fulfillment; her willing intervention suggests that Myrrha's tale represents a more than personal derangement. The manner in which the girl consummates her love confirms the connivance of cultural norms in its fulfillment. Not only is Cinyras quite willing to accept into his bed a girl whose age the nurse describes as "the same as Myrrha's" (p. 197), he does so while his own wife is away at a religious festival, refraining from sexual contact with her husband out of pious obligation. If Myrrha's desire for her father represents an unnatural confusion of the orderly progress of the generations, what of his ready acceptance of sleeping with a girl his daughter's age? But such male desire bears no social stigma. In one of the most disturbing moments in world literature, the poet reports that in the blind dark of the bed: "The father receives his own flesh in his incestuous bed, strives to calm her girlish fears, and speaks encouragingly to the shrinking girl. It chanced, by a name appropriate to her age, he called her 'daughter,' and she called him 'father,' that names might not be lacking to their guilt" (p. 198). The sexual relation between Myrrha and Cinyras, then, merely writes the truth of Roman practice in a large hand, as the poet's too-frequent protestations of its perversion ironically suggest. (Similarly, in book IX, the naive Iphis produces a moment of unconscious comedy when she laments her desire for another woman as something unprecedented in world history; lesbianism was of course known in ancient Rome.) It was expected that a Roman man would be the older, dominant partner both in marriage and other sexual relations, a gender-based power distinction taken largely for granted; the poem reveals the hidden obscenity of this customary practice simply by transforming the symbolic daughter into a literal one. Indeed, tale after tale in the *Metamorphoses* rehearses a brutal domination of women by men that is met with resistance of varying effect, perhaps most vividly in the story of Tereus, Procne, and Philomela, where the only revenge left open to the raped and mutilated princess and her sister, whose husband committed the atrocity, is to deny the criminal the product of their own sexual creation by killing the man's son and feeding him the roasted flesh, thus putting back inside his body the life that had issued from theirs. Moreover, numerous stories concern the opposition of either Juno or Diana to the fulfillment of a male's desire, the matron goddess and the virgin denying as far as they can the reduction of women's identities to the objects of male sexual desire, though often, particularly in Juno's case, striking more at the mistress than the mastering lover. It is Ovid's perhaps unique genius to offer his tales of transformed bodies both as metaphors for the pivotal moments of the human life cycle and as comments on the social construction of that life cycle in his own time.

And yet, metamorphosis may also be understood as a metaphor for the enterprise of Ovid's epic itself. Apollo, the harpist of reason's music; Pan and his pipes; the storyteller Hermes; the musician of abandon, Bacchus; the sculptor Pygmalion; the weavers Arachne and Philomela; the poets Orpheus and the Pierides; the rhetorician Ulysses; and numerous other narrators who consent to spin a strange tale or two: The *Metamorphoses* is filled with images of art and artists, whose work transforms the reality it appears to reflect. Even Perseus, waving the head of Medusa before his enemies to turn them to stone, is compared to a sculptor. Through these artist-figures, Ovid evinces both the range of uses to which the artistic transformation of reality may be put and provides models of his own narrative method. Particularly revealing in the latter area are the competition of Arachne with Athena and Lelex's narration of the story of Baucis and Philemon.

The beautiful tale of Baucis and Philemon, one of the epic's few instances of an enduring love not conditioned solely by the need to fulfill impulsive desires, attains even greater significance if one attends to the context of its telling. The river-god Acheloüs has just finished a tale of miraculous transformation when the skeptical Pirithoüs, a prince of Thessaly who conventionally represents the lowest boundary of civilized behavior, expresses his disbelief in the ability of the gods to alter shapes. The response to his charge seems baffling at first; rather than Acheloüs, a minor deity with a talent for taking other forms himself, turning into a wall of fire or a charging bull to refute the young man's charge, old Lelex responds with yet another story of a miraculous transformation. What's more, he was not even a witness to the miracle it concerns, let alone a participant in the tale; the best proof he can offer that it happened at all is having seen the site of its supposed occurrence. But, in a different sense, the story establishes its own truth. It may not accurately reflect historical events (Ovid's poetry often refers to such tales as those in the *Metamorphoses* as *fabulae*: "myths," in the sense of fictions), but it metaphorically encapsulates a more general truth than any actual event might convey. Baucis and Philemon, whose life of rural poverty Ovid captures in superbly observed detail, show their devotion to gods disguised as travelers by offering them full share in what little they have; in reward, they are spared the destruction that befalls their uncharitable neighbors, and their hovel is transformed into a temple and they themselves into its priests. This sort of transformation simply expresses to the outward eye what had been the inward truth all along: By reason of their pious behavior, Baucis and Philemon had always been priests of the gods and their ill-furnished room a temple. When the only wish they can ask the willing gods to grant is that neither might live to see the other's funeral, it is clear the gods can give them nothing they do not already possess. Even their eventual transformation into the closely planted pair of trees Lelex claims to have seen merely expresses the enduring character of the bond they shared all along.

Similarly, all the stories of the *Metamorphoses* transform the everchanging world into the fixed words of written poetry, a form less subject to the vagaries of time and memory than is the flux of existence. Indeed, the work teems with instances of language transforming reality in the most direct way: Medea (book VII), Scylla (book VIII), and Byblis (book IX), among others, turn their own inchoate desires into consequential realities by first putting them into words—words that deny the feelings they describe, but whose very articulation is the first step toward their admission as accepted facts. Thus, when Pythagoras sets aside "shades and empty names, the stuff that poets manufacture" (p. 293), one need take neither the philosopher's side and regard the very poem in which he speaks as mere entertainment nor take the poet's side and interpret the whole Pythagoras episode as an elaborate joke against pretentious vegetarians. One can take both sides without contradiction. The physical world may be a kaleidoscope of ever-changing appearances, as the opening of the poem and Pythagoras would have it, but art arrests its restless change into permanent form, not so much reflecting as molding the raw material of experience into an order whose principle is the associative logic of images.

But the closest image of his own enterprise Ovid provides is the weaver Arachne, who pits her skill against the patron goddess of the loom, Athena. The goddess, Jupiter's most dutiful and masculine daughter, having been born directly from his own head, works into her design a series of stories that show the triumph of authority, hierarchy, and the martial spirit—the stuff of conventional epic without the enlivening irony, the questioning of values, that a Homer or Virgil interweaves. The tales Arachne chooses, on the other hand, are pure Ovid; she begins with Jupiter's rape of Europa, which appears in book I of the *Metamorphoses* itself, and proceeds to detail the imposition of the male gods' sexual desire on their unwilling human victims so aptly that the fairly beaten Athena "was indignant at her success, and rent the embroidered web with its heavenly crimes" (p. 106). Nowhere does the poem so fully imply its intention: to show the outrages of power in their true colors, with no prettification or excuse. When Athena physically attacks her human superior in the art of spinning, Arachne chooses suicide, but the goddess, mildly repentant, transforms her into a spider, and the noose from which she hangs into a web. The structure of the epic itself, endless threads spinning outward from its central themes, resembles Arachne's web more than it does the narrative form of any previous example of the genre. If in the story of Arachne Ovid also unintentionally prophesied his own downfall at the hands of an arbitrary authority, his declaration at the poem's end that the *Metamorphoses* would withstand even the wrath of Jupiter—and, as it turned out, his surrogate, Augustus—is more than egotistical boasting, and not merely because the poem has in fact survived. Regarded from Ovid's viewpoint as the capacity to bring a less coercive order to the incoherence of existence than that imposed by political domination, poetry appears to be as eternal as any human achievement, and certainly longer-lived than any empire.

Robert Squillace teaches Cultural Foundations courses in the General Studies Program of New York University. He has published extensively on the field of modern British literature, most notably in his study *Modernism, Modernity and Arnold Bennett* (Bucknell University Press, 1997). His recent teaching has involved him deeply in the world of the ancients. He lives in Brooklyn with his wife, the medievalist Angela Jane Weisl. Squillace also wrote the Introduction and Notes for the Barnes & Noble Classics edition of Homer's *Odyssey*.

WHO'S WHO IN OVID'S
METAMORPHOSES

The Olympian Gods

By Ovid's lifetime, the main gods of the Roman pantheon had long since been accommodated to the fourteen divinities worshipped in Greek culture as dwelling on Mount Olympus. In most cases, the Greek tradition overshadowed whatever native attributes the deity in question had possessed before the full influence of Greek mythology came to be felt. Venus, for instance, had at one time been a relatively minor god associated with good fortune, but she essentially absorbed the identity of the Greek goddess of love, Aphrodite, so that in Ovid's era Venus and Aphrodite were merely considered the Latin and Greek names for the same being. Often, though, local worship of a god showed strongly regional beliefs, emphases, or political affiliations; hence, Apollo might appear in one instance as Actian Apollo (an incarnation of special appeal to Augustus) and in another as Sminthean Apollo, an epithet of Phrygian origin that alludes to the healer-god's victory over a plague of mice, *sminthos* being the Phrygian word for "mouse."

The descriptions that follow first give the Latin name of the god and then the Greek equivalent in parentheses. Only the most generally recognized attributes of the deity are outlined.

Apollo (Apollo): Associated with the power of rationality; patron of medicine, prophecy, and the lyre; drives the chariot of the sun (though Helios is usually regarded as the sun-god per se). Son of Jupiter and the minor goddess Latona (Leto); brother of Diana. Also called Phoebus or Phoebus Apollo.

Bacchus (Dionysus): Associated with irrational abandon and the crossing of customary boundaries of behavior; inspires a normally benign madness in his largely female worshippers (known as

Bacchantes or Maenads) that turns violent when challenged by (usually male) authority; patron of wine, flute and drums, and the drama. Known as the "twice-born"—in some traditions, because he is born first from Proserpina (Persephone) or Ceres, killed by the Titans, and later reborn from the human Semele; in others, because he is born first from Semele, then reborn after her death from the thigh of Jupiter himself. His worship originated in the Zagros Mountains and spread westward, which accounts for the many names under which he is known (Liber, Bromius, Nyseus, Lyaeus, etc.—see book IV).

Ceres (Demeter): Associated with the fertility of earth; root of the word "cereal." Daughter of Saturn, sister of Jupiter, mother of Proserpina, who is abducted by Pluto and becomes queen of the Underworld. The Greeks celebrated the Eleusinian mysteries in her honor.

Diana (Artemis): Associated with the moon; patron of childbirth, chastity, the hunt, and wild places. Daughter of Jupiter and the minor goddess Latona (Leto); sister of Apollo. In the *Metamorphoses*, frequently associated with women's attempts to avoid male domination, particularly of the sexual variety. Sometimes called Phoebe.

Juno (Hera): Originally a goddess associated, it is likely, with fertility and motherhood, but in the *Metamorphoses* relegated to punishing the victims of her husband's love life. Her avian emblem is the peacock, a brace of which draw her chariot (see book I for an account of how the bird received its gaudy plumage). Sister and wife of Jupiter, mother of Hephaestus and Ares (and of the minor goddess Hebe). Sometimes called Saturnia, daughter of Saturn.

Jupiter or **Jove** (Zeus): Associated with the sky, thunder and lightning, the planet Jupiter, and male sexual potency/activity; king of the gods. The son of the youngest of the Titans, Saturn (Cronus), he is saved from the fate of his siblings (who have all been swallowed by their father in order to prevent his own eventual overthrow) when his mother substitutes a stone for Jupiter, which Saturn swallows. Jupiter grows to adulthood secretly, then defeats his father, freeing his brothers and sisters from their abdominal prison. Married to his sister, Juno, Jupiter has too many children with too many different women (both divine and human) for easy calculation. Aside from Minerva and his daughters by Leda, they are practically all males.

Mars (Ares): Associated with the red planet that bears his name and with war. Son of Jupiter and Juno; brother of Vulcan, with whose wife, Venus, he has a notable affair. Almost always depicted in ancient texts as a brutish, unsympathetic figure.

Mercury (Hermes): Associated with the first planet from the sun (the one that orbits the fastest), secrecy, speed, and trickery. Patron of travelers and thieves; messenger of the gods. Son of Jupiter and Maia, one of the Pleiades. Sometimes called Cyllenius for his association with Cyllene.

Minerva (Athena): Associated with war, wisdom, strategy, and justice and jurisprudence. She was the patron of the city of Athens, to which she brought the gift of the olive tree; she also presided at the trial of Orestes, which established the principle that civil law must take precedence over family vengeance. A virgin goddess, she was born directly from the head of Jupiter and virtually personified his wisdom and foresight. (The Greek poet Hesiod reports in the *Theogony* that Jupiter swallowed the goddess Metis [wisdom], already pregnant with Athena, when he learned of a prophecy that she would later bear a son greater than his father; his loyal daughter was then born by her unusual route). Significantly, the obedient Minerva is not a terribly prominent figure in Ovid's poem. Often called Pallas.

Neptune (Poseidon): Chief god of the sea; also associated with earthquakes. Patron of sea-faring and of horses and horse-breeding; father of the Cyclopes, who forge his trident and Jupiter's thunderbolts. Son of Saturn, brother of Jupiter, with whom, as well as his other brother, Pluto, he casts lots for the dominion of the world after the demise of Saturn; Neptune draws the sea while Jupiter takes the sky and Pluto the Underworld. Ill-tempered and violent, Neptune has children with numerous partners, but few tales describe his relation with his wife, Amphitrite.

Pluto (Hades): God of the Underworld; associated with death, night, and silence. Son of Saturn, brother of Jupiter and Neptune; see the entry on Neptune for the story of how Pluto obtained his realm. The tale of his abduction of Proserpina, daughter of Ceres, appears in book V. Tradition records no children of Pluto, either with his wife or any lover. He was the least worshipped of the gods, reputedly having a temple dedicated to him only in the city of Elis. Sometimes called Dis.

Venus (Aphrodite): Goddess of sexual desire, associated with the islands of Cythera and Cyprus, as well as her eponymous planet. Origins of her worship are very ancient, going back to the Sumerian goddess Inanna, known in writing from at least 2000 B.C.E. Hesiod reports her birth from the severed genitals of Cronus' father, Uranus, which makes her a generation older than Jupiter and his siblings, but other traditions attribute her parentage to Jupiter and a shadowy figure named Dione. Mother of the divine Cupid and the human Aeneas, purported founder of Rome. Wife of Vulcan, though he apparently fathers none of her substantial brood of children.

Vesta (Hestia): Goddess of the hearth, associated with domesticity, the state, and the building of homes. The eldest child of Saturn, she remains a virgin goddess and never leaves Olympus itself—hence, the paucity of stories about her. Nevertheless, she was almost universally worshipped in the ancient Mediterranean as a stabilizing feminine presence in both home and community; her most prominent Roman votaries were the prestigious vestal virgins. Her antipathy toward Venus reflects the ancient double standard regarding the behavior of women—a woman could be devoted to home and husband or be an object of desire, but never both.

Vulcan (Hephaestus): God of the forge; patron of smiths and miners; associated with fire, metallurgy, and invention. Son of Jupiter and Juno, he is lamed when his father throws him off Mount Olympus for interfering on his mother's behalf in a marital quarrel. Because Lemnos was a center of his worship, legend has it that he landed there after his fall; sometimes he is known as "the Lemnian." Husband of Venus, though all his recorded children (none of them especially prominent in the mythic world) come from other unions. Also called Mulciber.

Characters Identified by Parentage or Associated Place

Ovid frequently refers to characters by means other than their own names, a feature that Miller's translation sometimes preserves. In particular, the poet identifies many characters either by denoting their ancestors or a location with which they were associated—for humans, usually their place of birth; for gods, a center of their worship. Roman practice was to name all daughters by the feminine version of the father's name; thus, all the daughters of Livius would be called Livia (they might be further distinguished by reference to their birth order). In calling Juno "Saturnia," then, Ovid is imposing his own society's customs on the gods themselves. By choosing on a particular textual occasion to identify a character in a way that recalls a specific facet of his or her origin, the poet can also influence the way readers interpret the figure at that moment. (Regardless of the possessive form the text uses—that is, whether "X's daughter" or "daughter of X"—the list below lists the name as "daughter of" or "son of.")

An excellent Web site for further identification and information is Greek Mythology Link, at http://homepage.mac.com/cparada/GML/index.html. In particular, the Dictionary tab answers all "who's who?" questions, using both Greek and Latin forms of the names.

Son of Abas: Acrisius.

Daughter of Acheloüs: Callirhoë (book IX).

Daughters of Acheloüs: The Sirens (book V).

Father of Achilles: Peleus.

Son of Achilles: Pyrrhus (in fact, the son of Neoptolemus, and so Achilles' grandson).

Grandson of Acrisius: Perseus.

Sons of Actor: Eurytus and Cteatus (or, by extension, Actor's later descendant, Patroclus [book XIII]).

Aeacides (descendant[s] of Aeacus): Peleus and his son, Achilles.

Sons of Aeacus: Phocus, Peleus, and Telamon (Peleus kills his half-brother, Phocus, leaving Aeacus with only two sons).

Daughter of Aeëtes: Medea.

Son of Aegeus: Theseus.

Aeolides (descendant of Aeolus): Sisyphus.

Daughter of Aeolus: Alcyone.

Grandson of Aeolus: Cephalus.

Son of Aeolus: Athamas (book IV); Misenus (book XIV).

Son of Aeson: Jason.

Daughter of Agamemnon: Iphigenia.

Daughter of Agenor: Europa.

Son of Agenor: Cadmus.

Daughter of Alcidamas: Ctesylla.

Alcides (descendant of Alceus): Hercules.

Daughter-in-law of Alcmena: Deianira.

Son of Alcmena: Hercules.

Son of Alemon: Myscelus.

Aloidae (descendants of Aloeus): Otus and Ephialtes (actually sons of Neptune via Aloeus' wife).

Daughter of Alpheus: Arethusa.

Son of the Amazon (Hippolyta): Hippolytus.

Son of Amphitryon: Hercules (more accurately, foster-son).

Son of Ampycus: Mopsus.

Son of Amyntor: Phoenix.

Son of Amythaon: Melampus.

Son of Andraemon: Thoas.

Son of Anius: Andros.

Sons of Aphareus: Lynceus and Idas.

Grandson of Apollo: Caunus.

Son of Apollo: Aesculapius.

Son of Arestor: Argus.

Daughter of Asopus: Aegina.

Son of Athamas: Palaemon.

Grandson of Atlas: Mercury (by extension, Mercury's son, Hermaphroditus, in book IV).

Atracides (citizen of Atrax): Caeneus.

Son of Atreus: Agamemnon (book XV).

Atrides (descendant of Atreus): Agamemnon is referred to simply as "Atrides," while Menelaus, his younger brother, is known as "the lesser Atrides."

Son of Autonoë: Actaeon.

Bacchiadae (descendants of Bacchus): Ruling family of Corinth.

Sons of Boreas: Zetes and Calais.

Daughters of Cadmus: Semele, Ino, Autonoë, Agave.

Grandson of Cadmus: Actaeon (book III).

Sons of Callirhoë: Amphoterus and Acarnan.

Daughter of Cebren: Hesperia.

Daughters of Cecrops: Aglaurus, Herse, and Pandrosus.

Daughter of Ceres: Proserpina.

Daughter of Chiron: Ocyrhoë.

Daughter of Cinyras: Myrrha.

Grandson of Cinyras: Ovid is indulging in a dark irony when he calls Adonis "grandson of Cinyras." Adonis is the child of Cinyras and his own daughter, Myrrha; thus he is *both* the son and grandson of the very same Cinyras.

Clarian: Associated with the island of Claros; said of Apollo.

Daughters of Clymene: The Heliades (that is, children of Helios).

Son of Clymene: Phaëton.

Daughter of Coeus: Latona.

Colchian: From the city of Colchis; used to mean Medea.

Son of Coronis: Aesculapius.

Daughter of Crataeis: Scylla.

Cumaean: From Cumae; used primarily for the Cumaean Sibyl (a soothsayer).

Cyllenius: Associated with Mount Cyllene; used for Mercury.

Cynthia: Associated with the mountain Cynthus: used for Diana.

Goddess of Cythera: Venus.

Son of the goddess of Cythera: Hermaphroditus (book IV).

Cytherea: Name associated with the island of Cythera and used for Venus.

Son of Cytherea (Venus): Aeneas.

Son of Danaë: Perseus.

Son of Deione: Miletus.

Delian: Associated with the island of Delos; used for Apollo and Diana.

Daughter of Deo: Proserpina.

Daughters of Doris: The Oceanids (nymphs of the sea).

Dulichian: From the island of Dulichius (near Ithaca); used for Ulysses.

Daughter of Dymas: Hecuba.

Son of Echion: Pentheus.

Daughter of Elatus: Caenis (see also Son of Elatus).

Son of Elatus: Caeneus (born his daughter, Caenis).

Epidaurian: Associated with the city of Epidaurius; used for Aesculapius.

Daughter of Epimetheus: Pyrrha.

Daughter of Erechtheus: Procris.

Erycina: Associated with Mount Eryx: used for Venus.

Daughter of Erysichthon: A shape-shifter; her name is not recorded.

Son of Europa: Minos.

Son of Eurymus: Telemus.

Daughter of Eurytus: Iole.

Son of Faunus: Acis (book XIII); Latinus (book XIV).

Gradivus: Mars.

Daughter of Granicus: Alexiroë.

Heliades: Daughters of Helios.

Son of Hermes (Mercury): Hermaphroditus.

Hesperides: The three daughters of Hesperus.

Son of Hippocoön: Enaesimus.

Hippotades (descendant of Hippotes): Aeolus.

Son of Hippotas: Aeolus (evidently, "Hippotas" is merely a variant spelling of the more usual "Hippotes").

Son of Hippotes: Aeolus.

Son of Hyperion: Helios.

Son of Iapetus: Prometheus.

Idalian: Associated with Mount Idalium (on Cyprus); used to mean Venus.

Sons of Ilia: Romulus and Remus (Romulus is the one who built Rome's walls).

Daughter of Inachus: Io (later transformed to Isis).

Grandson of Inachus: Phaëton.

Son of Iphitus: Coeranos.

Son of Ixion: Pirithoüs.

Daughter of Janus: Canens.

Daughter of Jove: Minerva.

Grandson of Jove: Peleus (book XI).

Son of Jove: Mercury (books I, II); Bacchus (book IV); Perseus (book IV); Hercules (book IX); Arcesius (book XII); Hercules (book XV).

Son of Julius (Caesar): Augustus/Octavian (by adoption).

Son of Juno: Vulcan (book IV).

Son of Laërtes: Ulysses.

Son of Laïus: Oedipus.

Daughter of Latinus: Lavinia.

Daughter of Latona: Diana.

Son of Latona: Apollo.

Sons of Leda: Castor and Pollux.

Lemnian: Associated with the island of Lemnos; used for Vulcan.

Son of the Lemnian: Erichthonius.

Lenaeus: One of the many names for Bacchus.

Liber: Another of the many names for Bacchus.

Son of Lucifer: Ceyx.

Lucina: Goddess of childbirth ("the bringer to light"); sometimes used as an epithet for Diana or Juno.

Grandson of Lycaon: Arcas.

Daughter of Macareus: Isse.

Daughter of Maeander: Cyanee.

Grandson of Maeander: Caunus.

Son of Maia: Mercury.

Son of Mars: Meleager.

Son of Megareus: Hippomenes.

Son of Mercury: Autolycus.

Son of Metion: Phorbas.

Daughter of Miletus: Byblis.

Daughter of Minos: Ariadne.

Daughters of Minyas: Alcithoë; the others have been variously identified and number either one or two.

Daughters of Mnemosyne ("Memory"): The nine muses: Calliope (epic), Clio (history), Euterpe (lyric), Melpomene (tragedy), Terpsichore (dance), Erato (love poetry), Polyhymnia (sacred music), Urania (astronomy), and Thalia (comedy).

Son of Nauplius: Palamedes.

Nelean: Associated with Neleus; used of his son, Nestor, or Neleus' kingdom, Pylos.

Sons of Neleus: Nestor and his brothers.

Daughter of Nephele: Helle.

Son of Neptune: Cygnus.

Neptunian: Descendant of Neptune: used for Theseus (book IX) and Hippomenes (book X).

Daughter of Nereus: Thetis.

Daughter of Nisus: Scylla.

Oebalides: Associated with Sparta (after its legendary king, Oebalus); used to mean Hyacinthus.

Son of Oecleus: Amphiaraus.

Son of Oeneus: Meleager. (Ovid also identifies him as the son of Mars, thus including both traditions of Meleager's parentage without acknowledging or resolving the contradiction thus created).

Grandson of Oeneus: Diomede.

Son of Oileus: The lesser Ajax (the greater Ajax is the son of Telamon).

Son of Olenus: Tectaphos.

Son of Ophion: Amycus.

Daughter of Ophius: Combe.

Daughters of Orion: Metioche and Menippe.

Paean: Apollo, referring to his identity as the god of medicine.

Pallantis: Descendant of the Titan named Pallas; used for Aurora, goddess of the dawn.

Pallas: Minerva.

Sons of Pallas: Clytos and Butes.

Daughters of Pandion: Philomel and Procne.

Son of Panthoüs: Euphorbus.

Paphian: Associated with the island of Paphos; used for Pygmalion.

Son of Parthaon: Oeneus.

Daughter of Pasiphaë: Phaedra.

Son of Peleus: Achilles.

Pelides: Descendant of Peleus; used for Achilles.

Father-in-law of Penelope: Laërtes.

Daughter of Peneus: Daphne.

Daughter of Perse: Hecate.

Phasian: Associated with the river Phasis (in Colchis); used for Medea.

Son of Pheres: Admetus.

Son of Philyra: Chiron.

Phoebe: Another name for Diana.

Son of Phoebus: Miletus (book IX) or Aesculapius (book XV).

Daughters of Phorcys: Medusa and the other Gorgons; also, the Gray sisters.

Son of the shining Pleiad: Mercury.

Grandson of Pleione: Mercury.

Son of Poeas: Philoctetes.

Granddaughter of Polypemon (Procrustes): Sinis.

Daughter of Priam: Polyxena (with Hecuba).

Son of Priam: Helenus (initially one of many sons of Priam, Helenus is so called because he is the only one to survive the Trojan War).

Daughters of Proetus: Eidothea and Cabiro are the only names recorded.

Son of Prometheus: Deucalion.

Samian: Associated with the isle of Samos; used for Pythagoras.

Daughter of Saturn: Juno.

Son of Saturn: Jupiter (books I, VIII); Pluto (book V); Picus (book XIV).

Saturnia: Descendant of Saturn; used to mean Juno.

Daughter of Schoeneus: Atalanta.

Son of Semele: Bacchus (Liber).

Sidonian: Associated with the Phoenician city of Sidon; used for Cadmus (book III) and Dido (book XIV).

Son of Sisyphus: Ulysses (abusive; Laërtes is Ulysses' literal father).

The Spanish shepherd: Used to mean Geryon.

Son of Sthenelus: Cycnus (book II) or Eurystheus (book IX).

Daughter of the Sun (Helios): Pasiphaë (book IX), Circe (books XIII, XIV).

Tantalides: Descendant of Tantalus; used to mean Agamemnon.

Daughter of Tantalus: Niobe.

Son of Telamon: The greater Ajax.

Daughter of Telestes: Ianthe.

Grandson of Tethys: Phaëton.

Teucri: Descendants of Teucer; collectively used to mean the Trojans.

Daughter of Thaumus: Iris.

Son of Theseus: Hippolytus.

Daughter of Thestius: Althaea.

Sons of Thestius: Plexippus and Toxeus.

Son of Thestor: Calchas.

Thestorides: Descendant of Thestor; used to mean Calchas.

Son of Thetis: Achilles.

Daughter of Tiresias: Manto.

Titania: Descendant of a Titan; used to mean Diana.

Trachinian: Associated with the city of Trachin; used for its king, Ceyx.

Son of Triopas: Erysichthon.

Tritonia: Associated with Lake Triton, in Africa; used to mean Minerva.

Tydides: Descendant of Tydeus; used for Diomede.

Granddaughter of Venus: Ino (later transformed into the sea-nymph Leucothoë).

Son of Venus: Cupid (book IX); Aeneas (books XIV, XV), and, by extension, Julius Caesar (book XV).

Son of Vulcan: Periphetes (also called Corynetes: "club-wielder").

A NOTE ON THE TRANSLATION

This edition of the *Metamorphoses* uses Frank Justus Miller's 1916 prose translation (reprinted without revision in 1921), which is still among the most admirably direct and accurate available. In Miller's time, however, a very comfortable majority of readers of English had grown up on the King James Version of the Bible; thus, they felt completely at home with the use of antiquated formal address ("thou," "thine," and so forth) and archaic vocabulary. Because this style is so much more alien to a contemporary readership, I have judged that retaining it would be distracting and have therefore updated the word choices to reflect modern usage. At the same time, in order to preserve the rhythm of Miller's prose, I have avoided any but the most necessary alterations of syntax, even where the word order may sound slightly out of date.

THE
METAMORPHOSES

BOOK I

MY MIND IS BENT to tell of bodies changed into new forms. O gods, for you yourselves have wrought the changes,[1] breathe on these my undertakings, and bring down my song in unbroken strains from the world's very beginning even unto the present time.

Before the sea was, and the lands, and the sky that hangs over all, the face of Nature showed alike in her whole round, which state have men called chaos: a rough, unordered mass of things, nothing at all but lifeless bulk and warring seeds of ill-matched elements heaped in one. No sun as yet shone forth upon the world, nor did the waxing moon renew her slender horns; not yet did the earth hang poised by her own weight in the circumambient air, nor had the ocean stretched her arms along the far reaches of the lands. And, though there was both land and sea and air, no one could tread that land, or swim that sea; and the air was dark. No form of things remained the same; all objects were at odds, for within one body cold things strove with hot, and moist with dry, soft things with hard, things having weight with weightless things.

God—or kindlier Nature—composed this strife; for he rent asunder land from sky, and sea from land, and separated the ethereal heavens from the dense atmosphere. When thus he had released these elements and freed them from the blind heap of things, he set them each in its own place and bound them fast in harmony. The fiery weightless element that forms heaven's vault leaped up and made place for itself upon the topmost height. Next came the air in lightness and in place. The earth was heavier than these, and, drawing with it the grosser elements, sank to the bottom by its own weight. The streaming water took the last place of all, and held the solid land confined in its embrace.

When he, whoever of the gods it was, had thus arranged in order and resolved that chaotic mass, and reduced it, thus resolved, to cosmic parts, he first moulded the earth into the form of a mighty ball

3

so that it might be of like form on every side. Then he bade the waters to spread abroad, to rise in waves beneath the rushing winds, and fling themselves around the shores of the encircled earth. Springs, too, and huge, stagnant pools and lakes he made, and hemmed down-flowing rivers within their shelving banks, whose waters, each far remote from each, are partly swallowed by the earth itself, and partly flow down to the sea; and being thus received into the expanse of a freer flood, beat now on shores instead of banks. Then did he bid plains to stretch out, valleys to sink down, woods to be clothed in leafage, and the rock-ribbed mountains to arise. And as the celestial vault is cut by two zones on the right and two on the left, and there is a fifth zone between, hotter than these, so did the providence of God mark off the enclosed mass with the same number of zones, and the same tracts were stamped upon the earth. The central zone of these may not be dwelt in by reason of the heat; deep snow covers two, two he placed between and gave them temperate climate, mingling heat with cold.

The air hung over all, which is as much heavier than fire as the weight of water is lighter than the weight of earth. There did the creator bid the mists and clouds to take their place, and thunder, that should shake the hearts of men, and winds which with the thunderbolts make chilling cold. To these also the world's creator did not allot the air that they might hold it everywhere. Even as it is, they can scarce be prevented, though they control their blasts, each in his separate tract, from tearing the world to pieces. So fiercely do these brothers strive together. But Eurus drew off to the land of the dawn and the realms of Araby, and where the Persian hills flush beneath the morning light. The western shores which glow with the setting sun are the place of Zephyrus: while bristling Boreas betook himself to Scythia and the farthest north. The land far opposite is wet with constant fog and rain, the home of Auster, the South-wind. Above these all he placed the liquid, weightless ether,[2] which has no trace of earthy dregs.

Scarce had he thus parted off all things within their determined bounds, when the stars, which had long been lying hid crushed down beneath the darkness, began to gleam throughout the sky. And, that no region might be without its own forms of animate life, the stars and divine forms occupied the floor of heaven, the sea fell to the shining fishes for their home, earth received the beasts, and the mobile air the birds.

A living creature of finer stuff than these, more capable of lofty thought, one who could have dominion over all the rest, was lacking yet. Then man was born: whether the god who made all else, designing a more perfect world, made man of his own divine substance, or whether the new earth, but lately drawn away from heavenly ether, retained still some elements of its kindred sky—that earth which the son of Iapetus mixed with fresh, running water, and moulded into the form of the all-controlling gods. And, though all other animals are prone, and fix their gaze upon the earth, he gave to man an uplifted face and bade him stand erect and turn his eyes to heaven. So, then, the earth, which had but lately been a rough and formless thing, was changed and clothed itself with forms of men before unknown.

Golden was that first age, which, with no one to compel, without a law, of its own will, kept faith and did the right. There was no fear of punishment, no threatening words were to be read on brazen tablets; no suppliant throng gazed fearfully upon its judge's face; but without judges lived secure. Not yet had the pine-tree, felled on its native mountains, descended from there into the watery plain to visit other lands; men knew no shores except their own. Not yet were cities begirt with steep moats; there were no trumpets of straight, no horns of curving brass, no swords or helmets. There was no need at all of armed men, for nations, secure from war's alarms, passed the years in gentle ease. The earth herself, without compulsion, untouched by hoe or plowshare, of herself gave all things needful. And men, content with food which came with no one's seeking, gathered the arbute fruit, strawberries from the mountain-sides, cornel-cherries, berries hanging thick upon the prickly bramble, and acorns fallen from the spreading tree of Jove. Then spring was everlasting, and gentle zephyrs with warm breath played with the flowers that sprang unplanted. Anon the earth, untilled, brought forth her stores of grain, and the fields, though unfallowed, grew white with the heavy, bearded wheat. Streams of milk and streams of sweet nectar flowed, and yellow honey was distilled from the verdant oak.

After Saturn had been banished to the dark land of death, and the world was under the sway of Jove,[3] the silver race came in, lower in the scale than gold, but of greater worth than yellow brass. Jove now shortened the bounds of the old-time spring, and through winter, summer, variable autumn, and brief spring completed the year in four seasons. Then first the parched air glared white with burning heat, and icicles hung down congealed by freezing winds. In that age men first sought the shelter of houses. Their homes had heretofore been caves, dense thickets, and branches bound together with bark. Then first the seeds of grain were planted in long furrows, and bullocks groaned beneath the heavy yoke.

Next after this and third in order came the brazen race, of sterner disposition, and more ready to fly to arms savage, but not yet impious. The age of hard iron came last. Straightway all evil burst forth into this age of baser vein: modesty and truth and faith fled the earth, and in their place came tricks and plots and snares, violence and cursed love of gain. Men now spread sails to the winds, though the sailor as yet scarce knew them; and keels of pine which long had stood upon high mountain-sides, now leaped insolently over unknown waves. And the ground, which had previously been a common possession like the sunlight and the air, the careful surveyor now marked out with long-drawn boundary-line. Not only did men demand of the bounteous fields the crops and sustenance they owed, but they delved as well into the very bowels of the earth; and the wealth which the creator had hidden away and buried deep amid the very Stygian shades, was brought to light, wealth that pricks men on to crime. And now baneful iron had come, and gold more baneful than iron; war came, which fights with both, and brandished in its bloody hands the clashing arms. Men lived on plunder. Guest was not safe from host, nor father-in-law from son-in-law; even among brothers it was rare to find affection. The husband longed for the death of his wife, she of her husband; murderous stepmothers brewed deadly poisons, and sons inquired into their fathers' years before the time. Piety lay vanquished, and the maiden Astraea, last of the immortals, abandoned the blood-soaked earth.

And, that high heaven might be no safer than the earth, they say that the Giants essayed the very throne of heaven, piling huge mountains, one on another, clear up to the stars. Then the Almighty Father hurled his thunderbolts, shattered Olympus, and dashed

Pelion down from underlying Ossa. When those dread bodies lay overwhelmed by their own bulk, they say that Mother Earth, drenched with their streaming blood, informed that warm gore anew with life, and, that some trace of her former offspring might remain, she gave it human form. But this new stock, too, proved contemptuous of the gods, very greedy for slaughter, and passionate. You might know that they were sons of blood.

When Saturn's son from his high throne saw this he groaned, and, recalling the infamous revels of Lycaon's table—a story still unknown because the deed was new—he conceived a mighty wrath worthy of the soul of Jove, and summoned a council of the gods. Nothing delayed their answer to the summons.

There is a high way, easily seen when the sky is clear. It is called the Milky Way, famed for its shining whiteness. By this way the gods fare to the halls and royal dwelling of the mighty Thunderer. On either side the palaces of the gods of higher rank are thronged with guests through folding-doors flung wide. The lesser gods dwell apart from these. Fronting on this way, the illustrious and strong heavenly gods have placed their homes. This is the place which, if I may make bold to say it, I would not fear to call the Palatia of high heaven.*

So, when the gods had taken their seats within the marble council chamber, the king himself, seated high above the rest and leaning on his ivory sceptre, shook thrice and again his awful locks, with which he moved the land and sea and sky. Then he opened his indignant lips, and thus spoke he: "I was not more troubled than now for the sovereignty of the world when each one of the serpent-footed giants was in act to lay his hundred hands upon the captive sky. For, although that was a savage enemy, their whole attack sprung from one body and one source. But now, wherever old Ocean roars around the earth, I must destroy the race of men. By the infernal streams that glide beneath the earth through Stygian groves, I swear that I have already tried all other means. But that which is incurable must be cut away with the knife, so the untainted part does not also draw infection. I have demigods, rustic

---

*District on the Palatine Hill where Augustus lived.

divinities, nymphs, fauns and satyrs, and sylvan deities upon the mountain-slopes. Since we do not yet esteem them worthy the honor of a place in heaven, let us at least allow them to dwell in safety in the lands allotted them. Or do you think that they will be safe, when against me, who wield the thunderbolt, who have and rule you as my subjects, Lycaon, well known for savagery, has laid his snares?"

All trembled, and with eager zeal demanded him who had been guilty of such bold infamy. So, when an impious band was mad to blot out the name of Rome with Caesar's blood, the human race was dazed with a mighty fear of sudden ruin, and the whole world shuddered in horror. Nor is the loyalty of your subjects, Augustus, less pleasing to you than that was to Jove. After he, by word and gesture, had checked their outcry, all held their peace. When now the clamour had subsided, checked by his royal authority, Jove once more broke the silence with these words: "He has indeed been punished; have no care for that. But what he did and what his punishment I will relate. An infamous report of the age had reached my ears. Eager to prove this false, I descended from high Olympus, and as a god disguised in human form travelled up and down the land. It would take too long to recount how great impiety was found on every hand. The infamous report was far less than the truth. I had crossed Maenala, bristling with the lairs of beasts, Cyllene, and the pine-groves of chill Lycaeus. Then I approached the seat and inhospitable abode of the Arcadian king, just as the late evening shades were ushering in the night. I gave a sign that a god had come, and the common folk began to worship me. Lycaon at first mocked at their pious prayers; and then he said: 'I will soon find out, and that by a plain test, whether this fellow be god or mortal. Nor shall the truth be at all in doubt.' He planned that night while I was heavy with sleep to kill me by an unexpected murderous attack. Such was the experiment he adopted to test the truth. And not content with that, he took a hostage who had been sent by the Molossian race, cut his throat, and some parts of him still warm with life, he boiled, and others he roasted over the fire. But no sooner had he placed these before me on the table than I, with my avenging bolt, overthrew the house upon its master and on his equally unworthy household gods.[4] The king himself flies in terror and, gaining the silent fields, howls aloud, attempting in vain to speak. His mouth of itself gathers foam, and with his accustomed greed for blood he turns against the sheep, delighting still in slaughter. His garments change to shaggy hair, his arms to legs. He turns into a wolf, and yet retains some traces of his former shape. There is the same grey hair, the same fierce face, the same gleaming eyes, the same picture of beastly savagery. One house has fallen; but not one house alone has deserved to perish. Wherever the plains of earth extend, the Furies* reign supreme. You would deem it a conspiracy of crime. Let them all pay, and quickly too, the penalties which they have deserved. So stands my purpose."

When he had done, some proclaimed their approval of his words, and added fuel to his wrath, while others played their parts by giving silent consent. And yet they all grieved over the threatened loss of the human race, and asked what would be the state of the world bereft of mortals. Who would bring incense to their altars? Was he planning to give over the world to the wild beasts to despoil? As they thus questioned, their king bade them be of good cheer (for the rest should be his care), for he would give them another race of wondrous origin far different from the first.

And now he was set to hurl his thunderbolts against the whole world; but he stayed his hand in fear unless perhaps the sacred heavens should take fire from so huge a conflagration, and burn from pole to pole. He remembered also that it was in the fates that a time would come when sea and land, the unkindled palace of the sky and the beleaguered structure of the universe should be destroyed by fire. And so he laid aside the bolts which Cyclopean hands had forged. He preferred a different punishment, to destroy the human race beneath the waves and to send down rain from every quarter of the sky.[5]

Straightway he shuts the North-wind up in the cave of Aeolus, and all blasts soever that put the clouds to flight; but he lets the South-wind loose. Forth flies the South-wind with dripping wings, his awful face shrouded in pitchy darkness. His beard is heavy with rain; water flows in streams down his hoary locks; dark clouds rest

---

*Underworld spirits who pursued criminals. Jove is saying that crime is everywhere.

upon his brow; while his wings and garments drip with dew. And, when he presses the low-hanging clouds with his broad hands, a crashing sound goes forth; and next the dense clouds pour forth their rain. Iris, the messenger of Juno, clad in robes of many hues, draws up water and feeds it to the clouds. The standing grain is overthrown; the crops which have been the object of the farmers' prayers lie ruined; and the hard labour of the tedious year has come to nothing.

The wrath of Jove is not content with the waters from his own sky; his sea-god brother aids him with auxiliary waves. He summons his rivers to council. When these have assembled at the palace of their king, he says: "Now is no time to employ a long harangue. Put forth all your strength, for there is need. Open wide your doors, away with all restraining dykes, and give full rein to all your river steeds." So he commands, and the rivers return, uncurb their fountains' mouths, and in unbridled course go racing to the sea.

Neptune himself smites the earth with his trident. She trembles, and at the stroke flings open wide a way for the waters. The rivers overleap all bounds and flood the open plains. And not only orchards, crops and herds, men and dwellings, but shrines as well and their sacred contents do they sweep away. If any house has stood firm, and has been able to resist that huge misfortune undestroyed, still do the overtopping waves cover its roof, and its towers lie hid beneath the flood. And now the sea and land have no distinction. All is sea, but a sea without a shore.

Here one man seeks a hill-top in his flight; another sits in his curved skiff, plying the oars where lately he has plowed; one sails over his fields of grain or the roof of his buried farmhouse, and one takes fish caught in the elm-tree's top. And sometimes it chanced that an anchor was embedded in a grassy meadow, or the curving keels brushed over the vineyard tops. And where but now the slender goats had browsed, the ugly sea-calves rested. The Nereids are amazed to see beneath the waters groves and cities and the haunts of men. The dolphins invade the woods, brushing against the high branches, and shake the oak-trees as they knock against them in their course. The wolf swims among the sheep, while tawny lions and tigers are borne along by the waves. Neither does the power of his lightning stroke avail the boar, nor his swift limbs the stag, since both are alike swept away by the flood; and the wandering bird, after long searching for a place to alight, falls with weary wings into the sea. The sea in unchecked liberty has now buried all the hills, and strange waves now beat upon the mountain-peaks. Most living things are drowned outright. Those who have escaped the water slow starvation at last overcomes through lack of food.

The land of Phocis separates the Boeotian from the Oetean fields, a fertile land, while still it was a land. But at that time it was but a part of the sea, a broad expanse of sudden waters. There Mount Parnasus lifts its two peaks skyward, high and steep, piercing the clouds. When here Deucalion and his wife, borne in a little skiff, had come to land—for the sea had covered all things else—they first worshipped the Corycian nymphs and the mountain deities, and the goddess, fate-revealing Themis, who in those days kept the oracles. There was no better man than he, none more scrupulous of right, nor than she was any woman more reverent of the gods. When now Jove saw that the world was all one stagnant pool, and that only one man was left from those who were but now so many thousands, and that but one woman too was left, both innocent and both worshippers of God, he rent the clouds asunder, and when these had been swept away by the North-wind he showed the land once more to the sky, and the heavens to the land. Then too the anger of the sea subsides, when the sea's great ruler lays by his three-pronged spear and calms the waves; and calling sea-hued Triton, showing forth above the deep, his shoulders thick overgrown with shell-fish, he bids him blow into his loud-resounding conch, and by that signal to recall the floods and streams. He lifts his hollow, twisted shell, which grows from the least and lowest to a broad-swelling whorl—the shell which, when in mid-sea it has received the Triton's breath, fills with its notes the shores that lie beneath the rising and the setting sun. So then, when it had touched the sea-god's lips wet with his dripping beard, and sounded forth the retreat which had been ordered, it was heard by all the waters both of land and sea; and all the waters by which it was heard it held in check. Now the sea has shores, the rivers, bank full, keep within their channels; the floods subside, and hill-tops spring into view; land rises up, the ground increasing as the waves decrease; and now at length, after long burial, the trees show their uncovered tops, whose leaves still hold the slime which the flood has left.

The world was indeed restored. But when Deucalion saw that it was an empty world, and that deep silence filled the desolated lands, he burst into tears and thus addressed his wife: "O sister, O my wife, O only woman left on earth, you whom the ties of common race and family, whom the marriage couch has joined to me, and whom now our very perils join: of all the lands which the rising and the setting sun behold, we two are the throng. The sea holds all the rest. And even this hold which we have upon our life is not as yet sufficiently secure. Even yet the clouds strike terror to my heart. What would be your feelings, now, poor soul, if the fates had willed that you be rescued all alone? How would you bear your fear, alone? who would console your grief? For be assured that if the sea should hold me also, I would follow you, my wife, and the sea should hold me also. Oh, would that by my father's arts I might restore the nations, and breathe, as did he, the breath of life into the moulded clay. But as it is, on us two only depends the human race. Such is the will of Heaven: and we remain sole samples of mankind." He spoke; and when they had wept awhile they resolved to appeal to the heavenly power and seek his aid through sacred oracles. Without delay side by side they went to the waters of Cephisus' stream, which, while not yet clear, still flowed within their familiar banks. From this they took some drops and sprinkled them on head and clothing. So having done, they bent their steps to the goddess's sacred shrine, whose gables were still discolored with foul moss, and upon whose altars the fires were dead. When they had reached the temple steps they both fell prone upon the ground, and with trembling lips kissed the chill stone and said: "If deities are appeased by the prayers of the righteous, if the wrath of the gods is thus turned aside, O Themis, tell us by what means our race may be restored, and bring aid, O most merciful, to a world overwhelmed."

The goddess was moved and gave this oracle: "Depart from here, and with veiled heads and loosened robes throw behind you as you go the bones of your great mother." Long they stand in dumb amaze; and first Pyrrha breaks the silence and refuses to obey the bidding of the goddess. With trembling lips she prays for pardon, but dares not outrage her mother's ghost by treating her bones as she is bid. Meanwhile they go over again the words of the oracle, which had been given so full of dark perplexities, and turn them over and over in their minds. At last Prometheus' son comforts the daughter of Epimetheus with reassuring words: "Either my wit is at fault, or else (oracles are holy and never counsel guilt!) our great mother is the earth, and I think that the bones which the goddess speaks of are the stones in the earth's body. It is these that we are bidden to throw behind us."

Although Pyrrha is moved by her husband's surmise, yet hope still wavers; so distrustful are they both as to the heavenly command. But what harm will it do to try? They go down, veil their heads, ungird their robes, and throw stones behind them just as the goddess had bidden. And the stones—who would believe it unless ancient tradition vouched for it?—began at once to lose their hardness and stiffness, to grow soft slowly, and softened to take on form. Then, when they had grown in size and become milder in their nature, a certain likeness to the human form, indeed, could be seen, still not very clear, but such as statues just begun out of marble have, not sharply defined, and very like roughly blocked-out images. That part of them, however, which was earthy and damp with slight moisture, was changed to flesh; but what was solid and incapable of bending became bone; that which was but now veins remained under the same name. And in a short time, through the operation of the divine will, the stones thrown by the man's hand took on the form of men, and women were made from the stones the woman threw. From this comes the hardness of our race and our endurance of toil; and we give proof from what origin we are sprung.

As to the other forms of animal life, the earth spontaneously produced these of divers kinds; after that old moisture remaining from the flood had grown warm from the rays of the sun, the slime of the wet marshes swelled with heat, and the fertile seeds of life, nourished in that life-giving soil, as in a mother's womb, grew and in time took on some special form. So when the seven-mouthed Nile has receded from the drenched fields and has returned again to its former bed, and the fresh slime has been heated by the sun's rays, farmers as they turn over the lumps of earth find many animate things; and among these some, but now begun, are upon the very verge of life, some are unfinished and lacking in their proper parts, and oft-times in the same body one part is alive and the other still nothing but raw earth. For when moisture and heat unite, life is conceived, and from these two sources all living things spring. And, though fire and water are naturally at enmity, still heat and moisture produce all things, and this inharmonious harmony is fitted to the growth of life. When, therefore, the earth, covered with mud from the recent flood, became heated up by the hot and genial rays of the sun, she brought forth innumerable forms of life; in part she restored the ancient shapes, and in part she created creatures new and strange.

She, indeed, would have wished not to do so, but you also she then bore, you, huge Python, you snake unknown before, who was a terror to new-created men; so huge a space of mountain-side did you fill. This monster the god of the glittering bow destroyed with arms never before used except against does and wild she-goats, crushing him with countless darts, nearly emptying his quiver, till the creature's poisonous blood flowed from the black wounds. And, that the fame of his deed might not perish through lapse of time, he instituted sacred games whose contests throngs beheld, called Pythian from the name of the serpent he had overthrown. At these games, every youth who had been victorious in boxing, running, or the chariot race received the honor of an oaken garland. For as yet the laurel-tree was not, and Phoebus was wont to wreathe his temples, comely with flowing locks, with a garland from any tree.

Now the first love of Phoebus was Daphne, daughter of Peneus, the river-god. It was no blind chance that gave this love, but the malicious wrath of Cupid. Delian Apollo, while still exulting over his conquest of the serpent, had seen him bending his bow with tight-drawn string, and had said: "What have you to do with the arms of men, you wanton boy? That weapon befits my shoulders; for I have strength to give unerring wounds to the wild beasts, my foes, and have but now laid low the Python swollen with countless darts, covering whole acres with plague-engendering form. You ought to be content with your torch to light the hidden fires of love, and not lay claim to my honors." And to him Venus' son replied: "Your dart may pierce all things else, Apollo, but mine shall pierce you; and by as much as all living things are less than gods, by so much less is your glory than mine." So saying he shook his wings and, dashing upward through the air, quickly alighted on the shady peak of Parnasus. There he took from his quiver two darts of opposite effect: one puts to flight, the other kindles the flame of love. The one which kindles love is of gold and has a sharp, gleaming point; the other is blunt and tipped with lead. This last the god fixed in the heart of Peneus' daughter, but with the other he smote Apollo, piercing even unto the bones and marrow. Straightway he burned with love; but she fled the very name of love, rejoicing in the deep fastnesses of the woods, and in the spoils of beasts which she had snared, vying with the virgin Phoebe. A single fillet bound her locks all unarranged. Many sought her; but she, averse to all suitors, impatient of control and without thought for man, roamed the pathless woods, nor cared at all that Hymen, love, or wedlock might be. Often her father said: "Daughter, you owe me a son-in-law"; and often: "Daughter, you owe me grandsons." But she, hating the wedding torch as if it were a thing of evil, would blush rosy red over her fair face, and, clinging around her father's neck with coaxing arms, would say: "O father, dearest, grant me to enjoy perpetual virginity. Her father has already granted this to Diana." He, indeed, yielded to her request. But that beauty of yours, Daphne, forbade the fulfilment of your desire, and your form did not fit with your prayer: Phoebus loves Daphne at sight, and longs to wed her; and what he longs for, that he hopes; and his own gifts of prophecy deceive him. And as the stubble of the harvested grain is kindled, as hedges burn with the torches which some traveller has chanced to put too near, or has gone off and left at break of day, so was the god consumed with flames, so did he burn in all his heart, and feed his fruitless love on hope. He looks at her hair hanging down her neck in disarray, and says: "What if it were arrayed?" He gazes at her eyes gleaming like stars, he gazes upon her lips, which but to gaze on does not satisfy. He marvels at her fingers, hands, and wrists, and her arms, bare to the shoulder; and what is hid he deems still lovelier. But she flees him swifter than the fleeting breeze, nor does she stop when he calls after her: "O nymph, O Peneus' daughter, stay! I who pursue you am no enemy. Oh stay! So does the lamb flee from the wolf; the deer from the lion; so do doves on fluttering wing flee from the eagle; so every creature flees its foes. But love is the cause of my pursuit. Ah me! I fear that you will fall, or brambles mar your innocent limbs, and I be cause of pain to you. The region here is rough through which you hurry. Run with less speed, I pray, and hold your flight. I, too,

will follow with less speed. No, stop and ask who your lover is. I am
no mountain-dweller, no shepherd I, no unkempt guardian here of
flocks and herds. You do not know, rash one, you do not know from
whom you flee, and for that reason you *do* flee. Mine is the
Delphian land, and Claros, Tenedos, and the realm of Patara ac-
knowledge me as lord. Jove is my father. By me what shall be, has
been, and what is are all revealed; by me the lyre responds in har-
mony to song. My arrow is sure of aim, but oh, one arrow, surer than
my own, has wounded my heart but now so fancy free. The art of
medicine is my discovery. I am called Help-Bringer throughout the
world, and all the potency of herbs is given unto me. Alas, that love
is curable by no herbs, and the arts which heal all others cannot heal
their lord!"

He would have said more, but the maiden pursued her frightened
way and left him with his words unfinished, even in her desertion
seeming fair. The winds bared her limbs, the opposing breezes set
her garments a-flutter as she ran, and a light air flung her locks
streaming behind her. Her beauty was enhanced by flight. But the
chase drew to an end, for the youthful god would not longer waste
his time in coaxing words, and urged on by love, he pursued at ut-
most speed. Just as when a Gallic hound has seen a hare in an open
plain, and seeks his prey on flying feet, but the hare, safety; he, just
about to fasten on her, now, even now thinks he has her, and grazes
her very heels with his outstretched muzzle; but she knows not
whether she be not already caught, and barely escapes from those
sharp fangs and leaves behind the jaws just closing on her: so ran
the god and maid, he sped by hope and she by fear. But he ran the
more swiftly, borne on the wings of love, gave her no time to rest,
hung over her fleeing shoulders and breathed on the hair that
streamed over her neck. Now was her strength all gone, and, pale
with fear and utterly overcome by the toil of her swift flight, seeing
her father's waters near, she cried: "O father, help! if your waters
hold divinity; change and destroy this beauty by which I pleased too
well." Scarce had she thus prayed when a down-dragging numbness
seized her limbs, and her soft sides were begirt with thin bark. Her
hair was changed to leaves, her arms to branches. Her feet, but now
so swift, grew fast in sluggish roots, and her head was now but a
tree's top. Her gleaming beauty alone remained.

But even now in this new form Apollo loved her; and placing his hand upon the trunk, he felt the heart still fluttering beneath the bark. He embraced the branches as if human limbs, and pressed his lips upon the wood. But even the wood shrank from his kisses. And the god cried out to this: "Since you cannot be my bride, you shall at least be my tree. My hair, my lyre, my quiver shall always be entwined with you, O laurel. With you shall Roman generals wreathe their heads, when shouts of joy shall acclaim their triumph, and long processions climb the Capitol. You at Augustus' portals shall stand a trusty guardian, and keep watch over the civic crown of oak which hangs between. And as my head is ever young and my locks unshorn, so you must keep the beauty of your leaves perpetual." Paean was done. The laurel waved her new-made branches, and seemed to move her head-like top in full consent.

There is a vale in Thessaly which steep-wooded slopes surround on every side. Men call it Tempe. Through this the River Peneus flows from the foot of Pindus with foam-flecked waters, and by its heavy fall forms clouds which drive along fine, smoke-like mist, sprinkles the tops of the trees with spray, and deafens even remoter regions by its roar. Here is the home, the seat, the inmost haunt of the mighty stream. Here, seated in a cave of overhanging rock, he was giving laws to his waters, and to his water-nymphs. To here came, first, the rivers of his own country, not knowing whether to congratulate or console the father of Daphne: the poplar-fringed Sperchios, the restless Enipeus, hoary Apidanus, gentle Amphrysos and Aeas; and later all the rivers which, by whatsoever way their current carries them, lead down their waters, weary with wandering, into the sea. Inachus only does not come; but, hidden away in his deepest cave, he augments his waters with his tears, and in utmost wretchedness laments his daughter, Io, as lost. He knows not whether she still lives or is among the shades. But, since he cannot find her anywhere, he thinks she must be nowhere, and his anxious soul forbodes things worse than death.

Now Jove had seen her returning from her father's stream, and said: "O maiden, worthy of the love of Jove, and destined to make some husband happy, seek now the shade of these deep woods"—and he pointed to the shady woods—"while the sun at his zenith's height is overwarm. But if you fear to go alone among the haunts of wild beasts, under a god's protection you shall tread in safety even the inmost woods. Nor am I of the common gods, but I am he who holds high heaven's sceptre in his mighty hand, and hurls the roaming thunderbolts. Oh, do not flee from me!"—for she was already in flight. Now had she left behind the pasture-fields of Lerna, and the Lyrcean plains thick-set with trees, when the god hid the wide land in a thick, dark cloud, caught the fleeing maid and ravished her.

Meanwhile Juno chanced to look down upon the midst of Argos, and marvelled that quick-rising clouds had wrought the aspect of night in the clear light of day. She knew that they were not river mists nor fogs exhaled from the damp earth; and at once she glanced around to see where her lord might be, as one who knew well his oft-discovered wiles. When she could not find him in the sky she said: "Either I am mistaken or I am being wronged"; and gliding down from the top of heaven, she stood upon the earth and bade the clouds disperse. But Jove had felt beforehand his spouse's coming and had changed the daughter of Inachus into a white heifer. Even in this form she still was beautiful. Saturnia looked awhile upon the heifer in grudging admiration; then asked whose she was and from where she came or from what herd, as if she did not know full well. Jove lyingly declared that she had sprung from the earth, that so he might forestall all further question as to her origin. Thereupon Saturnia asked for the heifer as a gift. What should he do? It would be a cruel task to surrender his love, but not to do so would arouse suspicion. Shame on one side prompts to give her up, but love on the other urges not. Shame by love would have been overcome; but if so poor a gift as a heifer were refused to her who was both his sister and his wife, perhaps she had seemed to be no heifer.

Though her rival was at last given up, the goddess did not at once put off all suspicion, for she feared Jove and further treachery, until she had given her over to Argus, the son of Arestor, to keep for her. Now Argus' head was set about with a hundred eyes, which took their rest in sleep two at a time in turn, while the others watched and remained on guard. In whatsoever way he stood he looked at Io; even when his back was turned he had Io before his eyes. In the day-time he allowed her to graze; but when the sun had set beneath the earth he shut her up and tied an ignominious halter round her neck. She fed on leaves of trees and bitter herbs, and instead of a couch the poor thing lay upon the ground, which was not always grassy, and drank water from the muddy streams. When she strove to stretch out suppliant arms to Argus, she had no arms to stretch; and when she attempted to voice her complaints, she only mooed. She would start with fear at the sound, and was filled with terror at her own voice. She came also to the bank of her father's stream, where she used to play; but when she saw, reflected in the water, her gaping jaws and sprouting horns, she fled in very terror of herself. Her Naiad sisters knew not who she was, nor yet her father, Inachus himself. But she followed him and her sisters, and offered herself to be petted and admired. Old Inachus had plucked some grass and held it out to her; she licked her father's hand and tried to kiss it. She could not restrain her tears, and, if only she could speak, she would tell her name and sad misfortune, and beg for aid. But instead of words, she did tell the sad story of her changed form with letters which she traced in the dust with her hoof. "Ah, woe is me!" exclaimed her father, Inachus; and, clinging to the weeping heifer's horns and snow-white neck: "Ah, woe is me! are you indeed my daughter whom I have sought all over the earth? You would have been, a lighter grief unfound than found. You are silent, and give me back no answer to my words; you only heave deep sighs, and, what alone you can, you moo in reply. I, in blissful ignorance, was preparing marriage rites for you, and had hopes, first of a son-in-law, and then of grandchildren. But now from the herd must I find you a husband, and from the herd must I look for grandchildren. And even by death I may not end my crushing woes. It is a dreadful thing to be a god, for the door of death is shut to me, and my grief must go on without end." As they thus wept together star-eyed Argus separated them and drove the daughter, torn from her father's arms, to more distant pastures. There he perched himself apart upon a high mountain-top, where at his ease he could keep watch on every side.

But now the ruler of the heavenly ones can no longer bear these great sufferings of Io, and he calls his son whom the shining Pleiad* bore, and bids him do Argus to death. Without delay Mercury puts on his winged sandals, takes in his potent hand his sleep-producing

---

*That is, Maia, mother of Mercury, later transformed into a star.

wand, and dons his magic cap. Thus arrayed, the son of Jove leaps down from sky to earth, where he removes his cap and lays aside his wings. Only his wand he keeps. With this, in the character of a shepherd, through the sequestered country paths he drives a flock of goats which he has collected as he came along, and plays upon his reed pipe as he goes. Juno's guardsman is greatly taken with the strange sound. "You, there," he calls, "whoever you are, you might as well sit beside me on this rock; for nowhere is there richer grass for the flock, and you see that there is shade convenient for shepherds."

So Atlas' grandson takes his seat, and fills the passing hours with talk of many things; and by making music on his pipe of reeds he tries to overcome those watchful eyes. But Argus strives valiantly against his slumberous languor, and though he allows some of his eyes to sleep, still he continues to watch with the others. He asks also how the reed pipe came to be invented; for at that time it had but recently been invented.

Then said the god: "On Arcadia's cool mountain-slopes, among the wood nymphs who dwelt on Nonacris, there was one much sought by suitors. Her sister nymphs called her Syrinx. More than once she had eluded the pursuit of satyrs and all the gods who dwell either in the bosky woods or fertile fields. But she patterned after the Delian goddess* in her pursuits and above all in her life of maidenhood. When girt after the manner of Diana, she would deceive the beholder, and could be mistaken for Latona's daughter, were not her bow of horn, were not Diana's of gold. But even so she was mistaken for the goddess.

"One day Pan saw her as she was coming back from Mount Lycaeus, his head wreathed with a crown of sharp pine-needles, and thus addressed her. . . ." It remained still to tell what he said and to relate how the nymph, spurning his prayers, fled through the pathless wastes until she came to Ladon's stream flowing peacefully along his sandy banks; how here, when the water checked her further flight, she besought her sisters of the stream to change her form; and how Pan, when now he thought he had caught Syrinx, instead of her held nothing but marsh reeds in his arms; and while

---

*Diana was associated with the island of Delos; hence, the epithet "Delian."

he sighed in disappointment, the soft air stirring in the reeds gave forth a low and complaining sound. Touched by this wonder and charmed by the sweet tones, the god exclaimed: "This union, at least, shall I have with you." And so the pipes, made of unequal reeds fitted together by a joining of wax, took and kept the name of the maiden. When Mercury was going on to tell this story, he saw that all those eyes had yielded and were closed in sleep. Straightway he checks his words, and deepens Argus' slumber by passing his magic wand over those sleep-faint eyes. And at once he strikes with his hooked sword the nodding head just where it joins the neck, and sends it bleeding down the rocks, defiling the rugged cliff with blood. Argus, you now lie low; the light which you had within your many fires is all put out; and one darkness fills your hundred eyes.

Saturnia took these eyes and set them on the feathers of her bird, filling his tail with star-like jewels. Straightway she flamed with anger, nor did she delay the fulfilment of her wrath. She set a terror-bearing fury to work before the eyes and heart of her Grecian rival, planted deep within her breast a goading fear, and sent her fleeing in terror through all the world. You alone, O Nile, did close her boundless toil. When she reached the stream, she flung herself down on her knees upon the river bank; with head thrown back she raised her face, which was all she could raise, to the high stars, and with groans and tears and agonized mooings she seemed to voice her griefs to Jove and to beg him to end her woes. Thereupon Jove threw his arms about his spouse's neck, and begged her at last to end her vengeance, saying: "Lay aside all fear for the future; she shall never be source of grief to you again"; and he called upon the Stygian pools to witness his oath.

The goddess's wrath is soothed; Io gains back her former looks, and becomes what she was before. The rough hair falls away from her body, her horns disappear, her great round eyes grow smaller, her gaping mouth is narrowed, her shoulders and her hands come back, and the hoofs are gone, being changed each into five nails. No trace of the heifer is left in her except only the fair whiteness of her body. And now the nymph, able at last to stand upon two feet, stands erect; yet fears to speak, in case she moo in the heifer's way, and with fear and trembling she resumes her long-abandoned speech.

Now, with fullest service, she is worshipped as a goddess by the linen-robed throng. A son, Epaphus, was born to her, thought to have sprung at length from the seed of mighty Jove, and throughout the cities dwelt in temples with his mother.[6] He had a companion of like mind and age named Phaëthon, child of the Sun. When this Phaëthon was once speaking proudly, and refused to give way to him, boasting that Phoebus was his father, the grandson of Inachus rebelled and said: "You are a fool to believe all your mother tells you, and are swelled up with false notions about your father." Phaëthon grew red with rage, but repressed his anger through very shame and carried Epaphus' insulting taunt straight to his mother, Clymene. "And that you may grieve the more, mother," he said, "I, the high-spirited, the bold of tongue, had no word to say. Ashamed am I that such an insult could have been uttered and yet could not be answered. But do you, if I am indeed sprung from heavenly seed, give me a proof of my high birth, and justify my claims to divine origin." So spoke the lad, and threw his arms around his mother's neck, begging her, by his own and Merops' life, by his sisters' nuptial torches, to give him some sure token of his birth. Clymene, moved (it is uncertain whether by the prayers of Phaëthon, or more by anger at the insult to herself), stretched out both arms to heaven, and, turning her eyes on the bright sun, exclaimed: "By the splendour of that radiant orb which both hears and sees me now, I swear to you, my boy, that you are sprung from the Sun, that being whom you behold, that being who sways the world. If I speak not the truth, may I never see him more, and may this be the last time my eyes shall look upon the light of day. But it is not difficult for you yourself to find your father's house. The place where he rises is not far from our own land. If you are so minded, go there and ask your question of the sun himself." Phaëthon leaps up in joy at his mother's words, already grasping the heavens in imagination; and after crossing his own Ethiopia and the land of Ind lying close beneath the sun, he quickly comes to his father's rising-place.

BOOK II

THE PALACE OF THE Sun stood high on lofty columns, bright with glittering gold and bronze that shone like fire. Gleaming ivory crowned the gables above; the double folding-doors were radiant with burnished silver. And the workmanship was more beautiful than the material. For upon the doors Mulciber* had carved in relief the waters that enfold the central earth, the circle of the lands and the sky that overhangs the lands. The sea holds the dark-hued gods: tuneful Triton, changeful Proteus, and Aegaeon, his strong arms thrown over a pair of huge whales; Doris and her daughters, some of whom are shown swimming through the water, some sitting on a rock drying their green hair, and some riding on fishes. They have not all the same appearance, and yet not altogether different; as it should be with sisters. The land has men and cities, woods and beasts, rivers, nymphs and other rural deities. Above these scenes was placed a representation of the shining sky, six signs of the zodiac on the right-hand doors, and six signs on the left.

Now when Clymene's son had climbed the steep path which leads to there, and had come beneath the roof of his sire whose fatherhood had been questioned, straightway he turned him to his father's face, but halted some little space away; for he could not bear the radiance at a nearer view. Clad in a purple robe, Phoebus sat on his throne gleaming with brilliant emeralds. To right and left stood Day and Month and Year and Century, and the Hours set at equal distances. Young Spring was there, wreathed with a floral crown; Summer, all unclad with garland of ripe grain; Autumn was there, stained with the trodden grape, and icy Winter with white and bristly locks.

---

*Another name for Vulcan, god of the forge.

Seated in the midst of these, the Sun, with the eyes which behold all things, looked on the youth filled with terror at the strange new sights, and said: "Why have you come? What do you seek in this high dwelling, Phaëthon—a son no father need deny?" The lad replied: "O common light of this vast universe, Phoebus, my father, if you grant me the right to use that name, if Clymene is not hiding her shame beneath an unreal pretence, grant me a proof, my father, by which all may know me for your true son, and take away this uncertainty from my mind." He spoke; and his father put off his glittering crown of light, and bade the boy draw nearer. Embracing him, he said: "You are both worthy to be called my son, and Clymene has told you your true origin. And, that you may not doubt my word, ask what gift you'd like, that you may receive it from my hand. And may that Stygian pool whereby gods swear, but which my eyes have never seen, be witness of my promise." Scarce had he ceased when the boy asked for his father's chariot, and the right to drive his winged horses for a day.

The father repented him of his oath. Thrice and again he shook his bright head and said: "Your words have proved mine to have been rashly said. If only I might retract my promise! For I confess, my son, that this alone would I refuse you. But I may at least strive to dissuade you. What you desire is not safe. You ask too great a gift, Phaëthon, and one which does not befit your strength and those so boyish years. Your lot is mortal: not for mortals is what you ask. In your simple ignorance you claim more than can be granted to the gods themselves. Though each of them may do as he will, yet none, but myself, has power to take his place in my chariot of fire. No, even the lord of great Olympus, who hurls dread thunderbolts with his awful hand, could not drive this chariot; and what have we greater than Jove? The first part of the road is steep, up which my steeds in all their morning freshness can scarce make their way. In mid-heaven it is exceeding high; to look down on sea and land from there oft-times causes even me to tremble, and my heart to quake with throbbing fear. The last part of the journey is precipitous, and needs an assured control. Then even Tethys, who receives me in her underlying waters, is wont to fear in case I fall headlong. Furthermore, the vault of heaven spins round in constant motion, drawing along the lofty stars which it whirls at dizzy speed. I make my way against this, nor does the swift motion which overcomes all else overcome me; but I drive clear contrary to the swift circuit of the universe. Suppose you have my chariot. What will you do? Will you be able to make your way against the whirling poles that their swift axis will not sweep away? Perhaps, too, you imagine there are groves there, and cities of the gods, and temples full of rich gifts? But no, the course lies amid lurking dangers and fierce beasts of prey. And if you should hold the way, and not go straying from the course, still you shall pass the horned Bull full in your path, the Haemonian Archer, the maw of the raging Lion, the Scorpion, curving his savage arms in long sweeps, and the Crab, reaching out in the opposite direction. Nor is it an easy thing for you to control the steeds, hot with those strong fires which they have within their breasts, which they breathe out from mouth and nostrils. Scarce do they suffer my control, when their fierce spirits have become heated, and their necks rebel against the reins. But you, O son, beware in case I be the giver of a fatal gift to you, and while there is still time amend your prayer. Do you truly seek sure pledges that you are a son of mine? Behold, I give sure pledges by my very fear; I show myself your father by my fatherly anxiety. See! look upon my face. And oh, if you could only look into my heart as well, and understand a father's cares therein! Then look around, see all that the rich world holds, and from those great and boundless goods of land and sea and sky ask anything. I will deny you nothing. But this one thing I beg you not to ask, which, if rightly understood, is a bane instead of blessing. A bane, my Phaëthon, that you seek as a boon. Why do you throw your coaxing arms about my neck, you foolish boy? No, doubt it not, it shall be given—I have sworn it by the Styx—whatever you choose. But, oh, make a wiser choice!"

The father's warning ended; yet he fought against the words, and urged his first request, burning with desire to drive the chariot. So then the father, delaying as far as might be, led forth the youth to that high chariot, the work of Vulcan. Its axle was of gold, the pole of gold; its wheels had golden tyres and a ring of silver spokes. Along the yoke chrysolites and jewels set in fair array gave back their bright glow to the reflected rays of Phoebus.

Now while the ambitious Phaëthon is gazing in wonder at the workmanship, behold, Aurora, who keeps watch in the reddening dawn, has opened wide her purple gates, and her courts glowing with rosy light. The stars all flee away, and the morning star closes their ranks as, last of all, he departs from his watch-tower in the sky.

When Titan saw him setting and the world grow red, and the slender horns of the waning moon fading from sight, he bade the swift Hours to yoke his steeds. The goddesses quickly did his bidding, and led the horses from the lofty stalls, breathing forth fire and filled with ambrosial food, and they put upon them the clanking bridles. Then the father anointed his son's face with a sacred ointment, and made it proof against the devouring flames; and he placed upon his head the radiant crown, heaving deep sighs the while, presaging woe, and said: "If you can at least obey your father's warnings, spare the lash, my boy, and more strongly use the reins. The horses hasten of their own accord; the hard task is to check their eager feet. And do not take your way straight through the five zones of heaven: the true path runs slantwise, with a wide curve, and, confined within the limits of three zones, avoids the southern heavens and the far north as well. This is your route. The tracks of my wheels you will clearly see. And, that the sky and earth may have equal heat, go not too low, nor yet direct your course along the top of heaven; for if you go too high you will burn up the skies, if too low the earth. In the middle is the safest path. And do not turn off too far to the right towards the writhing Serpent; nor on the left, where the Altar lies low in the heavens, guide your wheel. Hold on between the two. I commit all else to Fortune, and may she aid you, and guide you better than you guide yourself. While I am speaking dewy night has reached her goal on the far western shore. We may no longer delay. We are summoned. Behold, the dawn is glowing, and the shadows all have fled. Here, grasp the reins, or, if your purpose still may be amended, take my counsel, not my chariot, while you still can, while you still stand on solid ground, before you have mounted to the car which you have in ignorance foolishly desired. Let me give light to the world, which you may see in safety."

But the lad has already mounted the swift chariot, and, standing proudly, he takes the reins with joy into his hands, and thanks his unwilling father for the gift.

Meanwhile the sun's swift horses, Pyroïs, Eoüs, Aethon, and the fourth, Phlegon, fill all the air with their fiery whinnying, and paw impatiently against their bars. When Tethys, ignorant of her grandson's fate, dropped these and gave free course through the boundless skies, the horses dashed forth, and with swift-flying feet rent the clouds in their path, and, borne aloft upon their wings, they passed the east winds that have their rising in the same quarter. But the weight was light, not such as the horses of the sun could feel, and the yoke lacked its accustomed burden. And, as curved ships, without their proper ballast, roll in the waves, and, unstable because too light, are borne out of their course, so the chariot, without its accustomed burden, gives leaps into the air, is tossed aloft and is like a riderless car.

When they feel this, the team runs wild and leave the well-beaten track, and fare no longer in the same course as before. The driver is panic-stricken. He knows not how to handle the reins entrusted to him, nor where the road is; nor, if he did know, would he be able to control the steeds. Then for the first time the cold Bears grew hot with the rays of the sun, and tried, though all in vain, to plunge into the forbidden sea. And the Serpent, which lies nearest the icy pole, ever before harmless because sluggish with the cold, now grew hot, and conceived great frenzy from that fire. They say that you also, Boötes, fled in terror, slow though you were, and held back by your clumsy ox-cart.

But when the unhappy Phaëthon looked down from the top of heaven, and saw the lands lying far, far below, he grew pale, his knees trembled with sudden fear, and over his eyes came darkness through excess of light. And now he would prefer never to have touched his father's horses, and repents that he has discovered his true origin and prevailed in his prayer. Now, eager to be called the son of Merops, he is borne along just as a ship driven before the headlong blast, whose pilot has let the useless rudder go and abandoned the ship to the gods and prayers. What shall he do? Much of the sky is now behind him, but more is still in front! His thought measures both. And now he looks forward to the west, which he is destined never to reach, and at times back to the east. Dazed, he knows not what to do; he neither lets go the reins nor can he hold them, and he does not even know the horses' names. To add to his panic fear, he sees scattered everywhere in the sky strange figures of huge and savage beasts. There is one place where the Scorpion bends out his arms into two bows; and with tail and arms stretching out on both sides, he spreads over the space of two signs. When the boy sees this creature reeking with black poisonous sweat, and threatening to sting him with his curving tail, bereft of wits from chilling fear, down he dropped the reins.

When the horses feel these lying on their backs, they break loose from their course, and, with none to check them, they roam through unknown regions of the air. Wherever their impulse leads them, there they rush aimlessly, knocking against the stars set deep in the sky and snatching the chariot along through uncharted ways. Now they climb up to the top of heaven, and now, plunging headlong down, they course along nearer the earth. The Moon in amazement sees her brother's horses running below her own, and the scorched clouds smoke. The earth bursts into flame, the highest parts first, and splits into deep cracks, and its moisture is all dried up. The meadows are burned to white ashes; the trees are consumed, green leaves and all, and the ripe grain furnishes fuel for its own destruction. But these are small losses which I am lamenting. Great cities perish with their walls, and the vast conflagration reduces whole nations to ashes. The woods are ablaze with the mountains; Athos is ablaze, Cilician Taurus, and Tmolus, and Oeta, and Ida, dry at last, but previously covered with springs, and Helicon, haunt of the Muses, and Haemus, not yet linked with the name of Oeagrus. Aetna is blazing boundlessly with flames now doubled, and twin-peaked Parnasus and Eryx, Cynthus and Othrys, and Rhodope, at last destined to lose its snows, Mimas and Dindyma, Mycale and Cithaeron, famed for sacred rites. Nor does its chilling clime save Scythia; Caucasus burns, and Ossa with Pindus, and Olympus, greater than both; and the heaven-piercing Alps and cloud-capped Apennines.

Then indeed does Phaëthon see the earth aflame on every hand; he cannot endure the mighty heat, and the air he breathes is like the hot breath of a deep furnace. The chariot he feels growing white-hot beneath his feet. He can no longer bear the ashes and whirling sparks, and is completely shrouded in the dense, hot smoke. In this pitchy darkness he cannot tell where he is or where he is going, and is swept along at the will of his flying steeds.

It was then, as men think, that the peoples of Aethiopia became black-skinned, since the blood was drawn to the surface of their bodies by the heat. Then also Libya became a desert, for the heat dried up her moisture. Then the nymphs with dishevelled hair bewailed their fountains and their pools. Boeotia mourns the loss of Dirce; Argos, Amymone; Corinth, her Pirenian spring. Nor do rivers, whose lot had given them more spacious channels, remain unscathed. The Don's waters steam; old Peneus, too, Mysian Caïcus, and swift Ismenus; and Arcadian Erymanthus, Xanthus, destined once again to burn; tawny Lycormas, and Maeander, playing along upon its winding way; Thracian Melas and Laconian Eurotas. Babylonian Euphrates burns; Orontes burns, and swift Thermodon; the Ganges, Phasis, Danube; Alpheus boils; Sperchios' banks are aflame. The golden sands of Tagus melt in the intense heat, and the swans, which had been wont to throng the Maeonian streams in tuneful company, are scorched in mid Caÿster. The Nile fled in terror to the ends of the earth, and hid its head, and it is hidden yet. The seven mouths lie empty, filled with dust; seven broad channels, all without a stream. The same mischance dries up the Thracian rivers, Hebrus and Strymon; also the rivers of the west, the Rhine, Rhone, Po, and the Tiber, to whom had been promised the mastery of the world. Great cracks yawn everywhere, and the light, penetrating to the lower world, strikes terror into the infernal king and his consort. Even the sea shrinks up, and what was but now a great, watery expanse is a dry plain of sand. The mountains, which the deep sea had covered before, spring forth, and increase the numbers of the scattered Cyclades. The fish dive to the lowest depths, and the dolphins no longer dare to leap curving above the surface of the sea into their wonted air. The dead bodies of sea-calves float, with upturned belly, on the water's top. They say that Nereus himself and Doris and her daughters were hot as they lay hid in their caves. Thrice Neptune essayed to lift his arms and august face from out the water; thrice did he desist, unable to bear the fiery atmosphere.

Not so all-fostering Earth, who, encircled as she was by sea, amid the waters of the deep, amid her fast-contracting streams which had crowded into her dark bowels and hidden there, though parched by heat, heaved up her smothered face. Raising her shielding hand to her brow and causing all things to shake with her mighty trembling, she sank back a little lower than her wonted place, and then in awful tones she spoke: "If this is your will, and I have deserved all this, why, O king of all the gods, are your lightnings idle? If I must die by fire, oh, let me perish by your fire and lighten my suffering by thought of him who sent it. I scarce can open my lips to speak these words"—the hot smoke was choking her—"See my singed hair and all ashes in my eyes, all ashes over my face. Is this the return, this the reward you pay to my fertility and dutifulness? that I bear the wounds of the crooked plow and mattock, tormented year in, year out? that I provide kindly pasturage for the flocks, grain for mankind, incense for the altars of the gods? But, grant that I have deserved destruction, what has the sea, what has your brother done? Why are the waters which fell to him by the third lot so shrunken, and so much further from your sky? But if no consideration for your brother nor even for me has weight with you, at least have pity on your own heavens. Look around: the heavens are smoking from pole to pole. If the fire shall weaken these, the homes of the gods will fall in ruins. See, Atlas himself is troubled and can scarce bear up the white-hot vault upon his shoulders. If the sea perish and the land and the realms of the sky, then are we hurled back to primeval chaos. Save from the flames whatever yet remains and take thought for the safety of the universe."

So spoke the Earth and ceased, for she could no longer endure the heat; and she retreated into herself and into the depths nearer the land of shades. But the Almighty Father, calling on the gods to witness and him above all who had given the chariot, that unless he bring aid all things will perish by a grievous doom, mounts on high to the top of heaven, where it is his wont to spread the clouds over the broad lands, where he stirs his thunders and flings his hurtling bolts. But now he has no clouds with which to overspread the earth, nor any rains to send down from the sky. He thundered, and, balancing in his right hand a bolt, flung it from beside the ear at the charioteer and hurled him from the car and from life as well, and thus quenched fire with blasting fire. The maddened horses leap apart, wrench their necks from the yoke, and break away from the parted reins. Here lie the reins, there the axle torn from the pole; in another place the spokes of the broken wheels, and fragments of the wrecked chariot are scattered far and wide.

But Phaëthon, fire ravaging his ruddy hair, is hurled headlong and falls with a long trail through the air; as sometimes a star from the clear heavens, although it does not fall, still seems to fall. Him far from his native land, in another quarter of the globe, Eridanus receives and bathes his steaming face. The Naiads in that western land consign his body, still smoking with the flames of that forked bolt, to the tomb and carve this epitaph upon his stone:

HERE PHAËTHON LIES: IN PHOEBUS' CAR HE FARED,
AND THOUGH HE GREATLY FAILED, MORE GREATLY DARED.

The wretched father, sick with grief, hid his face; and, if we are to believe report, one whole day went without the sun. But the burning world gave light, and so even in that disaster was there some service. But Clymene, after she had spoken whatever could be spoken in such woe, melancholy and distraught and tearing her breast, wandered over the whole earth, seeking first his lifeless limbs, then his bones; his bones at last she found, but buried on a river-bank in a foreign land. Here she prostrates herself upon the tomb, drenches the dear name carved in the marble with her tears, and fondles it against her breast. The Heliades, her daughters, join in her lamentation, and pour out their tears in useless tribute to the dead. With bruising hands beating their naked breasts, they call night and day upon their brother, who nevermore will hear their sad laments, and prostrate themselves upon his sepulchre. Four times had the moon with waxing crescents reached her full orb; but they, as was their habit (for use had established habit), were mourning still. Then one day the eldest, Phaëthusa, when she would throw herself upon the grave, complained that her feet had grown cold and stark; and when the fair Lampetia tried to come to her, she was held fast as by sudden roots. A third, making to tear her hair, found her hands plucking at foliage. One complained that her ankles were encased in wood, another that her arms were changing to long branches. And while they look on those things in amazement bark closes round their loins, and, by degrees, their waists, breasts, shoulders, hands; and all that was free were their lips calling upon their mother. What can the frantic mother do but run, as impulse carries her, now here, now there, and print kisses on their lips? That is not enough: she tries to tear away the bark from their bodies and breaks off slender twigs with her hands. But as she does this bloody drops trickle forth as from a wound. And each one, as she is wounded, cries out: "Oh, spare me, mother; spare, I beg you. It is my body that you are tearing in the tree. And now farewell"—the bark closed over her latest words. Still their tears flow on, and these tears, hardened into amber by the sun, drop down from the new-made trees. The clear river receives them and bears them onward, one day to be worn by the brides of Rome.

Cycnus, the son of Sthenelus, was a witness of this miracle. Though he was kin to you, O Phaëthon, by his mother's blood, he was more closely joined in affection. He, abandoning his kingdom—for he ruled over the peoples and great cities of Liguria—went weeping and lamenting along the green banks of the Eridanus, and through the woods which the sisters had increased. And as he went his voice became thin and shrill; white plumage hid his hair and his neck stretched far out from his breast. A web-like membrane joined his reddened fingers, wings clothed his sides, and a blunt beak his mouth. So Cycnus became a strange new bird—the swan. But he did not trust himself to the upper air and Jove, since he remembered the fiery bolt which the god had unjustly hurled. His favorite haunts were the still pools and spreading lakes; and, hating fire, he chose the water for his home, as the opposite of flame.

Meanwhile Phoebus sits in gloomy mourning garb, shorn of his brightness, just as when he is darkened by eclipse. He hates himself and the light of day, gives over his soul to grief, to grief adds rage, and refuses to do service to the world. "Enough," he says; "from time's beginning has my lot been unrestful; I am weary of my endless and unrequited toils. Let any else who chooses drive the chariot of light. If no one will, and all the gods confess that it is beyond their power, let Jove himself do it, that, sometime at least, while he essays to grasp my reins, he may lay aside the bolts that are destined to rob fathers of their boys. Then will he know, when he has himself tried the strength of those fiery-footed steeds, that he who failed to guide them well did not deserve death."

As he thus speaks all the gods stand around him, and beg him humbly not to plunge the world in darkness. Jove himself seeks to excuse the bolt he hurled, and to his prayers adds threats in royal style. Then Phoebus yokes his team again, wild and trembling still with fear; and, in his grief, fiercely plies them with lash and goad, fiercely he plies them, reproaching and taxing them with the death of their master, his son.

But now the Almighty Father makes a round of the great battlements of heaven and examines to see if anything has been loosened by the might of fire. When he sees that these are firm with their immortal strength, he inspects the earth and the affairs of men. Yet Arcadia, above all, is his more earnest care. He restores her springs and rivers, which hardly dare as yet to flow; he gives grass again to the ground, leaves to the trees, and bids the damaged forests grow green again. And as he came and went upon his tasks he chanced to see a certain Arcadian nymph, and straightway the fire he caught grew hot to his very marrow. She had no need to spin soft wools nor to arrange her hair in studied elegance. A simple brooch fastened her gown and a white fillet held her loose-flowing hair. And in this garb, now with a spear, and now a bow in her hand, was she arrayed as one of Phoebe's warriors. Nor was any nymph who roamed over the slopes of Maenalus in higher favor with her goddess than was she. But no favor is of long duration.

The sun was high overhead, just beyond his zenith, when the nymph entered the forest that all years had left unfelled. Here she took her quiver from her shoulder, unstrung her tough bow, and lay down upon the grassy ground, with her head pillowed on her painted quiver. When Jove saw her there, tired out and unprotected: "Here, surely," he said, "my consort will know nothing of my guile; or if she learn it, well bought are taunts at such a price." Straightway he put on the features and dress of Diana and said: "Dear maid, best loved of all my followers, where have you been hunting to-day?" The maiden arose from her grassy couch and said: "Hail to you, my goddess, greater far than Jove, I say, though he himself should hear." Jove laughed to hear her, rejoicing to be prized more highly than himself; and he kissed her lips, not modestly, nor as a maiden kisses. When she began to tell him in what woods her hunt had been, he broke in upon her story with an embrace, and by this outrage betrayed himself. She, in truth, struggled against him with all her girlish might—had you been there to see, Saturnia, your judgment would have been more kind!—but whom could a girl overcome, or who could prevail against Jove? Jupiter won the day, and went back to the sky; she loathed the forest and the woods that knew her secret. As she retraced her path she almost forgot to take up the quiver with its arrows, and the bow she had hung up.

But see, Diana, with her train of nymphs, approaches along the
slopes of Maenalus, proud of her trophies of the chase. She sees our
maiden and calls to her. At first she flees in fear, in case this should
be Jove in disguise again. But when she sees the other nymphs com-
ing too, she is reassured and joins the band. Alas, how hard it is not
to betray a guilty conscience in the face! She walks with downcast
eyes, not, as was her wont, close to her goddess, and leading all the
rest. Her silence and her blushes give clear tokens of her plight; and,
were not Diana herself a maid, she could know her guilt by a thou-
sand signs; it is said that the nymphs knew it. Nine times since then
the crescent moon had grown full orbed, when the goddess, worn
with the chase and overcome by the hot sun's rays, came to a cool
grove through which a gently murmuring stream flowed over its
smooth sands. The place delighted her and she dipped her feet into
the water. Delighted too with this, she said to her companions:
"Come, no one is near to see; let us disrobe and bathe us in the
brook." The Arcadian blushed, and, while all the rest obeyed, she
only sought excuses for delay. But her companions forced her to
comply, and there her shame was openly confessed. As she stood
terror-stricken, vainly striving to hide her state, Diana cried:
"Begone! and pollute not our sacred pool"; and so expelled her from
her company.

The great Thunderer's wife had known all this long since; but she
had put off her vengeance until a fitting time. And now that time
was come; for, to add a sting to Juno's hate, a boy, Arcas, had been
born of her rival. Whereto when she turned her angry mind and her
angry eyes, "See there!" she cried, "nothing was left, adulteress, than
to breed a son, and publish my wrong by his birth, a living witness
to my lord's shame. But you shall suffer for it. For I will take away
the beauty with which you delight yourself, brazen girl, and him
who is my husband." So saying, she caught her by the hair full in
front and flung her face-foremost to the ground. And when the girl
stretched out her arms in prayer for mercy, her arms began to grow
rough with black shaggy hair; her hands changed into feet tipped
with sharp claws; and her lips, which but now Jove had praised, were
changed to broad, ugly jaws; and, that she might not move him with
entreating prayers, her power of speech was taken from her, and
only a harsh, terrifying growl came hoarsely from her throat. Still

her human feelings remained, though she was now a bear; with constant moanings she shows her grief, stretches up such hands as are left her to the heavens, and, though she cannot speak, still feels the ingratitude of Jove. Ah, how often, not daring to lie down in the lonely woods, she wandered before her home and in the fields that had once been hers! How often was she driven over the rocky ways by the baying of hounds and, huntress though she was, fled in affright before the hunters! Often she hid at sight of the wild beasts, forgetting what she was; and, though herself a bear, shuddered at sight of other bears which she saw on the mountain-slopes. She even feared the wolves, although her own father, Lycaon, ran with the pack.

And now Arcas, Lycaon's grandson, had reached his fifteenth year, ignorant of his mother's plight. While he was hunting the wild beasts, seeking out their favorite haunts, hemming the Arcadian woods with his close-wrought nets, he chanced upon his mother, who stopped still at sight of Arcas, and seemed like one that recognized him. He shrank back at those unmoving eyes that were fixed for ever upon him, and feared he knew not what; and when she tried to come nearer, he was just in the act of piercing her breast with his wound-dealing spear. But the Omnipotent stayed his hand, and together he removed both themselves and the crime, and together caught up through the void in a whirlwind, he set them in the heavens and made them neighbouring stars.

Then indeed did Juno's wrath wax hotter still when she saw her rival shining in the sky, and straight went down to Tethys, venerable goddess of the sea, and to old Ocean, whom oft the gods hold in reverence. When they asked her the cause of her coming, she began: "Do you ask me why I, the queen of heaven, am here? Another queen has usurped my heaven. Count my word false if tonight, when darkness has obscured the sky, you see not new constellations fresh set, to outrage me, in the place of honor in highest heaven, where the last and shortest circle encompasses the utmost pole. And is there any reason now why anyone should hesitate to insult Juno and should fear my wrath, who do but help where I would harm? Oh, what great things have I accomplished! What unbounded power is mine! She whom I drove out of human form has now become a goddess. So do I punish those who wrong me! Such is my vaunted might! It only remains for him to release her from her bestial form and restore her former features, as he did once before in Argive Io's case. Why, now that I am deposed, should he not wed and set her in my chamber, and become Lycaon's son-in-law? But do you, if the insult to your foster-child moves you, debar these bears from your green pools, disown stars which have gained heaven at the price of shame, and let not that harlot bathe in your pure stream."

The gods of the sea granted her prayer, and Saturnia, mounting her swift chariot, was borne back through the yielding air by her gaily decked peacocks, peacocks but lately decked with the slain Argus' eyes, at the same time that your plumage, talking raven, though white before, had been suddenly changed to black. For he had once been a bird of silvery-white plumage, so that he rivalled the spotless doves, nor yielded to the geese which one day were to save the Capitol with their watchful cries,[1] nor to the river-loving swan. But his tongue was his undoing. Through his tongue's fault the talking bird, which once was white, was now the opposite of white.

In all Thessaly there was no fairer maid than Coronis of Larissa. She surely found favor in your eyes, O Delphic god, so long as she was chaste—or undetected. But the bird of Phoebus discovered her unchastity, and was hasting with all speed, hard-hearted tattler, to his master to disclose the sin he had spied out. The gossiping crow followed him on flapping wings and asked the news. But when he heard the real object of the trip he said: "It's no profitable journey you are taking, my friend. Scorn not the forewarning of my tongue. See what I used to be and what I am now, and then ask the reason for it. You will find that good faith was my undoing. Once upon a time a child was born, named Erichthonius, a child without a mother.[2] Him Pallas hid in a box woven of Actaean osiers, and gave this to the three daughters of double-shaped Cecrops, with the strict command not to look upon her secret. Hidden in the light leaves that grew thick over an elm, I set myself to watch what they would do. Two of the girls, Pandrosos and Herse, watched the box in good faith, but the third, Aglauros, called her sisters cowards, and with her hand undid the fastenings. And within they saw a baby-boy and a snake stretched out beside him. I went and betrayed them to the goddess, and for my pains I was turned out of my place as Minerva's attendant and put after the bird of night! My punishment ought to be a warning to all birds not to invite trouble by talking too much. But perhaps (do you say?) she did not seek me out of her own accord, when I asked no such thing? Well, you may ask Pallas herself. Though she be angry with me now, she will not deny that, for all her anger. It is a well-known story. I once was a king's daughter, child of the famous Coroneus in the land of Phocis, and—no, do not scorn me—rich suitors sought me in marriage. But my beauty proved my curse. For once, while I paced, as is my wont, along the shore with slow steps over the sand's top, the god of the ocean saw me and grew hot. And when his prayers and coaxing words proved but waste of time, he offered force and pursued. I ran from him, leaving the hard-packed beach, and was quickly worn out, but all to no purpose, in the soft sand beyond. Then I cried out for help to gods and men, but my cries reached no mortal ear. But the virgin goddess heard a virgin's prayer and came to my aid. I was stretching my arms to heaven, when my arms began to darken with light feathers. I strove to cast my mantle from my shoulders, but it was feathers, too, which had already struck their roots deep into my skin. I tried to beat my bare breasts with my hands, but I found I had now neither breasts nor hands. I would run; and now the sand did not retard my feet as before, but I skimmed lightly along the top of the ground, and soon I floated on the air, soaring high; and so I was given to Minerva to be her blameless comrade. But of what use was that to me, if, after all, Nyctimene, who was changed into a bird because of her vile sins, has been put in my place? Or have you not heard the tale all Lesbos knows too well, how Nyctimene outraged the sanctity of her father's bed? And, bird though she now is, still, conscious of her guilt, she flees the sight of men and light of day, and tries to hide her shame in darkness, outcast by all from the whole radiant sky."[3]

In reply to all this the raven said: "On your own head, I pray, be the evil that warning portends; I scorn the idle prophecy," continued on his way to his master, and then told him that he had seen Coronis lying beside the youth of Thessaly. When that charge was heard the laurel glided from the lover's head; together countenance and color changed, and the quill dropped from the hand of the god. And as his heart became hot with swelling anger he seized his accustomed arms, strung his bent bow from the horns, and transfixed with unerring shaft the bosom which had been so often pressed to his own. The smitten maid groaned in agony, and, as the arrow was drawn out, her white limbs were drenched with her red blood. "It was right, O Phoebus," she said, "that I should suffer thus from you, but first I should have borne my child. But now two of us shall die in one." And while she spoke her life ebbed out with her streaming blood, and soon her body, its life all spent, lay cold in death.

The lover, alas! too late repents his cruel act; he hates himself because he listened to the tale and was so quick to break out in wrath. He hates the bird by which he has been compelled to know the offence that brought his grief; bow and hand he hates, and with that hand the hasty arrows too. He fondles the fallen girl, and too late tries to bring help and to conquer fate; but his healing arts are exercised in vain. When his efforts were of no avail, and he saw the pyre made ready with the funeral fires which were to consume her limbs, then indeed—for the cheeks of the heavenly gods may not be wet with tears—from his deep heart he uttered piteous groans; such groans as the young cow utters when before her eyes the hammer high poised from beside the right ear crashes with its resounding blow through the hollow temples of her suckling calf. The god pours fragrant incense on her unconscious breast, gives her the last embrace, and performs all the fit offices unfitly for the dead. But that his own son should perish in the same funeral fires he cannot brook. He snatched the unborn child from his mother's womb and from the devouring flames, and bore him for safe keeping to the cave of two-formed Chiron. But the raven, which had hoped only for reward from his truth-telling, he forbad to take their place among white birds.

Meantime the Centaur was rejoicing in his foster-child of heavenly stock, glad at the honor which the task brought with it, when lo! there comes his daughter, her shoulders overmantled with red-gold locks, whom once the nymph, Chariclo, bearing her to him upon the banks of the swift stream, had called thereafter Ocyrhoë. She was not satisfied to have learnt her father's art, but she sang prophecy. So when she felt in her soul the prophetic madness, and was warmed by the divine fire prisoned in her breast, she looked upon the child and cried: "O child, health-bringer to the whole world, speed your growth. Often shall mortal bodies owe their lives to you, and to you it shall be counted right to restore the spirits of the departed. But having dared this once in scorn of the gods, from power to give life a second time you shall be prevented by your grandsire's lightning. So, from a god you shall become but a lifeless corpse; but from this corpse you shall again become a god and twice renew your fates. You also, dear father, who is now immortal and destined by the law of your birth to last through all the ages, shall some day long for power to die, when you shall be in agony with all your limbs burning with the fatal Hydra's blood. But at last, from immortal the gods shall make you capable of death, and the three goddesses shall loose your thread." Still other fates remained to tell; but suddenly she sighed deeply, and with flowing tears said: "The fates forestall me and forbid me to speak more. My power of speech fails me. Not worth the cost were those arts which have brought down the wrath of heaven upon me. I would that I had never known the future. Now my human shape seems to be passing. Now grass pleases as food; now I am eager to race around the broad pastures. I am turning into a mare, my kindred shape. But why completely? Surely my father is half human." Even while she spoke, the last part of her complaint became scarce understood and her words were all confused. Soon they seemed neither words nor yet the sound of a horse, but as of one trying to imitate a horse. At last she clearly whinnied and her arms became legs and moved along the ground. Her fingers drew together and one continuous light hoof of horn bound together the five nails of her hand. Her mouth enlarged, her neck was extended, the train of her gown became a tail; and her locks as they lay roaming over her neck were become a mane on the right side. Now was she changed alike in voice and feature; and this new wonder gave her a new name as well.

The half-divine son of Philyra[4] wept and vainly called on you for aid, O lord of Delphi. For you could not revoke the edict of mighty Jove, nor, if you could, were you then at hand. In those days you were dwelling in Elis and the Messenian fields. Your garment was a shepherd's cloak, your staff a stout stick from the wood, and a pipe made of seven unequal reeds was in your hand. And while your thoughts were all of love, and while you discoursed sweetly on the pipe, the cattle you were keeping strayed, it is said, all unguarded into the Pylian fields. There Maia's son spied them, and by his native craft drove them into the woods and hid them there. Nobody saw the theft except one old man well known in that neighbourhood, called Battus by all the countryside. He, as a hired servant of the wealthy Neleus, was watching a herd of blooded mares in the glades and rich pasture-fields thereabouts. Mercury feared his tattling and, drawing him aside with cajoling hand, said: "Whoever you are, my man, if anyone should chance to ask you if you have seen any cattle going by here, say that you have not; and, that your kindness may not go unrewarded, you may choose out a sleek heifer for your pay"; and he gave him the heifer at once. The old man took it and replied: "Go on, stranger, and feel safe. That stone will tell of your thefts sooner than I"; and he pointed out a stone. The son of Jove pretended to go away, but soon came back with changed voice and form, and said: "My good fellow, if you have seen any cattle going along this way, help me out, and don't refuse to tell about it, for they were stolen. I'll give you a cow and a bull into the bargain if you'll tell." The old man, tempted by the double reward, said: "You'll find them over there at the foot of that mountain." And there, true enough, they were. Mercury laughed him to scorn and said: "Would you betray me to myself, you rogue? me to my very face?" So saying, he turned the faithless fellow into a flinty stone, which even to this day is called touch-stone; and the old reproach still rests upon the undeserving flint.

The god of the caduceus had taken himself away on level wings and now as he flew he was looking down upon the Munychian fields, the land that Minerva loves, and the groves of the learned Lyceum. That day chanced to be a festival of Pallas when young maidens bore to their goddess' temple mystic gifts in flower-wreathed baskets on their heads. The winged god saw them as they were returning home and directed his way towards them, not straight down but sweeping in such a curve as when the swift kite has spied the fresh-slain sacrifice, afraid to come down while the priests are crowded around the victim, and yet not venturing to go quite away, he circles around in air and on flapping wings greedily hovers over his hoped-for prey; so did the nimble Mercury fly round the Athenian hill, sweeping in circles through the same spaces of air. As Lucifer shines more brightly than all the other stars and as the golden moon outshines Lucifer, so much was Herse more lovely than all the maidens round her, the choice ornament in the solemn procession of her comrades. The son of Jove was astounded at her beauty, and hanging in mid-air he caught the flames of love; as when a leaden bullet is thrown by a Balearic sling, it flies along, is heated by its motion, and finds heat in the clouds which it had not before. Mercury now turns his course, leaves the air and flies to earth, nor seeks to disguise himself; such is the confidence of beauty. Yet though that trust be lawful, he assists it none the less with pains; he smooths his hair, arranges his robe so that it may hang neatly and so that all the golden border will show. He takes care to have in his right hand his smooth wand with which he brings on sleep or drives it away, and to have his winged sandals glittering on his trim feet.

In a retired part of the house were three chambers, richly adorned with ivory and tortoise-shell. The right-hand room of these Pandrosos occupied, Aglauros the left, and Herse the room between. Aglauros first saw the approaching god and made so bold as to ask his name and the cause of his visit. He, grandson of Atlas and Pleione, replied: "I am he who carry my father's messages through the air. My father is Jove himself. Nor will I conceal why I am here. Only do you consent to be true to your sister, and to be called the aunt of my offspring. I have come here for Herse's sake. I pray you favor a lover's suit." Aglauros looked at him with the same covetous eyes with which she had lately peeped at the secret of the golden-haired Minerva, and demanded a mighty weight of gold as the price of her service; meantime, she compelled him to leave the palace.

The warrior goddess now turned her angry eyes upon her, and breathed sighs so deep and perturbed that her breast and the aegis that lay upon her breast shook with her emotion. She remembered that this was the girl who had with profaning hands uncovered the secret at the time when, contrary to her command, she looked upon the son of the Lemnian, without mother born.[5] And now she would be in favor with the god and with her sister, and rich, besides, with the gold which in her greed she had demanded. Straightway Minerva sought out the cave of Envy, filthy with black gore. Her home was hidden away in a deep valley, where no sun shines and no breeze blows; a gruesome place and full of a numbing chill. No cheerful fire burns there, and the place is wrapped in thick, black fog. When the warlike maiden goddess came to the cave, she stood without, for she might not enter that foul abode, and beat upon the door with end of spear. The battered doors flew open; and there, sitting within, was Envy, eating snakes' flesh, the proper food of her venom. At the horrid sight the goddess turned away her eyes. But that other rose heavily from the ground, leaving the snakes' carcasses half consumed, and came forward with sluggish step. When she saw the goddess, glorious in form and armor, she groaned aloud and shaped her countenance to match the goddess' sigh. Pallor spreads across her face and her whole body seems to shrivel up. Her eyes are all awry, her teeth are foul with mould; green, poisonous gall overflows her breast, and venom drips down from her tongue. She never smiles, except at the sight of another's troubles; she never sleeps, disturbed with wakeful cares; unwelcome to her is the sight of men's success, and with the sight she pines away; she gnaws and is gnawed, herself her own punishment. Although she detested the loathsome thing, yet in curt speech Tritonia spoke to her: "Infect with your venom one of Cecrops' daughters. Such the task I set. I mean Aglauros." Without more words she fled the creature's presence and, pushing her spear against the ground, sprang lightly back to heaven.

The hag, eyeing her askance as she flees, mutters awhile, grieving to think on the goddess' joy of triumph. Then she takes her staff, thick-set with thorns, and, wrapped in a mantle of dark cloud, sets forth. Wherever she goes, she tramples down the flowers, causes the grass to wither, blasts the high waving trees, and taints with the foul pollution of her breath whole peoples, cities, homes. At last she spies Tritonia's city, splendid with art and wealth and peaceful joy; and she can scarce restrain her tears at the sight, because she sees no cause for others' tears. But, having entered the chamber of Cecrops' daughter, she performed the goddess' bidding, touched the girl's breast with her festering hand and filled her heart with pricking thorns. Then she breathed pestilential, poisonous breath into her nostrils and spread black venom through her very heart and bones. And, to fix a cause for her grief, Envy pictured to her imagination her sister, her sister's blest marriage and the god in all his beauty, magnifying the excellence of everything. Maddened by this, Aglauros eats her heart out in secret misery; careworn by day, careworn by night, she groans and wastes away most wretchedly with slow decay, like ice touched by the fitful sunshine. She is consumed by envy of Herse's happiness; just as when a fire is set under a pile of weeds, which give out no flames and waste away with slow consumption. She often longed to die that she might not behold such happiness; often to tell it, as if it were a crime, to her stern father. At last she sat down at her sister's threshold, to prevent the god's entrance when he should come. And when he coaxed and prayed with his most honeyed words, "Have done," she said, "for I shall never stir from here till I have foiled your purpose." "We'll stand by that bargain," Mercury quickly replied, and with a touch of his heavenly wand he opened the door. At this the girl struggled to get up, but found the limbs she bends in sitting made motionless with dull heaviness; she strove to stand erect, but her knees had stiffened; a numbing chill stole through her limbs, and her flesh was pale and bloodless. And, as an incurable cancer spreads its evil roots ever more widely and involves sound with infected parts, so did a deadly chill little by little creep to her breast, stopping all vital functions and choking off her breath. She no longer tried to speak, and, if she had tried, her voice would have found no way of utterance. Her neck was changed to stone, her features had hardened—there she sat, a lifeless statue. Nor was the stone white in color; her soul had stained it black.

When Mercury had inflicted this punishment on the girl for her impious words and spirit, he left the land of Pallas behind him, and flew to heaven on outflung pinions. Here his father calls him aside; and not revealing his love affair as the real reason, he says: "My son, always faithful to perform my bidding, delay not, but swiftly in accustomed flight glide down to earth and seek out the land that looks up at your mother's star from the left. The natives call it the land of Sidon. There you are to drive down to the sea-shore the herd of the king's cattle which you will see grazing at some distance on the mountain-side." He spoke, and quickly the cattle were driven from the mountain and headed for the shore, as Jove had directed, to a spot where the great king's daughter was accustomed to play in company with her Tyrian maidens. Majesty and love do not go well together, nor tarry long in the same dwelling-place. And so the father and ruler of the gods, who wields in his right hand the three-forked lightning, whose nod shakes the world, laid aside his royal majesty along with his sceptre, and took upon him the form of a bull. In this form he mingled with the cattle, lowed like the rest, and wandered around, beautiful to behold, on the young grass. His color was white as the untrodden snow, which has not yet been melted by the rainy south-wind. The muscles stood rounded upon his neck, a long dewlap hung down in front; his horns were small, but perfect in shape as if by an artist's hand, cleaner and more clear than pearls. His brow and eyes would inspire no fear, and his whole expression was peaceful. Agenor's daughter looked at him in wondering admiration, because he was so beautiful and friendly. But, although he seemed so gentle, she was afraid at first to touch him. Presently she drew near, and held out flowers to his snow-white lips. The disguised lover rejoiced and, as a foretaste of future joy, kissed her hands. Even so he could scarce restrain his passion. And now he jumps sportively about on the grass, now lays his snowy body down on the yellow sands; and, when her fear has little by little been allayed, he yields his breast for her maiden hands to pat and his horns to entwine with garlands of fresh flowers. The princess even dares to sit upon his back, little knowing upon whom she rests. The god little by little edges away from the dry land, and sets his borrowed hoofs in the shallow water; then he goes further out and soon is in full flight with his prize on the open ocean. She trembles with fear and looks back at the receding shore, holding fast a horn with one hand and resting the other on the creature's back. And her fluttering garments stream behind her in the wind.

BOOK III

AND NOW THE GOD, having put off disguise of the bull, owned himself for what he was, and reached the fields of Crete. But the maiden's father, ignorant of what had happened, bids his son, Cadmus, go and search for the lost girl, and threatens exile as a punishment if he does not find her—pious and guilty by the same act. After roaming over all the world in vain (for who could search out the secret loves of Jove?) Agenor's son becomes an exile, shunning his father's country and his father's wrath. Then in suppliant wise he consults the oracle of Phoebus, seeking thus to learn in what land he is to settle. Phoebus replies: "A heifer will meet you in the wilderness, one who has never worn the yoke or drawn the crooked plough. Follow where she leads, and where she lies down to rest upon the grass there see that you build your city's walls and call the land Boeotia." Hardly had Cadmus left the Castalian grotto when he saw a heifer moving slowly along, all unguarded and wearing on her neck no mark of service. He follows in her track with deliberate steps, silently giving thanks the while to Phoebus for showing him the way. And now the heifer had passed the fords of Cephisus and the fields of Panope, when she halted and, lifting towards the heavens her beautiful head with its spreading horns, she filled the air with her lowings; and then, looking back upon those who were following close behind, she kneeled and let her flank sink down upon the fresh young grass. Cadmus gave thanks, reverently pressed his lips upon this stranger land, and greeted the unknown mountains and the plains.

With intent to make sacrifice to Jove, he bade his attendants hunt out a spring of living water for libation. There was a primeval forest there, scarred by no axe; and in its midst a cave thick set about with shrubs and pliant twigs. With well-fitted stones it fashioned a low arch, from which poured a full-welling spring, and deep within dwelt a serpent sacred to Mars. The creature had a wondrous golden crest; fire flashed from his eyes; his body was all swollen with venom; his triple tongue flickered out and in and his teeth were ranged in triple row. When with luckless steps the wayfarers of the Tyrian race had reached this grove, they let down their vessels into the spring, breaking the silence of the place. At this the dark serpent thrust forth his head out of the deep cave, hissing horribly. The urns fell from the men's hands, their blood ran cold, and, horror-struck, they were seized with a sudden trembling. The serpent twines his scaly coils in rolling knots and with a spring curves himself into a huge bow; and, lifted high by more than half his length into the unsubstantial air, he looks down upon the whole wood, as huge, could you see him all, as is that serpent in the sky that lies outstretched between the twin bears. He makes no tarrying, but seizes on the Phoenicians, whether they are preparing for fighting or for flight or whether very fear holds both in check. Some he slays with his fangs, some he crushes in his constricting folds, and some he stifles with the deadly corruption of his poisoned breath.

The sun had reached the middle heavens and drawn close the shadows. And now Cadmus, wondering what has delayed his companions, starts out to trace them. For shield, he has a lion's skin; for weapon, a spear with glittering iron point and a javelin; and, better than all weapons, a courageous soul. When he enters the wood and sees the corpses of his friends all slain, and victorious above them their huge-bodied foe licking their piteous wounds with bloody tongue, he cries: "O you poor forms, most faithful friends, either I shall avenge your death or be your comrade in it." So saying, he heaved up a massive stone with his right hand and with mighty effort hurled its mighty bulk. Under such a blow, high ramparts would have fallen, towers and all; but the serpent went unscathed, protected against that strong stroke by his scales as by an iron doublet and by his hard, dark skin. But that hard skin cannot withstand the javelin too, which now is fixed in the middle fold of his tough back and penetrates with its iron head deep into his flank. The creature, mad with pain, twists back his head, views well his wound, and bites at the spear-shaft fixed therein. Then, when by violent efforts he had loosened this all round, with difficulty he tore it out; but the iron head remained fixed in the backbone. Then indeed fresh fuel was added to his native wrath; his throat swells with full veins, and white foam flecks his horrid jaws. The earth resounds with his scraping scales, and such rank breath as exhales from the Stygian cave befouls the tainted air. Now he coils in huge spiral folds; now shoots up, straight and tall as a tree; now he moves on with huge rush, like a stream in flood, sweeping down with his breast the trees in his path. Cadmus gives way a little, receiving his foe's rushes on the lion's skin, and holds in check the ravening jaws with his spear-point thrust well forward. The serpent is furious, bites vainly at the hard iron and catches the sharp spear-head between his teeth. And now from his venomous throat the blood begins to trickle and stains the green grass with spattered gore. But the wound is slight, because the serpent keeps backing from the thrust, drawing away his wounded neck, and by yielding keeps the stroke from being driven home nor allows it to go deeper. But Cadmus follows him up and presses the planted point into his throat; until at last an oak-tree stays his backward course and neck and tree are pierced together. The oak bends beneath the serpent's weight and the stout trunk groans beneath the lashings of his tail.

While the conqueror stands gazing on the huge bulk of his conquered foe, suddenly a voice sounds in his ears. He cannot tell from where it comes, but he hears it saying: "Why, O son of Agenor, do you gaze on the serpent you have slain? You too shall be a serpent for men to gaze on." Long he stands there, with quaking heart and pallid cheeks, and his hair rises up on end with chilling fear. But behold, the hero's helper, Pallas, gliding down through the high air, stands beside him, and she bids him plow the earth and plant therein the dragon's teeth, destined to grow into a nation. He obeys and, having opened up the furrows with his deep-sunk plow, he sows in the ground the teeth as he is bid, a man-producing seed. Then, a thing beyond belief, the plowed ground begins to stir; and first there spring up from the furrows the points of spears, then helmets with colored plumes waving; next shoulders of men and breasts and arms laden with weapons come up, and the crop grows with the shields of warriors. So when on festal days the curtain in the theatre is raised, figures of men rise up, showing first their faces, then little by little all the rest; until at last, drawn up with steady motion, the entire forms stand revealed, and plant their feet upon the curtain's edge.

Frightened by this new foe, Cadmus was preparing to take his arms. "Take not your arms," one of the earth-sprung brood cried out, "and take no part in our fratricidal strife." So saying, with his hard sword he clave one of his earth-born brothers, fighting hand to hand; and instantly he himself was felled by a javelin thrown from far. But he also who had slain this last had no longer to live than his victim, and breathed forth the spirit which he had but now received. The same dire madness raged in them all, and in mutual strife by mutual wounds these brothers of an hour perished. And now the youth, who had enjoyed so brief a span of life, lay writhing on their mother earth warm with their blood—all but five. One of these five was Echion, who, at Pallas' bidding, dropped his weapons to the ground and sought and made peace with his surviving brothers. These the Sidonian wanderer had as comrades in his task when he founded the city granted him by Phoebus' oracle.

And now Thebes stood complete; now you could seem, O Cadmus, even in exile, a happy man. You have obtained Mars and Venus, too, as parents of your bride; add to this blessing children worthy of so noble a wife, so many sons and daughters, the pledges of your love, and grandsons, too, now grown to budding manhood. But of a certainty man's last day must ever be awaited, and none be counted happy till his death, till his last funeral rites are paid.

One grandson of yours, Actaeon, amid all your happiness first brought you cause of grief, upon whose brow strange horns appeared, and whose dogs greedily lapped their master's blood. But if you seek the truth, you will find the cause of this in fortune's fault and not in any crime of his. For what crime was mere mischance?

It was on a mountain stained with the blood of many slaughtered beasts; midday had shortened every object's shade, and the sun was at equal distance from either goal. Then young Actaeon with friendly speech thus addressed his comrades of the chase as they fared through the trackless wastes: "Both nets and spears, my friends, are dripping with our quarry's blood, and the day has given us good luck enough. When once more Aurora, borne on her saffron car, shall bring back the day, we will resume our proposed task. Now Phoebus is midway in his course and cleaves the very fields with his burning rays. Cease then your present task and bear home the well-wrought nets." The men performed his bidding and ceased their toil.

There was a vale in that region, thick grown with pine and cypress with their sharp needles. It was called Gargaphie, the sacred haunt of high-girt Diana. In its most secret nook there was a well-shaded grotto, wrought by no artist's hand. But Nature by her own cunning had imitated art; for she had shaped a native arch of the living rock and soft tufa.* A sparkling spring with its slender stream babbled on one side and widened into a pool girt with grassy banks. Here the goddess of the wild woods, when weary with the chase, was wont to bathe her maiden limbs in the crystal water. On this day, having come to the grotto, she gives to the keeping of her armor-bearer among her nymphs her hunting spear, her quiver, and her unstrung bow; another takes on her arm the robe she has laid by; two unbind her sandals from her feet. But Theban Crocale, defter than the rest, binds into a knot the locks which have fallen down her mistress' neck, her own locks streaming free the while. Others bring water, Nephele, Hyale and Rhanis, Psecas and Phiale, and pour it out from their capacious urns. And while Titania is bathing there in her accustomed pool, lo! Cadmus' grandson, his day's toil deferred, comes wandering through the unfamiliar woods with unsure footsteps, and enters Diana's grove; for so fate would have it. As soon as he entered the grotto bedewed with fountain spray, the naked nymphs smote upon their breasts at sight of the man, and filled all the grove with their shrill, sudden cries. Then they thronged around Diana, seeking to hide her body with their own; but the goddess stood head and shoulders over all the rest. And red as the clouds which flush beneath the sun's slant rays, red as the rosy dawn, were the cheeks of Diana as she stood there in view without her robes. Then, though the band of nymphs pressed close about her, she stood turning aside a little and cast back her gaze; and though she would fain have had her arrows ready, what she had she took up, the water, and flung it into the young man's face. And as she poured the avenging drops upon his hair, she spoke these words foreboding his coming doom: "Now you are free to tell that you have seen me all unrobed—if you can tell." No more than this she spoke; but on the head which she had sprinkled she caused to grow the horns of the long-lived stag,

---

*Form of rock (often limestone) deposited by springs or lakes.

stretched out his neck, sharpened his ear-tips, gave feet in place of hands, changed his arms into long legs, and clothed his body with a spotted hide. And last of all she planted fear within his heart. Away in flight goes Autonoë's heroic son, marvelling to find himself so swift of foot. But when he sees his features and his horns in a clear pool, "Oh, woe is me!" he tries to say; but no words come. He groans—the only speech he has—and tears course down his changeling cheeks. Only his mind remains unchanged. What is he to do? Shall he go home to the royal palace, or shall he stay skulking in the woods? Shame blocks one course and fear the other.

But while he stands perplexed he sees his hounds. And first come Melampus and keen-scented Ichnobates, baying loud on the trail—Ichnobates a Cretan dog, Melampus a Spartan; then others come rushing on swifter than the wind: Pamphagus, Dorceus, and Oribasus, Arcadians all; staunch Nebrophonus, fierce Theron and Laelaps; Pterelas, the swift of foot, and keen-scented Agre; savage Hylaeus, but lately ripped up by a wild boar; the wolf-dog Nape and the trusty shepherd Poemenis; Harpyia with her two pups; Sicyonian Ladon, thin in the flanks; Dromas, Canace, Sticte, Tigris, Alce; white-haired Leucon, black Asbolus; Lacon, renowned for strength, and fleet Aëllo; Thoüs and swift Lycisce with her brother Cyprius; Harpalos, with a white spot in the middle of his black forehead; Melaneus and shaggy Lachne; two dogs from a Cretan father and a Spartan mother, Labros and Agriodus; shrill-tongued Hylactor, and others whom it were too long to name. The whole pack, keen with the lust of blood, over crags, over cliffs, over trackless rocks, where the way is hard, where there is no way at all, follow on. He flees over the very ground where he has oft-times pursued; he flees (the pity of it!) his own faithful hounds. He longs to cry out: "I am Actaeon! Recognize your own master!" But words fail his desire. All the air resounds with their baying. And first Melanchaetes fixes his fangs in his back, Theridamas next; Oresitrophus has fastened on his shoulder. They had set out later than the rest, but by a short-cut across the mountain had outstripped their course. While they hold back their master's flight, the whole pack collects, and all together bury their fangs in his body till there is no place left for further wounds. He groans and makes a sound which, though not human, is still one no deer could utter, and fills the heights he knows so well with mournful cries. And now, down on his knees in suppliant attitude, just like one in prayer, he turns his face in silence towards them, as if stretching out beseeching arms. But his companions, ignorant of his plight, urge on the fierce pack with their accustomed shouts, looking all around for Actaeon, and call, each louder than the rest, for Actaeon, as if he were far away—he turns his head at the sound of his name—and complain that he is absent and is missing through sloth the sight of the quarry brought to bay. Well, indeed, might he wish to be absent, but he is here; and well might he wish to see, not to feel, the fierce doings of his own hounds. They throng him on every side and, plunging their muzzles in his flesh, mangle their master under the deceiving form of the deer. Nor, as they say, till he had been done to death by many wounds, was the wrath of the quiver-bearing goddess appeased.

Common talk wavered this way and that: to some the goddess seemed more cruel than was just; others called her act worthy of her austere virginity; both sides found good reasons for their judgment. Jove's wife alone spake no word either in blame or praise, but rejoiced in the disaster which had come to Agenor's house; for she had now transferred her anger from her Tyrian rival to those who shared her blood. And lo! a fresh pang was added to her former grievance and she was smarting with the knowledge that Semele was pregnant with the seed of mighty Jove. Words of reproach were rising to her lips, but "What," she cried, "have I ever gained by reproaches? It is she who must feel my wrath. Herself, if I am duly called most mighty Juno, I must attack if I am fit to wield in my hand the jewelled sceptre, if I am queen of heaven, the sister and the wife of Jove—at least his sister. And yet, methinks, she is content with this stolen love, and the insult to my bed is but for a moment. But she has conceived—that still was lacking—and bears plain proof of her guilt in her full womb, and seeks—a fortune that has scarce been mine—to be made a mother from Jove. So great is her trust in beauty! But I will cause that trust to mock her: I am no daughter of Saturn if she go not down to the Stygian pool plunged there by her Jupiter himself."

On this she rose from her seat, and, wrapped in a saffron cloud, she came to the home of Semele. But before she put aside her concealing cloud she feigned herself an old woman, whitening her hair at the temples, furrowing her skin with wrinkles, and walking with bowed form and tottering steps. She spoke also in the voice of age and became even as Beroë, the Epidaurian nurse of Semele. When, after gossiping about many things, they came to mention of Jove's name, the old woman sighed and said: "I pray that it be Jupiter; but I am afraid of all such doings. Many, pretending to be gods, have found entrance into modest chambers. But to be Jove is not enough; make him prove his love if he is true Jove; as great and glorious as he is when welcomed by heavenly Juno, so great and glorious, pray him grant you his embrace, and first don all his splendours."

In such wise did Juno instruct the guileless daughter of Cadmus. She in her turn asked Jove for a gift, unnamed. The god replied: "Choose what you want, and you shall suffer no refusal. And that you may be more assured, I swear it by the divinity of the seething Styx, whose godhead is the fear of all the gods." Rejoicing in her evil fortune, too much prevailing and doomed to perish through her lover's compliance, Semele said: "In such guise as Saturnia beholds you when you seek her arms in love, so show yourself to me." The god would have checked her even as she spoke; but already her words had sped forth into uttered speech. He groans; for neither can she recall her wish, nor he his oath. And so in deepest distress he ascends the steeps of heaven, and with his beck drew on the mists that followed, then mingling clouds and lightnings and blasts of wind, he took last the thunder and that fire that none can escape. And yet whatever way he can he essays to lessen his own might, nor arms himself now with that bolt with which he had hurled down from heaven Typhoeus of the hundred hands, for that weapon were too deadly; but there is a lighter bolt, to which the Cyclops' hands had given a less devouring flame, a wrath less threatening. The gods call them his "Second Armory." With these in hand he enters the palace of Agenor's son, the home of Semele. Her mortal body bore not the onrush of heavenly power, and by that gift of wedlock she was consumed. The babe still not wholly fashioned is snatched from the mother's womb and (if report may be believed) sewed up in his father's thigh, there to await its full time of birth. In secret his mother's sister, Ino, watched over his infancy; later, he was confided to the nymphs of Nysa,* who hid him in their cave and nurtured him with milk.

---

*Legendary mountain in a distant, uncertain, but definitely non-European location.

Now while these things were happening on the earth by the decrees of fate, when the cradle of Bacchus, twice born, was safe, it chanced that Jove (as the story goes), while warmed with wine, put care aside and bandied good-humoured jests with Juno in an idle hour. "I maintain," said he, "that your pleasure in love is greater than that which we enjoy." She held the opposite view. And so they decided to ask the judgment of wise Tiresias. He knew both sides of love. For once, with a blow of his staff he had outraged two huge serpents mating in the green forest; and, wonderful to relate, from man he was changed into a woman, and in that form spent seven years. In the eighth year he saw the same serpents again and said: "Since in striking you there is such magic power as to change the nature of the giver of the blow, now will I strike you once again." So saying, he struck the serpents and his former state was restored and he became as he had been born. He therefore, being asked to arbitrate the playful dispute of the gods, took sides with Jove. Saturnia, they say, grieved more deeply than she should and than the issue warranted, and condemned the arbitrator to perpetual blindness. But the Almighty Father (for no god may undo what another god has done) in return for his loss of sight gave Tiresias the power to know the future, lightening the penalty by the honor.

He, famed far and near through all the Boeotian towns, gave answers that none could censure to those who sought his aid. The first to make trial of his truth and assured utterances was the nymph, Liriope, whom once the river-god, Cephisus, embraced in his winding stream and ravished, while imprisoned in his waters. When her time came the beauteous nymph brought forth a child, whom a nymph might love even as a child, and named him Narcissus. When asked whether this child would live to reach well-ripened age, the seer replied: "If he never knows himself." Long did the saying of the prophet seem but empty words. But what befell proved its truth—the event, the manner of his death, the strangeness of his infatuation. For Narcissus had reached his sixteenth year and might seem either boy or man. Many youths and many maidens sought his love; but in that slender form was pride so cold that no youth, no maiden touched his heart. Once as he was driving the frightened deer into his nets, a certain nymph of strange speech beheld him, resounding Echo, who could neither hold her peace when others spoke, nor yet begin to speak till others had addressed her.

Up to this time Echo had form and was not only a voice; and yet, though talkative, she had no other use of speech than now—only the power out of many words to repeat the last she heard. Juno had made her thus; for often when she might have surprised the nymphs in company with her lord upon the mountain-sides, Echo would cunningly hold the goddess in long talk until the nymphs were fled. When Saturnia realized this, she said to her: "That tongue of yours, by which I have been tricked, shall have its power curtailed and enjoy the briefest use of speech." The event confirmed her threat. Nevertheless she does repeat the last phrases of a speech and returns the words she hears. Now when she saw Narcissus wandering through the fields, she was inflamed with love and followed him by stealth; and the more she followed, the more she burned by a nearer flame; as when quick-burning sulphur, smeared round the tops of torches, catches fire from another fire brought near. Oh, how often does she long to approach him with alluring words and make soft prayers to him! But her nature forbids this, nor does it permit her to begin; but as it allows, she is ready to await the sounds to which she may give back her own words. By chance the boy, separated from his faithful companions, had cried: "Is anyone here?" and "Here!" cried Echo back. Amazed, he looks around in all directions and with loud voice cries "Come!"; and "Come!" she calls him calling. He looks behind him and, seeing no one coming, calls again: "Why do you run from me?" and hears in answer his own words again. He stands still, deceived by the answering voice, and "Here let us meet," he cries. Echo, never to answer other sound more gladly, cries: "Let us meet"; and to help her own words she comes forth from the woods that she may throw her arms around the neck she longs to clasp. But he flees at her approach and, fleeing, says: "Hands off! embrace me not! May I die before I give you power over me!" "I give you power over me!" she says, and nothing more. Thus spurned, she lurks in the woods, hides her shamed face among the foliage, and lives from that time on in lonely caves. But still, though spurned, her love remains and grows on grief; her sleepless cares waste away her wretched form; she becomes gaunt and wrinkled and all moisture fades from her body into the air. Only her voice and her bones remain: then, only voice; for they say that her bones were turned to stone. She hides in woods and is seen no more upon the mountain-sides; but all may hear her, for voice, and voice alone, still lives in her.

Thus had Narcissus mocked her, thus had he mocked other nymphs of the waves or mountains; thus had he mocked the companies of men. At last one of these scorned youth, lifting up his hands to heaven, prayed: "So may he himself love, and not gain the thing he loves!" The goddess, Nemesis, heard his righteous prayer. There was a clear pool with silvery bright water, to which no shepherds ever came, or she-goats feeding on the mountain-side, or any other cattle; whose smooth surface neither bird nor beast nor falling bough ever ruffled. Grass grew all around its edge, fed by the water near, and a coppice that would never suffer the sun to warm the spot. Here the youth, worn by the chase and the heat, lies down, attracted there by the appearance of the place and by the spring. While he seeks to slake his thirst another thirst springs up, and while he drinks he is smitten by the sight of the beautiful form he sees. He loves an unsubstantial hope and thinks that substance which is only shadow. He looks in speechless wonder at himself and hangs there motionless in the same expression, like a statue carved from Parian marble. Prone on the ground, he gazes at his eyes, twin stars, and his locks, worthy of Bacchus, worthy of Apollo; on his smooth cheeks, his ivory neck, the glorious beauty of his face, the blush mingled with snowy white: all things, in short, he admires for which he is himself admired. Unwittingly he desires himself; he praises, and is himself what he praises; and while he seeks, is sought; equally he kindles love and burns with love. How often did he offer vain kisses on the elusive pool? How often did he plunge his arms into the water seeking to clasp the neck he sees there, but did not clasp himself in them! What he sees he knows not; but that which he sees he burns for, and the same delusion mocks and allures his eyes. O fondly foolish boy, why vainly seek to clasp a fleeting image? What you seek is nowhere; but turn yourself away, and the object of your love will be no more. That which you behold is but the shadow of a reflected form and has no substance of its own. With you it comes, with you it stays, and it will go with you—if you can go.

No thought of food or rest can draw him from the spot; but, stretched on the shaded grass, he gazes on that false image with eyes that cannot look their fill and through his own eyes perishes. Raising himself a little, and stretching his arms to the trees, he cries: "Did anyone, O woods, ever love more cruelly than I? You know, for you have been the convenient haunts of many lovers. Do you in the ages past, for your life is one of centuries, remember anyone who has pined away like this? I am charmed, and I see; but what I see and what charms me I cannot find—so great a delusion holds my love. And, to make me grieve the more, no mighty ocean separates us, no long road, no mountain ranges, no city walls with close-shut gates; by a thin barrier of water we are kept apart. He himself is eager to be embraced. For, often as I stretch my lips towards the lucent wave, so often with upturned face he strives to lift his lips to mine. You would think he could be touched—so small a thing it is that separates our loving hearts. Whoever you are, come forth from there! Why, O peerless youth, do you elude me? or where do you go when I strive to reach you? Surely my form and age are not such that you should shun them, and me too the nymphs have loved. Some ground for hope you offer with your friendly looks, and when I have stretched out my arms to you, you stretch yours too. When I have smiled, you smile back; and I have often seen tears, when I weep, on your cheeks. My becks you answer with your nod; and, as I suspect from the movement of your sweet lips, you answer my words as well, but words which do not reach my ears.—Oh, I am he! I have felt it, I know now my own image. I burn with love of my own self; I both kindle the flames and suffer them. What shall I do? Shall I be wooed or woo? Why woo at all? What I desire, I have; the very abundance of my riches beggars me. Oh, that I might be parted from my own body! and, strange prayer for a lover, I would that what I love were absent from me! And now grief is sapping my strength; but a brief space of life remains to me and I am cut off in my life's prime. Death is nothing to me, for in death I shall leave my troubles; I would he that is loved might live longer; but as it is, we two shall die together in one breath."

He spoke and, half distraught, turned again to the same image. His tears ruffled the water, and dimly the image came back from the troubled pool. As he saw it thus depart, he cried: "Oh, where do you flee? Stay here, and do not desert him who loves you, cruel one! Still may it be mine to gaze on what I may not touch, and by that gaze feed my unhappy passion." While he thus grieves, he plucks away his tunic at its upper fold and beats his bare breast with pallid hands. His breast when it is struck takes on a delicate glow; just as apples sometimes, though white in part, flush red in other part, or as grapes hanging in clusters take on a purple hue when not yet ripe. As soon as he sees this, when the water has become clear again, he can bear no more; but, as the yellow wax melts before a gentle heat, as hoar frost melts before the warm morning sun, so does he, wasted with love, pine away, and is slowly consumed by its hidden fire. No longer has he that ruddy color mingling with the white, no longer that strength and vigour, and all that lately was so pleasing to behold; scarce does his form remain which once Echo had loved so well. But when she saw it, though still angry and unforgetful, she felt pity; and as often as the poor boy says "Alas!" again with answering utterance she cries "Alas!" and as his hands beat his shoulders she gives back the same sounds of woe. His last words as he gazed into the familiar spring were these: "Alas, dear boy, vainly beloved!" and the place gave back his words. And when he said "Farewell!" "Farewell!" said Echo too. He drooped his weary head on the green grass and death sealed the eyes that marvelled at their master's beauty. And even when he had been received into the infernal abodes, he kept on gazing on his image in the Stygian pool. His naiad-sisters beat their breasts and shore their locks in sign of grief for their dear brother; the dryads, too, lamented, and Echo gave back their sounds of woe. And now they were preparing the funeral pile, the brandished torches and the bier; but his body was nowhere to be found. In place of his body they find a flower, its yellow centre girt with white petals.

When this story was noised abroad it spread the well-deserved fame of the seer throughout the cities of Greece, and great was the name of Tiresias. Yet Echion's son, Pentheus, the scoffer at gods, alone of all men flouted the seer, laughed at the old man's words of prophecy, and taunted him with his darkness and loss of sight. But he, shaking his hoary head in warning, said: "How fortunate would you be if this light were dark to you also, so that you might not behold the rites of Bacchus! For the day will come—indeed, I foresee it is near—when the new god shall come here, Liber, son of Semele. Unless you worship him as is his due, you shall be torn into a thousand pieces and scattered everywhere, and shall with your blood defile the woods and your mother and your mother's sisters. So shall it come to pass; for you shall refuse to honor the god, and shall complain that in my blindness I have seen all too well." Even while he speaks the son of Echion flings him forth; but his words did indeed come true and his prophecies were accomplished.

The god is now come and the fields resound with the wild cries of revellers. The people rush out of the city in throngs, men and women, old and young, nobles and commons, all mixed together, and hasten to celebrate the new rites. "What madness, sons of the serpent's teeth, you seed of Mars, has dulled your reason?" Pentheus cries. "Can clashing cymbals, can the pipe of crooked horn, can shallow tricks of magic, women's shrill cries, wine-heated madness, vulgar throngs and empty drums—can all these vanquish men, for whom real war, with its drawn swords, the blare of trumpets, and lines of glittering spears, had no terrors? You, O elders, should I give you praise, who sailed the long reaches of the sea and planted here your Tyre, here your wandering Penates, and who now permit them to be taken without a struggle? Or you, the young men of fresher age and nearer to my own, for whom once it was seemly to bear arms and not the thyrsus, to be sheltered by helmets and not garlands? Be mindful, I pray, from what seed you are sprung, and show the spirit of the serpent, who in his single strength killed many foes. For his fountain and his pool he perished; but do you conquer for your glory's sake! He did to death brave men: do you but put to flight unmanly men and save your ancestral honor. If it be the fate of Thebes not to endure for long, I would the enginery of war and heroes might batter down her walls and that sword and fire might roar around her: then should we be unfortunate, but our honor without stain; we should bewail, not seek to conceal, our wretched state; then our tears would be without shame. But now our Thebes shall fall before an untried boy, whom neither arts of war assist nor spears nor horsemen, but whose weapons are scented locks, soft garlands, purple and gold inwoven in embroidered robes. But immediately—only you must stand aside—I will force him to confess that his father's name is borrowed and his sacred rites a lie. Did Acrisius have spirit enough to despise his empty godhead, and to shut the gates of Argos in his face, and shall Pentheus and all Thebes tremble at this wanderer's approach? Go quickly"—this to his slaves—"go, bring this plotter here, and in chains! Let there be no dull delay to my bidding." His grandsire addresses him in words of reprimand, and Athamas, and all his counsellors, and they vainly strive to curb his will. He is all the more eager for their warning; his mad rage is fretted by restraint and grows apace, and their very efforts at control but make him worse. So have I seen a river, where nothing obstructed its course, flow smoothly on with but a gentle murmur; but, where it was held in check by dams of timber and stone set in its way, foaming and boiling it went, fiercer for the obstruction.

But now the slaves come back, all covered with blood, and, when their master asks where Bacchus is, they say that they have not seen him; "but this companion of his," they say, "this priest of his sacred rites, we have taken," and they deliver up, his hands bound behind his back, one of Etruscan stock, a votary of Bacchus. Him Pentheus eyes awhile with gaze made terrible by his wrath; and, with difficulty withholding his hand from punishment, he says: "You, fellow, doomed to perish and by your death to serve as a warning to others, tell me your name, your parents, and your country; and why you devote yourself to this new cult." He fearlessly replies: "My name is Acoetes, and my country is Maeonia; my parents were but humble folk. My father left me no fields or sturdy bullocks to till them; no woolly sheep, no cattle. He himself was poor and used to catch fish with hook and line and rod and draw them leaping from the stream. His craft was all his wealth; and when he passed it on to me he said: 'Take this craft; it is all my fortune. Be you my heir and successor in it.' And in dying he left me nothing but the waters. This alone can I call my heritage. Soon, that I might not always stay planted on the selfsame rocks, I learned to steer ships with guiding hand; I studied the stars; the rainy constellation of the Olenian Goat, Taygete, the Hyades, the Bears; I learned the winds and from what directions they blow; I learned what harbours are best for ships. It chanced that while making for Delos I was driven out of my course to the shore of Chios and made the land with well-skilled oars. Light leaping, we landed on the wet shore and spent the night. As soon as the eastern sky began to redden I rose and bade my men go for fresh water, showing them the way that led to the spring. For my own task, from a high hill I observed the direction of the wind; then called my comrades and started back on board. 'Lo, here we are!' cried Opheltes, first of all the men, bringing with him a prize (so he considered it) which he had found in a deserted field, a little boy with form beautiful as a girl's. He seemed to stagger, as if overcome with wine and sleep, and could scarce follow him who led. I gazed on his garb, his face, his walk; and all I saw seemed more to me than mortal. This I perceived, and said to my companions: 'What divinity is in that mortal body I know not; but assuredly a divinity is therein. Whoever you are, be gracious to us and favor our undertakings. Grant pardon also to these men.' 'Do not pray for us,' said Dictys, than whom none was more quick to climb the topmost yard and slide down on firm-grasped rope. Libys seconded this speech; so did yellow-haired Melanthus, the look-out, and Alcimedon and Epopeus, who by his voice marked the time for the rowers and urged on their flagging spirits. And all the rest approved, so blind and heedless was their greed for booty. 'And yet I shall not permit this ship to be defiled by such sacrilege,' I said; 'here must my authority have greater weight.' And I resisted their attempt to come on board. Then did Lycabas break out into wrath, the most reckless man of the crew, who, driven from Tuscany, was suffering exile as a punishment for the foul crime of murder. He, while I withstood him, tore at my throat with his strong hands and would have hurled me overboard, if, scarce knowing what I did, I had not clung to a rope that held me back. The godless crew applauded Lycabas. Then at last Bacchus—for it was he—as if aroused from slumber by the outcry, and as if his wine-dimmed senses were coming back, said: 'What are you doing? Why this uproar? And tell me, O sailor-men, how did I get here and where are you planning to take me?' 'Be not afraid,' said Proreus, 'tell me what port you wish to make, and you shall be set off at any place you choose.' 'Then turn your course to Naxos,' said Liber; 'that is my home, and there shall you find, yourselves, a friendly land.' By the sea and all its gods the treacherous fellows swore that they would do this, and bade me get the painted vessel under sail. Naxos lay off upon the right; and as I was setting my sails towards the right Opheltes said: 'What are you doing, you fool? what madness'—and each one for himself supplied the words—'holds you? Take the left tack.' The most of them by nods and winks let me know what they wanted, and some whispered in my ear. I could not believe my senses and I said to them: 'Then let someone else take the helm'; and declared that I would have nor part nor lot in their wicked scheme. They all cried out upon me and kept up their wrathful mutterings. And one of them, Aethalion, broke out: 'I'd have you know, the safety of us all does not depend on you alone!' So saying, he came and took my place at the helm and, leaving the course for Naxos, steered off in another direction. Then the god, in mockery of them, as if he had just discovered their faithlessness, looked out upon the sea from the curved stern, and in seeming tears cried out: 'These are not the shores you promised me, you sailor-men; and this is not the land I sought. What have I done to be so treated? And what glory will you gain if you, grown men, deceive a little boy? if you, so many, overcome just one?' I was long since in tears; but the godless crew mocked my tears and swept the seas with speeding oars. Now by the god himself I swear (for there is no god more surely near than he) that what I speak is truth, though far beyond belief. The ship stands still upon the waves, as if a dry-dock held her. The sailors in amaze redouble their striving at the oars and make all sail, hoping thus to speed their way by twofold power. But ivy twines and clings about the oars, creeps upward with many a back-flung, catching fold, and decks the sails with heavy, hanging clusters. The god himself, with his brow garlanded with clustering berries, waves a wand wreathed with ivy-leaves. Around him lie tigers, the forms (though empty all) of lynxes and of fierce spotted panthers. The men leap overboard, driven on by madness or by fear. And first Medon's body begins to grow dark and his back to be bent in a well-marked curve. Lycabas starts to say to him: 'Into what strange creature are you turning?' But as he speaks his own jaws spread wide, his nose becomes hooked, and his skin becomes hard and covered with scales. But Libys, while he seeks to ply the sluggish oars, sees his hands suddenly shrunk in size to things that can no longer be called hands at all, but fins. Another, catching at a twisted rope with his arms, finds he has no arms and goes plunging backwards with limbless body into the sea: the end of his tail is curved like the horns of a half-moon. They leap about on every side, sending up showers of spray; they emerge from the water, only to return to the depths again; they sport like a troupe of dancers, tossing their bodies in wanton sport and drawing in and blowing out the water from their broad nostrils. Of but now twenty men—for the ship bore so many—I alone remained. And, as I stood quaking and trembling with cold fear, and hardly knowing what I did, the god spoke words of cheer to me and said: 'Be of good courage, and hold on your course to Naxos.' Arrived there, I have joined the rites and am one of the Bacchanalian throng."

Then Pentheus said: "We have lent ear to this long, rambling tale, that by such delay our anger might lose its might. You slaves, now hurry him away, rack his body with fearsome tortures, and so send him down to Stygian night." Straightway Acoetes, the Tyrrhenian, was dragged out and shut up in a strong dungeon. And while the slaves were getting the cruel instruments of torture ready, the iron, the fire—of their own accord the doors flew open wide; of their own accord, with no one loosing them, the chains fell from the prisoner's arms.

But Pentheus stood fixed in his purpose. He no longer sent messengers, but went himself to where Cithaeron, the chosen seat for the god's sacred rites, was resounding with songs and the shrill cries of worshippers. As a spirited horse snorts when the brazen trumpet with tuneful voice sounds out the battle and his eagerness for the fray waxes hot, so did the air, pulsing with the long-drawn cries, stir Pentheus, and the wild uproar in his ears heated his wrath white-hot.

About midway of the mountain, bordered with thick woods, was an open plain, free from trees, in full view from every side. Here, as Pentheus was spying with profane eyes upon the sacred rites, his mother was the first to see him, first to rush madly on him, first with hurled thyrsus to smite her son. "Ho, there, my sisters, come!" she cried, "see that huge boar prowling in our fields. Now must I rend him." The whole mad throng rush on him; from all sides they come and pursue the frightened wretch—yes, frightened now, and speaking milder words, cursing his folly and confessing that he has sinned. Sore wounded, he cries out: "O help, my aunt, Autonoë! Let the ghost of Actaeon move your heart." She knows not who Actaeon is, and tears the suppliant's right arm away; Ino in frenzy rends away his left. And now the wretched man has no arms to stretch out in prayer to his mother; but, showing his mangled stumps where his arms have been torn away, he cries: "Oh, mother, see!" Agave howls madly at the sight and tosses her head with wildly streaming hair. Off she tears his head, and holding it in bloody hands, she yells: "See, comrades, see my toil and its reward of victory!" Not more quickly are leaves, when touched by the first cold of autumn and now lightly clinging, whirled from the lofty tree by the wind than is Pentheus torn limb from limb by those impious hands. Taught by such a warning, the Thebans throng the new god's sacred rites, burn incense, and bow down before his shrines.

BOOK IV

BUT NOT MINYAS' DAUGHTER Alcithoë; she will not have the god's holy revels admitted; no, so bold is she that she denies Bacchus to be Jove's son! And her sisters are with her in the impious deed. The priest had bidden the people to celebrate a Bacchic festival: all serving-women must be excused from toil; with their mistresses they must cover their breasts with the skins of beasts, they must loosen the ribands of their hair, and with garlands upon their heads they must hold in their hands the vine-wreathed thyrsus. And he had prophesied that the wrath of the god would be merciless if he were disregarded. The matrons and young wives all obey, put by weaving and work-baskets, leave their tasks unfinished; they burn incense, calling on Bacchus, naming him also Bromius, Lyaeus, son of the thunderbolt, twice born, child of two mothers; they hail him as Nyseus also, Thyoneus of the unshorn locks, Lenaeus, planter of the joy-giving vine, Nyctelius, father Eleleus, Iacchus, and Euhan, and all the many names besides by which you are known, O Liber, throughout the towns of Greece.* For yours is unending youth, eternal boyhood; you are the most lovely in the lofty sky; your face is virgin-seeming, if without horns you stand before us. The Orient admits your sway, even to the bounds where remotest Ganges washes dark India. Pentheus you destroyed, you awful god, and Lycurgus, armed with the two-edged battle-axe (impious were they both), and hurled the Tuscan sailors into the sea. Lynxes, with bright reins harnessed, draw your car; bacchant women and satyrs follow you, and that old man† who, drunk with wine, supports his staggering limbs on his staff, and clings weakly to his misshapen ass.

---

*The names were accumulated as Bacchus worship spread from the Zagros Mountains.
†The satyr Silenus, drunken tutor and companion of Bacchus (Dionysus).

Wherever you go, glad shouts of youths and cries of women echo round, with drum of tambourine, the cymbals' clash, and the shrill piping of the flute.

"Oh, be with us, merciful and mild!" the Theban women cry; and perform the sacred rites as the priest bids them. Only the daughters of Minyas stay within, marring the festival, and out of due time ply their household tasks, spinning wool, thumbing the turning threads, or keep close to the loom, and press their maidens with work. Then one of them, drawing the thread the while with deft thumb, says: "While other women are deserting their tasks and thronging this so-called festival, let us also, who keep to Pallas, a truer goddess, lighten with various talk the serviceable work of our hands, and to beguile the tedious hours, let us take turns in telling stories, while all the others listen." The sisters agree and bid her be first to speak. She mused awhile which she should tell of many tales, for very many she knew. She was in doubt whether to tell of you, Dercetis of Babylon, who, as the Syrians believe, changed to a fish, all covered with scales, and swims in a pool; or how her daughter, changed to a pure white dove, spent her last years perched on high battlements; or how a certain nymph, by incantation and herbs too potent, changed the bodies of some boys into mute fishes, and at last herself became a fish; or how the mulberry-tree, which once had borne white fruit, now has fruit dark red, from the bloody stain. The last seems best. This tale, not commonly known as yet, she tells, spinning her wool the while.

"Pyramus and Thisbe—he, the most beautiful youth, and she, loveliest maid of all the East—dwelt in houses side by side, in the city which Semiramis is said to have surrounded with walls of brick.* Their nearness made the first steps of their acquaintance. In time love grew, and they would have been joined in marriage, too, but their parents forbade. Still, what no parents could forbid, sore smitten in heart they burned with mutual love. They had no go-between, but communicated by nods and signs; and the more they covered up the fire, the more it burned. There was a slender chink in the party-wall of the two houses, which it had at some former time received when it was building. This chink, which no one had ever discovered through all these years—but what does love not

*The city of Babylon, whose legendary founder was Queen Semiramis.

see?—you lovers first discovered and made it the channel of speech. Safe through this your loving words used to pass in tiny whispers. Often, when they had taken their positions, on this side Thisbe, and Pyramus on that, and when each in turn had listened eagerly for the other's breath, 'O envious wall,' they would say, 'why do you stand between lovers? How small a thing 'twould be for you to permit us to embrace each other, or, if this be too much, to open for our kisses! But we are not ungrateful. We owe it to you, we admit, that a passage is allowed by which our words may go through to loving ears.' So, separated all to no purpose, they would talk, and as night came on they said good-bye and printed, each on his own side of the wall, kisses that did not go through. The next morning had put out the starry beacons of the night, and the sun's rays had dried the frosty grass; they came together at the accustomed place. Then first in low whispers they lamented bitterly, then decided when all had become still that night to try to elude their guardians' watchful eyes and steal out of doors; and, when they had gotten out, they would leave the city as well; and that they might not run the risk of missing one another, as they wandered in the open country, they were to meet at Ninus' tomb* and hide in the shade of a tree. Now there was a tree there hanging full of snow-white berries, a tall mulberry, and not far away was a cool spring. They liked the plan, and slow the day seemed to go. But at last the sun went plunging down beneath the waves, and from the same waves the night came up.

"Now Thisbe, carefully opening the door, steals out through the darkness, seen of none, and arrives duly at the tomb with her face well veiled and sits down under the trysting-tree. Love made her bold. But see! here comes a lioness, her jaws all dripping with the blood of fresh-slain cattle, to slake her thirst at the neighbouring spring. Far off under the rays of the moon Babylonian Thisbe sees her, and flees with trembling feet into the deep cavern, and as she flees she leaves her cloak on the ground behind her. When the savage lioness has quenched her thirst by copious gulps of water, returning to the woods she comes by chance upon the light garment (but without the girl herself!) and tears it with bloody jaws.

---

*Ninus, the son of Semiramis, was the mythic founder of the eponymous Nineveh.

Pyramus, coming out a little later, sees the tracks of the beast plain in the deep dust and grows deadly pale at the sight. But when he saw the cloak too, smeared with blood, he cried: 'One night shall bring two lovers to death. But she of the two was more worthy of long life; on my head lies all the guilt. Oh, I have been the cause of your death, poor girl, in that I bade you come forth by night into this dangerous place, and did not myself come here first. Come, rend my body and devour my guilty flesh with your fierce fangs, O all you lions who have your lairs beneath this cliff! But it's a coward's part merely to pray for death.' He picks up Thisbe's cloak and carries it to the shade of the trysting-tree. And while he kisses the familiar garment and bedews it with his tears he cries: 'Drink now my blood too.' So saying, he drew the sword which he wore girt about him, plunged the blade into his side, and straightway, with his dying effort, drew the sword from his warm wound. As he lay stretched upon the earth the spouting blood leaped high; just as when a pipe has broken at a weak spot in the lead and through the small hissing aperture sends spurting forth long streams of water, cleaving the air with its jets. The fruit of the tree, sprinkled with the blood, was changed to a dark red color; and the roots, soaked with his gore, also tinged the hanging berries with the same purple hue.

"And now comes Thisbe from her hiding-place, still trembling, but fearful also that her lover will miss her; she seeks for him both with eyes and soul, eager to tell him how great perils she has escaped. And while she recognizes the place and the shape of the well-known tree, still the color of its fruit mystifies her. She doubts if it be this. While she hesitates, she sees somebody's limbs writhing on the bloody ground, and starts back, paler than boxwood, and shivering like the sea when a slight breeze ruffles its surface. But when after a little while she recognizes her lover, she smites her innocent arms with loud blows of grief, and tears her hair; and embracing the well-beloved form, she fills his wounds with tears, mingling these with his blood. And as she kissed his lips, now cold in death, she wailed: 'O my Pyramus, what mischance has reft you from me? Pyramus! answer me. It is your dearest Thisbe calling you. Oh, listen, and lift your drooping head!' At the name of Thisbe, Pyramus lifted his eyes, now heavy with death, and having looked upon her face, closed them again.

"Now when she saw her own cloak and the ivory scabbard empty of the sword, she said: 'It was your own hand and your love, poor boy, that took your life. I, too, have a hand brave for this one deed; I, too, have love. This shall give me strength for the fatal blow. I will follow you in death, and men shall say that I was the most wretched cause and comrade of your fate. Whom death alone had power to part from me, not even death shall have power to part from me. O wretched parents, mine and his, be entreated of this by the prayers of us both, that you begrudge us not that we, whom faithful love, whom the hour of death has joined, should be laid together in the same tomb. And do you, O tree, who now shade with your branches the poor body of one, and soon will shade two, keep the marks of our death and always bear your fruit of a dark color, meet for mourning, as a memorial of our double death.' She spoke, and fitting the point beneath her breast, she fell forward on the sword which was still warm with her lover's blood. Her prayers touched the gods and touched the parents; for the color of the mulberry fruit is dark red when it is ripe, and all that remained from both funeral pyres rests in a common urn."

The tale was done. Then, after a brief interval, Leuconoë began, while her sisters held their peace. "Even the Sun, who with his central light guides all the stars, has felt the power of love. The Sun's loves we will relate. This god was first, it's said, to see the shame of Mars and Venus; this god sees all things first. Shocked at the sight, he revealed her sin to the goddess' husband, Vulcan, Juno's son, and where it was committed. Then Vulcan's mind reeled and the work upon which he was engaged fell from his hands. Straightway he fashioned a net of fine links of bronze, so thin that they would escape detection of the eye. Not the finest threads of wool would surpass that work; no, not the web which the spider lets down from the ceiling beam. He made the web in such a way that it would yield to the slightest touch, the least movement, and then he spread it deftly over the couch. Now when the goddess and her paramour had come to this place, by the husband's art and by the net so cunningly prepared they were both caught and held fast in each other's arms. Straightway Vulcan, the Lemnian, opened wide the ivory doors and invited in the other gods. There lay the two in chains, disgracefully, and some one of the merry gods prayed that he might be so disgraced.

The gods laughed, and for a long time this story was the talk of heaven.

"But the goddess of Cythera did not forget the one who had spied on her, and took fitting vengeance on him; and he that betrayed her stolen love was equally betrayed in love. What now avails, O son of Hyperion, your beauty and brightness and radiant beams? For you, who inflames all lands with your fires, are yourself inflamed by a strange fire. You who should behold all things, gazes on Leucothoë alone, and on one maiden you fix those eyes which belong to the whole world. Soon rise too early in the eastern sky, and soon you sink too late beneath the waves, and through your long lingering over her you prolong the short wintry hours. Sometimes your beams fail utterly, your heart's darkness passing into your rays, and darkened you terrify the hearts of men. Nor is it that the moon has come between you and earth that you are dark; it is that love of yours alone that makes your face so wan. You delight in her alone. Now neither Clymene seems fair to you, nor the maid of Rhodes, nor Aeaean Circes' mother, though most beautiful, nor Clytie, who, although scorned by you, still seeks your love and even now bears its deep wounds in her heart.* Leucothoë makes you forgetful of them all, she whom most fair Eurynome bore in the land of spices. But, after the daughter came to womanhood, as the mother surpassed all in loveliness, so did the daughter surpass her. Her father, Orchamus, ruled over the cities of Persia, himself the seventh in line from ancient Belus.

"Beneath the western skies lie the pastures of the Sun's horses. Here not common grass, but ambrosia is their food. On this their bodies, weary with their service of the day, are refreshed and gain new strength for toil. While here his horses crop their celestial pasturage and Night takes her turn of toil, the god enters the apartments of his love, assuming the form of Eurynome, her mother. There he discovers Leucothoë, surrounded by her twelve maidens, spinning fine wool with whirling spindle. Then having kissed her, just as her mother would have kissed her dear daughter, he says: 'Mine is a private matter. Retire, you slaves, and let not a mother want the right to a private speech.' The slaves obey; and now the

---

*The figures mentioned are various sea-nymphs and minor deities.

god, when the last witness has left the room, declares: 'Lo, I am he who measure out the year, who behold all things, by whom the earth beholds all things—the world's eye. I tell you, you have found favor in my sight.' The nymph is filled with fear; distaff and spindle fall unheeded from her limp fingers. Her very fear becomes her. Then he, no longer tarrying, resumes his own form and his wonted splendour. But the maiden, though in terror at this sudden apparition, yet, overwhelmed by his radiance, at last without protest suffers the ardent wooing of the god.

"Clytie was jealous, for love of the Sun still burned uncontrolled in her. Burning now with wrath at the sight of her rival, she spread abroad the story, and especially to the father did she tell his daughter's shame. He, fierce and merciless, unheeding her prayers, unheeding her arms stretched out to the Sun, and unheeding her cry, 'He overbore my will,' with brutal cruelty buried her deep in the earth, and heaped on the spot a heavy mound of sand. The son of Hyperion rent this with his rays, and made a way by which you might put forth your buried head; but too late, for now, poor nymph, you could not lift your head, crushed beneath the heavy earth, and you lay there, a lifeless corpse. Nothing more pitiful than that sight, they say, did the driver of the swift steeds see since Phaëthon's burning death. He tried, indeed, by his warm rays to recall those death-cold limbs to the warmth of life. But since grim fate opposed all his efforts, he sprinkled the body and the ground with fragrant nectar, and preluding with many words of grief, he said: 'In spite of fate you shall reach the upper air.' Straightway the body, soaked with the celestial nectar, melted away and filled the earth around with its sweet fragrance. Then did a shrub of frankincense, with deep-driven roots, rise slowly through the soil and its top cleaved the mound.

"But Clytie, though love could excuse her grief, and grief her tattling, was sought no more by the great light-giver, nor did he find anything to love in her. For this cause she pined away, her love turned to madness. Unable to endure her sister nymphs, beneath the open sky, by night and day, she sat upon the bare ground, naked, bareheaded, unkempt. For nine whole days she sat, tasting neither drink nor food, her hunger fed by nothing but pure dew and tears, and moved not from the ground. Only she gazed on the face of her god as he went his way, and turned her face towards him. They say that her limbs grew fast to the soil and her deathly pallor changed in part to a bloodless plant; but in part it was red, and a flower, much like a violet, came where her face had been. Still, though roots hold her fast, she turns ever towards the sun and, though changed herself, preserves her love unchanged."

The story-teller ceased; the wonderful tale had held their ears. Some of the sisters say that such things could not happen; others declare that true gods can do anything. But Bacchus is not one of these. Alcithoë is next called for when the sisters have become silent again. Running her shuttle swiftly through the threads of her loom, she said: "I will pass by the well-known love of Daphnis, the shepherd-boy of Ida, whom a nymph, in anger at her rival, changed to stone: so great is the burning smart which jealous lovers feel. Nor will I tell how once Sithon, the natural laws reversed, lived of changing sex, now woman and now man. How you also, Celmis, now adamant, were once most faithful friend of little Jove; how the Curetes sprang from copious showers; how Crocus and his beloved Smilax were changed into tiny flowers.[1] All these stories I will pass by and will charm your minds with a tale that is pleasing because new.

"How the fountain of Salmacis is of ill-repute, how it enervates with its enfeebling waters and renders soft and weak all men who bathe therein, you shall now hear. The cause is hidden; but the enfeebling power of the fountain is well known. A little son of Hermes and of the goddess of Cythera the naiads nursed within Ida's caves. In his fair face mother and father could be clearly seen; his name also he took from them. When fifteen years had passed, he left his native mountains and abandoned his foster-mother, Ida, delighting to wander in unknown lands and to see strange rivers, his eagerness making light of toil. He came even to the Lycian cities and to the Carians, who dwell hard by the land of Lycia. Here he saw a pool of water crystal clear to the very bottom. No marshy reeds grew there, no unfruitful swamp-grass, nor spiky rushes; it is clear water. But the edges of the pool are bordered with fresh grass, and herbage ever green. A nymph dwells in the pool, one that loves not hunting, nor is wont to bend the bow or strive with speed of foot. She only of the naiads does not follow in swift Diana's train. Often, it's said, her sisters would chide her: 'Salmacis, take now either hunting-spear or

painted quiver, and vary your ease with the hardships of the hunt.'
But she takes no hunting-spear, no painted quiver, nor does she vary
her ease with the hardships of the hunt; but at times she bathes her
shapely limbs in her own pool; often combs her hair with a boxwood
comb, often looks in the mirror-like waters to see what best be-
comes her. Now, wrapped in a transparent robe, she lies down to rest
on the soft grass or the soft herbage. Often she gathers flowers; and
on this occasion, too, she chanced to be gathering flowers when she
saw the boy and longed to possess what she saw.

"Not yet, however, did she approach him, though she was eager
to do so, until she had calmed herself, until she had arranged her
robes and composed her countenance, and taken all pains to appear
beautiful. Then did she speak: 'O youth, most worthy to be believed
a god, if you are indeed a god, you must be Cupid; or if you are mor-
tal, happy are they who gave you birth, blest is thy brother, fortunate
indeed any sister of yours and she who nursed you. But far, oh, far
happier than they all is she, if any be your promised bride, if you
shall deem any worthy to be your wife. If there be any such, let mine
be stolen joy; if not, may I be yours, your bride, and may we be
joined in wedlock.' The maiden said no more. But the boy blushed
rosy red; for he knew not what love is. But still the blush became
him well. Such color have apples hanging in sunny orchards, or
painted ivory; such has the moon, eclipsed, red under white, when
brazen vessels clash vainly for her relief.[2] When the nymph begged
and prayed for at least a sister's kiss, and was in act to throw her
arms round his snowy neck, he cried: 'Have done, or I must flee and
leave this spot—and you.' Salmacis trembled at this threat and said:
'I yield the place to you, fair stranger,' and turning away, pretended
to depart. But even so she often looked back, and deep in a neigh-
bouring thicket she hid herself, crouching on bended knees. But the
boy, freely as if unwatched and alone, walks up and down on the
grass, dips his toes in the lapping waters, and his feet. Then quickly,
charmed with the coolness of the soothing stream, he threw aside
the thin garments from his slender form. Then was the nymph as
one spellbound, and her love kindled as she gazed at the naked
form. Her eyes shone bright as when the sun's dazzling face is re-
flected from the surface of a glass held opposite his rays. Scarce can
she endure delay, scarce bear her joy postponed, so eager to hold him

in her arms, so madly incontinent. He, clapping his body with hollow palms, dives into the pool, and swimming with alternate strokes flashes with gleaming body through the transparent flood, as if one should encase ivory figures or white lilies in translucent glass. 'I win, and he is mine!' cries the naiad, and casting off all her garments dives also into the waters: she holds him fast though he strives against her, steals reluctant kisses, fondles him, touches his unwilling breast, clings to him on this side and on that. At length, as he tries his best to break away from her, she wraps him round with her embrace, as a serpent, when the king of birds has caught her and is bearing her on high: which, hanging from his claws, wraps her folds around his head and feet and entangles his flapping wings with her tail; or as the ivy oft-times embraces great trunks of trees, or as the sea-polyp holds its enemy caught beneath the sea, its tentacles embracing him on every side. The son of Atlas resists as best he may and denies the nymph the joy she craves; but she holds on, and clings as if grown fast to him. 'Strive as you may, wicked boy,' she cries, 'still shall you not escape me. Grant me this, O gods, and may no day ever come that shall separate him from me or me from him.' The gods heard her prayer. For their two bodies, joined together as they were, were merged in one, with one face and form for both. As when one grafts a twig on some tree, he sees the branches grow one, and with common life come to maturity, so were these two bodies knit in close embrace: they were no longer two, nor such as to be called, one, woman, and one, man. They seemed neither, and yet both.

"When now he saw that the waters into which he had plunged had made him but half-man, and that his limbs had become enfeebled there, stretching out his hands and speaking, though not with manly tones, Hermaphroditus cried: 'Oh, grant this request, my father and my mother, to your son who bears the names of both: whoever comes into this pool as man may he go forth half-man, and may he weaken at touch of the water.' His parents heard the prayer of their two-formed son and charged the waters with that uncanny power."

Alcithoë was done; but still did the daughters of Minyas ply their tasks, despising the god and profaning his holy day: when suddenly unseen timbrels sounded harshly in their ears, and flutes, with curving horns, and tinkling cymbals; the air was full of the sweet scent of saffron and of myrrh; and, past all belief, their weft turned green, the hanging cloth changed into vines of ivy; part became grape-vines, and what were but now threads became clinging tendrils; vine-leaves sprang out along the warp, and bright-hued clusters matched the purple tapestry. And now the day was ended, and the time was come when you could not say whether it was dark or light; it was the borderland of night, yet with a gleam of day. Suddenly the whole house seemed to tremble, the oil-fed lamps to flare up, and all the rooms to be ablaze with ruddy fires, while ghostly beasts howled round. Meanwhile the sisters are seeking hiding-places through the smoke-filled rooms, in various corners trying to avoid the flames and glare of light. And while they seek to hide, a skinny covering overspreads their slender limbs, and thin wings enclose their arms. And in what fashion they have lost their former shape they know not for the darkness. No feathered pinions uplift them, yet they sustain themselves on transparent wings. They try to speak, but utter only the tiniest sound as befits their shrivelled forms, and give voice to their grief in thin squeaks. Houses, not forests, are their favorite haunts; and, hating the light of day, they flit by night and from late eventide derive their name.

Then, truly, was the divinity of Bacchus acknowledged throughout all Thebes, and his mother's sister, Ino, would be telling of the wonderful powers of the new god everywhere. She alone of all her sisters knew nothing of grief, except what she felt for them. She, proud of her children, of her husband, Athamas, and proud above all of her divine foster-son, is seen by Juno, who could not bear the sight. "That child of my rival," she said, communing with herself, "had power to change the Maeonian sailors and plunge them in the sea, to cause the flesh of a son to be torn in pieces by his own mother, and to enwrap the three daughters of Minyas with strange wings; and shall nothing be given to Juno, except to bemoan her wrongs still unavenged? Does that suffice me? Is this my only power? But he himself teaches me what to do. It is proper to learn even from an enemy. To what length madness can go he has proved enough and to spare by the slaughter of Pentheus. Why should not Ino be stung to madness too, and, urged by her fury, go where her kinswomen have led the way?"

There is a down-sloping path, by deadly yew-trees shaded, which leads through dumb silence to the infernal realms. The sluggish

Styx there exhales its vaporous breath; and by that way come down the spirits of the new-dead, shades of those who have received due funeral rites. This is a wide-extending waste, wan and cold; and the shades newly arrived know not where the road is which leads to the Stygian city where lies the dread palace of black Dis. This city has a thousand wide approaches and gates open on all sides; and as the ocean receives the rivers that flow down from all the earth, so does this place receive all souls; it is not too small for any people, nor does it feel the accession of a throng. There wander the shades bloodless, without body and bone. Some throng the forum, some the palace of the underworld king; others ply some craft in imitation of their former life.

To here, leaving her abode in heaven, Saturnian Juno endured to go; so much did she grant to her hate and wrath. When she made entrance there, and the threshold groaned beneath the weight of her sacred form, Cerberus reared up his threefold head and uttered his threefold baying. The goddess summoned the Furies, sisters born of Night, divinities deadly and implacable. Before hell's closed gates of adamant they sat, combing the while black snakes from their hair. When they recognized Juno approaching through the thick gloom, the goddesses arose. This place is called the Accursed Place. Here Tityos offered his vitals to be torn, lying stretched out over nine broad acres. Your lips can catch no water, Tantalus, and the tree that overhangs ever eludes you. You, Sisyphus, either push or chase the rock that must always be rolling down the hill again. There whirls Ixion on his wheel, both following himself and fleeing, all in one; and the Belides, for daring to work destruction on their cousin-husbands, with unremitting toil seek again and again the waters, only to lose them.[3]

On all these Saturnia looks with frowning eyes, but especially on Ixion; then, turning her gaze from him to Sisyphus, she says: "Why does this of all the brothers suffer unending pains, while Athamas dwells proudly in a rich palace—Athamas, who with his wife has always scorned my godhead?" And she explains the causes of her hatred and of her journey here, and what she wants. What she wanted was that the house of Cadmus should fall, and that the Fury-sisters should drive Athamas to madness. Commands, promises, prayers she poured out all in one, and begged the goddesses to aid her.

When Juno had done, Tisiphone, just as she was, shook her tangled grey locks, tossed back the straggling snakes from her face, and said: "There is no need of long explanations; consider done all that you ask. Leave this unlovely realm and go back to the sweeter airs of your native skies." Juno went back rejoicing; and as she was entering heaven, Iris, the daughter of Thaumus, sprinkled her all over with purifying water.

Straightway the fell Tisiphone seized a torch which had been steeped in gore, put on a robe red with dripping blood, girt round her waist a writhing snake, and started forth. Grief went along with her, Terror and Dread and Madness, too, with quivering face. She stood upon the doomed threshold. They say the very door-posts of the house of Aeolus* shrank away from her; the polished oaken doors grew dim and the sun hid his face. Ino was mad with terror at the monstrous sight, and her husband, Athamas, was filled with fear. They made to leave their palace, but the baleful Fury stood in their way and blocked their exit. And stretching her arms, wreathed with vipers, she shook out her locks: disturbed, the serpents hissed horribly. A part lay on her shoulders, part twined round her breast, hissing, vomiting venomous gore, and darting out their tongues. Then she tears away two serpents from the midst of her tresses, and with deadly aim hurls them at her victims. The snakes go gliding over the breasts of Ino and of Athamas and breathe upon them their pestilential breath. Their bodies suffer no wounds; it is their minds that feel the deadly stroke. The Fury, not content with this, had brought horrid poisons too—froth of Cerberus' jaws, the venom of the Hydra, strange hallucinations and utter forgetfulness, crime and tears, mad love of slaughter, all mixed together with fresh blood and green hemlock juice, and brewed in a brazen cauldron. And while they stood quaking there, over the breasts of both she poured this maddening poison brew, and made it sink to their being's core. Then, catching up her torch, she whirled it rapidly round and round and kindled fire by the swiftly moving fire. So, her task accomplished and her victory won, she retraced her way to the unsubstantial realm of mighty Dis, and there laid off the serpents she had worn.

---

*Founder of the royal house of Iolcus, father of Athamas.

Straightway cried Athamas, the son of Aeolus, madly raving in his palace halls: "Ho! my comrades, spread the nets here in these woods! I saw here but now a lioness with her two cubs"; and madly pursued his wife's tracks as if she were a beast of prey. His son, Learchus, laughing and stretching out his little hands in glee, he snatched from the mother's arms, and whirling him round and round through the air like a sling, he madly dashed the baby's head against a rough rock. Then the mother, stung to madness too, either by grief or by the sprinkled poison's force, howled wildly, and, quite bereft of sense, with hair streaming, she fled away, bearing you, little Melicerta, in her naked arms, and shouting, "Ho! Bacchus!" as she fled. At the name of Bacchus, Juno laughed in scorn and said: "So may your foster-son ever bless you!" A cliff hung over the sea, the lower part of which had been hollowed out by the beating waves, and sheltered the waters underneath from the rain. Its top stood high and sharp and stretched far out in front over the deep. To this spot—for madness had made her strong—Ino climbed, and held by no natural fears, she leaped with her child far out above the sea. The water where she fell was churned white with foam.

But Venus, pitying the undeserved sufferings of her granddaughter, thus addressed her uncle with coaxing words: "O Neptune, god of waters, whose power is second to heaven alone, I ask great things, I know; but do pity these my friends, whom you see plunged in the broad Ionian sea, and receive them among your sea-deities. Some favor is due to me from the sea, if in its sacred depths my being sprang once from foam, and in the Greek tongue I have a name from this." Neptune consented to her prayer and, taking from Ino and her son all that was mortal, gave them a being to be revered, changing both name and form; for he called the new god Palaemon, and his goddess-mother, Leucothoë.

The Theban women who had been Ino's companions followed on her track as best they could, and saw her last act from the edge of the rock. Nothing doubting that she had been killed, in mourning for the house of Cadmus they beat their breasts with their hands, tore their hair, and rent their garments; and they upbraided Juno, saying that she was unjust and too cruel to the woman who had wronged her. Juno could not brook their reproaches and said: "I will make yourselves the greatest monument of my cruelty."

No sooner said than done. For she who had been most devoted to
the queen cried: "I shall follow my queen into the sea"; and was just
about to take the leap when she was unable to move at all, and stood
fixed fast to the rock. A second, while she was preparing again to
smite her breasts as she had been doing, felt her lifted arms grow
stiff. Another had by chance stretched out her hands towards the
waters of the sea, but now it was a figure of stone that stretched out
hands to those same waters. Still another, plucking at her hair to
tear it out, you might see with sudden stiffened fingers still in act to
tear. Each turned to stone and kept the pose in which she was over-
taken. Still others were changed to birds, and they also, once
Theban women, now on light wings skim the water over that pool.

Cadmus was all unaware that his daughter and little grandson
had been changed to deities of the sea. Overcome with grief at the
misfortunes which had been heaped upon him, and awed by the
many portents he had seen, he fled from the city which he had
founded, as if the fortune of the place and not his own evil fate were
overwhelming him. Driven on through long wanderings, at last his
flight brought him with his wife to the borders of Illyria. Here,
overborne by the weight of woe and age, they reviewed the early
misfortunes of their house and their own troubles. Cadmus said:
"Was that a sacred serpent which my spear transfixed long ago
when, fresh come from Sidon, I scattered his teeth on the earth,
seed of a strange crop of men? If it be this the gods have been
avenging with such unerring wrath, I pray that I, too, may be a ser-
pent, and stretch myself in long snaky form—" Even as he spoke he
was stretched out in long snaky form; he felt his skin hardening and
scales growing on it, while iridescent spots besprinkled his darken-
ing body. He fell prone upon his belly, and his legs were gradually
moulded together into one and drawn out into a slender, pointed
tail. His arms yet remained; while they remained, he stretched them
out, and with tears flowing down his still human cheeks he cried:
"Come near, oh, come, my most wretched wife, and while still there
is something left of me, touch me, take my hand, while I have a
hand, while still the serpent does not usurp me quite." He wanted
to say much more, but his tongue was of a sudden cleft in two;
words failed him, and whenever he tried to utter some sad com-
plaint, it was a hiss; this was the only voice which Nature left him.

Then his wife, smiting her naked breasts with her hands, cried out: "O Cadmus, stay, unhappy man, and put off this monstrous form! Cadmus, what does this mean? Where are your feet? Where are your shoulders and your hands, your color, face, and, while I speak, your—everything? Why, O gods of heaven, do you not change me also into the same serpent form?" She spoke; he licked his wife's face and glided into her dear breasts as if familiar there, embraced her, and sought his wonted place about her neck. All who were there—for they had comrades with them—were filled with horror. But she only stroked the sleek neck of the crested dragon, and suddenly there were two serpents there with intertwining folds, which after a little while crawled off and hid in the neighbouring woods. Now also, as of yore, they neither fear mankind nor wound them, mild creatures, remembering what once they were.

But both in their altered form found great comfort in their grandson, whom conquered India now worshipped, whose temples Greece had filled with adoring throngs. There was one only, Acrisius, the son of Abas, sprung from the same stock, who forbade the entrance of Bacchus within the walls of his city, Argos, who violently opposed the god, and did not admit that he was the son of Jove. Nor did he admit that Perseus was son of Jove, whom Danaë had conceived of a golden shower. And yet, such is the power of truth, Acrisius in the end was sorry that he had repulsed the god and had not acknowledged his grandson. The one had now been received to a place in heaven; but the other, bearing the wonderful spoil of the snake-haired monster, was taking his way through the thin air on whirring wings. As he was flying over the sandy wastes of Libya, bloody drops from the Gorgon's head fell down; and the earth received them as they fell and changed them into snakes of various kinds. And for this cause the land of Libya is full of deadly serpents.

From there he was driven through the vast stretches of air by warring winds and borne, now this way, now that way, like a cloud of mist. He looked down from his great height upon the lands lying below and flew over the whole world. Thrice did he see the cold Bears, and thrice the Crab's spreading claws; time and again to the west, and as often back to the east was he carried. And now, as daylight was fading, fearing to trust himself to flight by night, he alighted on the borders of the West, in the realm of Atlas. Here he sought a little rest until the morning star should wake the fires of dawn and the dawn lead out the fiery car of day. Here, far surpassing all men in huge bulk of body, was Atlas, of the stock of Iapetus. He ruled this edge of the world and the sea which spread its waters to receive the Sun's panting horses and his weary car. A thousand flocks he had, and as many herds, wandering at will over the grassy plains; and no other realm was near to hem in his land. A tree he had whose leaves were of gleaming gold, concealing golden branches and golden fruits. "Good sir," said Perseus, addressing him, "if glory of high birth means anything to you, Jove is my father; or if you admire great deeds, you surely will admire mine. I crave your hospitality and a chance to rest." But Atlas bethought him of an old oracle, which Themis of Parnasus had given: "Atlas, the time will come when your tree will be spoiled of its gold, and he who gets the glory of this spoil will be Jove's son." Fearing this, Atlas had enclosed his orchard with massive walls and had put a huge dragon there to watch it; and he kept off all strangers from his boundaries. And now to Perseus, too, he said: "Go afar, in case the glory of your deeds, which you falsely brag of, and this Jupiter of yours be far from aiding you." He added force to threats, and was trying to thrust out the other, who held back and manfully resisted while he urged his case with soothing speech. At length, finding himself unequal in strength—for who would be a match in strength for Atlas?—he said: "Well, since so small a favor you will not grant to me, let me give you a gift"; and, himself turning his back, he held out from his left hand the ghastly Medusa-head. Straightway Atlas became a mountain huge as the giant had been; his beard and hair were changed to trees, his shoulders and arms to spreading ridges; what had been his head was now the mountain's top, and his bones were changed to stones. Then he grew to monstrous size in all his parts—for so, O gods, you had willed it—and the whole heaven with all its stars rested upon his head.

Now Aeolus, the son of Hippotas, had shut the winds in their everlasting prison, and the bright morning star that wakes men to their toil had risen in the heavens. Then Perseus bound on both his feet the wings he had laid by, girt on his hooked sword, and soon in swift flight was cleaving the thin air. Having left behind countless peoples all around him and below, he spied at last the Ethiopians and Cepheus' realm. There unrighteous Ammon* had bidden Andromeda, though innocent, to pay the penalty of her mother's words. As soon as Perseus saw her there bound by the arms to a rough cliff—except that her hair gently stirred in the breeze, and the warm tears were trickling down her cheeks, he would have thought her a marble statue—he took fire unwitting, and stood dumb. Smitten by the sight of her exquisite beauty, he almost forgot to move his wings in the air. Then, when he alighted near the maiden, he said: "Oh! those are not the chains you deserve to wear, but rather those that link fond lovers together! Tell me, for I would know, your country's name and yours, and why you are chained here." She was silent at first, for, being a maid, she did not dare address a man; she would have hidden her face modestly with her hands but that her hands were bound. Her eyes were free, and these filled with rising tears. As he continued to urge her, she, so that she should not seem to be trying to conceal some fault of her own, told him her name and her country, and what sinful boasting her mother had made of her own beauty. While she was yet speaking, there came a loud sound from the sea, and there, advancing over the broad expanse, a monstrous creature loomed up, breasting the wide waves. The maiden shrieked. The grieving father and the mother are at hand, both wretched, but she more justly so. They have no help to give, but only wailings and loud beatings of the breast, befitting the oc-casion, and they hang to the girl's chained form. Then speaks the stranger: "There will be long time for weeping by and by; but time for helping is very short. If I sought this maid as Perseus, son of Jove and that imprisoned one whom Jove filled with his life-giving shower; if as Perseus, victor over Gorgon of the snaky locks, and as he who has dared to ride the winds of heaven on fluttering wings, surely I should be preferred to all suitors as your son-in-law. But now I shall try to add to these great gifts the gift of service, too, if only the gods will favor me. That she be mine if saved by my valor is my bargain." The parents accept the condition—for who would refuse?—and beg him to save her, promising him a kingdom as dowry in addition.

---

*Egyptian god usually associated with Jupiter, as Isis was with Io.

But see! as a swift ship with its sharp beak plows the waves, driven by stout rowers' sweating arms, so does the monster come, rolling back the water from either side as his breast surges through. And now he was as far from the cliff as is the space through which a Balearic sling can send its whizzing bullet; when suddenly the youth, springing up from the earth, mounted high into the clouds. When the monster saw the hero's shadow on the surface of the sea, he savagely attacked the shadow. And as the bird of Jove, when it has seen in an open field a serpent sunning its mottled body, swoops down upon him from behind; and, so that the serpent might not twist back his deadly fangs, the bird buries deep his sharp claws in the creature's scaly neck; so did Perseus, plunging headlong in a swift swoop through the empty air, attack the roaring monster from above, and in his right shoulder buried his sword clear down to the curved hook. Smarting under the deep wound, the creature now reared himself high in air, now plunged beneath the waves, now turned like a fierce wild-boar when around him a noisy pack of hounds give tongue. Perseus eludes the greedy fangs by help of his swift wings; and where the vulnerable points lie open to attack, he smites with his hooked sword, now at the back, thick-set with bar-nacles, now on the sides, now where the tail is most slender and changes into the form of fish. The beast belches forth waters mixed with purple blood. Meanwhile Perseus' wings are growing heavy, soaked with spray, and he dares not depend further on his drenched pinions. He spies a rock whose top projects above the surface when the waves are still, but which is hidden by the roughened sea. Resting on this and holding an edge of the rock with his left hand, thrice and again he plunges his sword into the vitals of the monster. At this the shores and the high seats of the gods re-echo with wild shouts of applause. Cassiope and Cepheus rejoice and salute the hero as son-in-law, calling him prop and saviour of their house. The maiden also now comes forward, freed from chains, she, the prize as well as cause of his feat. He washes his victorious hands in water drawn for him; and, that the Gorgon's snaky head may not be bruised on the hard sand, he softens the ground with leaves, strews seaweed over these, and lays on this the head of Medusa, daughter of Phorcys.[4] The fresh weed twigs, but now alive and porous to the core, absorb the power of the monster and hardens at its touch and take a strange stiffness in their stems and leaves. And the sea-nymphs test the wonder on more twigs and are delighted to find the same thing happening to them all; and, by scattering these twigs as seeds, propagate the wondrous thing throughout their waters. And even till this day the same nature has remained in coral so that they harden when exposed to air, and what was a pliant twig beneath the sea is turned to stone above.

Now Perseus builds to three gods three altars of turf, the left to Mercury, the right to you, O warlike maid, and the central one to Jove. To Minerva he slays a cow, a young bullock to the winged god, and a bull to you, greatest of the gods. At once the hero claims Andromeda as the prize of his great deed, seeking no further dowry. Hymen and Love shake the marriage torch; the fires are fed full with incense rich and fragrant, garlands deck the dwellings, and everywhere lyre and flute and songs resound, blessed proofs of inward joy. The huge folding-doors swing back and reveal the great golden palace-hall with a rich banquet spread, where Cepheus' princely courtiers grace the feast.

When they have had their fill of food, and their hearts have expanded with Bacchus' generous gift, then Perseus seeks to know the manner of the region thereabouts, its peoples, customs, and the spirit of its men. The prince who answered him then said: "Now tell us, pray, O Perseus, by what wondrous valor, by what arts you won the Gorgon's snaky head." The hero, answering, told how beneath cold Atlas there was a place safe under the protection of the rocky mass. At the entrance to this place two sisters dwelt, both daughters of old Phorcys, who shared one eye between them. This eye by craft and stealth, while it was being passed from one sister to the other, Perseus stole away, and travelling far through trackless and secret ways, rough woods, and bristling rocks, he came at last to where the Gorgons lived. On all sides through the fields and along the ways he saw the forms of men and beasts changed into stone by one look at Medusa's face. But he himself had looked upon the image of that dread face reflected from the bright bronze shield his left hand bore; and while deep sleep held fast both the snakes and her who wore them, he smote her head clean from her neck, and from the blood of his mother swift-winged Pegasus and his brother sprang.[5]

The hero further told of his long journeys and perils passed, all true, what seas, what lands he had beheld from his high flight, what stars he had touched on beating wings. He ceased, while they waited still to hear more. But one of the princes asked him why Medusa only of the sisters wore serpents mingled with her hair. The guest replied: "Since what you ask is a tale well worth the telling, hear then the cause. She was once most beautiful in form, and the jealous hope of many suitors. Of all her beauties, her hair was the most beautiful—for so I learned from one who said he had seen her. It's said that in Minerva's temple Neptune, lord of the Ocean, ravished her. Jove's daughter turned away and hid her chaste eyes behind her aegis. And, that the deed might be punished as was due, she changed the Gorgon's locks to ugly snakes. And now to frighten her fear-numbed foes, she still wears upon her breast the snakes which she has made."

BOOK V

WHILE THE HEROIC SON of Danaë is relating these adventures among the Ethiopian chiefs, the royal halls are filled with confused uproar: not the loud sound that sings a song of marriage, but one that presages the fierce strife of arms. And the feast, turned suddenly to tumult, you could liken to the sea, whose peaceful waters the raging winds lash to boisterous waves. First among them is Phineus, brother of the king, rash instigator of strife, who brandishes an ashen spear with bronze point. "Behold," says he, "here am I, come to avenge the theft of my bride. Your wings shall not save you this time, nor Jove, changed to seeming gold." As he was in the act of hurling his spear, Cepheus cried out: "What are you doing, brother? What mad folly is driving you to crime? Is this the way you thank our guest for his brave deeds? Is this the dower you give for the maiden saved? If it's the truth you want, it was not Perseus who took her from you, but the dread deity of the Nereids, but horned Ammon, but that sea-monster who came to glut his maw upon my own flesh and blood. It was then you lost her when she was exposed to die; unless, perhaps, your cruel heart demands this very thing—her death, and seeks by my grief to ease its own. It seems it is not enough that you saw her chained, and that you brought no aid, uncle though you were, and promised husband: will you grieve, besides, that someone did save her, and will you rob him of his prize? If this prize seems so precious in your sight, you should have taken it from those rocks where it was chained. Now let the man who did take it, by whom I have been saved from childlessness in my old age, keep what he has gained by his deserving deeds and by my promise. And be assured of this: that he has not been preferred to you, but to certain death."

Phineus made no reply; but, looking now on him and now on Perseus, he was in doubt at which to aim his spear. Delaying a little space, he hurled it with all the strength that wrath gave at Perseus;

but in vain. When the weapon struck and stood fast in the bench, then at last Perseus leapt gallantly up and hurled back the spear, which would have pierced his foeman's heart; but Phineus had already taken refuge behind the altar, and, shame! the wretch found safety there. Still was the weapon not without effect, for it struck full in Rhoetus' face. Down he fell, and when the spear had been wrenched forth from the bone he writhed about and sprinkled the well-spread table with his blood. And now the mob was fired to wrath unquenchable. They hurled their spears, and there were some who said that Cepheus ought to perish with his son-in-law. But Cepheus had already withdrawn from the palace, calling to witness Justice, Faith, and the gods of hospitality that this was done against his protest. Then came warlike Pallas, protecting her brother with her shield, and making him stout of heart.

There was an Indian youth, Athis by name, whom Limnaee, a nymph of Ganges' stream, is said to have brought forth beneath her crystal waters. He was of surpassing beauty, which his rich robes enhanced, a sturdy boy of sixteen years, clad in a purple mantle fringed with gold; a golden chain adorned his neck, and a golden circlet held his locks in place, perfumed with myrrh. He was well skilled to hurl the javelin at the most distant mark, but with more skill could bend the bow. When now he was in the very act of bending his stout bow, Perseus snatched up a brand which lay smouldering on the altar and smote the youth, crushing his face to splintered bones.

When Assyrian Lycabas beheld him, his lovely features defiled with blood—Lycabas, his closest comrade and his declared true lover—he wept aloud for Athis, who lay gasping out his life beneath that bitter wound; then he caught up the bow which Athis had bent, and cried: "Now you have me to fight, and not long shall you plume yourself on a boy's death, which brings you more contempt than glory." Before he had finished speaking the keen arrow fleshed from the bowstring; but it missed its mark and stuck harmless in a fold of Perseus' robe. Acrisius' grandson quickly turned on him that hook which had been fleshed in Medusa's death, and drove it into his breast. But he, even in death, with his eyes swimming in the black darkness, looked round for Athis, fell down by his side, and bore to the shadows this comfort, that in death they were not divided.

Then Phorbas of Syene, Metion's son, and Libyan Amphimedon, eager to join in the fray, slipped and fell in the blood with which all the floor was wet. As they strove to rise the sword met them, driven through the ribs of one and through the other's throat.

But Eurytus, the son of Actor, who wielded a broad, two-edged battle-axe, Perseus did not attack with his hooked sword, but lifting high in both hands a huge mixing-bowl heavily embossed and ponderous, he hurled it crashing at the man. The red blood spouted forth as he lay dying on his back, beating the floor with his head. Then in rapid succession Perseus laid low Polydaemon, descended from Queen Semiramis, Caucasian Abaris, Lycetus who dwelt by Sperchios, Helices of unshorn locks, Phlegyas and Clytus, treading the while on heaps of dying men.

Phineus did not dare to come to close combat with his enemy, but hurled his javelin. This was ill-aimed and struck Idas, who all to no purpose had kept out of the fight, taking sides with neither party. He, gazing with angry eyes upon cruel Phineus, said: "Since I am forced into the strife, O Phineus, accept the foeman you have made, and score me wound for wound." And he was just about to hurl back the javelin which he had drawn out of his own body, when he fell fainting, his limbs all drained of blood.

Then also Hodites, first of the Ethiopians after the king, fell by the sword of Clymenus; Hypseus smote Prothoënor; Lyncides, Hypseus. Amid the throng was one old man, Emathion, who loved justice and revered the gods. He, since his years forbade warfare, fought with the tongue, and strode forward and cursed their impious arms. As he clung to the altar-horns with age-enfeebled hands Chromis struck off his head with his sword: the head fell straight on the altar, and there the still half-conscious tongue kept up its execrations and the life was breathed out in the midst of the altar-fires.

Next fell two brothers by Phineus' hand, Broteas and Ammon, invincible with gauntlets, if gauntlets could but contend with swords; and Ampycus, Ceres' priest, his temples wreathed with white fillets. You, too, Lampetides, not intended for such a scene as this, but for a peaceful task, to ply lute and voice: you had been bidden to grace the feast and sing the festal song. To him standing apart and holding his peaceful quill, Pettalus mocking cried: "Go sing the rest of your song to the Stygian shades," and pierced the left temple with his blade. He fell, and with dying fingers again essays the strings, and as he fell there was a lamentable sound. Nor did Lycormas, maddened at the sight, suffer him to perish unavenged; but, tearing out a stout bar from the door-post on the right, he broke the murderer's neck with a crashing blow. And Pettalus fell to the earth like a slaughtered bull. Cinyphian Pelates essayed to tear away another bar from the left post, but in the act his right hand was pierced by the spear of Corythus of Marmarida, and pinned to the wood. There fastened, Abas thrust him through the side; nor did he fall, but, dying, hung down from the post to which his hand was nailed. Melaneus, too, was slain, one of Perseus' side; and Dorylas, the richest man in the land of Nasamonia—Dorylas, rich in land, than whom none held a wider domain, none heaped so many piles of spices. Into his groin a spear hurled from the side struck; that place is fatal. When Bactrian Halcyoneus, who hurled the spear, beheld him gasping out his life and rolling his eyes in death, he said: "Only this land on which you lie of all your lands shall you possess," and left the lifeless body. Against him Perseus, swift to avenge, hurled the spear snatched from the warm wound, which, striking the nose, was driven through the neck, and stuck out on both sides. And, while fortune favored him, he slew also Clytius and Clanis, both born of one mother, but each with a different wound. For through both thighs of Clytius went the ashen spear, hurled by his mighty arm; the other dart Clanis crunched with his jaw. There fell also Mendesian Celadon; Astreus, too, whose mother was a Syrian, and his father unknown; Aethion, once wise to see what is to come, but now tricked by a false omen; Thoactes, armor-bearer of the king; Agyrtes, infamous for that he had slain his sire.*

Yet more remains, faint with toil though he is; for all are bent on crushing him alone. On all sides the banded lines assail him, in a cause that repudiated merit and plighted word. On his side his father-in-law with useless loyalty and his bride and her mother range themselves, and fill all the hall with their shrieks. But their cries are drowned in the clash of arms and the groans of dying men; while Bellona drenches and pollutes with blood the sacred home, and ever renews the strife.

---

*The incident of patricide to which Ovid refers is in fact obscure.

Now he stands alone where Phineus and a thousand followers close round him. Thicker than winter hail fly the spears, past right side and left, past eyes and ears. He stands with his back against a great stone column and, so protected in the rear, faces the opposing crowds and their impetuous attack. The attack is made on the left by Chaonian Molpeus, and by Arabian Ethemon on the right. Just as a tigress, pricked by hunger, that hears the bellowing of two herds in two several valleys, knows not which to rush upon, but burns to rush on both; so Perseus hesitates whether to smite on right or left; he stops Molpeus with a wound through the leg and was content to let him go; but Ethemon gives him no time, and comes rushing on, eager to wound him in the neck, and drives his sword with mighty power but careless aim, and breaks it on the edge of the great stone column: the blade flies off and sticks in its owner's throat. The stroke indeed is not deep enough for death; but as he stands there trembling and stretching out his empty hands (but all in vain), Perseus thrusts him through with Mercury's hooked sword.

But when Perseus saw his own strength was no match for the superior numbers of his foes, he exclaimed: "Since you yourselves force me to it, I shall seek aid from my own enemy. Turn away your faces, if any friend be here." So saying, he raised on high the Gorgon's head. "Seek someone else to frighten with your magic arts," cried Thescelus, and raised his deadly javelin in act to throw; but in that very act he stood immovable, a marble statue. Next after him Ampyx thrust his sword full at the heart of the great-souled Perseus; but in that thrust his right hand stiffened and moved neither this way nor that. But Nileus, who falsely claimed that he was sprung from the sevenfold Nile, and who had on his shield engraved the image of the stream's seven mouths, part silver and part gold, cried: "See, O Perseus, the source from which I have sprung. Surely a great consolation for your death will you carry to the silent shades, that you have fallen by so great a man"—his last words were cut off in mid-speech; you would suppose that his open lips still strove to speak, but they no longer gave passage to his words. These two Eryx rebuked, saying: "It's from defect of courage, not from any power of the Gorgon's head, that you stand rigid. Rush in with me and hurl to the earth this fellow and his magic arms!" He had begun the rush, but the floor held his feet fast and there he stayed, a motionless rock, an image in full armor.

These, indeed, deserved the punishment they received. But there was one, Aconteus, a soldier on Perseus' side, who, while fighting for his friend, chanced to look upon the Gorgon's face and hardened into stone. Astyages, thinking him still a living man, smote upon him with his long sword. The sword gave out a sharp clanging sound; and while Astyages stood amazed, the same strange power got hold on him, and he stood there still with a look of wonder on his marble face. It would take too long to tell the names of the rank and file who perished. Two hundred men survived the fight; two hundred saw the Gorgon and turned to stone.

But now at last Phineus repents him of this unrighteous strife. But what is he to do? He sees images in various attitudes and knows the men for his own; he calls each one by name, prays for his aid, and hardly believing his eyes, he touches those who are nearest him: marble, all! He turns his face away, and so stretching out sideways suppliant hands that confess defeat, he says: "Perseus, you are my conqueror. Remove that dreadful thing; that petrifying Medusa-head of yours—whosoever she may be, oh, take it away, I beg. It was not hate of you and lust for the kingly power that drove me to this war. It was my wife I fought for. Your claim was better in merit, mine in time. I am content to yield. Grant me now nothing, O bravest of men, save this my life. All the rest be yours." As he thus spoke, not daring to look at him to whom he prayed, Perseus replied: "Most craven Phineus, dismiss your fears; what I can give (and it is a great gift for your coward soul), I will grant: you shall not suffer by the sword. No, instead I will make of you a monument that shall endure for ages; and in the house of my father-in-law you shall always stand on view, that so my wife may find solace in the statue of her promised lord." So saying, he bore the Gorgon-head where Phineus had turned his fear-struck face. Then, even as he strove to avert his eyes, his neck grew hard and the very tears upon his cheeks were changed to stone. And now in marble was fixed the cowardly face, the suppliant look, the pleading hands, the whole cringing attitude.

Victorious Perseus, together with his bride, now returns to his ancestral city; and there, to avenge his grandsire, who little deserved this championship, he wars on Proetus.* For Proetus had driven his brother out by force of arms, and seized the stronghold of Acrisius.[1] But neither by the force of arms, nor by the stronghold he had basely seized, could he resist the baleful gaze of that dread snake-wreathed monster.

But you, O Polydectes, ruler of Little Seriphos, were not softened by the young man's valor, tried in so many feats, nor by his troubles; but you were hard and unrelenting in hate, and your unjust anger knew no end. You even refused him his honor, and declared that the death of Medusa was all a lie. "We will give you proof of that," then Perseus said; "protect your eyes!" (this to his friends). And with the Medusa-face he changed the features of the king to bloodless stone.[2]

During all this time Tritonia had been the comrade of her brother born of the golden shower. But now, wrapped in a hollow cloud, she left Seriphos, and, passing Cythnus and Gyarus on the right, by the shortest course over the sea she made for Thebes and Helicon, home of the Muses. On this mountain she alighted, and thus addressed the sisters versed in song: "The fame of a new spring has reached my ears, which broke out under the hard hoof of the winged horse of Medusa. This is the cause of my journey: I wished to see the marvellous thing. The horse himself I saw born from his mother's blood." Urania replied: "Whatever cause has brought you to see our home, O goddess, you are most welcome to our hearts. But the tale is true, and Pegasus did indeed produce our spring." And she led Pallas aside to the sacred waters. She long admired the spring made by the stroke of the horse's hoof; then looked round on the ancient woods, the grottoes, and the grass, spangled with countless flowers. She declared the daughters of Mnemosyne to be happy alike in their favorite pursuits and in their home. And thus one of the sisters answered her: "O you, Tritonia, who would so fitly join our band, if your merits had not raised you to far greater tasks, you tell the truth and justly praise our arts and our home. We have indeed a happy lot—were we but safe in it. But (such is the licence of the time) all things affright our virgin souls, and the vision of fierce Pyreneus is ever before our eyes, and I have not yet recovered from my fear. This bold king with his Thracian soldiery had captured

---

*A human king of Tiryns, not the shape-shifting god with a similar name (Proteus).

Daulis and the Phocian fields, and ruled that realm which he had unjustly gained. It chanced that we were journeying to the temple on Parnassus. He saw us going, and feigning a reverence for our divinity, he said: 'O daughters of Mnemosyne'—for he knew us—'stay your steps and do not hesitate to take shelter beneath my roof against the lowering sky and the rain'—for rain was falling—'gods have often entered a humbler home.' Moved by his words and by the storm, we yielded to the man and entered his portal. And now the rain had ceased, the south wind had been routed by the north, and the dusky clouds were in full flight from the brightening sky. We were fain to go on our way; but Pyreneus shut his doors, and offered us violence. This we escaped by donning our wings. He, as if he would follow us, took his stand on a lofty battlement and cried to us: 'What way you take, the same will I take also'; and, quite bereft of sense, he leaped from the pinnacle of the tower. Headlong he fell, crushing his bones and dyeing the ground in death with his accursed blood."

While the muse was still speaking, the sound of whirring wings was heard and words of greeting came from the high branches of the trees. Jove's daughter looked up and tried to see from where came the sound which was so clearly speech. She thought some human being spoke; but it was a bird. Nine birds, lamenting their fate, had alighted in the branches, magpies, which can imitate any sound they please. When Minerva wondered at the sight, the other addressed her, goddess to goddess: "It is but lately those creatures also, conquered in a strife, have been added to the throng of birds. Pierus, lord of the rich domain of Pella, was their father, and Euippe of Paeonia was their mother. Nine times brought to the birth, nine times she called for help on mighty Lucina. Swollen with pride of numbers, this throng of senseless sisters journeyed through all the towns of Haemonia and all the towns of Achaia to us, and thus defied us to a contest in song: 'Cease to deceive the unsophisticated rabble with your pretence of song. Come, strive with us, O Thespian* goddesses, if you dare. Neither in voice nor in skill can we be conquered, and our numbers are the same. If you are conquered,

---

*That is, from near Thespiae. The Muses are daughters of Jove and Mnemosyne (Memory).

yield us Medusa's spring and Boeotian Aganippe; or we will yield to you the Emathian plains even to snow-clad Paeonia; and let the nymphs be judges of our strife.'

"It was a shame to strive with them, but it seemed greater shame to yield. So the nymphs were chosen judges and took oath by their streams, and they set them down upon benches of living rock. Then without drawing lots she who had proposed the contest first began. She sang of the battle of the gods and giants, ascribing undeserved honor to the giants, and belittling the deeds of the mighty gods: how Typhoeus, sprung from the lowest depths of earth, inspired the heavenly gods with fear, and how they all turned their backs and fled, until, weary, they found refuge in the land of Egypt and the seven-mouthed Nile. How even there Typhoeus, son of earth, pursued them, and the gods hid themselves in lying shapes: 'Jove thus became a ram,' said she, 'the lord of flocks, and so Libyan Ammon even to this day is represented with curving horns; Apollo hid in a crow's shape, Bacchus in a goat; the sister of Phoebus, in a cat, Juno in a snow-white cow, Venus in a fish, Mercury in an ibis bird.'*

"So far had she sung, tuning voice to harp; we, the Aonian† sisters, were challenged to reply—but perhaps you have not leisure, and care not to listen to our song?" "No, have no doubt," Pallas exclaimed, "but sing now your song in due order." And she took her seat in the pleasant shade of the forest. The muse replied: "We gave the conduct of our strife to one, Calliope;‡ who rose and, with her flowing tresses bound in an ivy wreath, tried the plaintive chords with her thumb, and then, with sweeping chords, she sang this song: 'Ceres was the first to turn the glebe with the hooked plowshare; she first gave corn and kindly sustenance to the world; she first gave laws. All things are the gift of Ceres; she must be the subject of my song. Would that I could worthily sing of her; surely the goddess is worthy of my song.

" 'The huge island of Sicily had been heaped upon the body of the giant, and with its vast weight was resting on Typhoeus, who had dared to aspire to the heights of heaven. He struggles indeed,

---

*Compare book I's rather different account of the war of gods and giants.
†From the region of Aonia, where Parnassus, mountain of the muses, rises.
‡The muse of epic poetry. Her tale mimics Ovid's own narrative style.

and strives often to rise again; but his right hand is held down by
Ausonian Pelorus and his left by you, Pachynus. Lilybaeum rests on
his legs, and Aetna's weight is on his head.. Flung on his back be-
neath this mountain, the fierce Typhoeus spouts forth ashes and
vomits flames from his mouth. Often he puts forth all his strength
to push off the weight of earth and to roll the cities and great moun-
tains from his body: then the earth quakes, and even the king of the
silent land is afraid in case the crust of the earth split open in wide
seams and the light of day be let in to frighten the trembling shades.
Fearing this disaster, the king of the lower world had left his gloomy
realm and, drawn in his chariot with its sable steeds, was traversing
the land of Sicily, carefully examining its foundations. After he had
examined all to his satisfaction, and found that no points were giv-
ing way, he put aside his fears. Then Venus Erycina saw him wan-
dering to and fro, as she was seated on her sacred mountain, and
embracing her winged son, she exclaimed: "O son, both arms and
hands to me, and source of all my power, take now those shafts,
Cupid, with which you conquer all, and shoot your swift arrows into
the heart of that god to whom the final lot of the triple kingdom
fell. You rule the gods, and Jove himself; you conquer and control
the deities of the sea, and the very king that rules the deities of the
sea. Why does Tartarus hold back? Why do you not extend your
mother's empire and your own? The third part of the world is at
stake. And yet in heaven, such is our long-suffering, we are de-
spised, and with my own, the power of love is weakening. Do you
not see that Pallas and huntress Diana have revolted against me?
And Ceres' daughter, too, will remain a virgin if we suffer it; for she
aspires to be like them. But do you, in behalf of our joint sover-
eignty, if you take any pride in that, join the goddess to her uncle in
the bonds of love." So Venus spoke. The god of love loosed his
quiver at his mother's bidding and selected from his thousand ar-
rows one, the sharpest and the surest and the most obedient to the
bow. Then he bent the pliant bow across his knee and with his
barbed arrow smote Dis through the heart.

   "'Not far from Henna's walls there is a deep pool of water, Pergus
by name. Not Caÿster* on its gliding waters hears more songs of

---

*River in Lydia (a region of modern Turkey) associated with Ephesus.

swans than does this pool. A wood crowns the heights around its
waters on every side, and with its foliage as with an awning keeps
off the sun's hot rays. The branches afford a pleasing coolness, and
the well-watered ground bears bright-colored flowers. There spring
is everlasting. Within this grove Proserpina was playing, and gath-
ering violets or white lilies. And while with girlish eagerness she was
filling her basket and her bosom, and striving to surpass her mates
in gathering, almost in one act did Pluto see and love and carry her
away: so precipitate was his love. The terrified girl called plaintively
on her mother and her companions, but more often upon her
mother. And since she had torn her garment at its upper edge, the
flowers which she had gathered fell out of her loosened tunic; and
such was the innocence of her girlish years, the loss of her flowers
even at such a time aroused new grief. Her captor sped his chariot
and urged on his horses, calling each by name, and shaking the
dark-dyed reins on their necks and manes. Through deep lakes he
galloped, through the pools of the Palici, reeking with sulphur and
boiling up from a crevice of the earth, and where the Bacchiadae,
a race sprung from Corinth between two seas, had built a city
between two harbours of unequal size.*

" 'There is between Cyane and Pisaean Arethusa a bay of the sea,
its waters confined by narrowing points of land. Here was Cyane,
the most famous of the Sicilian nymphs, from whose name the pool
itself was called. She stood forth from the midst of her pool as far
as her waist, and recognizing the goddess cried to Dis: "No further
shall you go! You cannot be the son-in-law of Ceres against her will.
The maiden should have been wooed, not ravished. But, if it is
proper for me to compare small things with great, I also have been
wooed, by Anapis,† and I wedded him, too, yielding to prayer, how-
ever, not to fear, like this maiden." She spoke and, stretching her
arms on either side, blocked his way. No longer could the son of
Saturn hold his wrath, and urging on his terrible steeds, he whirled
his royal sceptre with strong right arm and smote the pool to its bot-
tom. The smitten earth opened up a road to Tartarus and received
the down-plunging chariot in her cavernous depths.

---

*Much of Sicily and southern Italy remained culturally Greek in Ovid's time.
†Minor deity of a river confluent with Cyane's; not otherwise known.

"'But Cyane, grieving for the rape of the goddess and for her fountain's rights thus set at nothing, nursed an incurable wound in her silent heart, and dissolved all away in tears; and into those very waters was she melted whose great divinity she had been but now. You might see her limbs softening, her bones becoming flexible, her nails losing their hardness. And first of all melt the slenderest parts: her dark hair, her fingers, legs and feet; for it is no great change from slender limbs to cool water. Next after these, her shoulders, back and sides and breasts vanish into thin watery streams. And finally, in place of living blood, clear water flows through her weakened veins and nothing is left that you can touch.

"'Meanwhile all in vain the affrighted mother seeks her daughter in every land, on every deep. Not Aurora, rising with dewy tresses, not Hesperus sees her pausing in the search. She kindles two pine torches in the fires of Aetna, and wanders without rest through the frosty shades of night; again, when the genial day had dimmed the stars, she was still seeking her daughter from the setting to the rising of the sun. Faint with toil and athirst, she had moistened her lips in no fountain, when she chanced to see a hut thatched with straw, and knocked at its lowly door. Then out came an old woman and beheld the goddess, and when she asked for water gave her a sweet drink with parched barley floating upon it. While she drank, a coarse, saucy boy stood watching her, and mocked her and called her greedy. She was offended, and threw what she had not yet drunk, with the barley grains, full in his face. Straightway his face was spotted, his arms were changed to legs, and a tail was added to his transformed limbs; he shrank to tiny size, that he might have no great power to harm, and became in form a lizard, though yet smaller in size. The old woman wondered and wept, and reached out to touch the marvellous thing, but he fled from her and sought a hiding-place. He has a name suited to his offence, since his body is starred with bright-colored spots.*

"'Over what lands and what seas the goddess wandered it would take long to tell. When there was no more a place to search in, she came back to Sicily, and in the course of her wanderings here she came to Cyane. If the nymph had not been changed to water, she would

---

*The Latin word *stellio* (newt) resembles *stella* (star).

have told her all. But, though she wished to tell, she had neither lips nor tongue, nor anything with which to speak. But still she gave clear evidence, and showed on the surface of her pool what the mother knew well, Persephone's girdle, which had chanced to fall upon the sacred waters. As soon as she knew this, just as if she had then for the first time learned that her daughter had been stolen, the goddess tore her unkempt locks and smote her breast again and again with her hands. She did not know as yet where her child was; still she reproached all lands, calling them ungrateful and unworthy of the gift of corn; but Sicily above all other lands, where she had found traces of her loss. So there with angry hand she broke in pieces the plows that turn the glebe, and in her rage she gave to destruction farmers and cattle alike, and bade the plowed fields to betray their trust, and blighted the seed. The fertility of this land, famous throughout the world, lay false to its good name: the crops died in early blade, now too much heat, now too much rain destroying them. Stars and winds were baleful, and greedy birds ate up the seed as soon as it was sown; tares and thorns and stubborn grasses choked the wheat.

"'Then did Arethusa, Alpheus' daughter,[3] lift her head from her Elean pool and, brushing her dripping locks back from her brows, thus addressed the goddess: "O you mother of the maiden sought through all the earth, you mother of fruits, now cease your boundless toils and do not be so grievously angry with the land which has been true to you. The land is innocent; against its will it opened to the robbery. It is not for my own country that I pray, for I came here a stranger. Pisa is my native land, and from Elis have I sprung; I dwell in Sicily a foreigner. But I love this country more than all; this is now my home, here is my dwelling-place. And now, I pray you, save it, O most merciful. Why I moved from my place and why I came to Sicily, through such wastes of sea, a fitting time will come to tell you, when you shall be free from care and of a more cheerful countenance. The solid earth opened a way before me, and passing through the lowest depths, I here lifted my head again and beheld the stars that had grown unfamiliar. Therefore, while I was gliding beneath the earth in my Stygian stream, I saw Proserpina there with these very eyes. She seemed sad indeed, and her face was still perturbed with fear; but yet she was a queen, the great queen of that world of darkness, the mighty consort of the tyrant of the underworld." The mother upon hearing these words stood as if turned to stone, and was for a long time like one bereft of reason. But when her overwhelming frenzy had given way to overwhelming pain, she set forth in her chariot to the realms of heaven. There, with clouded countenance, with dishevelled hair, and full of indignation, she appeared before Jove and said: "I have come, O Jupiter, as suppliant in behalf of my child and your own. If you have no regard for the mother, at least let the daughter touch her father's heart. And let not your care for her be less because I am her mother. See, my daughter, sought so long, has at last been found, if you call it finding more certainly to lose her, or if you call it finding merely to know where she is. That she has been stolen, I will bear, if only he will bring her back; for your daughter does not deserve to have a robber for a husband—if now she is not mine." And Jove replied: "She is, indeed, our daughter, yours and mine, our common pledge and care. But if only we are willing to give right names to things, this is no harm that has been done, but only love. Nor will he shame us for a son-in-law—do you but consent, goddess. Though all else be lacking, how great a thing it is to be Jove's brother! But what that other things are not lacking, and that he does not yield place to me—except only by the lot? But if you so greatly desire to separate them, Proserpina shall return to heaven, but on one condition only: if in the lower-world no food has as yet touched her lips. For so have the fates decreed."

"'He spoke; but Ceres was resolved to have her daughter back. Not so the fates; for the girl had already broken her fast, and while, simple child that she was, she wandered in the trim gardens, she had plucked a purple pomegranate hanging from a bending bough, and peeling off the yellowish rind, she had eaten seven of the seeds. The only one who saw the act was Ascalaphus, whom Orphne, not the least famous of the Avernal* nymphs, is said to have borne to her own Acheron within the dark groves of the lower-world.[4] The boy saw, and by his cruel tattling thwarted the girl's return to earth. Then was the queen of Erebus enraged, and changed the informer into an ill-omened bird; throwing in his face a handful of water

---

*From or belonging to Avernus, the Underworld.

from the Phlegethon, she gave him a beak and feathers and big eyes. Robbed of himself, he is now clothed in yellow wings; he grows into a head and long, hooked claws; but he scarce moves the feathers that sprout all over his sluggish arms. He has become a loathsome bird, prophet of woe, the slothful screech-owl, a bird of evil omen to men.

" 'He indeed can seem to have merited his punishment because of his tattling tongue. But, daughters of Acheloüs, why have you the feathers and feet of birds, though you still have maidens' features? Is it because, when Proserpina was gathering the spring flowers, you were among the number of her companions, O Sirens, skilled in song? After you had sought in vain for her through all the lands, that the sea also might know your search, you prayed that you might float on beating wings above the waves: you found the gods ready, and suddenly you saw your limbs covered with golden plumage. But, that you might not lose your tuneful voices, so soothing to the ear, and that rich dower of song, maiden features and human voice remained.

" 'But now Jove, holding the balance between his brother and his grieving sister, divides the revolving year into two equal parts. Now the goddess, the common divinity of two realms, spends half the months with her mother and with her husband, half. Straightway the bearing of her heart and face is changed. For she who but lately even to Dis seemed sad, now wears a joyful countenance; like the sun which, long concealed behind dark and misty clouds, disperses the clouds and reveals his face.

" 'Now kindly Ceres, happy in the recovery of her daughter, asks of you, Arethusa, why you fled, why you are now a sacred spring. The waters fall silent while their goddess lifts her head from her deep spring, and dries her green locks with her hands, and tells the old story of the Elean river's love. "I used to be one of the nymphs," she says, "who have their dwelling in Achaia, and no other was more eager in scouring the glades, or in setting the hunting-nets. But although I never sought the fame of beauty, although I was brave, I had the name of beautiful. Nor did my beauty, all too often praised, give me any joy; and my dower of charming form, in which other maids rejoice, made me blush like a country girl, and I deemed it wrong to please. Wearied with the chase, I was returning, I remember, from the Stymphalian wood; the heat was great and my toil had made it double. I came upon a stream flowing without eddy, and without sound, crystal-clear to the bottom, in whose depths you might count every pebble, waters which you would scarcely think to be moving. Silvery willows and poplars fed by the water gave natural shade to the soft-sloping banks. I came to the water's edge and first dipped my feet, then in I went up to the knees: not satisfied with this, I removed my robes, and hanging the soft garments on a drooping willow, naked I plunged into the waters. And while I beat them, drawing them and gliding in a thousand turns and tossing my arms, I thought I heard a kind of murmur deep in the pool. In terror I leaped on the nearer bank. Then Alpheus called from his waters: 'Where do you go in haste, Arethusa? Where in such haste?' Twice in his hoarse voice he called to me. As I was, without my robes, I fled; for my robes were on the other bank. So much the more he pressed on and burned with love; naked I seemed readier for his taking. So did I flee and so did he hotly press after me, as doves on fluttering pinions flee the hawk, as the hawk pursues the frightened doves. Even past Orchomenus, past Psophis and Cyllene, past the combs of Maenalus, chill Erymanthus and Elis, I kept my flight; nor was he swifter of foot than I. But I, being ill-matched in strength, could not long keep up my speed, while he could sustain a long pursuit. Yet through level plains, over mountains covered with trees, over rocks also and cliffs, and where there was no way at all, I ran. The sun was at my back. I saw my pursuer's long shadow stretching out ahead of me—unless it was fear that saw it—but surely I heard the terrifying sound of feet, and his deep-panting breath fanned my hair. Then, forspent with the toil of flight, I cried aloud: 'O help me or I am caught, help your armor-bearer, goddess of the nets, to whom so often you have given your bow to bear and your quiver, with all its arrows!' The goddess heard, and threw an impenetrable cloud of mist about me. The river-god circled around me, wrapped in the darkness, and at fault quested about the hollow mist. And twice he went round the place where the goddess had hidden me, unknowing, and twice he called, 'Arethusa! O Arethusa!' How did I feel then, poor wretch! Was I not as the lamb, when it hears the wolves howling around the fold? or the hare which, hiding in the brambles, sees the dogs' deadly muzzles and dares not make the slightest motion? But he went not far away, for he saw no traces of my feet further on; he watched the cloud and the place. Cold sweat poured down my beleaguered limbs and the dark drops rained down from my whole body. Wherever I put my foot a pool trickled out, and from my hair fell the drops; and sooner than I can now tell the tale I was changed to a stream of water. But sure enough he recognized in the waters the maid he loved; and laying aside the form of a man which he had assumed, he changed back to his own watery shape to mingle with me. My Delian goddess* cleft the earth, and I, plunging down into the dark depths, was borne here to Ortygia, which I love because it bears my goddess' name, and this first received me to the upper air."

"'With this, Arethusa's tale was done. Then the goddess of fertility yoked her two dragons to her car, curbing their mouths with the bit, and rode away through the air midway between heaven and earth, until she came at last to Pallas' city. Here she gave her fleet car to Triptolemus, and bade him scatter the seeds of grain she gave, part in the untilled earth and part in fields that had long lain fallow. And now high over Europe and the land of Asia the youth held his course and came to Scythia, where Lyncus ruled as king. He entered the royal palace. The king asked him how he came and why, what was his name and country: he said: "My country is far-famed Athens; Triptolemus, my name. I came neither by ship over the sea, nor on foot by land; the air opened a path for me. I bring the gifts of Ceres, which, if you sprinkle them over your wide fields, will give a fruitful harvest and food not wild." The barbaric king heard with envy. And, that he himself might be the giver of so great a good, he received his guest with hospitality, and when he was heavy with sleep, he attacked him with the sword. Him, in the very act of piercing the stranger's breast, Ceres transformed into a lynx; and back through the air she bade the Athenian drive her sacred team.'

"Our eldest sister here ended the song I have just rehearsed; then the nymphs with one voice agreed that the goddesses of Helicon had won. When the conquered sisters retorted with reviling, I made answer: 'Since it was not enough that you have earned punishment by your challenge and you add insults to your offence, and since our patience is not without end, we shall proceed to punishment and

---

*Goddess from the island of Delos—that is, Diana.

indulge our resentment.' The Pierides mocked, and scorned her threatening words. But as they tried to speak, and with loud outcries brandished their hands in saucy gestures, they saw feathers sprouting on their fingers, and plumage covering their arms; each saw another's face stiffening into a hard beak, and new forms of birds added to the woods. And while they strove to beat their breasts, uplifted by their flapping arms, they hung in the air, magpies, the noisy scandal of the woods. Even now in their feathered form their old-time gift of speech remains, their hoarse garrulity, their boundless passion for talk."

BOOK VI

Tᴙɪᴛᴏɴɪᴀ* ʜᴀᴅ ʟɪsᴛᴇɴᴇᴅ ᴛᴏ this tale, and had approved of the muses' song and their just resentment. And then to herself she said: "To praise is not enough; let me be praised myself and not allow my divinity to be scouted without punishment." So saying, she turned her mind to the fate of Maeonian Arachne, who she had heard would not yield to her the palm in the art of spinning and weaving wool. Neither for place of birth nor birth itself had the girl fame, but only for her skill. Her father, Idmon of Colophon, used to dye the absorbent wool for her with Phocaean purple. Her mother was now dead; but she was low-born herself, and had a husband of the same degree. Nevertheless, the girl, Arachne, had gained fame for her skill throughout the Lydian towns, although she herself had sprung from a humble home and dwelt in the hamlet of Hypaepa. Often, to watch her wondrous skill, the nymphs would leave their own vineyards on Tmolus' slopes, and the water-nymphs of Pactolus would leave their waters. And it was a pleasure not only to see her finished work, but to watch her as she worked; so graceful and deft was she. Whether she was winding the rough yarn into a new ball, or shaping the stuff with her fingers, reaching back to the distaff for more wool, fleecy as a cloud, to draw into long soft threads, or giving a twist with practised thumb to the graceful spindle, or embroidering with her needle: you could know that Pallas had taught her. Yet she denied it, and, offended at the suggestion of a teacher ever so great, she said: "Let her but strive with me; and if I lose there is nothing which I would not forfeit."

Then Pallas assumed the form of an old woman, put false locks of grey upon her head, took a staff in her hand to sustain her tottering limbs, and thus she began: "Old age has some things at least

---

*Another name for Minerva, of obscure derivation and meaning.

that are not to be despised; experience comes with riper years. Do not scorn my advice: seek all the fame you will among mortal men for handling wool; but yield place to the goddess, and with humble prayer beg her pardon for your words, reckless girl. She will grant you pardon if you ask it." But she regarded the old woman with sullen eyes, dropped the threads she was working, and, scarce holding her hand from violence, with open anger in her face she answered the disguised Pallas: "Doting in mind, you come to me, and spent with old age; and it is too long life that is your curse. Go, talk to your daughter-in-law, or to your daughter, if such you have. I am quite able to advise myself. To show you that you have done no good by your advice, we are both of the same opinion. Why does not your goddess come herself? Why does she avoid a contest with me?" Then the goddess exclaimed: "She has come!" and throwing aside her old woman's disguise, she revealed Pallas. The nymphs worshipped her godhead, and the Mygdonian women; Arachne alone remained unafraid, though she did start up and a sudden flush marked her unwilling cheeks and again faded: as when the sky grows crimson when the dawn first appears, and after a little while when the sun is up it pales again. Still she persists in her challenge, and stupidly confident and eager for victory, she rushes on her fate. For Jove's daughter refuses not, nor again warns her or puts off the contest any longer. They both set up the looms in different places without delay and they stretch the fine warp upon them. The web is bound upon the beam, the reed separates the threads of the warp, the woof is threaded through them by the sharp shuttles which their busy fingers ply, and when shot through the threads of the warp, the notched teeth of the hammering slay beat it into place. They speed on the work with their mantles close girt about their breasts and move back and forth their well-trained hands, their eager zeal beguiling their toil. There are inwoven the purple threads dyed in Tyrian kettles, and lighter colors insensibly shading off from these. As when after a storm of rain the sun's rays strike through, and a rainbow, with its huge curve, stains the wide sky, though a thousand different colors shine in it, the eye cannot detect the change from each one to the next; so like appear the adjacent colors, but the extremes are plainly different. There, too, they weave in pliant threads of gold, and trace in the weft some ancient tale.

Pallas pictures the hills of Mars on the citadel of Cecrops* and that old dispute over the naming of the land. There sit twelve heavenly gods on lofty thrones in awful majesty, Jove in their midst; each god she pictures with his own familiar features; Jove's is a royal figure. There stands the god of ocean, and with his long trident smites the rugged cliff, and from the cleft rock sea-water leaps forth; a token to claim the city for his own. To herself the goddess gives a shield and a sharp-pointed spear, and a helmet for her head; the aegis guards her breast; and from the earth smitten by her spear's point upsprings a pale-green olive-tree hanging thick with fruit; and the gods look on in wonder. Victory crowns her work. Then, that her rival may know by pictured warnings what reward she may expect for her mad daring, she weaves in the four corners of the web four scenes of contest, each clear with its own colors, and in miniature design. One corner shows Thracian Rhodope and Haemus, now huge, bleak mountains, but once audacious mortals who dared assume the names of the most high gods. A second corner shows the wretched fate of the Pygmaean queen, whom Juno conquered in a strife, then changed into a crane, and bade her war upon those whom once she ruled. Again she pictures how Antigone† once dared to set herself against the consort of mighty Jove, and how Queen Juno changed her into a bird; Ilium availed her nothing, nor Laomedon, her father; no, she is clothed in white feathers, and claps her rattling bill, a stork. The remaining corner shows Cinyras‡ bereft of his daughters; there, embracing the marble temple-steps, once their limbs, he lies on the stone, and seems to weep. The goddess then wove around her work a border of peaceful olive-wreath. This was the end; and so, with her own tree, her task was done.

Arachne pictures Europa cheated by the disguise of the bull: a real bull and real waves you would think them. The maid seems to be looking back upon the land she has left, calling on her companions, and, fearful of the touch of the leaping waves, to be drawing back her timid feet. She wrought Asterie, held by the struggling eagle; she wrought Leda, beneath the swan's wings.[1] She added

---

how, in a satyr's image hidden, Jove filled lovely Antiope with twin
offspring; how he was Amphitryon when he cheated you, Alcmena;
how in a golden shower he tricked Danaë; Aegina, as a flame;
Mnemosyne, as a shepherd; Deo's daughter, as a spotted snake.[2] You
also, Neptune, she pictured, changed to a grim bull with the Aeolian
maiden; now as Enipeus you beget the Aloidae, as a ram deceivedst
Bisaltis. The golden-haired mother of corn, most gentle, knew you
as a horse; the snake-haired mother of the winged horse knew you
as a winged bird; Melantho knew you as a dolphin.[3] To all these
Arachne gave their own shapes and appropriate surroundings. Here
is Phoebus like a countryman; and she shows how he wore now a
hawk's feathers, now a lion's skin; how as a shepherd he tricked
Macareus' daughter, Isse;[4] how Bacchus deceived Erigone with the
false bunch of grapes; how Saturn in a horse's shape begot the cen-
taur, Chiron.[5] The edge of the web with its narrow border is filled
with flowers and clinging ivy intertwined.

Not Pallas, nor Envy himself, could find a flaw in that work. The
golden-haired goddess was indignant at her success, and rent the
embroidered web with its heavenly crimes; and, as she held a shut-
tle of Cytorian boxwood, thrice and again she struck Idmonian
Arachne's head. The wretched girl could not endure it, and put a
noose about her bold neck. As she hung, Pallas lifted her in pity, and
said: "Live on, indeed, wicked girl, but continue to hang; and let this
same doom of punishment (that you may fear for future times as
well) be declared upon your race, even to remote posterity." So say-
ing, as she turned to go she sprinkled her with the juices of Hecate's
herb; and at once her hair, touched by the poison, fell off, and with
it both nose and ears; and the head shrank up; her whole body also
was diminished; the slender fingers clung to her side as legs; the rest
was belly. Still from this she ever spins a thread; and now, as a spider,
she exercises her old-time weaver's art.

All Lydia is in a tumult; the story spreads throughout the towns
of Phrygia and fills the whole world with talk. Now Niobe, before
her marriage, had known Arachne, when, as a girl, she dwelt in
Maeonia, near Mount Sipylus. And yet she did not take warning by
her countrywoman's fate to give place to the gods and speak them
reverently. Many things gave her pride; but in truth neither her hus-
band's art nor the high birth of both and their royal power and state

so pleased her, although all those did please, as her children did. And Niobe would have been called most blessed of mothers, had she not seemed so to herself. For Manto, daughter of Tiresias, whose eyes could see what was to come, had fared through the streets of Thebes inspired by divine impulse, and proclaiming to all she met: "Women of Thebes, go throng Latona's temple, and give to her and to her children twain incense and pious prayer, wreathing your hair with laurel. By my mouth Latona* speaks." They obey; all the Theban women deck their temples with laurel wreaths and burn incense in the altar flames, with words of prayer.

But lo! comes Niobe, thronged about with a numerous following, a notable figure in Phrygian robes wrought with threads of gold, and beautiful as far as anger suffered her to be; and she tosses her shapely head with the hair falling on either shoulder. She halts and, drawn up to her full height, casts her haughty eyes around and cries: "What madness this, to prefer gods whom you have only heard of to those whom you have seen? Or why is Latona worshipped at these altars, while my divinity still waits for incense? I have Tantalus to my father,† the only mortal ever allowed to touch the table of the gods; my mother is a sister of the Pleiades; most mighty Atlas is one grandfather, who supports the vault of heaven on his shoulders; my other grandsire is Jove himself, and I boast him as my father-in-law as well. The Phrygian nations hold me in reverent fear. I am queen of Cadmus' royal house, and the walls of Thebes, erected by the magic of my husband's lyre, together with its people, acknowledge me and him as their rulers. Wherever I turn my eyes in the palace I see great stores of wealth. Besides, I have beauty worthy of a goddess; add to all this that I have seven daughters and as many sons, and soon shall have sons- and daughters-in-law. Ask now what cause I have for pride; and then presume to prefer to me the Titaness, Latona, daughter of Coeus, whoever he may be—Latona, to whom the broad earth once refused a tiny spot for bringing forth her children. Neither heaven nor earth nor sea was open for this goddess of yours; she was outlawed from the universe, until Delos, pitying the wanderer, said to her: 'You are a vagrant on the

---

*Latona is the mother of Diana and Phoebus Apollo.
†Given her father's consignment to eternal torture (book IV), a dubious boast.

land; I, on the sea,' and gave her a place that stood never still. And there she bore two children, the seventh part only of my offspring. Surely I am happy. Who can deny it? And happy I shall remain. This also who can doubt? My very abundance has made me safe. I am too great for Fortune to harm; though she should take many from me, still many more will she leave to me. My blessings have banished fear. Even suppose that some part of this tribe of children could be taken from me, not even so despoiled would I be reduced to the number of two, Latona's throng, with which how far is she from childlessness? Away with you, hasten, you have sacrificed enough, and take off those laurels from your hair." They take off the wreaths and leave the sacrifice unfinished; but, as they may, they still worship the goddess with unspoken words.

The goddess was angry, and on the top of Cynthus she thus addressed Apollo and Diana: "Lo, I, your mother, proud of your birth and willing to yield place to no goddess but Juno only, I have had my divinity called in question; and through all coming ages I shall be denied worship at the altar, unless you, my children, come to my aid. Nor is this my only cause for resentment. This daughter of Tantalus has added insult to her injuries: she has dared to prefer her own children to you, and has called me childless—may that fall on her head!—and by her impious speech has displayed her father's unbridled tongue." To this story of her wrongs Latona would have added prayers; but here Phoebus cried: "Have done! a long complaint is but delay of punishment!" Phoebe said the same. Then, swiftly gliding through the air, they alighted on Cadmus' citadel, covered in clouds.

There was a broad and level plain near the walls, beaten by the constant tread of horses, where a host of wheels and the hard hoof had levelled the clods beneath them. There some of Amphion's seven sons mounted their strong horses, sitting firm on their backs bright with Tyrian purple, and guided them with rich gold-mounted bridles. While one of these, Ismenus, who was his mother's first-born son, was guiding his charger's course round the curving track and pulling hard on the foaming bit, "Ah me!" he cried, and, with an arrow fixed in his breast, he dropped the reins from his dying hands and slowly sank sidewise down to the earth over his horse's right shoulder. Next, hearing through the void air the sound of the rattling quiver, Sipylus gave full rein; as when a shipmaster, conscious of an approaching storm, flees at the sight of a cloud and crowds on all sail that he may catch each passing breeze. He gave full rein, and as he gave it the arrow that none may escape overtook him, and the shaft stuck quivering in his neck; while the iron point showed from his throat in front. He, leaning forward, as he was, pitched over the galloping horse's mane and legs, and stained the ground with his warm blood. Unhappy Phaedimus and Tantalus, who bore his grandsire's name, when they had finished their wonted task had passed to the youthful exercise of the shining wrestling-match. And now they were straining together, breast to breast, in close embrace, when an arrow, sped from the drawn bow, pierced them both just as they stood clasped together. They groaned together; together they fell writhing in pain to the ground; together as they lay they moved their dying eyes; together they breathed their last. Alphenor saw them die, and beating his breast in agony, he ran to lift up their cold bodies in his arms; and in this pious duty he fell; for Apollo pierced him through the midriff with a death-dealing blade. When this was removed, a piece of his lungs was drawn out sticking to the barbs, and his life-blood came rushing forth into the air. But one wound was not all that pierced youthful Damasichthon. He was struck where the lower leg just begins, and where the sinews of the hough give a soft spot; and while he was trying to draw out the fatal shaft with his hand, a second arrow was driven clear to the feathers through his throat. The blood drove it forth and gushing out spurted high in air in a long, slender stream. Ilioneus was the last; stretching out his arms in prayer doomed to be vain, he cried: "Oh, spare me, all you gods," not knowing that he need not pray to them all. The archer-god was moved to pity, but too late to recall his shaft. Still the youth fell smitten by a slight wound only, since the arrow did not deeply pierce his heart.

Rumour of the trouble, the people's grief, and the tears of her own friends informed the mother of this sudden disaster, amazed that it could have happened, and angry because the gods had dared so far, that they should have such power; for the father, Amphion, had already driven a dagger through his heart, and so in dying had ended his grief and life together. Alas, how different now was this Niobe from that Niobe who had but now driven the people from

Latona's altar, and had walked proudly through the city streets, enviable then to her friends, but now one for even her enemies to pity. She threw herself upon the cold bodies of her sons, wildly giving the last kisses to them all. From them she lifted her bruised arms to high heaven and cried: "Feed now upon my grief, cruel Latona, feed and glut your heart on my sorrow. Yes, glut your bloodthirsty heart! In my seven sons have I suffered sevenfold death. Exult, and triumph in your hateful victory. But why victory? In my misery I still have more than you in your felicity. After so many deaths, I triumph still!"

She spoke, and the taut bowstring twanged, which terrified all but Niobe alone; misery made her bold. The sisters were standing about their brothers' biers, with loosened hair and robed in black. One of these, while drawing out the shaft fixed in a brother's vitals, sank down with her face upon him, fainting and dying. A second, attempting to console her grieving mother, ceased suddenly, and was bent in agony by an unseen wound. She closed her lips till her dying breath had passed. One fell while trying in vain to flee. Another died upon her sister; one hid, and one stood trembling in full view. And now six had suffered various wounds and died; the last remained. The mother, covering her with her crouching body and her sheltering robes, cried out: "Oh, leave me one, the littlest! Of all my many children, the littlest I beg you spare—just one!" And even while she prayed, she for whom she prayed fell dead. Now does the childless mother sit down amid the lifeless bodies of her sons, her daughters, and her husband, in stony grief. Her hair stirs not in the breeze; her face is pale and bloodless, and her eyes are fixed and staring in her sad face. There is nothing alive in the picture. Her very tongue is silent, frozen to her mouth's roof, and her veins can move no longer; her neck cannot bend nor her arms move nor her feet go. Within also her vitals are stone. But still she weeps; and, caught up in a strong, whirling wind, she is rapt away to her own native land. There, set on a mountain's peak, she weeps; and even to this day tears trickle from the marble.

Then truly do all men and women fear the wrath of the goddess so openly displayed; and all more zealously than ever worship the dread divinity of the twin gods' mother. And, as usual, stirred by the later, they tell over former tales. Then one of them begins: "So also in the fertile fields of Lycia, peasants of olden time scorned the goddess and suffered for it. The story is little known because of the humble estate of the men concerned, but it is remarkable. I myself saw the pool and the place made famous by the wonder. For my father, who at that time was getting on in years and too weak to travel far, had bidden me go and drive down from that country some choice steers which were grazing there, and had given me a man of that nation to serve as guide. While I fared through the grassy glades with him, there, in the midst of a lake, an ancient altar was standing, black with the fires of many sacrifices, surrounded with shivering reeds. My guide halted and said with awe-struck whisper: 'Be merciful to me!' and in like whisper I said: 'Be merciful!' Then I asked my guide whether this was an altar to the Naiads, or Faunus, or some deity of the place, and he replied: 'No, young man; no mountain deity dwells in this altar. She claims its worship, whom the queen of heaven once shut out from all the world, whom wandering Delos would scarce accept at her prayer, when it was an island, lightly floating on the sea. There, reclining on the palm and Pallas' tree, in spite of their stepmother, she brought forth her twin babes. Even then the new-made mother is said to have fled from Juno, carrying in her bosom her infant children, both divine. And now, having reached the borders of Lycia, home of the Chimaera,[6] when the hot sun beat fiercely upon the fields, the goddess, weary of her long struggle, was faint by reason of the sun's heat and parched with thirst; and the hungry children had drained her breasts dry of milk. She chanced to see a lake of no great size down in a deep vale; some rustics were there gathering bushy osiers, with fine swamp-grass and rushes of the marsh. Latona came to the water's edge and kneeled on the ground to quench her thirst with a cooling drink. But the rustic rabble would not let her. Then she besought them: "Why do you deny me water? The enjoyment of water is a common right. Nature has not made the sun private to any, nor the air, nor soft water. This common right I seek; and yet I beg you to give it to me as a favor. I was not preparing to bathe my limbs or my weary body here in your pool, but only to quench my thirst. Even as I speak, my mouth is dry of moisture, my throat is parched, and m voice can scarce find utterance. A drink of water will be nectar me, and I shall confess that I have received life with it; yes, life will be giving me if you let me drink. These children too, let them touch your hearts, who from my bosom stretch out their little arms." And it chanced that the children did stretch out their arms. Who would not have been touched by the goddess' gentle words? Yet for all her prayers they persisted in denying with threats if she did not go away; they even added insulting words. Not content with that, they soiled the pool itself with their feet and hands, and stirred up the soft mud from the bottom, leaping about, all for pure mean-ness. Then wrath postponed thirst; for Coeus' daughter could nei-ther humble herself longer to those unruly fellows, nor could she endure to speak with less power than a goddess; but stretching up her hands to heaven, she cried: "Live then for ever in that pool." It fell out as the goddess prayed. It is their delight to live in water; now to plunge their bodies quite beneath the enveloping pool, now to thrust forth their heads, now to swim upon the surface. Often they sit upon the sedgy bank and often leap back into the cool lake. But even now, as of old, they exercise their foul tongues in quarrel, and all shameless, though they may be under water, even under the water they try to utter maledictions. Now also their voices are hoarse, their inflated throats swell up, and their constant quarrelling distends their wide jaws; they stretch their ugly heads, the necks seem to have disap-peared. Their backs are green; their bellies, the largest part of the body, are white; and as new-made frogs they leap in the muddy pool.'"

Then, when this unknown story-teller had told the destruction of the Lycian peasants, another recalled the satyr whom the son of Latona had conquered in a contest on Pallas' reed, and punished. "Why do you tear me from myself?" he cried. "Oh, I repent! Oh, a flute is not worth such price!" As he screams, his skin is stripped off the surface of his body, and he is all one wound: blood flows down on every side, the sinews lie bare, his veins throb and quiver with no skin to cover them: you could count the entrails as they palpitate, ᵈ the vitals showing clearly in his breast. The country people, the deities, fauns and his brother satyrs, and Olympus, whom ᵗ he still loved, the nymphs, all wept for him, and every ᵤ fed his woolly sheep or horned kine on those moun- ᶥl earth was soaked, and soaking caught those tears ᵖ into her veins. Changing these then to water, ᵢinto the free air. From there the stream within its sloping banks ran down quickly to the sea, and had the name of Marsyas, the clearest river in all Phrygia.

Straightway the company turns from such old tales to the present, and mourns Amphion dead with his children. They all blame the mother; but even then one man, her brother Pelops, is said to have wept for her, and, drawing aside his garment from his breast, to have revealed the ivory patch on the left shoulder. This at the time of his birth had been of the same color as his right, and of flesh. But later, when his father had cut him in pieces, they say that the gods joined the parts together again; they found all the others, but one part was lacking where the neck and upper arm unite. A piece of ivory was made to take the place of the part which could not be found; and so Pelops was made whole again.

Now all the neighbouring princes assembled, and the near-by cities urged their kings to go and offer sympathy: Argos and Sparta and Peloponnesian Mycenae; Calydon, which had not yet incurred Diana's wrath; fertile Orchomenos and Corinth, famed for works of bronze; warlike Messene, Patrae, and low-lying Cleonae; Nelean Pylos and Troezen, not yet ruled by Pittheus;[7] and all the other cities which are shut off by the Isthmus between its two seas, and those which are outside visible from the Isthmus between its two seas. But of all cities—who could believe it?—only you, Athens, did nothing. War hindered this friendly service, and barbaric hordes from oversea held the walls of Mopsopia in alarm. Now Tereus of Thrace had put these to flight with his relieving troops, and by the victory had a great name. And since he was strong in wealth and in men, and traced his descent, as it happened, from Gradivus, Pandion, king of Athens, allied him to himself by wedding him to Procne. But neither Juno, bridal goddess, nor Hymen, nor the Graces were present at that wedding. The Furies lighted them with torches stolen from a funeral; the Furies spread the couch, and the uncanny screech-owl brooded and sat on the roof of their chamber. Under this omen were Procne and Tereus wedded; under this omen was their child conceived. Thrace, indeed, rejoiced with them, and they themselves gave thanks to the gods; both the day on which Pandion's daughter was married to their illustrious king, and that day on which Itys was born, they made a festival: even so is our true advantage hidden.

Now Titan through five autumnal seasons had brought round the revolving years, when Procne coaxingly to her husband said: "If I have found any favor in your sight, either send me to visit my sister or let my sister come to me. You will promise my father that after a brief stay she shall return. If you give me a chance to see my sister you will confer on me a precious gift." Tereus accordingly bade them launch his ship, and plying oar and sail, he entered the Cecropian harbour and came to land on the shore of Piraeus. As soon as he came into the presence of his father-in-law they joined right hands, and the talk began with good wishes for their health. He had begun to tell of his wife's request, which was the cause of his coming, and to promise a speedy return should the sister be sent home with him, when lo! Philomela entered, attired in rich apparel, but richer still in beauty; such as we are wont to hear the naiads described, and dryads when they move about in the deep woods, if only one should give to them refinement and apparel like hers. The moment he saw the maiden Tereus was inflamed with love, quick as if one should set fire to ripe grain, or dry leaves, or hay stored away in the mow. Her beauty, indeed, was worth it; but in his case his own passionate nature pricked him on, and, besides, the men of his clime are quick to love: his own fire and his nation's burnt in him. His impulse was to corrupt her attendants' care and her nurse's faithfulness, and even by rich gifts to tempt the girl herself, even at the cost of all his kingdom; or else to ravish her and to defend his act by bloody war. There was nothing which he would not do or dare, smitten by this mad passion. His heart could scarce contain the fires that burnt in it. Now, impatient of delay, he eagerly repeated Procne's request, pleading his own cause under her name. Love made him eloquent, and as often as he asked more urgently than he should, he would say that Procne wished it so. He even added tears to his entreaties, as though she had bidden him to do this too. O gods, what blind night rules in the hearts of men! In the very act of pushing on his shameful plan Tereus gets credit for a kind heart and wins praise from wickedness. Ay, more—Philomela herself has the same wish; winding her arms about her father's neck, she coaxes him to let her visit her sister; by her own welfare (yes, and against it, too) she urges her prayer. Tereus gazes at her, and as he looks feels her already in his arms; as he sees her kisses and her arms about her father's neck, all this goads him on, food and fuel for his passion; and whenever she embraces her father he wishes that he were in the father's place—indeed, if he were, his intent would be no less impious. The father yields to the prayers of both. The girl is filled with joy; she thanks her father and, poor unhappy wretch, she deems that success for both sisters which is to prove a woeful happening for them both.

Now Phoebus' toils were almost done and his horses were pacing down the western sky. A royal feast was spread, wine in cups of gold. Then they lay them down to peaceful slumber. But although the Thracian king retired, his heart seethes with thoughts of her. Recalling her look, her movement, her hands, he pictures at will what he has not yet seen, and feeds his own fires, his thoughts preventing sleep. Morning came; and Pandion, wringing his son-in-law's hand as he was departing, consigned his daughter to him with many tears and said: "Dear son, since a natural plea has won me, and both my daughters have wished it, and you also have wished it, my Tereus, I give her to your keeping; and by your honor and the ties that bind us, by the gods, I pray you guard her with a father's love, and as soon as possible—it will seem a long time in any case to me—send back to me this sweet solace of my tedious years. And do you, my Philomela, if you love me, come back to me as soon as possible; it is enough that your sister is so far away." Thus he made his last requests and kissed his child good-bye, and gentle tears fell as he spoke the words; and he asked both their right hands as pledge of their promise, and joined them together and begged that they would remember to greet for him his daughter and her son. His voice broke with sobs, he could hardly say farewell, as he feared the forebodings of his mind.

As soon as Philomela was safely embarked upon the painted ship and the sea was churned beneath the oars and the land was left behind, Tereus exclaimed: "I have won! in my ship I carry the fulfilment of my prayers!" The barbarous fellow triumphs, he can scarce postpone his joys, and never turns his eyes from her, as when the ravenous bird of Jove has dropped in his high eyrie some hare caught in his hooked talons; the captive has no chance to escape, the captor gloats over his prize.

And now they were at the end of their journey, now, leaving the travel-worn ship, they had landed on their own shores; when the king dragged off Pandion's daughter to a hut deep hidden in the ancient woods; and there, pale and trembling and all fear, begging with tears to know where her sister was, he shut her up. Then, openly confessing his horrid purpose, he violated her, just a weak girl and all alone, vainly calling, often on her father, often on her sister, but most of all upon the great gods. She trembled like a frightened lamb, which, torn and cast aside by a grey wolf, cannot yet believe that it is safe; and like a dove which, with its own blood all smeared over its plumage, still palpitates with fright, still fears those greedy claws that have pierced it. Soon, when her senses came back, she dragged at her loosened hair, and like one in mourning, beating and tearing her arms, with outstretched hands she cried: "Oh, what a horrible thing you have done, barbarous, cruel wretch! Do you care nothing for my father's injunctions, his affectionate tears, my sister's love, my own virginity, the bonds of wedlock? You have confused all natural relations: I have become a concubine, my sister's rival; you, a husband to both. Now Procne must be my enemy. Why do you not take my life, that no crime may be left undone, you traitor? Aye, would that you had killed me before you wronged me so. Then would my shade have been innocent and clean. If those who dwell on high see these things, indeed, if there are any gods at all, if all things have not perished with me, sooner or later you shall pay dearly for this deed. I will myself cast shame aside and proclaim what you have done. If I should have the chance, I would go where people throng and tell it; if I am kept shut up in these woods, I will fill the woods with my story and move the very rocks to pity. The air of heaven shall hear it, and, if there is any god in heaven, he shall hear it too."

The savage tyrant's wrath was aroused by these words, and his fear no less. Pricked on by both these spurs, he drew his sword which was hanging by his side in its sheath, caught her by the hair, and twisting her arms behind her back, he bound them fast. At sight of the sword Philomela gladly offered her throat to the stroke, filled with the eager hope of death. But he seized her tongue with pincers, as it protested against the outrage, calling ever on the name of her father and struggling to speak, and cut it off with his merciless blade. The mangled root quivers, while the severed tongue lies palpitating on the dark earth, faintly murmuring; and, as the severed tail of a mangled snake is wont to writhe, it twitches convulsively, and with its last dying movement it seeks its mistress's feet. Even after this horrid deed—one would scarce believe it—the monarch is said to have worked his lustful will again and again upon the poor mangled form.

With such crimes upon his soul he had the face to return to Procne's presence. She on seeing him at once asked where her sister was. He groaned in pretended grief and told a made-up story of death; his tears gave credence to the tale. Then Procne tore from her shoulders the robe gleaming with a broad golden border and put on black weeds; she built also a cenotaph in honor of her sister, brought pious offerings to her imagined spirit, and mourned her sister's fate, not meet so to be mourned.

Now through the twelve signs, a whole year's journey, has the sun-god passed. And what shall Philomela do? A guard prevents her flight; stout walls of solid stone fence in the hut; speechless lips can give no token of her wrongs. But grief has sharp wits, and in trouble cunning comes. She hangs a Thracian web on her loom, and skilfully weaving purple signs on a white background, she thus tells the story of her wrongs. This web, when completed, she gives to her one attendant and begs her with gestures to carry it to the queen. The old woman, as she was bid, takes the web to Procne, not knowing what she bears in it. The savage tyrant's wife unrolls the cloth, reads the pitiable tale of her misfortune, and (a miracle that she could!) says not a word. Grief chokes the words that rise to her lips, and her questing tongue can find no words strong enough to express her outraged feelings. Here is no room for tears, but she hurries on to confound right and wrong, her whole soul bent on the thought of vengeance.

It was the time when the Thracian matrons were wont to celebrate the biennial festival of Bacchus.[8] Night was in their secret; by night Mount Rhodope would resound with the shrill clash of brazen cymbals; so by night the queen goes forth from her house, equips herself for the rites of the god and dons the array of frenzy; her head was wreathed with trailing vines, a deer-skin hung from her left side, a light spear rested on her shoulder. Swift she goes through the woods with an attendant throng of her companions, and driven on by the madness of grief, Procne, terrific in her rage, mimics your madness, O Bacchus! She comes to the secluded lodge at last, shrieks aloud and cries "Euhoe!" breaks down the doors, seizes her sister, arrays her in the trappings of a Bacchante, hides her face with ivy-leaves, and, dragging her along in amazement, leads her within her own walls.

When Philomela perceived that she had entered that accursed house the poor girl shook with horror and grew pale as death. Procne found a place, and took off the trappings of the Bacchic rites and, uncovering the shame-blanched face of her wretched sister, folded her in her arms. But Philomela could not lift her eyes to her sister, feeling herself to have wronged her. And, with her face turned to the ground, longing to swear and call all the gods to witness that that shame had been forced upon her, she made her hand serve for voice. But Procne was all on fire, could not contain her own wrath, and chiding her sister's weeping, she said: "This is no time for tears, but for the sword, for something stronger than the sword, if you have such a thing. I am prepared for any crime, my sister; either to fire this palace with a torch, and to cast Tereus, the author of our wrongs, into the flaming ruins, or to cut out his tongue and his eyes, to cut off the parts which brought shame to you, and drive his guilty soul out through a thousand wounds. I am prepared for some great deed; but what it shall be I am still in doubt."

While Procne was thus speaking Itys came into his mother's presence. His coming suggested what she could do, and regarding him with pitiless eyes, she said: "Ah, how like your father you are!" Saying no more, she began to plan a terrible deed and boiled with inward rage. But when the boy came up to her and greeted his mother, put his little arms around her neck and kissed her in his winsome, boyish way, her mother-heart was touched, her wrath fell away, and her eyes, though all unwilling, were wet with tears that flowed in spite of her. But when she perceived that her purpose was wavering through excess of mother-love, she turned again from her son to her sister; and gazing at both in turn, she said: "Why is one able to make soft, pretty speeches, while her ravished tongue dooms the other to silence? Since he calls me mother, why does she not call me sister? Remember whose wife you are, daughter of Pandion! Will you be faithless to your husband? But faithfulness to such a husband as Tereus is a crime." Without more words she dragged

Itys away, as a tigress drags a suckling fawn through the dark woods on Ganges' banks. And when they reached a remote part of the great house, while the boy stretched out pleading hands as he saw his fate, and screamed, "Mother! mother!" and sought to throw his arms around her neck, Procne smote him with a knife between breast and side—and with no change of face. This one stroke sufficed to slay the lad; but Philomela cut the throat also, and they cut up the body still warm and quivering with life. Part bubbles in brazen kettles, part sputters on spits; while the whole room drips with gore.

This is the feast to which the wife invites Tereus, little knowing what it is. She pretends that it is a sacred feast after their ancestral fashion, of which only a husband may partake, and removes all attendants and slaves. So Tereus, sitting alone in his high ancestral banquet-chair, begins the feast and gorges himself with flesh of his own flesh. And in the utter blindness of his understanding he cries: "Go, call Itys to me here!" Procne cannot hide her cruel joy, and eager to be the messenger of her bloody news, she says: "You have, within, him whom you want." He looks about and asks where the boy is. And then, as he asks and calls again for his son, just as she was, with streaming hair, and all stained with her mad deed of blood, Philomela springs forward and hurls the gory head of Itys straight into his father's face; nor was there ever any time when she longed more to be able to speak, and to express her joy in fitting words. Then the Thracian king overturns the table with a great cry and invokes the snaky sisters from the Stygian pit. Now, if he could, he would gladly lay open his breast and take from within the horrid feast and vomit forth the flesh of his son; now he weeps bitterly and calls himself his son's most wretched tomb; then with drawn sword he pursues the two daughters of Pandion. As they fly from him you would think that the bodies of the two Athenians were poised on wings: they were poised on wings! One flies to the woods, the other rises to the roof. And even now their breasts have not lost the marks of their murderous deed, their feathers are stained with blood. Tereus, swift in pursuit because of his grief and eager desire for vengeance, is himself changed into a bird. Upon his head a stiff crest appears, and a huge beak stands forth instead of his long sword. He is the hoopoë, with the look of one armed for war.

This woe shortened the days of old Pandion and sent him down to the shades of Tartarus before old age came to its full term. His sceptre and the state's control fell to Erechtheus, equally famed for justice and for prowess in arms. Four sons were born to him and four daughters also. Of these daughters two were of equal beauty, of whom you, Procris, made happy in wedlock Cephalus, the grandson of Aeolus. Boreas was not favored because of Tereus and the Thracians; and so the god was long kept from his beloved Orithyia, while he wooed and preferred to use prayers rather than force. But when he could accomplish nothing by soothing words, rough with anger, which was the north-wind's usual and more natural mood, he said: "I have deserved it! For why have I given up my own weapons, fierceness and force, rage and threatening moods, and had recourse to prayers, which do not at all become me? Force is my fit instrument. By force I drive on the gloomy clouds, by force I shake the sea, I overturn gnarled oaks, pack hard the snow, and pelt the earth with hail. So also when I meet my brothers in the open sky—for that is my battleground—I struggle with them so fiercely that the mid-heavens thunder with our meeting and fires leap bursting out of the hollow clouds. So also when I have entered the vaulted hollows of the earth, and have set my strong back beneath her lowest caverns, I fright the ghosts and the whole world, too, by my heavings. By this means I should have sought my wife. I should not have begged Erechtheus to be my father-in-law, but made him to be so." With these words or others no less boisterous, Boreas shook his wings, whose mighty flutterings sent a blast over all the earth, and ruffled the broad ocean. And trailing along his dusty mantle over the mountain-tops, he swept the land; and wrapped in darkness, the lover embraced with his tawny wings his Orithyia, who was trembling sore with fear. As he flew his own flames were fanned and burned stronger. Nor did the robber check his airy flight until he came to the people and the city of the Cicones.* There did the Athenian girl become the bride of the cold monarch, and mother, when she brought forth twin sons, who had all else of their mother, but their father's wings. Yet these wings, they say, were not born with their bodies; while the beard was not yet to be seen beneath

---

*Thracian tribe raided by Ulysses (Odysseus to the Greeks) in the *Odyssey* (book 9).

their yellow locks, both Calais and Zetes were wingless, but soon and at the same time wings began to spring out on either side after the fashion of birds, and the cheeks began to grow tawny. So these two youths, when boyhood was passed and they had grown to man's estate, went with the Minyans* over an unknown sea in that first ship to seek the bright gleaming fleece of gold.

---

*The Argonauts, companions of Jason, called Minyans after Minyas of Boeotia.

BOOK VII

AND NOW THE MINYANS were plowing the deep in their Thessalian ship. They had seen Phineus, spending his last days helpless in perpetual night; and the sons of Boreas had driven the harpies from the presence of the unhappy king. Having experienced many adventures under their illustrious leader Jason, they reached at last the swift waters of muddy Phasis.[1] There, while they were approaching the king and demanding the fleece that Phrixus had given to him, while the dreadful condition with its great tasks was being proposed to the Minyans, meanwhile the daughter of King Aeëtes conceived an overpowering passion. Long she fought against it, and when by reason she could not rid her of her madness she cried: "In vain, Medea, do you fight. Some god or other is opposing you; I wonder if this is not what is called love, or at least something like this. For why do the mandates of my father seem too harsh? They certainly are too harsh. Why do I fear that he may perish whom I have but now seen for the first time? What is the cause of all this fear? Come, thrust from your maiden breast these flames that you feel, if you can, unhappy girl. Ah, if I could, I should be more myself. But some strange power holds me down against my will. Desire persuades me one way, reason another. I see the better and approve it, but I follow the worse. Why do you, a royal maiden, burn for a stranger, and think upon marriage with a foreign world? This land also can give you something to love. Whether he live or die is in the lap of the gods. Yet may he live! This I may pray for even without loving him. For what has Jason done? Who that is not heartless would not be moved by Jason's youth, his noble birth, his manhood? Who, though the rest were lacking, would not be touched by his beauty? Certainly he has touched my heart. But unless I help him he will be breathed on by the bulls' fiery breath, and he will have to meet an enemy of his own sowing sprung from the earth, or he will be given as prey like any wild beast to the greedy dragon. If I permit this, then shall I confess that I am the child of a tigress and that I have iron and stone in my heart. But why can I not look on as he dies, and why is such a sight defilement for my eyes? Why do I not urge on the bulls against him, and the fierce earth-born warriors, and the sleepless dragon? Heaven forefend! and yet that is not matter for my prayers, but for my deeds. Shall I then betray my father's throne? and shall an unknown stranger be preserved by my aid, that, when saved by me, he may sail off without me, and become another's husband, while I, Medea, am left for punishment? If he can do that, if he can prefer another woman to me, let him perish, ungrateful man. But no: his look, his loftiness of soul, his grace of form are not such that I need fear deceit or forgetfulness of my service. And he shall give me his pledge beforehand, and I will compel the gods to be witnesses of our troth. Why do you fear when all is safe? Now for action, and away with all delay! Jason shall always owe himself to you, he shall join you to himself in solemn wedlock. Then you shall be hailed as his deliverer through the cities of Greece by throngs of women. And shall I then sail away and leave my sister here, my brother, father, gods, and native land? Indeed my father is a stern man, indeed my native land is barbarous, my brother is still a child, my sister's goodwill is on my side; and the greatest god is within me! I shall not be leaving great things, but going to great things: the title of saviour of the Achaean youth, acquaintance with a better land, cities, whose fame is mighty even here, the culture and arts of civilized countries, and the man I would not give in exchange for all that the wide world holds—the son of Aeson; with him as my husband I shall be called the beloved of heaven, and with my head shall touch the stars. But what of certain mountains, which, they say, come clashing together in mid-sea; and Charybdis, the sailor's dread, who now sucks in and again spews forth the waves; and greedy Scylla, girt about with savage dogs, baying in the Sicilian seas! No; holding that which I love, and resting in Jason's arms, I shall fare over the long reaches of the sea; in his safe embrace I shall fear nothing; or if I fear at all, I shall fear for my husband only. But do you call it marriage, Medea, and do you give fair-seeming names to your fault? No, rather, look ahead and see how great a wickedness you are approaching and flee it while you may." She spoke, and before her eyes stood righteousness, filial affection, and modesty; and love, defeated, was now on the point of flight.

She took her way to an ancient altar of Hecate, the daughter of Perse, hidden in the deep shades of a forest.[2] And now she was strong of purpose and the flames of her vanquished passion had died down; when she saw the son of Aeson and the dying flame leaped up again. Her cheeks grew red, then all her face became pale again; and as a tiny spark, which has lain hidden beneath the ashes, is fed by a breath of wind, then grows and regains its former strength as it is fanned to life; so now her smouldering love, which you would have thought all but dying, at sight of the young hero standing before her blazed up again. It chanced that the son of Aeson was more beautiful than usual that day: you could pardon her for loving him. She gazed upon him and held her eyes fixed on his face as if she had never seen him before; and in her infatuation she thought the face she gazed on more than mortal, nor could she turn herself away from him. But when the stranger began to speak, grasped her right hand, and in low tones asked for her aid and promised marriage in return, she burst into tears and said: "I see what I am about to do, nor shall ignorance of the truth be my undoing, but love itself. You shall be preserved by my assistance; but when preserved, fulfil your promise." He swore he would be true by the sacred rites of the threefold goddess, by whatever divinity might be in that grove, by the all-beholding father of his father-in-law who was to be, by his own successes and his mighty perils. She believed; and straight he received the magic herbs and learnt their use, then withdrew full of joy into his lodging.

The next dawn had put to flight the twinkling stars. Then the throngs gathered into the sacred field of Mars and took their stand on the heights. In the midst of the company sat the king himself, clad in purple, and conspicuous with his ivory sceptre.—See! here come the brazen-footed bulls, breathing fire from nostrils of adamant. The very grass shrivels up at the touch of their hot breath. And as full furnaces are wont to roar, or as limestones burned in the lime-kiln hiss and grow hot when water is poured upon them; so did the bulls' chests and parched throats rumble with the fires pent up within. Nevertheless the son of Aeson went forward to meet them.

As he came towards them the fierce beasts turned upon him terrible faces and sharp horns tipped with iron, pawed the dusty earth with their cloven feet, and filled the place with their fiery bellowings. The Minyans were stark with fear; he went up to the bulls, not feeling their hot breath at all, so great is the power of charmed drugs; and stroking their hanging dewlaps with fearless hand, he placed the yoke on their necks and made them draw the heavy plow and cut through the field that had never felt iron before. The Colchians are amazed; but the Minyans shouted aloud and increased their hero's courage. Next he took from a brazen helmet the serpent's teeth and sowed them broadcast in the plowed field. The earth softened these seeds steeped in virulent poison and the teeth swelled up and took on new forms. And just as in its mother's body an infant gradually assumes human form, and is perfected within through all its parts, and does not come forth to the common air until it is fully formed; so, when the forms of men had been completed in the womb of the pregnant earth, they rose up on the teeming soil and, what is yet more wonderful, each clashed weapons that had been brought forth with him. When the Greeks saw them preparing to hurl sharp-pointed spears at the head of the Thessalian hero, their faces fell with fear and their hearts failed them. She also, who had safeguarded him, was sore afraid; and when she saw him, one man, attacked by so many foes, she grew pale, and sat there suddenly cold and bloodless. And, in case the charmed herbs which she had given him should not be strong enough, she chanted a spell to help them and called in her secret arts. But he hurled a heavy rock into the midst of his enemies and so turned their fury away from him upon themselves. The earth-born brethren perished by each other's wounds and fell fighting in internecine strife. Then did the Greeks congratulate the victorious youth, catching him in their arms and clinging to him in eager embraces. You also, barbarian maiden, would gladly have embraced the victor; your modesty stood in the way. Still, you would have embraced him; but respect for common talk held you back. What was allowed you did, gazing on him with silent joy and thanking your spells and the gods who gave them.

There remained the task of putting to sleep the ever-watchful dragon with magic herbs. This creature, distinguished by a crest, a three-forked tongue and hooked fangs, was the awful guardian of the golden tree. After Jason had sprinkled upon him the Lethaean juice of a certain herb and thrice had recited the words that bring peaceful slumber, which stay the swollen sea and swift-flowing rivers, then sleep came to those eyes which had never known sleep before, and the heroic son of Aeson gained the golden fleece. Proud of this spoil and bearing with him the giver of his prize, another spoil, the victor and his wife in due time reached the harbour of Iolchos.*

The Thessalian mothers and aged fathers bring gifts in honor of their sons' safe return, and burn incense heaped on the altar flames, and the victim with gilded horns which they have vowed is slain. But Aeson is absent from the rejoicing throng, being now near death and heavy with the weight of years. Then says the son of Aeson: "O wife, to whom I freely own my deliverance is due, although you have already given me all, and the sum of your benefits has exceeded all my hopes; still, if your spells can do this—and what can they not do?—take some portion from my own years of life and give this to my father." And he could not restrain his tears. Medea was moved by the petitioner's filial love, and the thought of Aeëtes deserted came into her mind, how different from Jason's! Still, not confessing such feelings, she replied: "What impious words have fallen from your lips, my husband? Can I then transfer to any man, think you, a portion of your life? Neither would Hecate permit this, nor is your request right. But a greater gift than what you ask, my Jason, will I try to give. By my art and not your years I will try to renew your father's long span of life, if only the three-formed goddess will help me and grant her present aid in this great deed which I dare attempt."

There were yet three nights before the horns of the moon would meet and make the round orb. When the moon shone at her fullest and looked down upon the earth with unbroken shape, Medea went forth from her house clad in flowing robes, barefoot, her hair unadorned and streaming down her shoulders; and all alone she wandered out into the deep stillness of midnight. Men, birds, and beasts were sunk in profound repose; there was no sound in the hedgerow; the leaves hung mute and motionless; the dewy air was still. Only

---

*Jason's home city, in Thessaly.

the stars twinkled. Stretching up her arms to these, she turned thrice about, thrice sprinkled water caught up from a flowing stream upon her head and thrice gave tongue in wailing cries. Then she kneeled down upon the hard earth and prayed: "O Night, faithful preserver of mysteries, and you bright stars, whose golden beams with the moon succeed the fires of day; you three-formed Hecate, who knows our undertakings and comes to the aid of the spells and arts of magicians; and you, O Earth, who provides the magicians with your potent herbs; you breezes and winds, you mountains and streams and pools; all you gods of the groves, all you gods of the night: be with me now. With your help when I have willed it, the streams have run back to their fountain-heads, while the banks wondered; I lay the swollen, and stir up the calm seas by my spell; I drive the clouds and bring on the clouds; the winds I dispel and summon; I break the jaws of serpents with my incantations; living rocks and oaks I root up from their own soil; I move the forests, I bid the mountains shake, the earth to rumble and the ghosts to come forth from their tombs.[3] You also, Luna, do I draw from the sky, though the clanging bronze of Temesa strive to aid your throes; even the chariot of the Sun, my grandsire,* pales at my song; Aurora pales at my poisons. You dulled the bulls' flames at my command; you pressed under the curved plow those necks which had endured no weight. You turned the savage onslaught of the serpent-born band against themselves; you lulled the watcher who knew no sleep, and beguiling the defender sent the golden prize back to the cities of Greece. Now I have need of juices by whose aid old age may be renewed and may turn back to the bloom of youth and regain its early years. And you will give them; for not in vain have the stars gleamed in reply, not in vain is my car at hand, drawn by winged dragons." There was the car, sent down from the sky. When she had mounted therein and stroked the bridled necks of the dragon team, shaking the light reins with her hands she was whirled aloft. She looked down on Thessalian Tempe lying below, and turned her dragons towards regions that she knew. All the herbs that Ossa bore, and high Pelion, Othrys and Pindus and Olympus, greater than Pindus, she surveyed: and those that pleased her, some she

---

*Aeëtes, Medea's father, was the offspring of Helios, the sun-god.

plucked up by the roots and some she cut off with the curved blade of a bronze pruning-hook. Many grasses also she chose from the banks of the Apidanus, many from Amphrysus. Nor were you, Enipeus, left without toll; Peneus also, and Sperchios gave something, and the reedy banks of Boebe. From Euboean Anthedon she culled a grass that gives long life, a herb not yet made famous by the change which it produced in Glaucus' body.*

And now nine days and nine nights had seen her traversing all lands, drawn in her car by her winged dragons, when she returned. The dragons had not been touched except by the odour of the herbs, and yet they sloughed off their skins of many long years. As she came Medea stopped before the threshold and the door; covered by the sky alone, she avoided her husband's embrace, and built two turf altars, one on the right to Hecate and one on the left to Youth. She wreathed these with boughs from the wild wood, then hard by she dug two ditches in the earth and performed her rites; plunging her knife into the throat of a black sheep, she drenched the open ditches with his blood. Next she poured upon it bowls of liquid wine, and again bowls of milk still warm, while at the same time she uttered her incantations, called up the deities of the earth, and prayed the king of the shades with his stolen bride not to be in haste to rob the old man's body of the breath of life.

When she had appeased all these divinities by long, low-muttered prayers, she bade her people bring out under the open sky old Aeson's worn-out body; and having buried him in a deep slumber by her spells, like one dead she stretched him out on a bed of herbs. Far away she bade Jason go, far away all the attendants, and warned them not to look with profane eyes upon her secret rites. They retired as she had bidden. Medea, with streaming hair after the fashion of the Bacchantes, moved round the blazing altars, and dipping many-cleft sticks in the dark pools of blood, she lit the gory sticks at the altar flames. Thrice she purified the old man with fire, thrice with water, thrice with sulphur.

Meanwhile the strong potion in the bronze pot is boiling, leaping and frothing white with the swelling foam. In this pot she boils roots cut in a Thessalian vale, together with seeds, flowers, and

---

*Ovid narrates the transformation of Glaucus in book XIII.

strong juices. She adds to these ingredients pebbles sought for in the farthest Orient and sands which the ebbing tide of Ocean leaves. She adds hoar frost gathered under the full moon, the wings of the uncanny screech-owl with the flesh as well, and the entrails of a werewolf which has the power of changing its wild-beast features into a man's. There also in the pot is the scaly skin of a slender Cinyphian water-snake, the liver of a long-lived stag, to which she adds also eggs and the head of a crow nine generations old. When with these and a thousand other nameless things the barbarian woman had prepared her more than mortal plan, she stirred it all up with a branch of the fruitful olive long since dry and well mixed the top and bottom together. And lo, the old dry stick, when moved about in the hot broth, grew green at first, in a short time put forth leaves, and then suddenly was loaded with teeming olives. And wherever the froth bubbled over from the hollow pot, and the hot drops fell upon the ground, the earth grew green and flowers and soft grass sprang up. When she saw this, Medea unsheathed her knife and cut the old man's throat; then, letting the old blood all run out, she filled his veins with her brew. When Aeson had drunk this in part through his lips and part through the wound, his beard and hair lost their hoary grey and quickly became black again; his lean-ness vanished, away went the pallor and the look of neglect, the deep wrinkles were filled out with new flesh, his limbs had the strength of youth. Aeson was filled with wonder, and remembered that this was he forty years ago.

Now Bacchus had witnessed this marvel from his station in the sky, and learning from this that his own nurses might be restored to their youthful years, he obtained this desire from the Colchian woman.

That malice might have its turn, the Phasian woman feigned a quarrel with her husband, and fled as a suppliant to the house of Pelias. There, since the king himself was heavy with years, his daughters gave her hospitable reception. These girls the crafty Colchian in a short time won over by a false show of friendliness; and while she was relating among the most remarkable of her achievements the rejuvenation of Aeson, dwelling particularly on that, the daughters of Pelias were induced to hope that by skill like this their own father might be made young again. And they beg this gift, bidding her name the price, no matter how great. She made no reply for a little while and seemed to hesitate, keeping the minds of her suppliants in suspense by feigned deep meditation. When she had at length given her promise, she said to them: "That you may have the greater confidence in this gift, the oldest leader of the flock among your sheep shall become a lamb again by my drugs." Straightway a woolly ram, worn out with untold years, was brought forward, his great horns curving round his hollow temples. When the witch cut his scrawny throat with her Thessalian knife, barely staining the weapon with his scanty blood, she plunged his carcass into a kettle of bronze, throwing in at the same time juices of great potency. These made his body shrink, burnt away his horns, and with his horns, his years. And now a thin bleating was heard from within the pot; and, even while they were wondering at the sound, out jumped a lamb and ran frisking away to find some udder to give him milk.

Pelias' daughters looked on in amazement; and now that these promises had been performed, they urged their request still more eagerly than before. Three times had Phoebus unyoked his steeds after their plunge in Ebro's stream, and on the fourth night the stars were shining bright in the sky, when the treacherous daughter of Aeëtes set some clear water over a hot fire and put therein herbs of no potency. And now a death-like sleep held the king, his body all relaxed, and with the king his guards, sleep which incantations and the potency of magic words had given. The king's daughters, as they were bid, entered his chamber with the Colchian and stood around his bed. "Why do you hesitate now, you laggards?" Medea said. "Come, draw your swords, and let out his old blood that I may re-fill his empty veins with young blood again. In your own hands rests your father's life and youth. If you have any filial love, and if the hopes are not vain that you are cherishing, come, do your duty by your father; drive out age at your weapon's point; let out his enfeebled blood with the stroke of the blade." Spurred on by these words, as each was filial she became first in the unfilial act, and that she might not be wicked did the wicked deed. Nevertheless, none could bear to see her own blows; they turned their eyes away; and so with averted faces they blindly struck with cruel hands. The old man, streaming with blood, still raised himself on his elbow and half mangled tried to get up from his bed; and with all those swords round him, he stretched out his pale arms and cried: "What are you doing, my daughters? What arms you to your father's death?" Their courage left them, their hands fell. When he would have spoken further, the Colchian cut his throat and plunged his mangled body into the boiling water.

But had she not gone away through the air drawn by her winged dragons, she would not have escaped punishment. High up she sped over shady Pelion, the home of Chiron, over Othrys and the regions made famous by the adventure of old Cerambus. (He, by the aid of the nymphs borne up into the air on wings, at the time when the heavy earth had sunk beneath the overwhelming sea, escaped Deucalion's flood undrowned.)* Aeolian Pitane she passed by on the left, with its huge serpent image made of stone; and Ida's grove, where Bacchus, to conceal his son's theft, changed the bullock into the seeming form of a stag; where the father of Corythus lay buried beneath a small mound of sand; where Maera spread terror through the fields by her strange barking; over the city of Eurypylus where the women of Cos wore horns what time the band of Hercules withdrew; over Rhodes, beloved of Phoebus; and the Telchines of Ialysus whose eyes, blighting all things by their very glance, Jupiter in scorn and hatred plunged beneath his brother's waves. She passed also the walls of ancient Carthaea on the island of Cea, where father Alcidamas was sometime to marvel that a peaceful dove could have sprung from his daughter's body. Next Hyrie's lake she saw, and Tempe, which Cycnus' sudden change into a swan made famous. For there Phyllius, at the command of a boy, had tamed and brought him wild birds and a savage lion; being commanded to tame a wild bull also, he had tamed him, but angry that so often his love was spurned, he withheld the last gift of the bull from the boy who asked it; whereupon the boy in anger said, "You will wish you had given it," and leaped at once from a cliff. They all thought that he had fallen; but changed to a swan he remained floating in the air on snowy wings. But Hyrie, his mother, not knowing that her son was saved, melted away in tears and became a pool of the same name. Near these regions lies Pleuron, where Combe, the daughter of

*The nymphs later changed Cerambus into a beetle for offending them.

Ophius, escaped death at the hands of her sons on fluttering wings. After that, she sees the fertile island of Calaurea, sacred to Latona, the island that saw the king and his wife both changed into birds. On her right lies Cyllene, which Menephron was doomed to defile with incest after the wild beasts' fashion. Far off from here she looks down on the Cephisus, bewailing the fate of his grandson changed by Apollo into a plump sea-calf; and upon the home of Eumelus, who lamented that his son now dwelt in air.[4]

At length, upborne by the snaky wings, she reached Corinth of the sacred spring. Here, according to ancient tradition, in the earliest times men's bodies sprang from mushrooms. But after the new wife had been burnt by the Colchian witchcraft, and the two seas had seen the king's palace aflame, she stained her impious sword in the blood of her sons; and then, after this horrid vengeance, the mother fled Jason's sword. Borne away by her dragons sprung from Titans' blood, she entered the citadel of Pallas, which beheld you, most righteous Phene, and you, old Periphas, flying side by side, and the granddaughter of Polypemon upborne by new-sprung wings. Aegeus received her, that one deed enough to doom him; but he was not content with hospitality: he made her his wife as well.

And now came Theseus, a son that his father knew not; who by his manly prowess had established peace on the Isthmus between its two seas. Bent on his destruction, Medea mixed in a cup a poison which she had brought long ago from the Scythian shores. This poison, they say, came from the mouth of the Echidnean dog. There is a cavern with a dark, yawning throat and a way down-sloping, along which Hercules, the hero of Tiryns, dragged Cerberus with chains wrought of adamant, while the great dog fought and turned away his eyes from the bright light of day. He, goaded on to mad frenzy, filled all the air with his threefold howls, and sprinkled the green fields with white foam. Men think that these flecks of foam grew; and, drawing nourishment from the rich, rank soil, they gained power to hurt; and because they spring up and flourish on hard rocks, the country folk call them aconite. This poison, through the treachery of his wife, father Aegeus himself presented to his son as though to a stranger. Theseus had taken and raised the cup in his unwitting hand, when the father recognized the tokens of his own family on the ivory hilt of the sword which Theseus wore, and he

dashed the vile thing from his lips. But Medea escaped death in a
dark whirlwind her witch songs raised.

But the father, though he rejoiced at his son's deliverance, was
still horror-struck that so monstrous an iniquity could have been so
nearly done. He kindled fires upon the altars, made generous gifts
to the gods; his axes struck at the brawny necks of bulls with rib-
bons about their horns. It is said that no day ever dawned for the
Athenians more glad than that. The elders and the common folk
made merry together. Together they sang their songs, with wit in-
spired by wine: "You, O most mighty Theseus, Marathon extols for
the blood of the Cretan bull; and that the farmer of Cromyon may
till his fields without fear of the sow is your gift and your deed.
Through you the land of Epidaurus saw Vulcan's club-wielding son
laid low; the banks of Cephisus saw the merciless Procrustes slain;
Eleusis, the town of Ceres, beheld Cercyon's death. By your hand
fell that Sinis of great strength turned to evil uses, who could bend
the trunks of trees, and force down to earth the pine-tops to shoot
men's bodies far out through the air. A way lies safe and open now
to Alcathoë and the Lelegeïan walls, now that Sciron is no more. To
this robber's scattered bones both land and sea denied a resting-
place; but, long tossed about, it is said that in time they hardened
into cliffs; and the cliffs still bear the name of Sciron. If we should
wish to count your praises and your years, your deeds would exceed
your years. For you, brave hero, we give public thanks and prayers,
to you we drain our cups of wine." The palace resounds with the ap-
plause of the people and the prayers of the happy revellers; nowhere
in the whole city is there any place for gloom.

And yet—so true it is that there is no pleasure unalloyed, and
some care always comes to mar our joys—Aegeus' rejoicing over his
son's return was not unmixed with care. Minos was threatening war.
Strong in men and ships, he was yet most strong in fatherly resent-
ment and with just arms was seeking to avenge the death of his son
Androgeos.[5] But first he sought for friendly aid for his warfare; and
he scoured the sea in the swift fleet in which his chief strength lay.
He joined to his cause Anaphe and Astypalaea, the first by prom-
ises, the second by threats of war; the low-lying Myconus and the
chalky fields of Cimolus; Syros covered with wild thyme, level
Seriphos, Paros of the marble cliffs, and that place which impious

Sithonian Arne betrayed, and having received the gold which she in her greed had demanded, was changed into a bird which even now delights in gold, a black-footed, black-winged daw.

But Oliaros and Didymae, Tenos, Andros, Gyaros and Peparethos, rich in glossy olives, gave no aid to the Cretan fleet. Sailing then to the left, Minos sought Oenopia, the realm of the Aeacidae. Men of old time had called the place Oenopia; but Aeacus himself styled it Aegina by his mother's name.* At his approach a rabble rushed forth, eager to see and know so famous a man. Him Telamon met, and Peleus, younger than Telamon, and Phocus, third in age. Aeacus himself came also, slow with the weight of years, and asked him what was the cause of his coming. Reminded of his fatherly grief, the ruler of a hundred cities sighed and thus made answer: "I beg you aid the arms which for my son's sake I have taken up; and be a part of my pious warfare. Repose for the dead I ask." To him Aeacus replied: "You ask in vain that which my city cannot give; for no land is more closely linked to the Athenians than this: so strong are the treaties between us." The other, disappointed, turned away saying: "Your treaty shall cost you dear"; for he thought it were better to threaten war than to wage it and to waste his strength there untimely. Still the Cretan fleet could be seen from the Oenopian walls, when, driven on under full sail, an Attic ship arrived and entered the friendly port, bringing Cephalus and his country's greetings. The men of the house of Aeacus, though it was long since they had seen Cephalus, yet knew him, grasped his hand, and brought him into their father's house. The hero advanced, the centre of all eyes, retaining even yet the traces of his old beauty and charm, bearing a branch of his country's olive, and, himself the elder, flanked on right and left by two of lesser age, Clytos and Butes, sons of Pallas.

After they had exchanged greetings, Cephalus delivered the message of the Athenians, asking for aid and quoting the ancestral league and treaty between their two nations. He added that not only Athens but the sovereignty over all Greece was Minos' aim. When thus his eloquence had commended his cause, Aeacus, his left hand resting on the sceptre's hilt, exclaimed: "Ask not our aid, but take it,

---

*For the heritage of Aeacus, see endnote 2 to book VI.

Athens; and boldly count your own the forces which this island holds, and all things which the state of my affairs supplies. Warlike strength is not lacking; I have soldiers enough for myself and for my enemy. Thanks to the gods, the times are happy, and without excuse for my refusal." "May it prove even so," said Cephalus, "and may your city multiply in men. In truth, as I came here, I was rejoiced to meet youth so fair, so matched in age. And yet I miss many among them whom I saw before when last I visited your city." Aeacus groaned and with sad voice thus replied: "It was an unhappy beginning, but better fortune followed. Would that I could tell you the last without the first! Now I will take each in turn; and, not to delay you with long circumlocution, they are but bones and dust whom with kindly interest you ask for. And oh, how large a part of all my kingdom perished with them! A dire pestilence came on my people through angry Juno's wrath, who hated us for that our land was called by her rival's name. So long as the scourge seemed of mortal origin and the cause of the terrible plague was still unknown, we fought against it with the physician's art. But the power of destruction exceeded our resources, which were completely baffled. At first heaven rested down upon the earth in thick blackness, and held the sluggish heat confined in the clouds. And while the moon four times waxed to a full orb with horns complete, and four times waned from that full orb, hot south winds blew on us with pestilential breath. Consistently with this, the baleful infection reached our springs and pools; thousands of serpents crawled over our deserted fields and defiled our rivers with their poison. At first the swift power of the disease was confined to the destruction of dogs and birds, sheep and cattle, or among the wild beasts. The luckless plowman marvels to see his strong bulls fall in the midst of their task and sink down in the furrow. The woolly flocks bleat feebly while their wool falls off of itself and their bodies pine away. The horse, once of high courage and of great renown on the race-course, has now lost his victorious spirit and, forgetting his former glory, groans in his stall, doomed to an inglorious death. The boar forgets his rage, the hind to trust his fleetness, the bears to attack the stronger herds. Lethargy holds all. In woods and fields and roads foul carcasses lie; and the air is defiled by the stench. And, strange to say, neither dogs nor ravenous birds nor grey wolves did touch them. The bodies lie rotting on the ground, blast with their stench, and spread the contagion far and near.

"At last, now grown stronger, the pestilence attacks the wretched countrymen, and lords it within the great city's walls. As the first symptoms, the vitals are burnt up, and a sign of the lurking fire is a red flush and panting, feverish breath. The tongue is rough and swollen with fever; the lips stand apart, parched with hot respiration, and catch gasping at the heavy air. The stricken can endure no bed, no covering of any kind, but throw themselves face down on the hard ground; but their bodies gain no coolness from the ground; rather is the ground heated by their bodies. No one can control the pest, but it fiercely breaks out upon the very physicians, and their arts do but injure those who use them. The nearer one is to the sick and the more faithfully he serves them, the more quickly is he himself stricken unto death. And as the hope of life deserts them and they see the end of their malady only in death, they indulge their desires, and they have no care for what is best—for nothing is best. Everywhere, shameless they lie, in fountain-basins, in streams and roomy wells; nor by drinking is their thirst quenched so long as life remains. Many of these are too weak to rise, and die in the very water; and yet others drink even that water. To many poor wretches so great is the irksomeness of their hateful beds that they jump out, or, if they have not strength enough to stand, they roll out on the ground. They flee from their own homes: for each man's home seems a place of death to him. Since the cause of the disease is hidden, that small spot is held to blame. You might have seen them wandering half dead along the ways while they could keep on their feet, others lying on the ground and weeping bitterly, turning their dull eyes upward with a last weak effort, and stretching out their arms to the sky that hung over them like a pall—here, there, wherever death has caught them, breathing out their lives.

"What were my feelings then? Was it not natural that I should hate life and long to be with my friends? Wherever I turned my eyes there was a confused heap of dead, as mellow apples fall when the boughs are shaken, and acorns from the wind-tossed oak. You see a temple over there, raised on high, approached by a long flight of steps. It is sacred to Jupiter. Who did not bear his fruitless offerings to those altars? How often a husband for his wife's sake, a father for his son, while still uttering his prayer, has died before the implacable altars, and in his hand a portion of the incense was unused! How often the sacrificial bulls brought to the temples, while yet the priest was praying and pouring pure wine between their horns, have fallen without waiting for the stroke! While I myself was sacrificing to Jove on my own behalf and for my country and my three sons, the victim uttered dreadful bellowings and, suddenly falling without any stroke of mine, it barely stained the knife with its scanty blood; the diseased entrails also had lost the marks of truth and the warnings of the gods: for to the very vitals does the grim pest go. Before the temple doors I saw the corpses cast away, indeed, before the very altars, that their death might be even more odious. Some hung themselves, driving away the fear of death by death and going out to meet their approaching fate. The dead bodies were not borne out to burial in the accustomed way; for the gates would not accommodate so many funerals. They either lie on the ground unburied, or else they are piled high on funeral pyres without honors. And by this time there is no reverence for the dead; men fight for pyres, and with stolen flames they burn. There are none left to mourn the dead. Unwept they go wandering out, the souls of matrons and of brides, of men both young and old. There was no more space for graves, nor wood for fires.

"Dazed by such an overwhelming flood of woe, I cried to Jove: 'O Jove, if it is not falsely said that you loved Aegina, daughter of Asopus, and if you, great father, are not ashamed to be our father, either give me back my people or consign me also to the tomb.'[6] He gave a sign with lightning and a peal of thunder in assent. 'I accept the sign,' I said, 'and may those tokens of your mind towards us be happy signs. The omen which you give me I take as pledge.' It chanced there was an oak near by with branches unusually widespread, sacred to Jove and of Dodona's stock. Here we spied a swarm of grain-gathering ants in a long column, bearing heavy loads with their tiny mouths, and keeping their own path along the wrinkled bark. Wondering at their numbers, I said: 'O most excellent father, grant me just as many subjects, and fill my empty walls.' The lofty oak trembled and moved its branches, rustling in the windless air. My limbs were horror-smit with quaking fear and my hair stood on end. Yet I kissed the earth and the oak-tree; nor did I own my hopes to myself, and yet I did hope and I cherished my desires within my mind. Night came and sleep claimed our care-worn bodies. Before my eyes the same oak-tree seemed to stand, with just as many branches and with just as many creatures on its branches, to shake with the same motion, and to scatter the grain-bearing column on the ground below. These seemed suddenly to grow larger and ever larger, to raise themselves from the ground and stand with form erect, to throw off their leanness, their many feet, their black color, and to take on human limbs and a human form. Then sleep departed. Once awake I thought lightly of my vision, bewailing that there was no help in the gods. But there was a great confused noise in the palace, and I seemed to hear the voices of men to which I was long unused. And while I half believed that this also was a trick of sleep, Telamon came running and, throwing open the door, exclaimed: 'O father, more than you believed or hoped for shall you see. Come out!' I went without, and there just such men as I had seen in my dream I now saw and recognized with my waking eyes. They approached and greeted me as king. I gave thanks to Jove, and to my new subjects I portioned out my city and my fields, forsaken by their former occupants; and I called them Myrmidons, nor did I cheat the name of its origin. You have seen their bodies; the habits which they had before they still keep, a thrifty race, inured to toil, keen in pursuit of gain and keeping what they get. These men will follow you to the wars well matched in years and courage, as soon as the east wind which brought you so fortunately here"—for the east wind it was that brought him—"shall have changed to the south."

With such and other talk they filled the lingering day. The last hours of the day were given to feasting, the night to sleep. When the golden sun had shown his light, the east wind was still blowing and kept the sails from the homeward voyage. The sons of Pallas came to Cephalus, who was the older, and Cephalus with the sons of Pallas went together to the king. But deep sleep still held the king. Phocus, son of Aeacus, received them at the threshold; for Telamon and his brother were marshalling the men for war.[7] Into the inner court and beautiful apartments Phocus conducted the Athenians, and there they sat them down together. There Phocus noticed that Cephalus carried in his hand a javelin with a golden head, and a shaft made of some strange wood. After some talk, he said abruptly: "I am devoted to the woods and the hunting of wild beasts. Still, I have for some time been wondering from what wood that weapon you hold is made. Surely if it were of ash it would be of deep yellow hue; if it were of cornel-wood there would be knots upon it. What wood it is made of I cannot tell; but my eyes have never seen a javelin for throwing more beautiful than that." And one of the Athenian brothers replied: "You will admire the weapon's use more than its beauty; it goes straight to any mark, and chance does not guide its flight; and it flies back, all bloody, with no hand to bring it." Then indeed young Phocus was eager to know why it was so, and where it came from, who was the giver of so wonderful a gift. Cephalus told what the youth asked, but he was ashamed to tell at what price he gained it. He was silent; then, touched with grief for his lost wife, he burst into tears and said: "It is this weapon makes me weep, you son of a goddess—who could believe it?—and long will it make me weep if the fates shall give me long life. This destroyed me and my dear wife together. And oh, that I had never had it! My wife was Procris, or, if by more likely chance the name of Orithyia has come to your ears, the sister of the ravished Orithyia.* If you should compare the form and bearing of the two, Procris herself is the more worthy to be ravished away. It is she that her father, Erechtheus, joined to me; it is she that love joined to me. I was called happy, and happy I was. But the gods decreed it otherwise, or, perhaps, I should be happy still. It was in the second month after our marriage rites. I was spreading my nets to catch the antlered deer, when from the top of ever-blooming Hymettus the golden goddess of the dawn, having put the shades to flight, beheld me and carried me away, against my will: may the goddess pardon me for telling the simple truth; but as truly as she shines with the blush of roses on her face, as truly as she holds the portals of the day and night, and drinks the juices of nectar, it was Procris I loved; Procris was in my heart, Procris was ever on my lips. I kept talking of my wedding and its fresh joys of love and the first union of my now deserted couch. The goddess was provoked and exclaimed: 'Cease your complaints, ungrateful boy; keep your Procris! but, if my mind can

---

*Ovid tells Orithyia's story in book VI.

foresee at all, you will come to wish that you had never had her'; and
in a rage she sent me back to her. As I was going home, and turned
over in my mind the goddess' warning, I began to fear that my wife
herself had not kept her marriage vows. Her beauty and her youth
made me fear unfaithfulness; but her character forbade that fear.
Still, I had been absent long, and she from whom I was returning
was herself an example of unfaithfulness; and besides, we lovers fear
everything. I decided to make a cause for grievance and to tempt her
chaste faith by gifts. Aurora helped me in this jealous undertaking
and changed my form; (I seemed to feel the change). And so, un-
recognizable I entered Athens, Pallas' sacred city, and went into my
house. The household itself was blameless, showed no sign of any-
thing amiss, was only anxious for its lost lord. With much difficulty
and by a thousand wiles I gained the presence of Erechtheus'
daughter; and when I looked upon her my heart failed me and I al-
most abandoned the test of her fidelity which I had planned.
I scarce kept from confessing the truth, from kissing her as was her
due. She was sad; but no woman could be more beautiful than was
she in her sadness. She was all grief with longing for the husband
who had been torn away from her. Imagine, Phocus, how beautiful
she was, how that grief itself became her. Why should I tell how
often her chastity repelled my temptations? To every plea she said:
'I keep myself for one alone. Wherever he is I keep my love for one.'
What husband in his senses would not have found that test of her
fidelity enough? But I was not content and strove on to my own un-
doing! By promising to give fortunes for her favor, and at last, by
adding to my promised gifts, I forced her to hesitate. Then, victor
to my sorrow, I exclaimed: 'False one, he that is here is a feigned
adulterer! I was really your husband! By my own witness, traitress,
you are detected!' She, not a word. Only in silence, overwhelmed
with shame, she fled her treacherous husband and his house. In hate
for me, loathing the whole race of men, she wandered over the
mountains, devoted to Diana's pursuits. Then in my loneliness the
fire of love burned more fiercely, penetrating to the marrow. I craved
pardon, owned that I had sinned, confessed that I too might have
yielded in the same way under the temptation of gifts, if so great
gifts were offered to me. When I had made this confession and she
had sufficiently avenged her outraged feelings, she came back to me

and we spent sweet years together in harmony. She gave me beside, as though she had given but small gifts in herself, a wonderful hound which her own Cynthia had given, and said as she gave: 'He will surpass all other hounds in speed.' She gave me a javelin also, this one which, as you see, I hold in my hands. Would you know the story of both gifts? Hear the wonderful story: you will be moved by the strangeness of the deed.

"Oedipus, the son of Laïus, had solved the riddle which had been inscrutable to the understanding of all before; fallen headlong she lay, the dark prophet, forgetful of her own riddle.* Straightway a second monster was sent against Aonian Thebes (and surely kind Themis does not let such things go unpunished!) and many country dwellers were in terror of the fierce creature, fearing both for their own and their flocks' destruction. We, the neighbouring youths, came and encircled the broad fields with our hunting-nets. But that swift beast leaped over the nets, over the very tops of the toils which we had spread. Then we let slip our hounds from the leash; but she escaped their pursuit and mocked the hundred dogs with speed like any bird. Then all the hunters called upon me for my Laelaps (that is the name of the hound my wife had given me). Long since he had been struggling to get loose from the leash and straining his neck against the strap that held him. Scarce was he well released when we could not tell where he was. The warm dust kept the imprint of his feet, he himself had quite disappeared from sight. No spear is swifter than he, nor leaden bullets thrown by a whirled sling, or the light reed shot from a Gortynian bow. There was a high hill near by, whose top overlooked the surrounding plain. Up it I climbed and gained a view of that strange chase, in which the beast seemed now to be caught and now to slip from the dog's very teeth. Nor does the cunning creature flee in a straight course off into the distance, but it eludes the pursuer's jaws and wheels sharply round, so that its enemy may lose his spring. The dog presses him hard, follows him step for step, and, while he seems to hold him, does not hold, and snaps at the empty air. I turned to my javelin's aid. As my right hand was balancing it, while I was fitting my fingers into the loop,

---

*Later Oedipus himself brought plague to Thebes by unwittingly marrying his mother.

I turned my eyes aside for a single moment; and when I turned them back again to the same spot—oh, wonderful! I saw two marble images in the plain; the one you would think was fleeing, the other catching at the prey. Doubtless some god must have willed, if there was any god with them, that both should be unconquered in their race." Thus far he spoke and fell silent. "But what charge have you to bring against the javelin itself?" asked Phocus. The other thus told what charge he had against the javelin:

"My joys, Phocus, were the beginning of my woe. These I will describe first. Oh, what a joy it is, son of Aeacus, to remember the blessed time when during those first years I was happy in my wife, as I should be, and she was happy in her husband. Mutual cares and mutual love bound us together. Not Jove's love would she have preferred to mine; nor was there any woman who could lure me away from her, no, not if Venus herself should come. An equal passion burned in both our two hearts. In the early morning, when the sun's first rays touched the tops of the hills, with a young man's eagerness I used to go hunting in the woods. Nor did I take attendants with me, or horses or keen-scented dogs or knotted nets. I was safe with my javelin. But when my hand had had its fill of slaughter of wild creatures, I would come back to the cool shade and the breeze that came forth from the cool valleys. I wooed the breeze, blowing gently on me in my heat; the breeze I waited for. She was my labour's rest. 'Come, Aura,' I remember I used to cry, 'come soothe me; come into my breast, most welcome one, and, as indeed you do, relieve the heat with which I burn.' Perhaps I would add, for so my fates drew me on, more endearments, and say: 'You are my greatest joy; you refresh and comfort me; you make me love the woods and solitary places. It is always my joy to feel your breath upon my face.' Some one overhearing these words was deceived by their double meaning; and, thinking that the word 'Aura' so often on my lips was a nymph's name, was convinced that I was in love with some nymph. Straightway the rash tell-tale went to Procris with the story of my supposed unfaithfulness and reported in whispers what he had heard. A credulous thing is love. Smitten with sudden pain (as I heard the story), she fell down in a swoon. Reviving at last, she called herself wretched, victim of cruel fate; complained of my unfaithfulness, and, excited by an empty charge, she feared a mere nothing, feared an empty name and grieved, poor girl, as over a real rival. And yet she would often doubt and hope in her depth of misery that she was mistaken; she refused to believe the story she had heard, and, unless she saw it with her own eyes, would not think her husband guilty of such sin. The next morning, when the early dawn had banished night, I left the house and sought the woods; there, successful, as I lay on the grass, I cried: 'Come, Aura, come and soothe my toil'—and suddenly, while I was speaking, I thought I heard a groan. 'Come, dearest one,' I cried again. And as the fallen leaves made a slight rustling sound, I thought it was some beast and hurled my javelin at the place. It was Procris, and, clutching at the wound in her breast, she cried, 'Oh, woe is me.' When I recognized the voice of my faithful wife, I rushed headlong towards the sound, beside myself with horror. There I found her dying, her disordered garments stained with blood, and oh, the pity! trying to draw the very weapon she had given me from her wounded breast. With loving arms I raised her body, dearer to me than my own, tore open the garment from her breast and bound up the cruel wound, and tried to staunch the blood, praying that she would not leave me stained with her death. She, though strength failed her, with a dying effort forced herself to say these few words: 'By the union of our love, by the gods above and my own gods, by all that I have done for you, and by the love that still I bear you in my dying hour, the cause of my own death, I beg you, do not let this Aura take my place.' And then I knew at last that it was a mistake in the name, and I told her the truth. But what availed then the telling? She fell back in my arms and her last faint strength fled with her blood. So long as she could look at anything she looked at me and breathed out her unhappy spirit on my lips. But she seemed to die content and with a happy look upon her face."

This story the hero told with many tears. And now Aeacus came in with his two sons and his new levied band of soldiers, which Cephalus received with their valiant arms.

BOOK VIII

NOW WHEN LUCIFER HAD banished night and ushered in the shining day, the east wind fell and moist clouds arose. The peaceful south wind offered a safe return to Cephalus and the mustered troops of Aeacus, and, speeding their voyage, brought them, sooner than they had hoped, to their desired haven. Meanwhile King Minos was laying waste the coast of Megara, and was trying his martial strength against the city of Alcathoüs, where Nisus reigned. This Nisus had growing on his head, amid his locks of honored grey, a brilliant purple lock on whose preservation rested the safety of his throne.

Six times had the new moon shown her horns, and still the fate of war hung in the balance; so long did Victory hover on doubtful wings between the two. There was a royal tower reared on the tuneful walls where Latona's son was said to have laid down his golden lyre, whose music still lingered in the stones. Often to this tower the daughter of King Nisus used to climb and set the rocks resounding with a pebble, in the day when peace was. Also after the war began she would often look out from this place upon the rough martial combats. And now, as the war dragged on, she had come to know even the names of the warring chieftains, their arms, their horses, their dress, their Cretan quivers. And above all others did she know the face of their leader, Europa's son,* yes, better than she should. If he had hidden his head in a crested casque, Minos in a helmet was lovely to her eyes: or if he carried his shining golden shield, the shield became him well. Did he hurl his tough spear with tense muscles, the girl admired the strength and the skill he showed. Did he bend the wide-curving bow with arrow fitted to the string, thus she would swear that Phoebus stood with arrows in his hand. But

*By Jupiter; see the end of book II and the start of book III.

when unhelmed he showed his face, when clad in purple he bestrode his milk-white steed gorgeous with broidered trappings, and managed the foaming bit, then was Nisus' daughter hardly her own, hardly mistress of a sane mind. Happy the javelin which he touched and happy the reins which he held in his hand, she thought. She longed, were it but allowed, to speed her maiden steps through the foemen's line; she longed to leap down from her lofty tower into the Cretan camp, to open the city's bronze-bound gates to the enemy, to do any other thing which Minos might desire. And, as she sat gazing at the white tents of the Cretan king, she said: "Whether I should rejoice or grieve at this woeful war, I cannot tell. I grieve because Minos is the foe of her who loves him; but if there were no war, he would never have been known to me. Suppose he had me as a hostage, then he could give up the war; I should be in his company, should be a pledge of peace. If she who bore you, O loveliest of all the world, was such as you are, good reason was it that the god burned for her. Oh, thrice happy should I be, if only I might fly through the air and stand within the camp of the Cretan king, and confess my love, and ask what dower he would wish to be paid for me. Only let him not ask my country's citadel. For may all my hopes of wedlock perish ere I gain it by treachery. And yet oft-times many have found it good to be overcome, when an appeased victor has been merciful. Surely he wages a just war for his murdered son; and he is strong both in his cause and in the arms that defend his cause. We shall be conquered, I am sure. And if that doom awaits our city, why shall his warrior hand unbar these walls of ours, and not my love? Far better will it be without massacre and suspense and the cost of his own blood for him to conquer. In that case truly I should not fear in case someone should pierce your breast unwittingly, dear Minos; for, if not unwitting, who so cruel that he could bring himself to throw his pitiless spear at you?" She likes the plan, and decides to give up herself with her country as her dowry, and so to end the war. But merely to will is not enough. "A watch guards the entry; my father holds the keys of the city gates. Him only do I fear, unhappy! Only he delays the wish of my heart. Would to God I had no father! But surely everyone is his own god; Fortune resists half-hearted prayers. Another girl in my place, fired with so great a love, would long since have destroyed, and that with joy, whatever stood in the

way of her love. And why should another be braver than I? Through
fire and sword would I dare go. And yet here there is no need of fire
or sword. I need but my father's lock of hair. That is to me more
precious than gold; that purple lock will make me blest, will give
me my heart's desire."

While she thus spoke night came on, most potent healer of our
cares; and with the darkness her boldness grew. The first rest had
come, when sleep holds the heart weary with the cares of day: the
daughter steals silently into her father's chamber, and—oh, the hor-
rid crime!—she despoils him of the tress where his life lay. With this
cursed prize, through the midst of her foes, so sure is she of a wel-
come for her deed, she goes straight to the king; and thus she ad-
dresses him, startled at her presence: "Love has led me to this deed.
I, Scylla, daughter of King Nisus, do here deliver to your hands my
country and my house. I ask no reward except for you. Take as the
pledge of my love this purple lock, and know that I am giving to you
not a lock, but my father's life." And in her sin-stained hand she held
out the prize to him. Minos recoiled from the proffered gift, and, in
horror at the sight of so unnatural an act, he replied: "May the gods
banish you from their world, O foul disgrace of our age! May both
land and sea be denied to you! Be sure that I shall not permit so vile
a monster to set foot on Crete, my world, the cradle of Jove's infancy."

He spoke; and when this most upright lawgiver had imposed
laws upon his conquered foes, he bade loose the hawsers of the fleet,
and the rowers to man the bronze-bound ships. When Scylla saw
that the ships were launched and afloat, and that the king refused
her the reward of her sin, having prayed until she could pray no
more, she became violently enraged, and stretching out her hands,
with streaming hair and mad with passion, she exclaimed: "Where
do you flee, abandoning the giver of your success, O you whom I put
before my fatherland, before my father? Where do you flee, you
cruel man, whose victory is my sin, it's true, but is my merit also?
Does not the gift I gave move you, do not my love and all my hopes
depend on you alone? Deserted, where shall I go? Back to my fa-
therland? It lies overthrown. But suppose it still remained: it is
closed to me by my treachery. To my father's presence? him whom
I betrayed to you? My countrymen hate me, and with just cause; the
neighbouring peoples fear my example. I am banished from all the

world, that Crete alone might be open to me. And if you forbid me
Crete as well, and, O ungrateful, leave me here, Europa is not your
mother, but the inhospitable Syrtis, the Armenian tigress and
storm-tossed Charybdis. You are no son of Jove, nor was your
mother tricked by the false semblance of a bull. That story of your
birth is a lie: it was a real bull that begot you, a fierce, wild thing that
loved no heifer. Inflict my punishment, O Nisus, my father! Rejoice
in my woes, O walls that I have but now betrayed! For I confess
I have merited your hate and I deserve to die. But let some one of
those whom I have foully injured slay me. Why should you, who
have triumphed through my sin, punish my sin? Let this act which
was a crime against my country and my father be but a service in
your eyes. She is a true mate for you who with unnatural passion de-
ceived the savage bull by that shape of wood and bore a hybrid off-
spring in her womb.[1] Does my voice reach your ears? Or do the
same winds blow away my words to emptiness that fill your sails,
you ingrate? Now, now I do not wonder that Pasiphaë preferred the
bull to you, for you were a more savage beast than he. Alas for me!
He orders his men to haste away! and the waves resound as the oars
dash into them, and I and my land are both fading from his sight.
But it is in vain; you have forgotten my deserts in vain; I shall fol-
low you against your will, and clinging to the curving stern, I shall
be drawn over the long reaches of the sea." Scarce had she spoken
when she leaped into the water, swam after the ship, her passion
giving strength, and clung, hateful and unwelcome, to the Cretan
boat. When her father saw her—for he was hovering in the air,
having but now been changed into an osprey with tawny wings—he
came on that he might tear her, as she clung there, with his hooked
beak. In terror she let go her hold upon the boat, and as she fell the
light air seemed to hold her up and keep her from touching the
water. She was like a feather! Changed to a feathered bird, she is
called Ciris, and takes this name from the shorn lock of hair.

Minos duly paid his vows to Jove, a hundred bulls, when he dis-
embarked upon the Cretan strand; and he hung up his spoils of war
to adorn his palace. But now his family's disgrace had grown big,
and the queen's foul adultery was revealed to all by her strange
hybrid monster-child. Minos planned to remove this shame from
his house and to hide it away in a labyrinthine enclosure with blind

passages. Daedalus, a man famous for his skill in the builder's art, planned and performed the work. He confused the usual passages and deceived the eye by a conflicting maze of divers winding paths. Just as the watery Maeander plays in the Phrygian fields, flows back and forth in doubtful course and, turning back on itself, beholds its own waves coming on their way, and sends its uncertain waters now towards their source and now towards the open sea: so Daedalus made those innumerable winding passages, and was himself scarce able to find his way back to the place of entry, so deceptive was the enclosure he had built.

In this labyrinth Minos shut up the monster of the bull-man form and twice he fed him on Athenian blood; but the third tribute, demanded after each nine years, brought the creature's overthrow. And when, by the virgin Ariadne's help, the difficult entrance, which no former adventurer had ever reached again, was found by winding up the thread, straightway the son of Aegeus, taking Minos' daughter, spread his sails for Dia; and on that shore he cruelly abandoned his companion. To her, deserted and bewailing bitterly, Bacchus brought love and help. And, that she might shine among the deathless stars, he sent the crown she wore up to the skies. Through the thin air it flew; and as it flew its gems were changed to gleaming fires and, still keeping the appearance of a crown, it took its place between the Kneeler and the Serpent-holder.*

Meanwhile Daedalus, hating Crete and his long exile, and longing to see his native land, was shut in by the sea. "Though he may block escape by land and water," he said, "yet the sky is open, and by that way will I go. Though Minos rules over all, he does not rule the air." So saying, he sets his mind at work upon unknown arts, and changes the laws of nature. For he lays feathers in order, beginning at the smallest, short next to long, so that you would think they had grown upon a slope. Just so the old-fashioned rustic pan-pipes with their unequal reeds rise one above another. Then he fastened the feathers together with twine and wax at the middle and bottom; and, thus arranged, he bent them with a gentle curve, so that they looked like real birds' wings. His son, Icarus, was standing by and, little knowing that he was handling his own peril, with gleeful face

---

*Respectively, the constellations Hercules and Ophiuchus.

would now catch at the feathers which some passing breeze had blown about, now mould the yellow wax with his thumb, and by his sport would hinder his father's wondrous task. When now the finishing touches had been put upon the work, the master workman himself balanced his body on two wings and hung poised on the beaten air. He taught his son also and said: "I warn you, Icarus, to fly in a middle course, because, if you go too low, the water may weight your wings; if you go too high, the fire may burn them. Fly between the two. And I bid you not to shape your course by Boötes or Helice or the drawn sword of Orion, but fly where I shall lead." At the same time he tells him the rules of flight and fits the strange wings on his boy's shoulders. While he works and talks the old man's cheeks are wet with tears, and his fatherly hands tremble. He kissed his son, which he was destined never again to do, and rising on his wings, he flew on ahead, fearing for his companion, just like a bird which has led forth her fledglings from the high nest into the unsubstantial air. He encourages the boy to follow, instructs him in the fatal art of flight, himself flapping his wings and looking back on his son. Now some fisherman spies them, angling for fish with his flexible rod, or a shepherd, leaning upon his crook, or a plowman, on his plow-handles—spies them and stands stupefied, and believes them to be gods that they could fly through the air. And now Juno's sacred Samos had been passed on the left, and Delos and Paros; Lebinthus was on the right and Calymne, rich in honey, when the boy began to rejoice in his bold flight and, deserting his leader, led by a desire for the open sky, directed his course to a greater height. The scorching rays of the nearer sun softened the fragrant wax which held his wings. The wax melted; his arms were bare as he beat them up and down, but, lacking wings, they took no hold on the air. His lips, calling to the last upon his father's name, were drowned in the dark blue sea, which took its name from him. But the unhappy father, now no longer father, called: "Icarus, Icarus, where are you? In what place shall I seek you? Icarus," he called again; and then he spied the wings floating on the deep, and cursed his skill. He buried the body in a tomb, and the land was called from the name of the buried boy.

As he was consigning the body of his ill-fated son to the tomb, a chattering partridge looked out from a muddy ditch and clapped her wings uttering a joyful note. She was at that time a strange bird, of a kind never seen before, and but lately made a bird; a lasting reproach to you, Daedalus. For the man's sister, ignorant of the fates, had sent him her son to be trained, a lad of teachable mind, who had now passed his twelfth birthday. This boy, moreover, observed the backbone of a fish and, taking it as a model, cut a row of teeth in a thin strip of iron and thus invented the saw. He also was the first to bind two arms of iron together at a joint, so that, while the arms kept the same distance apart, one might stand still while the other should trace a circle. Daedalus envied the lad and thrust him down headlong from the sacred citadel of Minerva, with a lying tale that the boy had fallen. But Pallas, who favors the quick of wit, caught him up and made him a bird, and clothed him with feathers in midair. His old quickness of wit passed into his wings and legs, but he kept the name which he had before.* Still the bird does not lift her body high in flight nor build her nest on trees or on high points of rock; but she flutters along near the ground and lays her eggs in hedgerows; and, remembering that old fall, she is ever fearful of lofty places.

Now the land of Aetna received the weary Daedalus, where King Cocalus took up arms in the suppliant's defence and was esteemed most kind.[2] Now also Athens, thanks to Theseus, had ceased to pay her doleful tribute. The temple is wreathed with flowers, the people call on Minerva, goddess of battles, with Jove and the other gods, whom they worship with sacrificial blood, with gifts and burning incense. Quick-flying fame had spread the name of Theseus through all the towns of Greece, and all the peoples of rich Achaia prayed his help in their own great perils. Suppliant Calydon sought his help with anxious prayers, although she had her Meleager. The cause of seeking was a monster boar, the servant and avenger of outraged Diana. For they say that Oeneus, king of Calydon, in thanksgiving for a bounteous harvest-time, paid the first-fruits of the grain to Ceres, paid his wine to Bacchus, and her own flowing oil to golden-haired Minerva. Beginning with the rural deities, the honor they craved was paid to all the gods of heaven; only Diana's altar was passed by (they say) and left without its incense. Anger also can

---

*The boy's name, Perdix, is the Latin for "partridge."

move the gods. "But we shall not bear this without vengeance," she said; "and though unhonored, it shall not be said that we are un-avenged." And the scorned goddess sent over Oeneus' fields an avenging boar, as great as the bulls which feed on grassy Epirus, and greater than those of Sicily. His eyes glowed with blood and fire; his neck was stiff and high; his bristles stood up like lines of stiff spear-shafts; amid deep, hoarse grunts the hot foam flecked his broad shoulders; his tusks were long as the Indian elephant's, lightning flashed from his mouth, the herbage shrivelled beneath his breath. Now he trampled down the young corn in the blade, and now he laid waste the full-grown crops of some farmer who was doomed to mourn, and cut off the ripe grain in the ear. In vain the threshing-floor, in vain the granary awaited the promised harvests. The heavy bunches of grapes with their trailing vines were cast down, and berry and branch of the olive whose leaf never withers. He vents his rage on the cattle, too. Neither herdsmen nor dogs can protect them, nor can the fierce bulls defend their herds. The people flee in all directions, nor do they count themselves safe until protected by a city's walls. Then at last Meleager and a picked band of youths as-sembled, fired with the love of glory: the twin sons of Leda, wife of Tyndarus, one famous for boxing, the other for horsemanship; Jason, the first ship's builder; Theseus and Pirithoüs, inseparable friends; the two sons of Thestius; Lynceus and swift-footed Idas, sons of Aphareus; Caeneus, no longer a woman; warlike Leucippus and Acastus, famed for his javelin; Hippothoüs and Dryas; Phoenix, the son of Amyntor; Actor's two sons and Elean Phyleus. Telamon was also there, and the father of great Achilles; and, along with the son of Pheres and Boeotian Iolaüs, were Eurytion, quick in action, and Echion, of unconquered speed; Locrian Lelex, Panopeus, Hyleus and Hippasus, keen for the fray; Nestor, then in the prime of his years; and those whom Hippocoön sent from ancient Amyclae; the father-in-law of Penelope, and Arcadian Ancaeus; Ampycus' prophetic son, and the son of Oecleus, who had not yet been ruined by his wife;[3] and Atalanta of Tegea, the pride of the Arcadian woods.[4] A polished buckle clasped her robe at the neck; her hair, plainly dressed, was caught up in one knot. From her left shoulder hung an ivory quiver, resounding as she moved, with its shafts, and her left hand held a bow. Such was she in dress. As for her face, it was one which you could truly say was maidenly for a boy or boyish for a maiden. As soon as his eyes fell on her, the Calydonian hero straightway longed for her (but God forbade); he felt the flames of love steal through his heart; and "O happy man," he said, "if ever that maiden shall deem any man worthy to be hers." Neither the occasion nor his own modesty permitted him more words; the greater task of the mighty conflict urged him to action.

There was a dense forest, that past ages had never touched with the axe, rising from the plain and looking out on the downward-sloping fields. When the heroes came to this, some stretched the hunting-nets, some slipped the leashes from the dogs, some followed the well-marked trail as they longed to come at their dangerous enemy. There was a deep dell, where the rain-water from above drained down; the lowest part of this marshy spot was covered with a growth of pliant willows, sedge-grass and swamp-rushes, osiers and tall bulrushes, with an undergrowth of small reeds. From this covert the boar was roused and launched himself with a mad rush against his foes, like lightning struck out from the clashing clouds. The grove is laid low by his onrush, and the trees crash as he knocks against them. The heroes raise a halloo and with unflinching hands hold their spears poised with the broad iron heads well forward. The boar comes rushing on, scatters the dogs one after another as they strive to stop his mad rush, and thrusts off the baying pack with his deadly sidelong stroke. The first spear, thrown by Echion's arm, missed its aim and struck glancing on the trunk of a maple-tree. The next, if it had not been thrown with too much force, seemed sure of transfixing the back where it was aimed. It went too far. Jason of Pagasae was the marksman. Then Mopsus cried: "O Phoebus, if I have ever worshipped and do still worship you, grant me with unerring spear to reach my mark." So far as possible the god heard his prayer. His spear did strike the boar, but without injury; for Diana had wrenched the iron point from the javelin as it sped, and pointless the wooden shaft struck home. But the beast's savage anger was roused, and it burned hotter than the lightning. Fire gleamed from his eyes, seemed to breathe from his throat. And, as a huge rock, shot from a catapult sling, flies through the air against walls or turrets filled with soldiery; so with irresistible and death-dealing force the beast rushed on the youths, and overbore

Eupalamus and Pelagon, who were stationed on the extreme right. Their comrades caught them up as they lay. But Enaesimus, the son of Hippocoön, did not escape the boar's fatal stroke. As he in fear was just turning to run he was hamstrung and his muscles gave way beneath him. Pylian Nestor came near perishing before he ever went to the Trojan War; but, putting forth all his strength, he leaped by his spear-pole into the branches of a tree which stood near by, and from this place of safety he looked down upon the foe he had escaped. The raging beast whetted his tusks on an oak-tree's trunk; and, threatening destruction and emboldened by his freshly sharpened tusks, ripped up the thigh of the mighty Hippasus with one sweeping blow. But now the twin brothers, not yet set in the starry heavens, came riding up, both conspicuous among the rest, both on horses whiter than snow, both poising their spears, which they threw quivering through the air. And they would have struck the boar had the bristly monster not taken refuge in the dense woods, where neither spear nor horse could follow him. Telamon did attempt to follow, and in his eagerness, careless where he went, he fell prone on the ground, caught by a projecting root. While Peleus was helping him to rise, Atalanta notched a swift arrow on the cord and sent it speeding from her bent bow. The arrow just grazed the top of the boar's back and remained stuck beneath his ear, staining the bristles with a trickle of blood. Nor did she show more joy over the success of her own stroke than Meleager. He was the first to see the blood, the first to point it out to his companions, and to say: "Due honor shall your brave deed receive." The men, flushed with shame, spurred each other on, gaining courage as they cried out, hurling their spears in disorder. The mass of missiles made them of no effect, and kept them from striking as they were meant to do. Then Ancaeus, the Arcadian, armed with a two-headed axe raging to meet his fate, cried out: "Learn now, O youths, how far a man's weapons surpass a girl's; and leave this task to me. Though Latona's daughter herself shield this boar with her own arrows, in spite of Diana shall my good right arm destroy him." So, swollen with pride and with boastful lips, he spoke: and, heaving up in both hands his two-edged axe, he stood on tiptoe, poised to strike. The boar made in upon his bold enemy, and, as the nearest point for death, he fiercely struck at the upper part of the groins with his two tusks.

Ancaeus fell; his entrails poured out amid streams of blood and the ground was soaked with gore. Then Ixion's son, Pirithoüs, advanced against the foe, brandishing a hunting-spear in his strong right hand. To him Theseus cried out in alarm: "Keep away, O dearer to me than my own self, my soul's other half; it is no shame for brave men to fight at long range. Ancaeus' rash valor has proved his curse." He spoke and hurled his own heavy shaft with its sharp bronze point. Though this was well aimed and seemed sure to reach the mark, a leafy branch of an oak-tree turned it aside. Then the son of Aeson hurled his javelin, which chance caused to swerve from its aim and fatally wound an innocent dog, passing clear through his flanks and pinning him to the ground. But the hand of Meleager had a different fortune: he threw two spears, the first of which stood in the earth, but the second stuck squarely in the middle of the creature's back. Straightway, while the boar rages and whirls round and round, spouting forth foam and fresh blood in a hissing stream, the giver of the wound presses his advantage, pricks his enemy on to madness, and at last plunges his gleaming hunting-spear right through the shoulder. The others vent their joy by wild shouts of applause and crowd around to press the victor's hand. They gaze in wonder at the huge beast lying stretched out over so much ground, and still think it hardly safe to touch him. But each dips his spear in the blood.

Then Meleager, standing with his foot upon that death-dealing head, spoke thus to Atalanta: "Take the prize that is mine by right, O fair Arcadian, and let my glory be shared with you." And then he presented her with the spoils: the skin with its bristling spikes, and the head remarkable for its huge tusks. She rejoiced in the gift and no less in the giver; but the others begrudged it, and an angry murmur rose through the whole company. Then two, the sons of Thestius, stretching out their arms, cried with a loud voice: "Let be, girl, and do not usurp our honors. And be not deceived by trusting in your beauty, in the event this lovesick giver be far from helping you." And they took from her the gift, and from him the right of giving. This was more than that son of Mars could bear, and, gnashing his teeth with rage, he cried: "Learn then, you that plunder another's rights, the difference between deeds and threats," and plunged his impious blade deep in Plexippus' heart, who was taken off his guard. Then, as Toxeus stood hesitating what to do, wishing to avenge his brother, but at the same time fearing to share his brother's fate, Meleager gave him scant time to hesitate, but, while his spear was still warm with its first victim's slaughter, he warmed it again in his comrade's blood.

Althaea in the temple of the gods was offering thanksgiving for her son's victory, when she saw the corpses of her brothers carried in. She beat her breast and filled the city with woeful lamentation, and changed her gold-spangled robes for black. But when she learned who was their murderer, her grief all fell away and was changed from tears to the passion for vengeance.

There was a billet of wood which, when the daughter of Thestius lay in childbirth, the three sisters threw into the fire and, spinning the threads of life with firm-pressed thumb, they sang: "An equal span of life we give to you and to this wood, O babe new-born." When the three goddesses had sung this prophecy and vanished, the mother snatched the blazing brand from the fire, and quenched it in water. Long had it lain hidden away in a secret place and, guarded safe, had safeguarded your life, O youth. And now the mother brought out this billet and bade her servants make a heap of pine-knots and fine kindling, and lit the pile with cruel flame. Then four times she made to throw the billet in the flames and four times she held her hand. Mother and sister strove in her, and the two names tore one heart this way and that. Often her cheeks grew pale with fear of the impious thing she planned; as often blazing wrath gave its own color to her eyes. Now she looked like one threatening some cruel deed, and now you would think her pitiful. And when the fierce anger of her heart had dried up her tears, still tears would come again. And as a ship, driven by the wind, and against the wind by the tide, feels the double force and yields uncertainly to both, so Thestius' daughter wavered betwixt opposing passions; now quenched her wrath and now fanned it again. At last the sister in her overcomes the mother, and, that she may appease with blood the shades of her blood-kin, she is pious in impiety. For when the devouring flames grow hot, she cries: "Be that the funeral pyre of my own flesh." And, as she held the fateful billet in her relentless hand and stood, unhappy wretch, before the sepulchral fires, she said: "O triple goddesses of vengeance, Eumenides, behold these fearful rites. I avenge and I do a wicked deed: death must be atoned by death; to crime must crime be added, death to death. Through woes on woes heaped up let this accursed house go on to ruin! Shall happy Oeneus rejoice in his victorious son and Thestius be childless? 'Twill be better for you both to grieve. Only do you, my brothers' manes, fresh-made ghosts, appreciate my service, and accept the sacrifice I offer at so heavy cost, the baleful tribute of my womb. Ah me, where am I hurrying? Brothers, forgive a mother's heart! My hands refuse to finish what they began. I confess that he deserves to die; but that I should be the agent of his death, I cannot bear. And shall he go scathless then? Shall he live, victorious and puffed up with his own success, and lord it in Calydon, while you are nothing but a handful of ashes, shivering ghosts? I will not suffer it. Let the wretch die and drag to ruin with him his father's hopes, his kingdom and his fatherland! Where is my mother-love? Where are parents' pious cares? Where are those pangs which ten long months I bore? O that you had perished in your infancy by those first fires, and I had suffered it! You lived by my gift; now you shall die by your own desert; pay the price of your deed. Give back the life I twice gave you, once at your birth, once when I saved the brand; or else add me to my brothers' pyre. I both desire to act, and cannot. Oh, what shall I do? Now I can see only my brothers' wounds, the sight of that deed of blood: and now love and the name of mother break me down. Woe is me, my brothers! It is ill that you should win, but win you shall; only let me have the solace that I grant to you, and let me follow you!" She spoke, and turning away her face, with trembling hand she threw the fatal billet into the flames. The brand either gave or seemed to give a groan as it was caught and consumed by the unwilling fire.

Unconscious, far away, Meleager burns with those flames; he feels his vitals scorching with hidden fire, and overcomes the great pain with fortitude. But yet he grieves that he must die a cowardly and bloodless death, and he calls Ancaeus happy for the wounds he suffered. With groans of pain he calls with his dying breath on his aged father, his brothers and loving sisters and his wife, perhaps also upon his mother. The fire and his pains increase, and then die down. Both fire and pain go out together; his spirit gradually slips away into the thin air as white ashes gradually overspread the glowing coals.

Lofty Calydon is brought low. Young men and old, chieftains and commons, lament and groan; and the Calydonian women, dwellers by Euenus' stream, tear their hair and beat their breasts. The father, prone on the ground, defiles his white hair and his aged head with dust, and laments that he has lived too long. For the mother, now knowing her awful deed, has punished herself, driving a dagger through her heart. Not if some god had given me a hundred mouths each with its tongue, a master's genius, and all Helicon's inspiration, could I describe the piteous prayers of those poor sisters. Careless of decency, they beat and bruise their breasts; and, while their brother's corpse remains, they caress that corpse over and over, kiss him and kiss the bier as it stands before them. And, when he is ashes, they gather the ashes and press them to their hearts, throw themselves on his tomb in abandonment of grief and, clasping the stone on which his name has been carved, they drench the name with their tears. At length Diana, satisfied with the destruction of Parthaon's house, made feathers spring on their bodies—all but Gorge and great Alcmena's daughter-in-law—stretched out long wings over their arms, gave them a horny beak, and sent them transfigured into the air.[5]

Meanwhile Theseus, having done his part in the confederate task, was on his way back to Tritonia's city where Erechtheus ruled. But Acheloüs,* swollen with rain, blocked his way and delayed his journey. "Enter my house, illustrious hero of Athens," said the river-god, "and do not entrust yourself to my greedy waters. The current is wont to sweep down solid trunks of trees and huge boulders in zigzag course with crash and roar. I have seen great stables that stood near by the bank swept away, cattle and all, and in that current neither strength availed the ox nor speed the horse. Many a strong man also has been overwhelmed in its whirling pools when swollen by melting snows from the mountain-sides. It is safer for you to rest until the waters shall run within their accustomed bounds, until its own bed shall hold the slender stream." The son of Aegeus replied: "I will use both your house, Acheloüs, and your advice." And he did use them both. He entered the river-god's dark dwelling, built of porous pumice and rough tufa; the floor was damp

---

*Acheloüs was the god of an eponymous river between Calydon and Athens.

with soft moss, conchs and purple-shells panelled the ceiling. Now had the blazing sun traversed two-thirds of his daily course, when Theseus and his comrades of the chase disposed themselves upon the couches. Ixion's son lay here, and there Lelex, the hero of Troezen, took his place, his temples already sprinkled with grey; and others who had been deemed worthy of equal honor by the Acarnanian river-god, who was filled with joy in his noble guest. Without delay barefoot nymphs set the feast upon the tables, and then when the food had been removed, they set out the wine in jewelled cups. Then the noble hero, looking forth upon the wide water spread before his eyes, pointed with his finger and said: "What place is that? Tell me the name which that island bears. And yet it seems not to be one island." The river-god replied: "No, what you see is not one island. There are five islands lying there together; but the distance hides their divisions. And, that you may wonder the less at what Diana did when she was slighted, those islands once were nymphs, who, when they had slaughtered ten bullocks and had invited all the other rural gods to their sacred feast, forgot me as they led the festal dance. I swelled with rage, as full as when my flood flows at the fullest; and so, terrible in wrath, terrible in flood, I tore forests from forests, fields from fields; and with the place they stood on, I swept the nymphs away, who at last remembered me then, into the sea. There my flood and the sea, united, cleft the undivided ground into as many parts as now you see the Echinades over there amid the waves. But, as you yourself see, away, look, far away beyond the others is one island that I love: the sailors call it Perimele. She was beloved by me, and from her I took the name of maiden. Her father, Hippodamas, was enraged with this, and he hurled his daughter to her death down from a high cliff into the deep. I caught her, and supporting her as she swam, I cried: 'O god of the trident, to whom the lot gave the kingdom next to the world, even the wandering waves, bring aid, I pray, to one drowned by a father's cruelty; give her a place, O Neptune, or else let her become a place herself.' While I prayed a new land embraced her floating form and a solid island grew from her transformed shape."

With these words the river was silent. The story of the miracle had moved the hearts of all. But one mocked at their credulity, a scoffer at the gods, one reckless in spirit, Ixion's son, Pirithoüs.

"These are but fairy-tales you tell, Acheloüs," he said, "and you concede too much power to the gods, if they give and take away the forms of things." All the rest were shocked and disapproved such words, and especially Lelex, ripe both in mind and years, who replied: "The power of heaven is indeed immeasurable and has no bounds; and whatever the gods decree is done. And, that you may believe it, there stand in the Phrygian hill-country an oak and a linden-tree side by side, surrounded by a low wall. I have myself seen the spot; for Pittheus sent me to Phrygia, where his father once ruled.* Not far from the place I speak of is a marsh, once a habitable land, but now water, the haunt of divers and coots. Here Jupiter came in the guise of a mortal, and with his father came Atlas' grandson, he that bears the caduceus, his wings laid aside. To a thousand homes they came, seeking a place for rest; a thousand homes were barred against them. Still one house received them, humble indeed, thatched with straw and reeds from the marsh; but pious old Baucis and Philemon, of equal age, were in that cottage wedded in their youth, and in that cottage had grown old together; there they made their poverty light by owning it, and by bearing it in a contented spirit. It was of no use to ask for masters or for servants in that house; they two were the whole household, together they served and ruled. And so when the heavenly ones came to this humble home and, stooping, entered in at the lowly door, the old man set out a bench and bade them rest their limbs, while over this bench busy Baucis threw a rough covering. Then she raked aside the warm ashes on the hearth and fanned yesterday's coals to life, which she fed with leaves and dry bark, blowing them into flame with the breath of her old body. Then she took down from the roof some fine-split wood and dry twigs, broke them up and placed them under the little copper kettle. And she took the cabbage which her husband had brought in from the well-watered garden and lopped off the outside leaves. Meanwhile the old man with a forked stick reached down a chine of smoked bacon, which was hanging from a blackened beam and, cutting off a little piece of the long-cherished pork, he put it to cook in the boiling water. Meanwhile they beguiled the intervening time with their talk and patted down a mattress of

---

*Pittheus' father was Pelops; his land, Troezen, was where Theseus grew up.

soft sedge-grass, which they placed on a couch with frame and feet of willow. They threw drapery over this, which they were not accustomed to bring out except on festal days; but even this was a cheap thing and well-worn, a very good match for the willow couch. The gods reclined. The old woman, with her skirts tucked up, with trembling hands set out the table. But one of its three legs was too short; so she propped it up with a potsherd. When this had levelled the slope, she wiped it, thus levelled, with green mint. Next she placed on the board some olives, green and ripe, truthful Minerva's berries,[6] and some autumnal cornel-cherries pickled in the lees of wine; endives and radishes, cream cheese and eggs, lightly roasted in the warm ashes, all served in earthen dishes. After these viands, an embossed mixing-bowl of the same costly ware was set on together with cups of beechwood coated on the inside with yellow wax. A moment and the hearth sent its steaming viands on, and wine of no great age was brought out, which was then pushed aside to give a small space for the second course. Here were nuts and figs, with dried dates, plums and fragrant apples in broad baskets, and purple grapes just picked from the vines; in the centre of the table was a comb of clear white honey. Besides all this, pleasant faces were at the board and lively and abounding goodwill.

"Meanwhile they saw that the mixing-bowl, as often as it was drained, kept filling of its own accord, and that the wine welled up of itself. The two old people saw this strange sight with amaze and fear, and with upturned hands they both uttered a prayer, Baucis and the trembling old Philemon, and they craved indulgence for their fare and meagre entertainment. They had one goose, the guardian of their tiny estate;* and him the hosts were preparing to kill for their divine guests. But the goose was swift of wing, and quite wore the slow old people out in their efforts to catch him. He eluded their grasp for a long time, and finally seemed to flee for refuge to the gods themselves. Then the gods told them not to kill the goose. 'We are gods,' they said, 'and this wicked neighbourhood shall be punished as it deserves; but to you shall be given exemption from this punishment. Leave now your dwelling and come with us to that tall mountain there.' They both obeyed and, propped on their

---

*See the tale of Alcyone (book XI) for another reference to watch-geese.

staves, they struggled up the long slope. When they were a bowshot distant from the top, they looked back and saw the whole country-side covered with water, only their own house remaining. And, while they wondered at this, while they wept for the fate of their neighbours, that old house of theirs, which had been small even for its two occupants, was changed into a temple. Marble columns took the place of the forked wooden supports; the straw grew yellow and became a golden roof; there were gates richly carved, a marble pave-ment covered the ground. Then calmly the son of Saturn spoke: 'Now ask of us, you good old man, and you, wife, worthy of your good husband, any gift you will.' When he had spoken a word with Baucis, Philemon announced their joint decision to the gods: 'We ask that we may be your priests, and guard your temple; and, since we have spent our lives in constant company, we pray that the same hour may bring death to both of us—that I may never see my wife's tomb, nor be buried by her.' Their request was granted. They had the care of the temple as long as they lived. And at last, when, spent with extreme old age, they chanced to stand before the sacred edi-fice talking of old times, Baucis saw Philemon putting forth leaves, Philemon saw Baucis; and as the tree-top formed over their two faces, while still they could they cried with the same words: 'Farewell, dear mate,' just as the bark closed over and hid their lips. Even to this day the Bithynian peasant in that region points out two trees standing close together, and growing from one double trunk. These things were told me by staid old men who could have had no reason to deceive. With my own eyes I saw votive wreaths hanging from the boughs, and placing fresh wreaths there myself, I said: 'Those whom the gods care for are gods; let those who have worshipped be worshipped.'"

Lelex made an end: both the tale and the teller had moved them all; Theseus especially. When he would hear more of the wonderful doings of the gods, the Calydonian river-god, propped upon his elbow, thus addressed him: "Some there are, bravest of heroes, whose form has been once changed and remained in its new state. To others the power is given to assume many forms, as to you, Proteus, dweller in the earth-embracing sea. For now men saw you as a youth, now as a lion; now you were a raging boar, now a serpent whom men would fear to touch; now horns made you a bull; often you could appear as a stone, often, again, a tree; sometimes, assuming the form of flowing water, you were a stream, and sometimes a flame, the water's enemy.

"No less power had the wife of Autolycus, Erysichthon's daughter. This Erysichthon* was a man who scorned the gods and burnt no sacrifice on their altars. He, so the story goes, once violated the sacred grove of Ceres with the axe and profaned those ancient trees with iron. There stood among these a mighty oak with strength matured by centuries of growth, itself a grove. Round about it hung woollen fillets, votive tablets, and wreaths of flowers, witnesses of granted prayers. Often beneath this tree dryads held their festival dances; often with hand linked to hand in line they would encircle the great tree whose mighty girth was full fifteen ells. It towered as high above other trees as they were higher than the grass that grew beneath. Yet not for this did Triopas' son withhold his axe, as he bade his slaves cut down the sacred oak. But when he saw that they shrank back, the wretch snatched an axe from one of them and said: 'Though this be not only the tree that the goddess loves, but even the goddess herself, now shall its leafy top touch the ground.' He spoke; and while he poised his axe for the slanting stroke, the oak of Deo trembled and gave forth a groan; at the same time its leaves and its acorns grew pale, its long branches took on a pallid hue. But when that impious stroke cut into the trunk, blood came streaming forth from the severed bark, even as when a huge sacrificial bull has fallen at the altar, and from his smitten neck the blood pours forth. All were astonished, and one, bolder than the rest, tried to stop his wicked deed and stay his cruel axe. But the Thessalian looked at him and said: 'Take that to pay you for your pious thought!' and, turning the axe from the tree against the man, lopped off his head. Then, as he struck the oak blow after blow, from within the tree a voice was heard: 'I, a nymph most dear to Ceres, dwell within this wood, and I prophesy with my dying breath, and find my death's solace in it, that punishment is at hand for what you do.' But he accomplished his crime; and at length the tree, weakened by countless blows and drawn down by ropes, fell and with its weight laid low a wide stretch of woods around.

---

*The story of Erysichthon inspired the Stephen King novel and film *Thinner*.

"All the dryad sisters were stupefied at their own and their forest's loss and, mourning, clad in black robes, they went to Ceres and prayed her to punish Erysichthon. The beautiful goddess consented, and with a nod of her head shook the fields heavy with ripening grain. She planned in her mind a punishment that might make men pity (but that no man could pity him for such deeds), to rack him with dreadful Famine. But, since the goddess herself could not go to her (for the fates do not permit Ceres and Famine to come together), she summoned one of the mountain deities, a rustic oread, and thus addressed her: 'There is a place on the farthest border of icy Scythia, a gloomy and barren soil, a land without corn, without trees. Sluggish Cold dwells there and Pallor, Fear, and gaunt Famine. So, bid Famine hide herself in the sinful stomach of that impious wretch. Let no abundance satisfy her, and let her overcome my utmost power to feed. And, that the vast journey may not daunt you, take my chariot and my winged dragons and guide them aloft.' And she gave the reins into her hands. The nymph, borne through the air in her borrowed chariot, came to Scythia, and on a bleak mountain-top which men call Caucasus, unyoked her dragon steeds. Seeking out Famine, she saw her in a stony field, plucking with nails and teeth at the scanty herbage. Her hair hung in matted locks, her eyes were sunken, her face ghastly pale; her lips were wan and foul, her throat rough with scurf; her skin was hard and dry so that the entrails could be seen through it; her skinny hip-bones bulged out beneath her hollow loins, and her belly was but a belly's place; her breast seemed to be hanging free and just to be held by the framework of the spine; her thinness made her joints seem large, her knees were swollen, and her ankles were great bulging lumps.

"When the nymph saw her in the distance (for she did not dare approach her), she delivered to her the goddess' commands. And, though she tarried but a little while, though she kept far from her and had but now arrived, still she seemed to feel the famine. Then, mounting high in air, she turned her course and drove the dragons back to Thessaly.

"Famine did the bidding of Ceres, although their tasks are ever opposite, and flew through the air on the wings of the wind to the appointed mansion. Straight she entered the chamber of the impious king, who was sunk in deep slumber (for it was night); there she wrapped her skinny arms about him and filled him with herself, breathing upon his throat planted hunger. When her duty was done, she left the fertile world, and returned to the homes of want and her familiar caverns.

"Still gentle Sleep, hovering on peaceful wings, soothes Erysichthon. And in his sleep he dreams of feasting, champs his jaws on nothing, wearies tooth upon tooth, cheats his gullet with fancied food; for his banquet is nothing but empty air. But when he awakes, a wild craving for food lords it in his ravenous jaws and in his burning stomach. Straightway he calls for all that sea and land and air can furnish; with loaded tables before him, he complains still of hunger; in the midst of feasts seeks other feasts. What would be enough for whole cities, enough for a whole nation, is not enough for one. The more he sends down into his maw the more he wants. And as the ocean receives the streams from a whole land and is not filled with his waters, but swallows up the streams that come to it from afar; and as the all-devouring fire never refuses fuel, but burns countless logs, seeks ever more as more is given it, and is more greedy by reason of the quantity: so do the lips of impious Erysichthon receive all those banquets, and ask for more. All food in him is but the cause of food, and ever does he become empty by eating.

"And now famine and his belly's deep abyss had exhausted his ancestral stores; but even then ravenous Famine remained unexhausted and his raging greed was still unappeased. At last, when all his fortunes had been swallowed up, there remained only his daughter, worthy of a better father. Penniless, he sold even her. The high-spirited girl refused a master, and stretching out her hands over the neighbouring waves, she cried: 'Save me from slavery, O you who has already stolen my virginity.' This Neptune had taken; he did not refuse her prayer; and though her master following her had seen her but now, the god changed her form, gave her the features of a man and garments proper to a fisherman. Her master, looking at this person, said: 'Ho, you who conceal the dangling hook in a little bait, you that handle the rod; so may the sea be calm, so be the fish trustful in the wave for your catching, and feel no hook until you strike: where is she, tell me, who but now stood on this shore with mean garments and disordered hair, for I saw her standing upon the shore, and her tracks go no farther!' She perceived by this that the god's gift was working well, and, delighted that one asked her of herself, answered his question in these words: 'Whoever you are, excuse me, sir; I have not taken my eyes from this pool to look in any direction. I have been altogether bent on my fishing. And that you may believe me, so may the god of the sea assist this art of mine, as it is true that for a long time back no man has stood upon this shore except myself, and no woman, either.' Her master believed, and turning upon the sands, he left the spot, completely deceived. Then her former shape was given back to her. But when her father perceived that his daughter had the power to change her form, he sold her often and to many masters. But now in the form of a mare, now bird, now cow, now deer, away she went, and so found food, though not fairly, for her greedy father. At last, when the strength of the plague had consumed all these provisions, and but added to his fatal malady, the wretched man began to tear his own flesh with his greedy teeth and, by consuming his own body, fed himself.

"But why do I dwell on tales of others? I myself, young sirs, have often changed my form; but my power is limited in its range. For sometimes I appear as you see me now; sometimes I change to a serpent; again I am leader of a herd and put my strength into my horns—horns, I say, so long as I could. But now one of the weapons of my forehead is gone, as you yourself can see." He ended with a groan.

BOOK IX

THE NEPTUNIAN HERO ASKED the god why he groaned and what was the cause of his mutilated forehead. And thus the Calydonian river, binding up his rough locks with a band of reeds, made answer: "It is an unpleasant task you set; for who would care to chronicle his defeats? Still I will tell the story as it happened: nor was it so much a disgrace to be defeated as it was an honor to have striven at all, and the thought that my conqueror was so mighty is a great comfort to me. Deianira (if you have ever heard of her) was once a most beautiful maiden and the envied hope of many suitors. When along with them I entered the house of the father of the maid I sought, I said: 'Take me for son-in-law, O son of Parthaon.'* Hercules said the same, and the others yielded their claims to us two. He pleaded the fact that Jove was his father, pleaded his famous labours and all that he had overcome at the command of his stepmother. In reply I said: 'It is a shame for a god to give place to a mortal' (Hercules had not yet been made a god); 'you behold in me the lord of the waters which flow down their winding courses through your realm. If I wed your daughter, it will be no stranger from foreign shores; but I shall be one of your own countrymen, a part of your own kingdom. Only let it not be to my disadvantage that Queen Juno does not hate me and that no labours are imposed upon me in consequence of her hate. For Jove, from whom you boast that you have sprung, O son of Alcmena, is either not your father, or is so to your disgrace. Through your mother's sin you claim your father. Choose, then, whether you prefer to say that your claim to Jove is false, or to confess yourself the son of shame.' As I thus spoke he eyed me for a long while with lowering gaze and, unable to control his hot wrath

---

*Presumably Oeneus, the father of Deianira (though traditions of her parentage vary).

longer, he answered just these words: 'My hand is better than my tongue. Let me but win in fighting and you may win in speech'; and he came at me fiercely. I was ashamed to draw back after having spoken so boldly; and so I threw off my green coat, put up my arms, held my clenched hands out in front of my breast in position, and so prepared me for the fight. He caught up some dust in the hollow of his hand and threw it over me and in turn himself became yellow with the tawny sand. And now he caught at my neck, now at my quick-moving legs (or you would think he did), and attacked me at every point. My weight protected me and I was attacked in vain. Just like a cliff I stood, which, though the roaring waves dash against it, stands secure, safe in its own bulk. We draw apart a little space, then rush together again to the fray and stand firm in our tracks, each determined not to yield. Foot locked with foot, fingers with fingers clenched, brow against brow, with all my body's forward-leaning weight I pressed upon him. Like that have I seen two strong bulls rush together when they strive for the sleekest heifer in the pasture as the prize of conflict. The herd looks on in fear and trembling, not knowing to which one victory will award so great dominion. Three times without success did Alcides strive to push away from him my opposing breast; at the fourth attempt he shook off my embrace, broke my hold, and, giving me a sharp buffet with his hand (I am determined to tell it as it was), he whirled me round and clung with all his weight upon my back. If you will believe me (for I am not trying to gain any credit by exaggeration), I seemed to bear the weight of a mountain on my back. With difficulty I thrust in my arms streaming with sweat, with difficulty I broke his hard grip from my body. He pressed close upon me as I panted for breath, gave me no chance to regain my strength, and got me around the neck. Then at length I fell to my knees upon the earth and bit the dust. Finding myself no match for him in strength, I had recourse to my arts, and glided out of his grasp in the form of a long snake. But when I wound my body into twisting coils, and darted out my forked tongue and hissed fiercely at him, the hero of Tiryns only laughed, and mocking at my arts he said: 'It was the task of my cradle days to conquer snakes; and though you should outdo all other serpents, Acheloüs, how small a part of that Lernaean monster would you, just one snake, be?[1] For it throve on the wounds I gave;

nor was any one of its hundred heads cut off without its neck being the stronger by two succeeding heads. This creature, branching out with serpents sprung from death and thriving on destruction, I overmastered and, having overmastered, destroyed. And what do you think will become of you who, having assumed but a lying serpent form, make use of borrowed arms, who are masked in a shifting form?' So saying he fixed his vice-like grip upon my throat. I was in anguish, as if my throat were in a forceps' grip, and struggled to tear my jaws from his fingers. Conquered in this form also, there remained to me my third refuge, the form of a savage bull. And so in bull form I fought him. He threw his arms around my neck on the left, kept up with me as I ran at full speed, dragging upon me; and, finally, forced down my hard horns and thrust them into the earth and laid me low in the deep dust. Nor was this enough: holding my tough horn in his pitiless right hand, he broke it off and tore it from my forehead, mutilating me. This horn the naiads took, filled it with fruit and fragrant flowers, and hallowed it. And now the goddess of glad Abundance is enriched with my horn."

So spoke the river-god; and lo, a nymph girt like Diana, one of the attendants with locks flowing free, appeared and served them from her bounteous horn with all the fruits of Autumn, and wholesome apples for the second course. The dawn came on, and, as the first rays of the sun smote the mountain-tops, the youths took their departure; for they did not wait until the river should flow in peaceful current and all the flood-waters should subside. And Acheloüs hid his rustic features and his head, scarred from the wrenched-off horn, beneath his waves.

He was humbled indeed by the loss of his beauteous horn, which had been taken from him, though scathless in all else, a loss which he could hide with willow boughs and reeds entwined about his head. But, O savage Nessus, a passion for the same maiden utterly destroyed you, pierced through the body by a flying arrow. For, seeking his native city with his bride, the son of Jove had come to the swift waters of Euenus. The stream was higher than its wont, swollen with winter rains, full of wild eddies, and quite impassable. As the hero stood undaunted for himself, but anxious for his bride, Nessus came up, strong of limb and well acquainted with the fords, and said: "By my assistance, Alcides,*

---

*Hercules' name from birth until his meeting with the Delphic oracle.

she shall be set on that bank; and do you use your strength and swim across!" The Theban accordingly entrusted to Nessus' care the Calydonian maid, pale and trembling, fearing the river and the centaur himself. At once, just as he was, burdened with his quiver and the lion's skin (for he had tossed his club and curving bow across to the other bank), the hero said: "Since I have undertaken it, these waters shall be overcome." And in he plunged; nor did he seek out where the stream was easiest, and scorned to take advantage of the smoother waters. And now he had just gained the other bank, and was picking up his bow which he had thrown across, when he heard his wife's voice calling; and to Nessus, who was in act to betray his trust, he shouted: "Where is your vain confidence in your fleetness carrying you, you ravisher? To you, two-formed Nessus, I am talking: listen, and do not dare come between me and mine. If no fear of me has weight with you, at least your father's whirling wheel should prevent the outrage you intend.* You shall not escape, however much you trust in your horse's fleetness. With my deadly wound, if not with my feet, I shall overtake you." Suiting the action to his last words, he shot an arrow straight into the back of the fleeing centaur. The barbed point protruded from his breast. This he tore out, and spurting forth from both wounds came the blood mixed with the deadly poison of the Lernaean hydra. Nessus caught this, and muttering, "I shall not die unavenged," he gave his tunic, soaked with his blood, to Deianira as a gift, potent to revive waning love.

Meanwhile, long years had passed; the deeds of the mighty Hercules had filled the earth and had sated his stepmother's hate. Returning victorious from Oechalia, he was preparing to pay his vows to Jove at Cenaeum, when tattling Rumour came on ahead to your ears, Deianira, Rumour, who loves to mingle false and true and, though very small at first, grows huge through lying, and she reported that the son of Amphitryon[2] was enthralled by love of Iole.[3] The loving wife believes the tale, and completely overcome by the report of this new love, she indulges her tears at first and, poor creature, pours out her grief in a flood of weeping. But soon she says: "Why do I weep? My rival will rejoice at my tears. But since she is on her way here I must make haste and devise some plan

---

*Hercules refers to Ixion (see book IV), progenitor of all the Centaurs.

while I may, and while as yet another woman has not usurped my couch. Shall I complain or shall I grieve in silence? Shall I go back to Calydon or tarry here? Shall I leave my house or, if I can nothing more, stay and oppose her? What if, O Meleager, remembering that I am your sister, I make bold to plan some dreadful deed, and by killing my rival prove how much a woman's outraged feelings and grief can do?" Her mind has various promptings; but to all other plans she prefers to send to her husband the tunic soaked in Nessus' blood, in the hope that this may revive her husband's failing love; and to Lichas, ignorant of what he bears, with her own hands she all unwittingly commits the cause of her future woe, and with hon-eyed words the unhappy woman bids him take this present to her lord. The hero innocently received the gift and put on his shoulders the tunic soaked in the Lernaean hydra's poison.

He was offering incense and prayers amid the kindling flames and pouring wine from the libation bowl upon the marble altar: then was the virulence of that pest aroused and, freed by the heat, went stealing throughout the frame of Hercules. While he could, with his habitual manly courage he held back his groans. But when his endurance was conquered by his pain, he overthrew the altar and filled woody Oeta with his cries. At once he tries to tear off the deadly tunic; but where it is torn away, it tears the skin with it and, ghastly to relate, it either sticks to his limbs, from which he vainly tries to tear it, or else lays bare his torn muscles and huge bones. His very blood hisses and boils with the burning poison, as when a piece of red-hot metal is plunged into a pool. Without limit the greedy flames devour his vitals; the dark sweat pours from his whole body; his burnt sinews crackle and, while his very marrow melts with the hidden, deadly fire, he stretches suppliant hands to heaven and cries: "Come, feast, Saturnia, upon my destruction; feast, I say; look down, cruel one, from your lofty seat, behold my miserable end, and glut your savage heart! Or, if I merit pity even from my enemy—that is, from you—take away this hateful life, sick with its cruel suffer-ings and born for toil. This will be a gift to me, surely a fitting gift for a stepmother to bestow! Was it for this I slew Busiris, who de-filed his temples with strangers' blood? that I deprived the dread Antaeus of his mother's strength? that I did not fear the Spanish shepherd's triple form, nor your triple form, O Cerberus? Was it for this, O hands, that you broke the strong bull's horns? that Elis knows your toil, the waves of Stymphalus, the Parthenian woods? that by your prowess the gold-wrought girdle of Thermodon was secured, and that fruit guarded by the dragon's sleepless eyes? Was it for this that the centaurs could not prevail against me, nor the boar that wasted Arcadia? that it did not avail the hydra to grow by loss and gain redoubled strength? What, when I saw the Thracian's horses fat with human blood and those mangers full of mangled corpses and, seeing, threw them down and slew the master and the steeds themselves? By these arms the monster of Nemea lies crushed; upon this neck I upheld the sky! The cruel wife of Jove is weary of imposing toils; but I am not yet weary of performing them. But now a strange and deadly thing is at me, which neither by strength can I resist, nor yet by weapons nor by arms. Deep through my lungs steals the devouring fire, and feeds through all my frame. But Eurystheus is alive and well! And there are those who can believe that there are gods!"[4] He spoke and in sore distress went ranging along high Oeta; just as a bull carries about the shaft that has pierced his body, though the giver of the wound has fled. See him there on the mountains oft uttering heart-rending groans, oft roaring in agony, oft struggling to tear off his garments, uprooting great trunks of trees, stretching out his arms to his native skies.

Of a sudden he caught sight of Lichas cowering with fear and hiding beneath a hollow rock, and with all the accumulated rage of suffering he cried: "Was it you, Lichas, who brought this fatal gift? And shall you be called the author of my death?" The young man trembled, grew pale with fear, and timidly attempted to excuse his act. But while he was yet speaking and striving to clasp the hero's knees, Alcides caught him up and, whirling him thrice and again about his head, he hurled him far out into the Euboean sea, like a missile from a catapult. The youth stiffened as he yet hung in air; and as drops of rain are said to congeal beneath the chilling blast and change to snow, then whirling snowflakes condense to a soft mass and finally are packed in frozen hail: so, hurled by strong arms through the empty air, bloodless with fear, his vital moisture dried, he changed, old tradition says, to flinty rock. Even to this day in the Euboean sea a low rock rises from the waves, keeping the semblance of a human form; this rock, as if it were sentient, the sailors fear to

tread on, and they call it Lichas. But you, illustrious son of Jove, cut
down the trees which grew on lofty Oeta, built a huge funeral pyre,
and bade the son of Poeas, who set the torch beneath, to take in rec-
ompense your bow, capacious quiver and arrows, destined once
again to see the realm of Troy.[5] And as the pyre began to kindle with
the greedy flames, you spread the Nemean lion's skin on the top
and, with your club for pillow, laid you down with peaceful counte-
nance, as if, amid cups of generous wine and crowned with garlands,
you were reclining on a banquet-couch.

And now on all sides the spreading flames were crackling fiercely,
and licking at the careless limbs that scorned their power. The gods
felt fear for the earth's defender. Then Saturnian Jove, well pleased
(for he knew their thoughts), addressed them: "Your solicitude is a
joy to me, O gods of heaven, and I rejoice with all my heart that
I am called king and father of a grateful race of gods, and that my
offspring is safe under your protecting favor also. For, though you
offer this tribute to his own mighty deeds, still I myself am much
beholden to you. But let not your faithful hearts be filled with need-
less fear. Scorn not those flames! He who has conquered all things
shall conquer these fires which you see; nor shall he feel Vulcan's
power except in the part his mother gave him. Immortal is the part
which he took from me, and that is safe and beyond the power of
death, which no flame can destroy. And when this is done with
earth I shall receive him on the heavenly shores, and I trust that this
act of mine will be pleasing to all the gods. But if there is anyone, if
there is anyone, I say, who is going to be sorry that Hercules is made
a god, why then, he will begrudge the prize, but he will at least know
that it was given deservedly, and will be forced to approve the deed."
The gods assented; even Juno seemed to take all else complacently,
but not complacently the last words of Jove, and she grieved that she
had been singled out for rebuke. Meanwhile, whatever the flames
could destroy, Mulciber had now consumed, and no shape of
Hercules that could be recognized remained, nor was there anything
left which his mother gave. He kept traces only of his father; and as
a serpent, its old age sloughed off with its skin, revels in fresh life,
and shines resplendent in its bright new scales; so when the
Tirynthian put off his mortal frame, he gained new vigour in his
better part, began to seem of more heroic size, and to become awful

in his godlike dignity. Him the Almighty Father sped through the hollow clouds with his team of four, and set him amid the glittering stars.

Atlas felt his weight. But not even now did Eurystheus, the son of Sthenelus, put away his wrath; but his bitter hatred for the father he still kept up towards his race. Now, spent with long-continued cares, Argive Alcmena had in Iole one to whom she could confide her troubles, to whom she could relate her son's labours witnessed by all the world, and her own misfortunes. For by Hercules' command, Hyllus had received Iole to his arms and heart, and to him she was about to bear a child of that noble race. Thus spoke Alcmena to her: "May the gods be merciful to you at least and give you swift deliverance in that hour when in your need you call on Ilithyia,* goddess of frightened mothers in travail, whom Juno's hatred made so bitter against me. For when the natal hour of toil-bearing Hercules was near and the tenth sign was being traversed by the sun, my burden was so heavy and what I bore so great that you could know Jove was the father of the unborn child; nor could I longer bear my pangs. No, even now as I tell it, cold horror holds my limbs and my pains return even as I think of it. For seven nights and days I was in torture; then, spent with anguish, I stretched my arms to heaven and with a mighty wail I called upon Lucina and the three guardian deities of birth. Lucina came, indeed, but pledged in advance to give my life to cruel Juno. There she sat upon the altar before the door, listening to my groans, with her right knee crossed over her left, and with her fingers interlocked; and so she stayed the birth. Charms also, in low muttered words, she chanted, and the charms prevented my deliverance. I fiercely strove and, mad with pain, I shrieked out vain revilings against ungrateful Jove. I longed to die, and my words would have moved the unfeeling rocks. The Theban matrons stood around me, appealed to heaven, and strove to stay my grief. There was one of my attendants born of the common folk, Galanthis, with hair of reddish hue, active always in obedience to my commands, well loved by me for her faithful services. She felt assured that unjust Juno was working some spell against me; and as she was passing in and out the house, she saw the goddess

---

*In Latin, the Greek Ilithyia is more commonly called Lucina.

seated on the altar holding her clinched hands upon her knees, and said to her: 'Whoever you are, congratulate our mistress: Argive Alcmena is relieved; her prayers are answered and her child is born.' Up leaped the goddess of birth, unclinched her hands and spread them wide in consternation; my bonds were loosed and I was delivered of my child. They said Galanthis laughed in derision of the cheated deity. And as she laughed the cruel goddess caught her by the hair and dragged her on the ground; and, as the girl strove to rise, she kept her there and changed her arms into the forelegs of an animal. Her old activity remained and her hair kept its former hue; but her former shape was changed. And because she had helped her labouring mistress with her deceitful lips, through her mouth must she bring forth her young. And still, as of yore, she makes our dwelling-place her home."[6]

She spoke and, stirred by the warning fate of her former attendant, groaned deeply. And as she grieved her daughter-in-law thus addressed her: "And yet, my mother, it is the changed form of one not of our blood you grieve for. What if I should tell you of the strange misfortunes of my own sister? And yet my tears and grief check me and almost prevent my speech. She was her mother's only child (for I was born of my father's second wife), Dryope, the most beautiful of all the Oechalian maids. Her, a maid no more through the violence of him who rules at Delphi and at Delos,* Andraemon took and was counted happy in his wife.† There is a pool whose shelving banks take the form of sloping shores, the top of which a growth of myrtle crowns. Dryope had come here innocent of the fates and, that you may be the more indignant, with the intention of gathering garlands for the nymphs. In her arms she bore a pleasing burden, her infant boy not yet a full year old, and nursed him at her breast. Near the margin of the pool a plant of the water-lotus grew full of bright blossoms, the harbingers of fruit. To please her little son the mother plucked some of these blossoms, and I was in the act to do the same (for I was with her), when I saw drops of blood falling from the flowers and the branches shivering with horror.

---

*That is, Apollo.
†Andraemon's father, Oxylus, helped Hercules' sons win control of the Peloponessus.

For, you must know, as the slow rustics still relate, Lotis, a nymph, while fleeing from Priapus' vile pursuit, had taken refuge in this shape, changed as to features but keeping still her name.[7]

"But my sister knew nothing of this. And when she started back in terror and, with prayers to the nymphs, strove to leave the place, her feet clung, root-like, to the ground; she struggled to tear herself away, but nothing moved except the upper part of her body; the slow-creeping bark climbed upward from her feet and covered all her loins. When she saw this, she strove to tear her hair with her hands, but only filled her hands with leaves; for leaves now covered all her head. But the boy, Amphissos (for so his grandsire, Eurytus, had named him), felt his mother's breast grow hard, nor could he any longer draw his milky feast. I stood and saw your cruel fate, my sister, nor could I bring you any aid at all. And yet, so far as I could, I delayed the change by holding your growing trunk and branches fast in my embrace; and (shall I confess it?) I longed to hide me beneath that selfsame bark.

"But lo, her husband, Andraemon, and her most unhappy father came seeking for Dryope; and Dryope, in response to their questionings, I showed them as the lotus-tree. They printed kisses on the warm wood and, prostrate on the ground, they clung about the roots of their darling tree. And now my dear sister had only her face remaining, while all the rest was tree. Your tears rained down upon the leaves made from your poor body; and while they could, and your lips afforded utterance for your voice, it poured forth these complaints into the air: 'If oaths of wretched sufferers have any force, I swear by the gods that I have not merited this dreadful thing. In utter innocence I am suffering, and in innocence I have always lived. If I say not the truth, parched with the drought may I lose my foliage and may I be cut down by the axe and burned. But take this infant from his mother's limbs and give him to a nurse. Beneath my tree let him often come and take his milk; beneath my tree let him play. And when he learns to talk, have him greet his mother and sadly say: "Here in this tree-trunk is my mother hid." Still let him fear the pool, pluck no blossoms from the trees, and think all flowers are goddesses in disguise! Farewell, dear husband, and you, sister, and my father! No, if you love me still, protect my branches from the sharp knife, my foliage from the browsing sheep.

And, since it is not permitted me to bend down to you, reach up to me and let me kiss you while I may; and reach me once more my little son! Now I can say no more; for over my white neck the soft bark comes creeping, and I am buried in its overtopping folds. You need not close my eyes with your hands; without your service let the bark creep up and close my dying eyes!' In the same moment did she cease to speak and cease to be; and long did the new-made branches keep the warmth of the transformed body."

While Iole was telling this wonderful tale, and while Alcmena, herself also in tears, was drying with her sympathetic hand the tears of the daughter of Eurytus, a startling circumstance banished the grief of both. For there, in the deep doorway, stood a youth, almost a boy, with delicate down covering his cheeks, Iolaüs, restored in features to his youthful prime. Hebe, Juno's daughter, won by her husband's prayers, had given him this good; and when she was on the point of swearing that to no one after him would she bestow such gifts, Themis checked her vow. "For," said she, "Thebes is even now embroiled in civil strife, Capaneus shall be invincible but by the hand of Jove himself; the two brothers shall die by mutual wounds;[8] the prophet-king shall in the flesh behold his own spirits, engulfed by the yawning earth; and his son shall avenge parent on parent, filial and accursed in the selfsame act; stunned by these evil doings, banished from reason and from home, he shall be hounded by the Furies and by his mother's ghost until his wife shall ask of him the fatal golden necklace and the sword of Phegeus shall have drained his kinsman's blood. And then at last shall Callirhoë, daughter of Acheloüs, by prayer obtain from mighty Jove that her infant sons may attain at once to manly years, that so their victorious father's death be not long unavenged. Jove, thus prevailed upon, shall claim in advance for these the gifts of his stepdaughter and daughter-in-law, and shall in an act change beardless boys to men."[9]

When Themis, who knew what was to come, thus spoke with prophetic lips, a confused murmur of varying demands arose among the gods, and they inquired why they were not allowed to grant the same good to others. Pallantis lamented her husband's hoary age; mild Ceres bewailed Iasion's whitening locks; Mulciber demanded renewed life for Erichthonius, and Venus, too, with care for the future, stipulated that old Anchises' years should be restored.[10] Each god had his own favorite; and the noisy, partisan strife kept on, until Jupiter opened his lips and spoke: "Oh, if you have any reverence for me, what are you coming to? Does anyone suppose that he can so far prevail as to alter Fate's decrees? It was by the will of Fate that Iolaüs was restored to the years which he had passed, by Fate also Callirhoë's sons are destined to leap to manhood from infancy, and not by any ambition or strife of theirs. You, too (I say this that you may be of better mind), and me also the Fates control. If I could change them, old age would not bend low my Aeacus; Rhadamanthus, too, would enjoy perpetual youth, together with my Minos, who, because of the galling weight of age, is now despised and no longer reigns in his former state."*

Jove's words appeased the gods; nor could anyone complain when he saw Rhadamanthus, Aeacus, and Minos spent with years. Now Minos, while in his prime, had held great nations in fear of him by his very name; but at that time he was infirm with age and in fear of Miletus, son of Deione and Phoebus, proud of his youthful strength and parentage; and, though he believed that the youth was planning a rebellion against his kingdom, still he did not dare to banish him from his ancestral home. But of your own accord you fled, Miletus, and in your swift vessel crossed the Aegean sea and on the shores of Asia built a city which still bears its founder's name. There, while wandering along the banks of her father's winding stream, Cyanee, a nymph of unrivalled beauty, daughter of Maeander, who oft returns upon his former course, was known by you; and of this union Byblis and Caunus, twin progeny, were born.

Byblis is a warning that girls should not love unlawfully, Byblis, smitten with a passion for her brother, the grandson of Apollo. She loved him not as a brother, nor as a sister should. At first, indeed, she did not recognize the fires of love, nor think it wrong often to kiss him, often to throw her arms about her brother's neck, and she was long deceived by the semblance of sisterly affection. But gradually this affection changed to love: carefully adorned she came to see her brother, too anxious to seem lovely in his sight; and if any other seemed more beautiful to him, she envied her. But not yet did she have a clear vision of herself, felt no desire, prayed for no joy of

---

*These three sons of Jupiter instead become the judges of the dead.

love; but yet the hidden fire burned on. Now she called him her lord, now hated the name of brother, and wished him to call her Byblis, rather than sister.

Still in her waking hours she does not let her mind dwell on impure desires; but when she is relaxed in peaceful slumber, she often has visions of her love: she sees herself clasped in her brother's arms and blushes, though she lies sunk in sleep. When sleep has fled, she lies still for long and pictures again the visions of her slumber and at last, with wavering mind, she exclaims: "Oh, wretched girl that I am! What means this vision of the night? Oh, but I would not have it so! Why do I have such dreams? He is indeed beautiful, even to eyes that look unkindly on him, and is pleasing, and I could love him if he were not my brother; and he would be worthy of me; but it is my curse that I am his sister. If only when I am awake I make trial of no such thing, still may sleep often return with a dream like that! There's no one to tell in sleep, and there is no harm in imagined joy. O Venus and winged Cupid with your soft mother, how happy I was! How real my joy seemed! How my very heart melted within me as I lay! How sweet to remember it! And yet it was but a fleeting pleasure, and night was headlong and envious of the joys before me.

"Oh, if I could only change my name and be joined to you, how good a daughter I could be to your father, how good a son you could be to mine! we should have all things in common, if heaven allowed, except our grandparents. I should want you to be better born than I! You will be someone's husband, I suppose, O most beautiful; but to me, who have unfortunately drawn the same parents as yourself, you will never be anything but brother: what is our curse, that alone we shall have in common. What then do my dreams mean for me!—But what weight have dreams? or have dreams really weight? The gods forbid!—But surely the gods have loved their sisters; so Saturn married Ops, blood-kin of his; Oceanus, Tethys; the ruler of Olympus, Juno. But the gods are a law unto themselves! Why should I try to measure human fashions by divine and far different customs? Either my passion will flee from my heart if I forbid its presence, or if I cannot do this, I pray that I may die before I yield, and be laid out dead upon my couch, and as I lie there may my brother kiss my lips. And yet that act requires the will of two! Supposing it please me, it will seem a crime to him.

"Yet the Aeolidae* did not shun their sisters' chambers! But how do I know these things? Why do I quote these examples? Where am I tending? Get you far away, immodest love, and let not my brother be loved at all, except in sisterly fashion! And yet if he himself had first been smitten with love for me, I might perhaps smile upon his passion. Let me myself, then, woo him, since I should not have rejected his wooing! And can you speak? can you confess? Love will compel me: I can! or if shame holds my lips, a private letter shall confess my secret love."

This plan meets her approval; upon this her wavering mind decides. She half-way rises and, leaning upon her left elbow, says: "Let him see: let us confess our mad passion! Ah me! Where am I slipping? What hot love does my heart conceive?" And she proceeds to set down with a trembling hand the words she has thought out. In her right hand she holds her pen, in her left an empty waxen tablet. She begins, then hesitates and stops; writes on and hates what she has written; writes and erases; changes, condemns, approves; by turns she lays her tablets down and takes them up again. What she would do she knows not; on the point of action, she decides against it. Shame and bold resolution mingle in her face. She had begun with "sister"; but "sister" she decided to erase, and wrote these words on the amended wax: "A health to you, which, if you give it not to her, she will not have, one sends to you who loves you. Shamed, oh, she is ashamed to tell her name. And if you seek to know what I desire, I would that nameless I might plead my cause, and not be known as Byblis until my fond hopes were sure.

"You might have had knowledge of my wounded heart from my pale, drawn face, my eyes oft filled with tears, my sighs for no seeming cause, my frequent embraces and my kisses which you might have known, had you but marked them, were more than sisterly. Yet, though my heart was sore distressed, though full of hot passion, I have done everything (the gods are my witnesses) to bring myself to sanity. Long have I fought, unhappy that I am, to escape love's cruel charge, and I have borne more than you would think a girl could bear. But I have been overborne and am forced to confess my love, and with timid prayers to beg help of you. For you alone can

---

*Sons and daughters of the wind god Aeolus; they married each other.

save, you only can destroy your lover. Choose which you will do. It is no enemy who prays to you, but one who, though most closely joined to you, seeks to be more fully joined and to be bound by a still closer tie. Let old men know propriety and talk of what is fitting, what is right and wrong, and preserve the nice discrimination of the laws. But love is compliant and heedless for those of our age. What is allowed we have not yet discovered, and we believe all things allowed; and in this we do but follow the example of the gods. You and I have no harsh father, no care for reputation, no fear to hold us back. And yet that there may be cause for fear, beneath the sweet name of brother and sister we shall conceal our stolen love. I have full liberty to talk apart with you; we may embrace and kiss in open view of all. How much still is lacking? Pity her who confesses to you her love, but who would not confess if the utmost love did not compel her; and let it not be written on my sepulchre that for your sake I died."

The tablet was full when she had traced these words doomed to disappointment, the last line coming to the very edge. Straightway she stamped the shameful letter with her seal which she moistened with her tears (for moisture failed her tongue). Then, blushing hotly, she called one of her attendants and with timorous and coaxing voice said: "Take these tablets, most faithful servant, to my—"; and after a long silence added, "brother." While she was giving them, the tablets slipped from her hands and fell. Though much perturbed by the omen, she still sent the letter. The servant, finding a fitting time, went to the brother and delivered to him the message of confession. The grandson of Maeander, in a passion of sudden rage, threw down the tablets which he had taken and read half through, and, scarcely restraining his hands from the trembling servant's throat, he cried: "Flee while you may, you rascally promoter of a lawless love! But if your fate did not involve our own disgrace, you should have paid the penalty for this with death." He fled in terror and reported to his mistress her brother's savage answer. When Byblis heard that her love had been repulsed, she grew pale, and her whole body trembled in the grip of an icy chill. But when her senses came back, her mad love came back with equal force; and then with choked and feeble utterance she spoke: "Deservedly I suffer! For why did I so rashly tell him of this wound of mine? Why was I in such a haste to commit to tablets what should have been concealed?

I should first have tried his disposition towards me by obscure hints. That my voyage might have a favorable wind, I should first have tested with a close-reefed sail what the wind was, and so have fared in safety; but now with sails full spread I have encountered unexpected winds. And so my ship is on the rocks; with the full force of ocean am I overwhelmed, and have no power to turn back upon my course.

"No, by the clearest omens I was warned not to confess my love, at the time when the letter fell from my hand as I bade my servant bear it, and taught me that my hopes must fall as well. Should not that day or my whole purpose—say rather, should not the day have been postponed? God himself warned me and gave me clear signs had I not been mad with love. And yet I should have told him with my own lips, I should in person have confessed my passion, and not have trusted my inmost heart to waxen tablets! He should have seen my tears, he should have seen his lover's face; I could have spoken more than any tablets could hold; I could have thrown my arms about his unwilling neck and, if I were rejected, I could have seemed at the point of death, could have embraced his feet and, lying prostrate there, have begged for life. I should have done all things, which together might have won his stubborn soul if one by one they could not. Perhaps the servant whom I sent made some mistake: did not approach him rightly; chose an unfitting time, I suppose, sought an hour when his mind was full of other things.

"All this has wrought against me. For he is no tigress' son; he has no heart of hard flint or solid iron or adamant; no lioness has suckled him. He shall be conquered! I must go to him again; nor shall I weary in my attempts while I have breath left in my body. For if it were not too late to undo what I have done, it was the best thing not to have begun at all; but now that I have begun, the second best is to win through with what I have begun. Though I should now abandon my suit, he cannot help remembering always how far I have already dared. And in that case, just because I did give up, I shall seem either to have been fickle in my desire, or else to have been trying to tempt him and catch him in a snare. Whichever of these he thinks of me, he certainly will not believe that I have been overcome by that god who more than all others rules and inflames our hearts, but that I was moved by lust alone. In short, I cannot now undo the wrong that I have done. I have both written and have wooed him: and rash I was to do so. Though I do nothing more, I cannot seem other than guilty in his sight. As for the rest, I have much to hope and nothing to fear." Thus does she argue; and (so great is her uncertainty of soul), while she is sorry that she tried at all, she wants to try again. The wretched girl tries every art within her power, but is repeatedly repulsed. At length, when there seemed to be no limit to her importunity, the youth fled from his native land and from this shameful wooing, and founded a new city in another land.

Then, they say, the wretched daughter of Miletus lost all control of reason; she tore her garments from her breast, and in mad passion beat her arms. Now before all the world she rages and publicly proclaims her unholy love. She forsakes her land and her hated home and follows after her fleeing brother. And just as, crazed by your thyrsus, O son of Semele, your Ismarian worshippers throng your triennial orgies, so the women of Bubassus beheld Byblis go shrieking through the broad fields. Leaving these behind, she wandered through the land of Caria, by the well-armed Leleges and the country of the Lycians. And now she had passed by Cragus and Limyre and Xanthus' stream and the ridge where dwelt Chimaera, that fire-breathing monster with lion's head and neck and serpent's tail. Clear beyond the wooded ridge she went, and then at last, wearied with pursuing, you fell, O Byblis, and lay there with your hair streaming over the hard ground and your face buried in the fallen leaves. Often the Lelegeian nymphs try to lift her in their soft arms, often advise her how she may cure her love and offer comfort to her unheeding soul. Byblis lies without a word, clutching the green herbs with her fingers, and watering the grass with her flowing tears. The naiads are said to have given her a vein of tears which could never dry; for what greater gift had they to bestow? Straightway, as drops of pitch drip forth from the gashed pine-bark; as sticky bitumen oozes from rich heavy earth; or as, at the approach of the soft breathing west-wind, the water which had stood frozen with the cold now melts beneath the sun; so Phoebean Byblis, consumed by her own tears, is changed into a fountain, which to this day in those valleys has the name of its mistress, and issues forth from under a dark ilex-tree.

The story of this unnatural passion would, perhaps, have been the talk of Crete's hundred towns, if Crete had not lately had a wonder of its own in the changed form of Iphis. For there once lived in the Phaestian country, not far from the royal town of Gnosus, a man named Ligdus, otherwise unknown, of free-born but humble parentage; nor was his property any greater than his birth. But he was of blameless life and trustworthy. When now the time drew near when his wife should give birth to a child, he warned and instructed her with these words: "There are two things which I would ask of Heaven: that you may be delivered with the least possible pain, and that your child may be a boy. Girls are more trouble, and fortune has denied them strength. Therefore (and may Heaven save the mark!), if by chance your child should prove to be a girl (I hate to say it, and may I be pardoned for the impiety), let her be put to death." He spoke, and their cheeks were bathed in tears, both his who ordered and hers to whom the command was given. Nevertheless, Telethusa ceaselessly implored her husband (though all in vain) not so to straiten her expectation; but Ligdus remained steadfast in his determination. And now the time was at hand when the child should be born, when at midnight, in a vision of her dreams, she saw or seemed to see the daughter of Inachus standing before her bed, accompanied by a solemn train of sacred beings. She had crescent horns upon her forehead, and a wheaten garland yellow with bright gold about her head, a sight of regal beauty. Near her were seen the dog Anubis, sacred Bubastis, dappled Apis, and the god who enjoins silence with his finger on his lips; there also were the sacred rattles, and Osiris, ceaseless object of his worshippers' desire, and the Egyptian serpent swelling with sleep-producing venom.[11] She seemed to be thoroughly awake and to see all things about her clearly as the goddess spoke to her: "O Telethusa, one of my own worshippers, put away your grievous cares, and think not to obey your husband's orders. And do not hesitate, when Lucina has delivered you, to save your child, whatever it shall be. I am the goddess who brings help and succour to those who call upon me; nor shall you have cause to complain that you have worshipped a thankless deity." Having so admonished her, the goddess left the chamber. Then joyfully the Cretan woman arose from her bed, and, raising her innocent hands in suppliance to the stars, she prayed that her vision might come true.

When now her pains increased and the birth was accomplished, and the child proved to be a girl (though without the father's knowledge), the mother, with intent to deceive, bade them feed the boy. Circumstances favored her deceit, for the nurse was the only one who knew of the trick. The father paid his vows and named the child after its grandfather: the grandfather had been Iphis. The mother rejoiced in the name; for it was of common gender and she could use it without deceit. And so the trick, begun with pious fraud, remained undetected. The child was dressed like a boy, and its face would have been counted lovely whether you assigned it to a girl or boy.

Meanwhile thirteen years passed by; and then your father found you a bride, O Iphis, in golden-haired Ianthe, a girl the most praised among the Phaestian women for the rich dower of her beauty, the daughter of Cretan Telestes. The two were of equal age and equal loveliness, and from the same teachers had they received their first instruction in childish rudiments. And so love came to both their hearts all unsuspected and filled them both with equal longing. But they did not both love with equal hope: Ianthe looked forward confidently to marriage and the fulfilment of her troth, and believed that she whom she thought to be a man would some day be her husband. Whereas Iphis loved without hope of her love's fulfilment, and for this very reason loved all the more—a girl madly in love with another girl. Scarcely holding back her tears, "Oh, what will be the end of me," she said, "whom a love possesses that no one ever heard of, a strange and monstrous love? If the gods wished to save me they should have saved me; if not, and they wished to ruin me, they should at least have given me some natural woe, within the bounds of experience. Cows do not love cows, nor mares, mares; but the ram desires the sheep, and his own doe follows the stag. So also birds mate, and in the whole animal world there is no female smitten with love for female. I would I were no female! Nevertheless, that Crete might produce all monstrous things, the daughter of the Sun loved a bull—a female to be sure, and male; my passion is more mad than that, if the truth be told. Yet she had some hope of her love's fulfilment; yet she enjoyed her bull by a trick and the disguise of the heifer, and it was the lover who was deceived. Though all the ingenuity in the world should be collected here, though Daedalus himself should fly back on waxen wings, what could he do? With all his learned arts could he make me into a boy from a girl? or could he change you, Ianthe?

"No, then, be strong of soul, take courage, Iphis, and banish from your heart this hopeless, foolish love. See what you were born, unless you yourself deceive yourself as well as others; seek what is lawful, and love as a woman ought to love! It is hope of fulfilment that begets love, and hope that keeps it alive. And of this hope the nature of things deprives you. No guardian keeps you from her dear embrace, no watchfulness of a jealous husband, no cruel father; nor does she herself deny your suit. And yet you cannot have her, nor can you be happy, though all things should favor you, though gods and men should work for you. And even now none of my prayers have been denied; the gods, compliant, have given me whatever was theirs to give; and what I wish my father wishes, she herself and her father all desire. But nature will not have it so, nature, more mighty than they all, who alone is working my distress. And lo, the longed-for time is come, my wedding-day is at hand, and soon Ianthe will be mine—and yet not mine. In the midst of water I shall thirst. Why do you come, Juno, goddess of brides, and Hymen, to these wedding rites, where no man takes the woman for his bride, but where both are brides?" She broke off speech with these words. The other maiden burned with equal love, and prayed, Hymen, that you would make haste to come. And Telethusa, fearing what Ianthe sought, put off the time, now causing delay because of a pretended sickness, often giving for reason some ill-omened vision she had seen. But now she had exhausted every possible excuse, and the postponed wedding-day was close at hand, and but one more day remained. Then the mother took the encircling fillets from her own and her daughter's heads, and with flowing locks she prayed, clinging to the altar: "O Isis, who dwells in Paraetonium and the Mareotic fields and Pharos and the sevenfold waters of the Nile, help us, I pray, and heal our sore distress. You, goddess, you and these your symbols once I saw and recognized them all—the clashing sound, your train, the torches, [the rattling] of the sistra—and with retentive mind I noted your commands. That this, my daughter still looks on the light, that I have not been punished, behold, is all because of your counsel and your gift. Pity us two, and help us with your aid!" Tears followed on her words. The goddess seemed to move, indeed, did move her altar, the doors of the temple shook, her moon-shaped horns shot forth gleams of light and the sistrum rattled noisily. Not yet quite free from care and yet rejoicing in the good omen, the mother left the temple; and Iphis walked beside her as she went, but with a longer stride than was her wont. Her face seemed of a darker hue, her strength seemed greater, her very features sharper, and her locks, all unadorned, were shorter than before. She seemed more vigorous than was her girlish wont. In fact, you who but lately were a girl are now a boy! Go, make your offerings at the shrines; rejoice with gladness unafraid! They make their offerings at the shrines and add a votive tablet; the tablet had this inscription: THESE GIFTS AS MAN DID IPHIS PAY WHICH ONCE AS MAID HE VOWED. The morrow's sun had revealed the broad world with its rays, when Venus, Juno, and Hymen met at the marriage fires, and the boy Iphis gained his Ianthe.

BOOK X

SO THROUGH THE BOUNDLESS air Hymen, clad in a saffron mantle, departed and took his way to the country of the Ciconians, and was summoned by the voice of Orpheus, though all in vain. He was present, it is true; but he brought neither the hallowed words, nor joyous faces, nor lucky omen. The torch also which he held kept sputtering and filled the eyes with smoke, nor would it catch fire for any brandishing. The outcome of the wedding was worse than the beginning; for while the bride was strolling through the grass with a group of naiads in attendance, she fell dead, smitten in the ankle by a serpent's tooth. When the bard of Rhodope had mourned her to the full in the upper world, that he might try the shades as well he dared to go down to the Stygian world through the gate of Taenarus. And through the unsubstantial throngs and the ghosts who had received burial, he came to Persephone and him who rules those unlovely realms, lord of the shades. Then, singing to the music of his lyre, he said: "O divinities who rule the world which lies beneath the earth, to which we all fall back who are born mortal, if it is lawful and you permit me to lay aside all false and doubtful speech and tell the simple truth: I have not come down here to see dark Tartara, nor yet to bind the three necks of Medusa's monstrous offspring, rough with serpents. The cause of my journey is my wife, into whose body a trodden serpent shot his poison and so snatched away her budding years. I have desired strength to endure, and I will not deny that I have tried to bear it. But Love has overcome me, a god well-known in the upper world, but whether here or not I do not know; and yet I surmise that he is known here as well, and if the story of that old-time ravishment is not false, you, too, were joined by love. By these fearsome places, by this huge void and these vast and silent realms, I beg of you, unravel the fates of my Eurydice, too quickly run. We are in all things due to you, and though we tarry on earth a little while, slow or swift we speed to one abode. Here we all make our way; this is our final home; yours is the longest sway over the human race. She also shall be yours to rule when of ripe age she shall have lived out her allotted years. I ask the enjoyment of her as a wish; but if the fates deny this privilege for my wife, I am resolved not to return. Rejoice in the death of two."

As he spoke thus, accompanying his words with the music of his lyre, the bloodless spirits wept; Tantalus did not catch at the fleeing wave; Ixion's wheel stopped in wonder; the vultures did not pluck at the liver; the Belides rested from their urns, and you, O Sisyphus, sat upon your stone. Then first, tradition says, conquered by the song, the cheeks of the Eumenides were wet with tears; nor could the queen nor he who rules the lower world refuse the suppliant. They called Eurydice. She was among the new shades and came with steps halting from her wound. Orpheus, the Thracian, then received his wife and with her this condition, that he should not turn his eyes backward until he had gone forth from the valley of Avernus, or else the gift would be in vain. They took the up-sloping path through places of utter silence, a steep path, indistinct and clouded in pitchy darkness. And now they were nearing the margin of the upper earth, when he, afraid that she might fail him, eager for sight of her, turned back his longing eyes; and instantly she slipped into the depths. He stretched out his arms, eager to catch her or to feel her clasp; but, unhappy one, he clasped nothing but the yielding air. And now, dying a second time, she made no complaint against her husband; for of what could she complain but that she was beloved? She spake one last "farewell" which scarcely reached her husband's ears, and fell back again to the place from which she had come.

By his wife's double death Orpheus was stunned, like that frightened creature who saw the three-headed dog with chains on his middle neck, whose numbing terror left him only when his former nature left, and the petrifying power crept through his body; or like that Olenos, who took sin upon himself and was willing to seem guilty; and like you, luckless Lethaea, too boastful of your beauty, once two hearts joined in close embrace, but now two stones which well-watered Ida holds. Orpheus prayed and wished in vain to cross the Styx a second time, but the keeper drove him back. Seven days he sat there on the bank in filthy rags and with no taste of food.

Care, anguish of soul, and tears were his nourishment. Complaining that the gods of Erebus were cruel, he betook himself to high Rhodope and wind-swept Haemus.

Three times had the sun finished the year and come to watery Pisces; and Orpheus had shunned all love of womankind, whether because of his ill success in love, or whether he had given his troth once for all. Still, many women felt a passion for the bard; many grieved for their love repulsed. He set the example for the people of Thrace of giving his love to tender boys, and enjoying the spring-time and first flower of their youth.

A hill there was, and on the hill a wide-extending plain, green with luxuriant grass; but the place was devoid of shade. When here the heaven-descended bard sat down and smote his sounding lyre, shade came to the place. There came the Chaonian oak, the grove of the Heliades, the oak with its deep foliage, the soft linden, the beech, the virgin laurel-tree, the brittle hazel, the ash, suitable for spear-shafts, the smooth silver-fir, the ilex-tree bending with acorns, the pleasant plane, the many-colored maple, river-haunting willows, the lotus, lover of the pools, the evergreen boxwood, the slender tamarisk, the double-hued myrtle, the viburnum with its dark-blue berries. You also, pliant-footed ivy, came, and along with you tendrilled grapes, and the elm-trees, draped with vines; the mountain-ash, the forest-pines, the arbute-tree, loaded with ruddy fruit, the pliant palm, the prize of victory, the bare-trunked pine with broad, leafy top, pleasing to the mother of the gods, since Attis, dear to Cybele, exchanged for this his human form and stiffened in its trunk.[1]

Amid this throng came the cone-shaped cypress, now a tree, but once a boy, beloved by that god who strings the lyre and strings the bow. For there was a mighty stag, sacred to the nymphs who haunt the Carthaean plains, whose wide-spreading antlers gave ample shade to his own head. His antlers gleamed with gold, and down on his shoulders hung a gem-mounted collar set on his rounded neck. Upon his forehead a silver boss bound with small thongs was worn, and worn there from his birth. Pendent from both his ears, about his hollow temples, were gleaming pearls. He, quite devoid of fear and with none of his natural shyness, frequented men's homes and let even strangers stroke his neck. But more than to all the rest,

O Cyparissus, loveliest of the Cean race, was he dear to you. It was you who led the stag to fresh pasturage and to the waters of the clear spring. Now would you weave bright garlands for his horns; now, sitting like a horseman on his back, now here, now there, would gleefully guide his soft mouth with purple reins.

It was high noon on a summer's day, when the spreading claws of the shore-loving Crab were burning with the sun's hot rays. Weary, the stag had lain down upon the grassy earth and was drinking in the coolness of the forest shade. Him, all unwittingly, the boy, Cyparissus, pierced with a sharp javelin, and when he saw him dying of the cruel wound, he resolved on death himself. What did not Phoebus say to comfort him! How he warned him to grieve in moderation and consistently with the occasion! The lad only groaned and begged this as the good he most desired from heaven, that he might mourn for ever. And now, as his life forces were exhausted by endless weeping, his limbs began to change to a green color, and his locks, which but now overhung his snowy brow, were turned to a bristling crest, and he became a stiff tree with slender top looking to the starry heavens. The god groaned and, full of sadness, said: "You shall be mourned by me, shall mourn for others, and your place shall always be where others grieve."

Such was the grove the bard had drawn, and he sat, the central figure in an assembly of wild beasts and birds. And when he had tried the chords by touching them with his thumb, and his ears told him that the notes were in harmony although they were of different pitch, he raised his voice in this song: "From Jove, O Muse, my mother—for all things yield to the sway of Jove—inspire my song! Oft have I sung the power of Jove before; I have sung the giants in a heavier strain, and the victorious bolts hurled on the Phlegraean plains. But now I need the gentler touch, for I would sing of boys beloved by gods, and maidens inflamed by unnatural love and paying the penalty of their lust.

"The king of the gods once burned with love for Phrygian Ganymede, and something was found which Jove would rather be than what he was. Still he did not deign to take the form of any bird except that which could bear his thunderbolts. Without delay he cleft the air on his lying wings and stole away the Trojan boy, who even now, though against the will of Juno, mingles the nectar and attends the cups of Jove.

"You also, youth of Amyclae, Phoebus would have set in the sky, if grim fate had given him time to set you there. Still in what fashion you may you are immortal: as often as spring drives winter out and the Ram succeeds the watery Fish, so often do you come up and blossom on the green turf. Above all others did my father love you, and Delphi, set at the very centre of the earth, lacked its presiding deity while the god was haunting Eurotas' stream and Sparta, the unwalled. No more has he thought for zither or for bow. Entirely heedless of his usual pursuits, he refuses not to bear the nets, nor hold the dogs in leash, nor go as comrade along the rough mountain ridges. And so with long association he feeds his passion's flame. And now Titan was about midway between the coming and the banished night, standing at equal distance from both extremes; they strip themselves and, gleaming with rich olive oil, they try a contest with the broad discus. This, well poised, Phoebus sent flying through the air and cleft the opposite clouds with the heavy iron. Back to the wonted earth after long time it fell, revealing the hurler's skill and strength combined. Straightway the Taenarian youth, heedless of danger and moved by eagerness for the game, ran out to take up the discus. But it bounded back into the air from the hard earth beneath full in your face, O Hyacinthus. The god grows deadly pale even as the boy, and catches up the huddled form; now he seeks to warm you again, now tries to staunch your dreadful wound, now strives to stay your parting soul with healing herbs. But his arts are of no avail; the wound is past all cure. Just as when in a garden, if someone has broken off violets or brittle poppies or lilies, still hanging from the yellow stems, fainting they suddenly droop their withered heads and can no longer stand erect, but gaze, with tops bowed low, upon the earth: so the dying face lies prone, the neck, its strength all gone, cannot sustain its own weight and falls back upon the shoulders. 'You are fallen, defrauded of your youth's prime, Oebalides,' says Phoebus, 'and in your wound I see my guilt; you are my cause of grief and self-reproach; my hand must be proclaimed the cause of your destruction. I am the author of your death. And yet, what is my fault, unless my playing with you can be called a fault, unless my loving you can be called a fault? And oh, that I might give up my life for you, so well-deserving, or give it up with you! But since we are held from this by the laws of fate, you shall be always with me, and shall stay on my mindful lips. You shall my lyre, struck by my hand, you shall my songs proclaim. And as a new flower, by your markings shall you imitate my groans. Also the time will come when a most valiant hero shall be linked with this flower, and by the same markings shall he be known.'[2] While Apollo thus spoke with truth-telling lips, behold, the blood, which had poured out on the ground and stained the grass, ceased to be blood, and in its place there sprang a flower brighter than Tyrian dye. It took the form of the lily, except that the one was of purple hue, while the other was silvery white. Phoebus, not satisfied with this—for it was he who wrought the honoring miracle—himself inscribed his grieving words upon the leaves, and the flower bore the marks, AI AI, letters of lamentation, drawn thereon. Sparta, too, was proud that Hyacinthus was her son, and even to this day his honor still endures; and still, as the anniversary returns, as did their sires, they celebrate the Hyacinthia in solemn festival.

"But if you should chance to ask Amathus, rich in veins of ore, if she is proud of her Propoetides, she would repudiate both them and those whose foreheads once were deformed by two horns, from which they also took their name, Cerastae. Before their gates there used to stand an altar sacred to Jove, the god of hospitality; if any stranger, ignorant of the crime, had seen this altar all smeared with blood, he would suppose that suckling calves or two-year-old sheep of Amathus had been sacrificed thereon. It was the blood of slaughtered guests! Outraged by these impious sacrifices, fostering Venus was preparing to desert her cities and her Ophiusian plains; 'but,' she said, 'wherein have these pleasant regions, wherein have my cities sinned? What crime is there in them? Rather let this impious race pay the penalty by exile or by death, or by some punishment midway betwixt death and exile. And what other can that be than the penalty of a changed form?' While she hesitates to what she shall change them, her eyes fall upon their horns, and she reminds herself that these can still be left to them. And so she changes their big bodies into savage bulls.

"But the foul Propoetides dared to deny the divinity of Venus. In consequence of this, through the wrath of the goddess they are said to have been the first to prostitute their bodies and their fame; and as their shame vanished and the blood of their faces hardened, they were turned with but small change to hard stones.

"Pygmalion had seen these women spending their lives in shame, and, disgusted with the faults which in such full measure nature had given the female mind, he lived unmarried and long was without a partner of his couch. Meanwhile, with wondrous art he successfully carves a figure out of snowy ivory, giving it a beauty more perfect than that of any woman ever born. And with his own work he falls in love. The face is that of a real maiden, whom you would think living and desirous of being moved, if modesty did not prevent. So does his art conceal his art. Pygmalion looks in admiration and is inflamed with love for this semblance of a form. Often he lifts his hands to the work to try whether it be flesh or ivory; nor does he yet confess it to be ivory. He kisses it and thinks his kisses are returned. He speaks to it, grasps it and seems to feel his fingers sink into the limbs when he touches them; and then he fears that he might leave marks or bruises on them. Now he addresses it with fond words of love, now brings it gifts pleasing to girls, shells and smooth pebbles, little birds and many-hued flowers, and lilies and colored balls, with tears of the Heliades that drop down from the trees. He drapes its limbs also with robes, puts gemmed rings upon its fingers and a long necklace around its neck; pearls hang from the ears and chains adorn the breast. All these are beautiful; but no less beautiful is the statue unadorned. He lays it on a bed spread with coverlets of Tyrian hue, calls it the consort of his couch, and rests its reclining head upon soft, downy pillows, as if it could enjoy them.

"And now the festal day of Venus had come, which all Cyprus thronged to celebrate; heifers with spreading horns covered with gold had fallen 'neath the death-stroke on their snowy necks, and the altars smoked with incense. Pygmalion, having brought his gift to the altar, stood and falteringly prayed: 'If ye, O gods, can give all things, I pray to have as wife—' he did not dare add 'my ivory maid,' but said, 'one like my ivory maid.' But golden Venus (for she herself was present at her feast) knew what that prayer meant; and, as an omen of her favoring deity, thrice did the flame burn brightly and leap high in air. When he returned he sought the image of his maid, and bending over the couch he kissed her. She seemed warm to his touch. Again he kissed her, and with his hands also he touched her breast. The ivory grew soft to his touch and, its hardness vanishing, gave and yielded beneath his fingers, as Hymettian wax grows soft under the sun and, moulded by the thumb, is easily shaped to many forms and becomes usable through use itself. The lover stands amazed, rejoices still in doubt, fears he is mistaken, and tries his hopes again and yet again with his hand. Yes, it was real flesh! The veins were pulsing beneath his testing finger. Then did the Paphian hero pour out copious thanks to Venus, and again pressed with his lips real lips at last. The maiden felt the kisses, blushed and, lifting her timid eyes up to the light, she saw the sky and her lover at the same time. The goddess graced with her presence the marriage she had made; and ere the ninth moon had brought her crescent to the full, a daughter was born to them, Paphos, from whom the island takes its name.

"Cinyras was her son and, had he been without offspring, might have been counted fortunate. A horrible tale I have to tell. Far away be daughters, far away, fathers; or, if your minds find pleasure in my songs, do not give credence to this story, and believe that it never happened; or, if you do believe it, believe also in the punishment of the deed. If, however, nature allows a crime like this to show itself, I congratulate the Ismarian people, and this our city; I congratulate this land on being far away from those regions where such iniquity is possible. Let the land of Panchaia* be rich in balsam, let it bear its cinnamon, its costum, its frankincense exuding from the trees, its flowers of many sorts, provided it bear its myrrh-tree, too: a new tree was not worth so great a price. Cupid himself avers that his weapons did not harm you, Myrrha, and clears his torches from that crime of yours. One of the three sisters with firebrand from the Styx and with swollen vipers blasted you. It is a crime to hate one's father, but such love as this is a greater crime than hate. From every side the pick of princes desire you; from the whole Orient young men are here vying for your couch; out of them all choose one for your husband, Myrrha, only let not one be among them all. She, indeed, is fully aware of her vile passion and fights against it and says within herself: 'To what is my purpose tending? What am I planning? O gods, I pray you, and piety and the sacred rights of parents, keep this sin from me and fight off my crime, if indeed it is a crime. But I am not sure, for piety refuses to condemn such love as this.

---

*Panchaia, an island east of Arabia, evokes a remote Near Eastern locale.

Other animals mate as they will, nor is it thought base for a heifer to endure her sire, nor for his own offspring to be a horse's mate; the goat goes in among the flocks which he has fathered, and the very birds conceive from those from whom they were conceived. Happy they who have such privilege! Human civilization has made spiteful laws, and what nature allows, the jealous laws forbid. And yet they say that there are tribes among whom mother with son, daughter with father mates, so that natural love is increased by the double bond. Oh, wretched me, that it was not my lot to be born there, and that I am thwarted by the mere accident of place! Why do I dwell on such things? Avaunt, lawless desires! Worthy to be loved is he, but as a father.—Well, if I were not the daughter of great Cinyras, to Cinyras could I be joined. But as it is, because he is mine, he is not mine; and, while my very propinquity is my loss, would I as a stranger be better off? It is well to go far away, to leave the borders of my native land, if only I may flee from crime; but unhappy passion keeps the lover here, that I may see Cinyras face to face, may touch him, speak with him and kiss him, if nothing else is granted. But can you hope for anything else, you unnatural girl? Think how many ties, how many names you are confusing! Will you be the rival of your mother, the mistress of your father? Will you be called the sister of your son, the mother of your brother? And have you no fear of the sisters with black snakes in their hair, whom guilty souls see brandishing cruel torches before their eyes and faces? But you, while you have not yet sinned in body, do not conceive sin in your heart, and defile not great nature's law with unlawful longing. Grant that you wish it: facts themselves forbid. He is a righteous man and heedful of moral law—and oh, how I wish a like passion were in him!'

"She spoke; but Cinyras, whom a throng of worthy suitors caused to doubt what he should do, inquired of her herself, naming them over, whom she wished for husband. She is silent at first and, with gaze fixed on her father's face, wavers in doubt, while the warm tears fill her eyes. Cinyras, attributing this to maidenly alarm, bids her not to weep, dries her cheeks and kisses her on the lips. Myrrha is too rejoiced at this and, being asked what kind of husband she desires, says: 'One like you.' But he approves her word, not understanding it, and says: 'May you always be so filial.' At the word 'filial' the girl, conscious of her guilt, casts down her eyes.

"It was midnight, and sleep had set free men's bodies from their cares; but the daughter of Cinyras, sleepless through the night, is consumed by ungoverned passion, renews her mad desires, is filled now with despair, now with desire to try, feels now shame and now desire, and finds no plan of action; and, just as a great tree, smitten by the axe, when all but the last blow has been struck, wavers which way to fall and threatens every side, so her mind, weakened by many blows, leans unsteadily now this way and now that, and falteringly turns in both directions; and no end nor rest for her passion can she find but death. She decides on death. She rises from her couch, resolved to hang herself, and, tying her girdle to a ceiling-beam, she says: 'Farewell, dear Cinyras, and know why I die,' and is in the act of fitting the rope about her death-pale neck.

"They say that the confused sound of her words came to the ears of the faithful nurse who watched outside her darling's door. The old woman rises and opens the door; and when she sees the preparations for death, all in the same moment she screams, beats her breasts and rends her garments, and seizes and snatches off the rope from the girl's neck. Then at last she has time to weep, time to embrace her and ask the reason for the noose. The girl is stubbornly silent, gazes fixedly on the ground, and grieves that her attempt at death, all too slow, has been detected. The old woman insists, bares her white hair and thin breasts, and begs by the girl's cradle and her first nourishment that she trust to her nurse her cause of grief. The girl turns away from her pleadings with a groan. The nurse is determined to find out, and promises more than confidence. 'Tell me,' she says, 'and let me help you; my old age is not without resources. If it be madness, I have healing-charms and herbs; or if someone has worked an evil spell on you, you shall be purified with magic rites; or if the gods are wroth with you, wrath may be appeased by sacrifice. What further can I think? Surely your household fortunes are prosperous as usual; your mother and your father are alive and well.' At the name of father Myrrha sighed deeply from the bottom of her heart. Even now the nurse had no conception of any evil in the girl's soul, and yet she had a presentiment that it was some love affair, and with persistent purpose she begged her to tell her whatever it was. She took the weeping girl on her aged bosom, and so holding her in her feeble arms she said: 'I know, you are in love! and

in this affair I shall be entirely devoted to your service, have no fear;
nor shall your father ever know.' With a bound the mad girl leaped
from her bosom and, burying her face in her couch, she said: 'Please,
go away or stop asking why I grieve. It is a crime, what you want so
much to know.' The old woman is horrified and, stretching out her
hands trembling with age and fear, she falls pleadingly at her
nursling's feet, now coaxing and now frightening her if she does not
tell; she both threatens to report the affair of the noose and attempt
at death, and promises her help if she will confess her love. The girl
lifts her head and fills her nurse's bosom with her rising tears; often
she tries to confess, and often checks her words and hides her
shamed face in her robes. Then she says: 'O mother, blest in your
husband!'—only so much, and groans. Cold horror stole through
the nurse's frame (for she understood), and her white hair stood up
stiffly over all her head, and she said many things to banish, if she
might, the mad passion. The girl knew that she was truly warned;
still she was resolved on death if she could not have her desire. 'Live
then,' said the other, 'have your'—she did not dare say 'father'; she
said no more, calling on Heaven to confirm her promises.

"It was the time when married women were celebrating that
annual festival of Ceres at which with snowy bodies closely robed
they bring garlands of wheaten ears as the first offerings of their
fruits, and for nine nights they count love and the touch of man
among things forbidden. In that throng was Cenchreis, wife of the
king, in constant attendance on the secret rites. And so since the
king's bed was deprived of his lawful wife, the over-officious nurse,
finding Cinyras drunk with wine, told him of one who loved him
truly, giving a false name, and praised her beauty. When he asked
the maiden's age, she said: 'The same as Myrrha's.' Bidden to fetch
her, when she had reached home she cried: 'Rejoice, my child, we
win!' The unhappy girl felt no joy in all her heart, and her mind was
filled with sad forebodings; but still she did also rejoice; so incon-
sistent were her feelings.

"It was the time when all things are at rest, and between the
Bears Boötes had turned his wain with down-pointing pole. She
came to her guilty deed. The golden moon fled from the sky; the
stars hid themselves behind black clouds; night was without her
usual fires. You were the first, Icarus, to cover your face, and you,

Erigone, deified for your pious love of your father.* Thrice was Myrrha stopped by the omen of the stumbling foot; thrice did the funereal screech-owl warn her by his uncanny cry: still on she went, her shame lessened by the black shadows of the night. With her left hand she holds fast to her nurse, and with the other she gropes her way through the dark. Now she reaches the threshold of the chamber, now she opens the door, now is led within. But her knees tremble and sink beneath her; color and blood flee from her face, and her senses desert her as she goes. The nearer she is to her crime, the more she shudders at it, repents her of her boldness, would gladly turn back unrecognized. As she holds back, the aged crone leads her by the hand to the side of the high bed and, delivering her over, says: 'Take her, Cinyras, she is yours'; and leaves the doomed pair together. The father receives his own flesh in his incestuous bed, strives to calm her girlish fears, and speaks encouragingly to the shrinking girl. It chanced, by a name appropriate to her age, he called her 'daughter,' and she called him 'father,' that names might not be lacking to their guilt.

"Forth from the chamber she went, full of her father, with crime conceived within her womb. The next night repeated their guilt, nor was that the end. At length Cinyras, eager to recognize his mistress after so many meetings, brought in a light and beheld his crime and his daughter. Speechless with woe, he snatched his bright sword from the sheath which hung near by. Myrrha fled and escaped death by grace of the shades of the dark night. Groping her way through the broad fields, she left palm-bearing Arabia and the Panchaean country; then, after nine months of wandering, in utter weariness she rested at last in the Sabaean land.† And now she could scarce bear the burden of her womb. Not knowing what to pray for, and in a strait betwixt fear of death and weariness of life, she summed up her wishes in this prayer: 'O gods, if any there be who will listen to my prayer, I do not refuse the dire punishment I have deserved; but in case, surviving, I offend the living, and, dying, I offend the dead, drive me from both realms; change me and refuse me both life and death!' Some god did listen to her prayer; her last petition had its

---

*Both now constellations; regarding Erigone, see endnote 5 to book VI.
†Region of what is now northwestern Yemen.

answering gods. For even as she spoke the earth closed over her legs; roots burst forth from her toes and stretched out on either side the supports of the high trunk; her bones gained strength, and, while the central pith remained the same, her blood changed to sap, her arms to long branches, her fingers to twigs, her skin to hard bark. And now the growing tree had closely bound her heavy womb, had buried her breast and was just covering her neck; but she could not endure the delay and, meeting the rising wood, she sank down and plunged her face in the bark. Though she has lost her old-time feelings with her body, still she weeps, and the warm drops trickle down from the tree. Even the tears have fame, and the myrrh which distils from the tree-trunk keeps the name of its mistress and will be remembered through all the ages.

"But the misbegotten child had grown within the wood, and was now seeking a way by which it might leave its mother and come forth. The pregnant tree swells in mid-trunk, the weight within straining on its mother. The birth-pangs cannot voice themselves, nor can Lucina be called upon in the words of one in travail. Still, like a woman in agony, the tree bends itself, groans oft, and is wet with falling tears. Pitying Lucina stood near the groaning branches, laid her hands on them, and uttered charms to aid the birth. Then the tree cracked open, the bark was rent asunder, and it gave forth its living burden, a wailing baby-boy. The naiads laid him on soft leaves and anointed him with his mother's tears. Even Envy would praise his beauty, for he looked like one of the naked loves portrayed on canvas. But, that dress may make no distinction, you should either give the one a light quiver or take it from the other.

"Time glides by imperceptibly and cheats us in its flight, and nothing is swifter than the years. That son of his sister and his grandfather, who was but lately concealed within his parent tree, but lately born, then a most lovely baby-boy, is now a youth, now man, now more beautiful than his former self; now he excites even Venus' love, and avenges his mother's passion. For while the goddess' son, with quiver on shoulder, was kissing his mother, he chanced unwittingly to graze her breast with a projecting arrow. The wounded goddess pushed her son away; but the scratch had gone deeper than she thought, and she herself was at first deceived. Now, smitten with the beauty of a mortal, she cares no more for the borders of Cythera, nor does she seek Paphos, girt by the deep sea, nor fish-haunted Cnidos, nor Amathus, rich in precious ores. She stays away even from the skies; Adonis is preferred to heaven. She holds him fast, is his companion and, though her wont has always been to take her ease in the shade, and to enhance her beauty by fostering it, now, over mountain ridges, through the woods, over rocky places set with thorns, she ranges with her garments girt up to her knees after the manner of Diana. She also cheers on the hounds and pursues those creatures which are safe to hunt, such as the headlong hares, or the stag with high-branching horns, or the timid doe; but from strong wild boars she keeps away, and from ravenous wolves, and she avoids bears, armed with claws, and lions reeking with the slaughter of cattle. She warns you, too, Adonis, to fear these beasts, if only it were of any avail to warn. 'Be brave against timorous creatures,' she says; 'but against bold creatures boldness is not safe. Do not be rash, dear boy, at my risk; and do not provoke those beasts which nature has well armed, so your glory does not come at great cost to me. Neither youth nor beauty, nor the things which have moved Venus, move lions and bristling boars and the eyes and minds of wild beasts. Boars have the force of a lightning stroke in their curving tusks, and the impetuous wrath of tawny lions is irresistible. I fear and hate them all.' When he asks her why, she says: 'I will tell, and you shall marvel at the monstrous outcome of an ancient crime. But now I am aweary with my unaccustomed toil; and see, a poplar, happily at hand, invites us with its shade, and here is grassy turf for couch. I would fain rest here on the grass with you.' So saying, she reclined upon the ground and on him, and, pillowing her head against his breast and mingling kisses with her words, she told the following tale:

" 'You may, perhaps, have heard of a maid who surpassed swift-footed men in the contest of the race.* And that was no idle tale, for she did surpass them. Nor could you say whether her fleetness or her beauty was more worthy of your praise. Now when this maid consulted the oracle about a husband, the god replied: "A husband will be your curse, O Atalanta; flee from the intercourse of husband; and yet you will not flee, and, though living, you will lose yourself."

---

*Atalanta; see book VIII. Tradition also identifies her as an Argonaut.

Terrified by the oracle of the god, she lived unwedded in the shady woods, and with harsh terms she repulsed the insistent throng of suitors. "I am not to be won," she said, "till I be conquered first in speed. Contest the race with me. Wife and couch shall be given as prize unto the swift, but death shall be the reward of those who lag behind. Be that the condition of the race." She, in truth, was pitiless, but such was the witchery of her beauty, even on this condition a rash throng of suitors came to try their fate. Now Hippomenes had taken his seat as a spectator of this cruel race, and had exclaimed: "Who would seek a wife at so great peril to himself?" and he had condemned the young men for their headstrong love. But when he saw her face and her disrobed form, such beauty as is mine, or as would be yours if you were a woman, he was amazed and, stretching out his hands, he cried: "Forgive me, you whom but now I blamed. I did not yet realize the worth of the prize you strove for." As he praises, his own heart takes fire and he hopes that none of the youths may outstrip her in the race, and is filled with jealous fears. "But why is my fortune in this contest left untried?" he cries. "God himself helps those who dare." While thus Hippomenes was weighing the matter in his mind, the girl sped by on winged feet. Though she seemed to the Aonian youth to go not less swiftly than a Scythian arrow, yet he admired her beauty still more. And the running gave a beauty of its own. The breeze bore back the streaming pinions on her flying feet, her hair was tossed over her white shoulders; the bright-bordered ribbons at her knees were fluttering, and over her fair girlish body a pink flush came, just as when a purple awning, drawn over a marble hall, stains it with borrowed hues. While the stranger marked all this, the last goal was passed, and Atalanta was crowned victor with a festal wreath. But the conquered youths with groans paid the penalty according to the bond.

"'Not deterred by the experience of these, however, Hippomenes stood forth and, fixing his eyes upon the girl, exclaimed: "Why do you seek an easily won renown by conquering sluggish youth? Come, strive with me! If fortune shall give me the victory, 'twill be no shame for you to be overcome by so great a foe. For Megareus of Onchestus* is my father and his grandfather is Neptune; thus I am

---

*King of an eponymous city in Boeotia.

the great-grandson of the king of the waters. Nor is my manly
worth less than my race. Or, if I shall be defeated, you will have a
great and memorable name for the conquest of Hippomenes." As he
said this, the daughter of Schoeneus gazed on him with softening
eyes, being in a strait betwixt her desire to conquer and to be con-
quered. And thus she spoke: "What god, envious of beauteous
youths, wishes to destroy this one, and prompts him to seek wed-
lock with me at the risk of his own dear life? I am not worth so great
a price, if I am the judge. Nor is it his beauty that touches me—and
yet I could be touched by this as well—but the fact that he is still
but a boy. It is not he himself who moves me, but his youth. What
of his manly courage and his soul fearless of death? What that he
claims by birth to be the fourth from the monarch of the seas? What
of his love for me, and that he counts marriage with me of so great
worth that he would perish if cruel fate denies me to him?
O stranger, go from here while still you may; flee from this bloody
wedlock. Marriage with me is a fatal thing. No other maiden will
refuse to wed you, and it may well be that a wiser girl will seek your
love.—Yet why this care for you, since so many have already per-
ished? Let him look to himself! let him perish, too, since by the
death of so many suitors he was not warned, and cares so little for
his life.—And shall he die, because he wished to live with me, and
suffer undeserved death as the penalty of love? My victory will be
attended by unbearable hatred against me. But the fault is none of
mine. O sir, I would that you might desist, or, since you are so madly
set upon it, would that you might prove the swifter! Ah, how girl-
ish is his youthful face! Ah, poor Hippomenes, I would that you had
never looked on me! You were so worthy of life. But if I were of hap-
pier fortune, and if the harsh fates did not deny me marriage, you
were the only he with whom I should want to share my couch." So
speaks the maid; and, all untutored, feeling for the first time the im-
pulse of love, ignorant of what she does, she loves and knows it not.

"'Meanwhile the people and her father demanded the accus-
tomed race. Then did the Neptunian youth, Hippomenes, with sup-
pliant voice call on me: "O may Cytherea," he said, "be near, I pray,
and assist the thing I dare and smile upon the love which she has
given." A kindly breeze bore this soft prayer to me and I confess it
moved my heart. And there was but scanty time to give him aid.

There is a field, the natives call it the field of Tamasus, the richest portion of the Cyprian land, which in ancient times men set apart to me and bade my temples be enriched with this. Within this field there stands a tree gleaming with golden leaves and its branches crackle with the same bright gold. Fresh come from there, I chanced to have in my hand three golden apples which I had plucked. Revealing myself to no one except to him, I approached Hippomenes and taught him how to use the apples. The trumpets had sounded for the race, when they both, crouching low, flashed forth from their stalls and skimmed the surface of the sandy course with flying feet. You would think that they could graze the sea with unwet feet and pass lightly over the ripened heads of the standing grain. The youth was cheered on by shouts of applause and the words of those who cried to him: "Now, now is the time to bend to the work, Hippomenes! Go on! Now use your utmost strength! No tarrying! You're sure to win!" It is a matter of doubt whether the heroic son of Megareus or the daughter of Schoeneus took more joy of these words. Oh, how often, when she could have passed him, did she delay and after gazing long upon his face reluctantly leave him behind! And now dry, panting breath came from his weary throat and the goal was still far away. Then at length did Neptune's scion throw one of the three golden apples. The maid beheld it with wonder and, eager to possess the shining fruit, she turned out of her course and picked up the flying golden thing. Hippomenes passed her by while the spectators roared their applause. She by a burst of speed made up for her delay and the time that she had lost, and again left the youth behind her. Again she delayed at the tossing of the second apple, followed and passed the man. The last part of the course remained. "Now be near me, goddess, author of my gift!" he said, and obliquely into a side of the field, returning from which she would lose much time, with all his youthful strength he threw the shining gold. The girl seemed to hesitate whether or no she should go after it. I forced her to take it up, and added weight to the fruit she carried, and so impeded her equally with the weight of her burden and with her loss of time. And, so that my story may not be longer than the race itself, the maiden was outstripped; the victor led away his prize.

" 'And was I not worthy, Adonis, of being thanked and of having the honor of incense paid to me? But, forgetful of my services, he neither thanked nor offered incense to me. Then was I changed to sudden wrath and, smarting under the slight, and resolved not to be slighted in the future, I decided to make an example of them, and urged myself on against them both. They were passing by a temple deep hidden in the woods, which in ancient times illustrious Echion had built to the mother of the gods in payment of a vow; and the long journey persuaded them to rest. There incontinent desire seized on Hippomenes, who was under the spell of my divinity. Hard by the temple was a dimly lighted, cave-like place, built of soft native rock, hallowed by ancient religious veneration, where the priest had set many wooden images of the olden gods. This place he entered; this holy presence he defiled by lust. The sacred images turned away their eyes. The tower-crowned Mother* was on the verge of plunging the guilty pair beneath the waves of Styx; but the punishment seemed light. And so tawny manes covered their necks but now smooth, their fingers curved into claws, their arms changed to legs, their weight went chiefly to their chests, with tails they swept the surface of the sandy ground. Harsh were their features, rough growls they gave for speech, and for marriage chamber they haunted the wild woods. And now as lions, to others terrible, with tamed mouths they champed the bits of Cybele. These beasts, and with them all other savage things which turn not their backs in flight, but offer their breasts to battle, for my sake, dear boy, avoid, in case your manly courage be the ruin of us both.'

"Thus the goddess warned and through the air, drawn by her swans, she took her way; but the boy's manly courage would not brook advice. It chanced his hounds, following a well-marked trail, roused up a wild boar from his hiding-place; and, as he was rushing from the wood, the young grandson of Cinyras pierced him with a glancing blow. Straightway the fierce boar with his curved snout rooted out the spear wet with his blood, and pursued the youth, now full of fear and running for his life; deep in the groin he sank his long tusks, and stretched the dying boy upon the yellow sand. Borne through the middle air by flying swans on her light car, Cytherea had not yet come to Cyprus, when she heard afar the groans of the dying youth and turned her white swans to go to him. And when

*Cybele; see endnote 1 to book X.

from the high air she saw him lying lifeless and weltering in his blood, she leaped down, tore both her garments and her hair and beat her breasts with cruel hands. Reproaching fate, she said: 'But all shall not be in your power. My grief, Adonis, shall have an enduring monument, and each passing year in memory of your death shall give an imitation of my grief. But your blood shall be changed to a flower. Or was it once allowed to you, Persephone, to change a maiden's form to fragrant mint,* and shall the change of my hero, offspring of Cinyras, be grudged to me?' So saying, with sweet-scented nectar she sprinkled the blood; and this, touched by the nectar, swelled as when clear bubbles rise up from yellow mud. With no longer than an hour's delay a flower sprang up of blood-red hue such as pomegranates bear which hide their seeds beneath the tenacious rind. But short-lived is their flower; for the winds from which it takes its name shake off the flower so delicately clinging and doomed too easily to fall."†

---

*The story is obscure, but it concerns a nymph named Minthe.
†The flower is the anemone.

WHILE WITH SUCH SONGS the bard of Thrace drew the trees, held beasts enthralled and constrained stones to follow him, behold, the crazed women of the Cicones, with skins flung over their breasts, saw Orpheus from a hill-top, fitting songs to the music of his lyre. Then one of these, her tresses streaming in the gentle breeze, cried out: "See, see the man who scorns us!" and hurled her spear straight at the tuneful mouth of Apollo's bard; but this, wreathed in leaves, marked without harming him. Another threw a stone, which, even as it flew through the air, was overcome by the sweet sound of voice and lyre, and fell at his feet as if 'twould ask forgiveness for its mad attempt. But still the assault waxed reckless: their passion knew no bounds; mad fury reigned. And all their weapons would have been harmless under the spell of song; but the huge uproar of the Berecyntian flutes, mixed with discordant horns, the drums, and the breast-beatings and howlings of the Bacchanals, drowned the lyre's sound; and then at last the stones were reddened with the blood of the bard whose voice they could not hear. First away went the multitudinous birds still spellbound by the singer's voice, with the snakes and the train of beasts, the glory of Orpheus' audience, harried by the Maenads; then these turned bloody hands against Orpheus and flocked around like birds when in the day they see the bird of night wandering in the daylight; and as when in the amphitheatre in the early morning of the spectacle the doomed stag in the arena is the prey of dogs. They rushed upon the bard and hurled at him their wands wreathed with green vines, not made for such use as this. Some threw clods, some branches torn from trees, and some threw stones. And, that real weapons might not be wanting to their madness, it chanced that oxen, toiling beneath the yoke, were plowing up the soil; and not far from these, stout peasants were digging the hard earth and sweating at their work. When these beheld the advancing horde, they fled away and left behind the implements of their toil. Scattered through the deserted fields lay hoes, long mattocks and heavy grubbing-tools. These the savage women caught up and, first tearing in pieces the oxen who threatened them with their horns, they rushed back to slay the bard; and, as he stretched out his suppliant hands, uttering words then, but never before, unheeded, and moving them not a whit by his voice, the impious women struck him down. And (oh, the pity of it!) through those lips, to which rocks listened, and to which the hearts of savage beasts responded, the soul, breathed out, went faring forth in air.

The mourning birds wept for you, Orpheus, the throng of beasts, the flinty rocks, and the trees which had so often gathered to your songs; yes, the trees shed their leaves as if so tearing their hair in grief for you. They say that the rivers also were swollen with their own tears, and that naiads and dryads alike mourned with dishevelled hair and with dark-bordered garments. The poet's limbs lay scattered all around; but his head and lyre, O Hebrus, you received, and (a marvel!) while they floated in mid-stream the lyre gave forth some mournful notes, mournfully the lifeless tongue murmured, mournfully the banks replied. And now, borne onward to the sea, they left their native stream and gained the shore of Lesbos near the city of Methymna. Here, as the head lay exposed upon a foreign strand, a savage serpent attacked it and its streaming locks still dripping with the spray. But Phoebus at last appeared, drove off the snake just in the act to bite, and hardened and froze to stone, just as they were, the serpent's widespread, yawning jaws.

The poet's shade fled beneath the earth, and recognized all the places he had seen before; and, seeking through the blessed fields, found Eurydice and caught her in his eager arms. Here now side by side they walk; now Orpheus follows her as she precedes, now goes before her, now may in safety look back upon his Eurydice.

However, Bacchus did not suffer such crime as this to go unavenged. Grieved at the loss of the bard of his sacred rites, he straightway bound fast all those Thracian women, who saw the impious deed, with twisted roots. For he prolonged their toes and, in so far as each root followed down, he thrust their tips into the solid earth. And as a bird, when it has caught its foot in the snare which the cunning fowler has set for it, and feels that it is caught, flaps and flutters, but draws its bonds tighter by its struggling; so, as each of these women, fixed firmly in the soil, had stuck fast, with wild affright, but all in vain, she attempted to flee. The tough roots held her, and though she struggled, kept firm their grasp. And when she asked where were her fingers, where her feet, her nails, she saw the bark come creeping up her shapely legs; striving to smite her thighs with hands of grief, she smote on oak. Her breasts also became of oak; oaken her shoulders. Her arms you would think had been changed to long branches—nor would your thought be wrong.

Nor is this enough for Bacchus. He leaves their very fields and with a worthier band seeks the vineyards of his own Timolus and his Pactolus; although this was not at that time a golden stream, nor envied for its precious sands. His usual company, satyrs and bacchanals, thronged round him; but Silenus was not there. Him, stumbling with the weight of years and wine, the Phrygian rustics took captive, bound him with wreaths, and led him to Midas, their king. To this Midas, together with the Athenian Eumolpus, Thracian Orpheus had taught the rites of Bacchus. When now the king recognized the comrade and assistant of his revels, right merrily to celebrate the coming of his guest he ordered a festival which they kept for ten continuous days and nights. And now the eleventh dawn had driven away the ranks of stars on high, when the king with joyful heart came to the Lydian fields and gave Silenus back to his dear foster-child.

Then did the god, rejoicing in his foster-father's safe return, grant to the king the free choice of a good, a pleasing, but useless gift. Midas, fated to make an ill use of his gift, exclaimed: "Grant that whatsoever I may touch with my body may be turned to yellow gold." Bacchus granted his prayer and gave him the baleful gift, grieving the while that he had not asked better. The Berecyntian hero gaily went his way, rejoicing in his fatal gift, and tried its promised powers by touching this and that. Scarcely daring to believe, from a low oak-branch he broke off a green twig: the twig was changed to gold. He picked up a stone from the ground: the stone, also, showed a light golden hue. He touched a clod: beneath that magic touch the clod became a mass of gold. He plucked some ripe wheat-heads: it was a golden harvest. He picked an apple from a tree and held it in his hand: you would suppose the Hesperides had given it. If he laid his fingers on the lofty pillars, the pillars gleamed before his eyes. When he bathed his hands in water, the water flowing over his hands could cheat a Danaë. His mind itself could scarcely grasp its own hopes, dreaming of all things turned to gold. As he rejoiced, his slaves set a table before him loaded with meats; nor was bread wanting. Then indeed, if he touched the gift of Ceres with his hand, the gift of Ceres went stiff and hard; or if he tried to bite a piece of meat with hungry teeth, where his teeth touched the food they touched but yellow plates of gold. He mingled pure water with the wine of Bacchus, giver of his gift; but through his jaws you would see the molten gold go trickling.

Amazed by this strange mishap, rich and yet wretched, he seeks to flee his wealth and hates what he but now has prayed for. No store of food can relieve his hunger; his throat is parched with burning thirst, and through his own fault he is tortured by hateful gold. Lifting his hands and shining arms to heaven, he cries: "Oh, pardon me, Lenaeus, father! I have sinned. Yet have mercy, I pray you, and save me from this curse that looks so fair." The gods are kind: Bacchus restored him to his former condition when he confessed his fault, and he relieved him of the gift which he had given in fulfilment of his pledge. "And, that you may not remain encased in gold which you have so foolishly desired," he said, "go to the stream which flows by mighty Sardis town, take your way along the Lydian hills up the tumbling stream until you come to the river's source. There plunge your head and body beneath the foaming fountain where it comes leaping forth, and by that act wash your sin away." The king went to the stream as he was bid. The power of the golden touch imbued the water and passed from the man's body into the stream. And even to this day, receiving the seed of the original vein, the fields grow hard and yellow, their soil soaked with water of the golden touch.

But Midas, hating wealth, haunted the woods and fields, worshipping Pan, who has his dwelling in the mountain caves. But stupid his wits still remained, and his foolish mind was destined again as once before to harm its master. For Tmolus, looking far out upon the sea, stands stiff and high, with steep sides extending with one slope to Sardis, and on the other reaches down to little Hypaepae. There, while Pan was singing his songs to the soft nymphs and playing airy interludes upon his reeds close joined with wax, he dared speak slightingly of Apollo's music in comparison with his own, and came into an ill-matched contest with Tmolus as the judge.

The old judge took his seat upon his own mountain-top, and shook his ears free from the trees. His dark locks were encircled by an oak-wreath only, and acorns hung around his hollow temples. He, looking at the shepherd-god, exclaimed: "There is no delay on the judge's part." Then Pan made music on his rustic pipes, and with his rude notes quite charmed King Midas, for he chanced to hear the strains. After Pan was done, venerable Tmolus turned his face towards Phoebus; and his forest turned with his face. Phoebus' golden head was wreathed with laurel of Parnasus, and his mantle, dipped in Tyrian dye, swept the ground. His lyre, inlaid with gems and Indian ivory, he held in his left hand, while his right hand held the plectrum. His very pose was that of an artist. Then with trained thumb he plucked the strings and, charmed by those sweet strains, Tmolus ordered Pan to lower his reeds before the lyre.

All approved the judgment of the sacred mountain-god. And yet it was challenged and called unjust by Midas' voice alone. The Delian god did not suffer ears so dull to keep their human form, but lengthened them out and filled them with shaggy, grey hair; he also made them unstable at the base and gave them power of motion. Human in all else, in this one feature was he punished, and wore the ears of a slow-moving ass. Disfigured and ashamed, he strove to hide his temples beneath a purple turban, but the slave who was wont to trim his hair beheld his shame. And he, since he dared not reveal the disgraceful sight, yet eager to tell it out and utterly unable to keep it to himself, went off and dug a hole in the ground and into the hole, with low, muttered words, he whispered of his master's ears which he had seen. Then by throwing back the earth he buried the evidence of his voice and, having thus filled up the hole again, he silently stole away. But a thick growth of whispering reeds began to spring up there, and these, when at the year's end they came to their full size, betrayed the sower, for, stirred by the gentle breeze, they repeated his buried words and exposed the story of his master's ears.

His vengeance now complete, Latona's son retires from Tmolus and, cleaving the liquid air, without crossing the narrow sea of Helle, daughter of Nephele, he came to earth in the country of Laomedon. Midway between the Sigean and Rhoetean promontories

was an ancient altar sacred to the Panomphaean Thunderer. There
Apollo saw Laomedon beginning to build the walls of his new city,
Troy; and, perceiving that the mighty task was proceeding with
great difficulty, and demanded no slight resources, he, together with
the trident-bearing father of the swollen sea, put on mortal form
and built the walls for the Phrygian king, having first agreed upon
a sum of gold for the walls. There stood the work. But the king re-
pudiated his debt and, as a crowning act of perfidy, swore that he
had never promised the reward. "But you shall not go unpunished,"
the sea-god said, and he set all his waters flowing against the shores
of miserly Troy. He flooded the country till it looked like a sea,
swept away the farmers' crops and whelmed their fields beneath his
waters. Nor was this punishment enough; the king's daughter also
must be sacrificed to a monster of the deep. But while she was
bound there to the hard rocks, Alcides set her free, and then de-
manded his promised wage, the horses that were agreed upon. But
the great task's price was again refused, and so the hero took the
twice-perjured walls of conquered Troy. Nor did Telamon, the part-
ner of his campaign, go without reward, and Hesione was given
him. For Peleus was honored with a goddess for his bride, and was
not more proud of his grandfather's name than of his father-
in-law;* since it had not fallen to only one to be grandson of Jove,
but to only him had it fallen to have a goddess for his wife.

For old Proteus had said to Thetis: "O goddess of the waves, con-
ceive: you shall be the mother of a youth who, when to manhood
grown, shall outdo his father's deeds and shall be called greater than
he." Because of this, in case the earth should produce anything
greater than himself, though he had felt the hot fires of love deep in
his heart, Jove shunned the arms of Thetis, goddess of the sea, and
bade his grandson, the son of Aeacus, assume the place of lover in
his stead, and seek a union with this virgin of the deep.

There is a bay on the Thessalian coast, curved like a sickle into
two bays with arms running out; 'twould be a safe port for ships if
the water were deeper. The sea spreads smooth over the sandy bottom;
the shore is firm, such as leaves no trace of feet, delays no journey, is

---

*The grandfather is Jupiter, who fathered Aeacus; the father-in-law is the sea-god
Nereus.

free from seaweed. A myrtle wood grows close at hand, thick-hung with two-colored berries. There is a grotto in this grove, whether made by nature or art one may not surely say, but rather by art. To this grot oftentimes, riding your bridled dolphin, O Thetis, naked you were wont to come. There and then Peleus seized you as you lay wrapped in slumber; and since, though entreated by his prayers, you refused him, he prepared to force your will, entwining your neck with both his arms. And if you had not, by often changing your form, had recourse to your accustomed arts, he would have worked his daring will on you. But now you took the form of a bird: still he held fast to the bird. Now you were a sturdy tree; around the tree did Peleus tightly cling. Your third disguise was a spotted tigress' form: in fear of that Peleus loosed his hold on you. Then did he pray unto the gods of the sea with wine poured out upon the water, with entrails of sheep, and with the smoke of incense; until the Carpathian seer from his deep pools rose and said to him: "O son of Aeacus, you shall yet gain the bride that you desire. Only you must, when she lies within the rocky cave, deep sunk in sleep, bind her in her unconsciousness with snares and close-clinging thongs. And though she take a hundred lying forms, do not let her escape you, but hold her close, whatever she may be, until she take again the form she had at first." So spoke Proteus and hid his face beneath the waves, as he let his waters flow back again over his final words.

Now Titan was sinking low and kept the western sea beneath his down-sloping chariot, when the fair Nereid, seeking again the grot, lay down upon her accustomed couch. There scarce had Peleus well laid hold on her virgin limbs, when she began to assume new forms, until she perceived that she was held firmly bound and that her arms were pinioned wide. Then at length she groaned and said: "It is not without some god's assistance that you conquer," and gave herself up as Thetis. Her, thus owning her defeat, the hero caught in his embrace, attained his desire, and begat on her the great Achilles.

Peleus was blessed in his son, blessed in his wife, and to him only good befell, if you except the crime of the murdered Phocus. Driven from his father's house with his brother's blood upon his hands, he found asylum in the land of Trachin. Here ruled in peaceful, blood-less sway Ceyx, son of Lucifer,* with all his father's bright gladness

---

*Not Satan; rather, the equivalent to the Greek Hesperus. More on Ceyx follows.

in his face. But at that time he was sad and unlike himself, for he was mourning the taking off of his brother. To him the son of Aeacus came, worn with his cares and journeyings, and entered his city with but a few retainers following. He left the flocks of sheep and the cattle which he had brought with him in a shady vale not far from the city's walls; then, when first he was allowed to approach the monarch, stretching out with suppliant hand an olive-branch wound with woollen fillets, he told him who he was and from what father sprung. He concealed only his crime, and lied concerning the reason for his flight. He begged for a chance to support himself in city or in field. To him the Trachinian monarch with kind words replied: "The opportunities of our realm lie open, Peleus, even to humble folk, and we do not rule an inhospitable kingdom. To this our kindly disposition you add the strong incentive of an illustrious name and descent from Jove. Then waste no time in prayer. You shall have all you seek. Take your share in all, such as it is; and I wish it were better!" He spoke and wept. When Peleus and his companions asked him the cause of his great grief, he answered them: "Perhaps you think that that bird, which lives on rapine and is the terror of all birds, was always a feathered creature. He was once a man (and, so fixed is character, his only qualities were harshness, eagerness for war, readiness for violence), by name Daedalion. We two were born of that god who wakes the dawn and passes last from the sky.* I was by nature peaceful and my care was always for preserving peace and for my wife. But cruel war was my brother's pleasure. His fierce courage subdued kings and nations, and now in changed form it pursues the doves of Thisbe. He had a daughter, Chione, a girl most richly dowered with beauty, who had a thousand suitors when she had reached the marriageable age of fourteen years. It chanced that Phoebus and the son of Maia, returning the one from Delphi, the other from high Cyllene, beheld her both at once and both at once were filled with love of her. Apollo put off his hope of love till night-time, but the other brooked no delay, and touched the maiden's face with his sleep-compelling wand. She lay beneath the god's magic touch and endured his violence. Now night had spangled the heavens with the stars when Phoebus, assuming an old

---

*That is, Lucifer; the same star could also be identified as Venus.

woman's form, gained his forestalled joy. When the fullness of time was come, a son was born to the wing-footed god, Autolycus, of crafty nature, well versed in cunning wiles. For he could make white of black and black of white, a worthy heir of his father's art. To Phoebus also, for the birth was twin, was born Philammon, famous for song and zither. But what profits it that she bore two sons, that she found favor with two gods, that she herself was sprung from a brave sire and shining grandsire? Is not glory a curse as well? It has been a curse to many, surely to her! For she boldly set herself above Diana and criticized the goddess' beauty. But to her the goddess, moved by hot rage, exclaimed: 'Then by our deeds we'll please you.' Upon the word she bent her bow, sent an arrow swift flying from the string, and pierced that guilty tongue with the shaft. The tongue was stilled, nor voice nor attempted words came more. Even as she tried to speak her life fled forth with her blood. Wretched, I embraced her, feeling her father's grief in my heart, and to my dear brother I spoke words of comfort. The father heard them as the crags hear the murmurs of the sea, and kept ever bewailing his lost child. But when he saw her burning, four times he made to rush into the blazing pile. Four times thrust back, he took to mad flight and, like a bullock whose neck is pierced by hornets' stings, over trackless ways he rushed. Even then he seemed to me to run faster than human powers allow, and you would have thought his feet had taken wings. So then he fled us all and quickly, bent on destruction, he gained Parnasus' top. Apollo, pitying him, when Daedalion had hurled himself from that high cliff, made him a bird, held him suspended there on sudden wings, and gave him a hooked beak, gave him curved claws, but he left him his old-time courage and strength greater than his body. And now as a hawk, friendly to none, he vents his cruel rage on all birds and, suffering himself, makes others suffer, too."

While the son of Lucifer was telling this marvellous story of his brother, Phocian Onetor, Peleus' herdsman, came running in with breathless haste, crying: "Peleus, Peleus! I come to tell you dreadful news." Peleus bade him tell his news, while the Trachinian king himself waited in trembling anxiety. The herdsman went on: "I had driven the weary herd down to the curving shore when the high sun was midway in his course, beholding as much behind him as still lay before. A part of the cattle had kneeled down upon the yellow sands, and lying there were looking out upon the broad, level sea; part was wandering slowly here and there, while others still swam out and stood neck-deep in water. A temple stood near the sea, not resplendent with marble and gold, but made of heavy timbers, and shaded by an ancient grove. The place was sacred to Nereus and the Nereids (these a sailor told me were the gods of that sea, as he dried his nets on the shore). Hard by this temple was a marsh thick-set with willows, which the backwater of the sea made into a marsh. From this a loud, crashing noise filled the whole neighbourhood with fear: a huge beast, a wolf! he came rushing out, smeared with marsh-mud, his great, murderous jaws all bloody and flecked with foam, and his eyes blazing with red fire. He was mad with rage and hunger, but more with rage. For he stayed not to sate his dire hunger on the slain cattle, but mangled the whole herd, slaughtering all in wanton malice. Some of us, also, while we strove to drive him off, were sore wounded by his deadly fangs and given over to death. The shore, the shallow water, and the swamps, resounding with the bellowings of the herd, were red with blood. But delay is fatal, nor is there time to hesitate. While still there's something left, let us all together rush on to arms, to arms! and make a combined attack upon the wolf!" So spoke the rustic. Peleus was not stirred by the story of his loss; but, conscious of his crime, he well knew that the bereaved Nereid was sending this calamity upon him as a sacrificial offering to her slain Phocus. The Oetaean king bade his men put on their armor and take their deadly spears in hand, and at the same time was making ready to go with them himself. But his wife, Alcyone, roused by the loud outcries, came rushing out of her chamber, her hair not yet all arranged, and, sending this flying loose, she threw herself upon her husband's neck, and begged him with prayers and tears that he would send aid but not go himself, and so save two lives in one. Then said the son of Aeacus to her: "Your pious fears, O queen, become you; but have no fear. I am not ungrateful for your proffered help; but I have no desire that arms be taken in my behalf against the strange monster. I must pray to the goddess of the sea." There was a tall tower, a lighthouse on the top of the citadel, a welcome landmark for storm-tossed ships. They climbed up to its top, and then with cries of pity looked out upon the cattle lying dead upon the shore, and saw the killer revelling with bloody jaws, and with his long shaggy hair stained red with blood. There, stretching out his hands to the shores of the open sea, Peleus prayed to the sea-nymph, Psamathe, that she put away her wrath and come to his help. She, indeed, remained unmoved by the prayers of Peleus; but Thetis, adding her prayers for her husband's sake, obtained the nymph's forgiveness. But the wolf, though ordered off from his fierce slaughter, kept on, mad with the sweet taste of blood; until, just as he was fastening his fangs upon the torn neck of a heifer, the nymph changed him into marble. The body, except for its color, remained the same in all respects; but the color of the stone proclaimed that now he was no longer wolf, that now he no longer need be feared. But still the fates did not suffer the banished Peleus to continue in this land. The wandering exile went on to Magnesia, and there, at the hands of the Haemonian king, Acastus, he gained full absolution from his bloodguiltiness.[1]

Meanwhile King Ceyx was much disturbed and anxious, not only about the strange thing that happened to his brother, but also about others that had happened since his brother's fate. Accordingly, that he might consult the sacred oracles, the refuge of mankind in trouble, he planned to journey to the Clarian god.* For the infamous Phorbas with the followers of Phlegyas was making the journey to the Delphic oracle unsafe. But before he started he told his purpose to you, his most faithful wife, Alcyone. Straightway she was chilled to the very marrow of her bones, her face grew pale as boxwood and her cheeks were wet with her flowing tears. Three times she tried to speak, three times watered her face with weeping; at last, her loving complaints broken by her sobs, she said: "What fault of mine, O dearest husband, has brought your mind to this? Where is that care for me which used to stand first of all? Can you now abandon your Alcyone with no thought of her? Is it your pleasure now to go on a long journey? Am I now dearer to you when absent from you? But, I suppose, your journey is by land, and I shall only grieve, not fear for you, and my cares shall have no terror in them. The sea affrights me, and the stern visage of the deep; and but lately I saw some broken planks upon the beach, and often have I read men's

---

*Apollo; Clarus (in Asia Minor) receives the suppliants ordinarily bound for Delphi.

names on empty tombs. And let not your mind have vain confidence in that the son of Hippotes is your father-in-law, who holds the stout winds behind prison bars, and when he will can calm the sea. For when once the winds have been let out and have gained the open deep, no power can check them, and every land and every sea is abandoned to their will. Indeed, they harry the very clouds of heaven and rouse the red lightnings with their fierce collisions. The more I know them (for I do know them, and have often seen them when a child in my father's home) the more I think them to be feared. But if no prayers can change your purpose, dear husband, and if you are over-bent on going, take me with you, too! For surely we shall then be storm-tossed together, nor shall I fear anything but what I feel, and together we shall endure whatever comes, together over the broad billows we shall fare."

With these words and tears of the daughter of Aeolus the star-born husband was deeply moved; for the fire of love burned no less brightly in his heart. And yet he was unwilling either to give up his proposed journey on the sea or to take Alcyone as sharer of his perils. His anxious love strove to comfort her with many soothing words, but for all that he did not win her approval. He added this comforting condition, also, by which alone he gained his loving wife's consent: "Every delay, I know, will seem long to us; but I swear to you by my father's fires, if only the fates will let me, I will return before the moon shall twice have filled her orb." When by these promises of return her hope had been awakened, straightway he ordered his ship to be launched and duly supplied with her equipment. But when Alcyone saw this, as if forewarned of what was to come, she fell to trembling again; her tears flowed afresh and, embracing her husband in the depth of woe, she said a sad farewell at last and then fainted away completely. But the young men, though Ceyx sought excuses for delay, in double rows drew back the oars to their strong breasts and rent the waters with their rhythmic strokes. Then Alcyone lifted her tear-wet eyes and saw her husband standing on the high-curved poop and waving his hand in first signal to her, and she waved tokens back again. When the land drew further off, and her eyes could no longer make out his features, while yet she could she followed with her gaze the fast-receding ship. When even this was now so distant that it could not be seen, still she watched the sails floating along at the top of the mast. When she could not even see the sails, heavy-hearted she sought her lonely couch and threw herself upon it. The couch and the place renewed her tears, for they reminded her of the part that was gone from her.

They had left the harbour and the breeze had set the cordage rattling. At that the captain shipped his oars, ran the yard up to the top of the mast and spread all his sails to catch the freshening breeze. The ship was now skimming along about midway of the sea, and the land on either side was far away, when, as night came on, the water began to whiten with the roughening waves and the wind, driving ahead, to blow with increased violence. "Lower the yard at once," the captain cries, "and tight reef the sail." So he orders, but the blast blowing in his face drowns out his orders, nor does the uproar of the sea let his voice be heard. Still, of their own will, some hastily draw in the oars, some close the oar-holes, and some reef the sails. Here one is bailing out the water and pouring the sea into the sea, while another hastily secures the spars. While these things are being done, all in confusion, the storm is increasing in violence and from every quarter the raging winds make their attacks and stir up the angry waves. The captain himself is in terror and admits that he does not know how the vessel stands, nor what either to order or forbid; so great is the impending weight of destruction, so much more mighty than all his skill. All is a confused uproar—shouts of men, rattling of cordage, roar of the rushing waves, and crash of thunder. The waves run mountain-high and seem to reach the very heavens, and with their spray to sprinkle the lowering clouds. Now the water is tawny with the sands swept up from the bottom of the sea, and now blacker than the very waters of the Styx. At other times the waves spread out, white with the hissing foam. The Trachinian ship herself also is driven on in the grasp of chance. Now, lifted high, as from a mountain-top she seems to look down into deep valleys and the pit of Acheron; now, as she sinks far down and the writhing waters close her in, she seems to be looking up to the top of heaven from the infernal pools.* Often with mighty thuds the vessel's sides resound, beaten by crashing waves as heavily as when sometimes an iron ram or ballista smites a battered fortress. And as savage lions,

---

*Styx and Acheron are rivers of the Underworld.

gaining new strength as they come rushing to the attack, are wont to breast the hunters' arms and ready spears; so, when the waves had been lashed to fury by the opposing winds, they rushed against the bulwarks of the barque and towered high over it. And now the tightening wedges of the hull spring loose and yawning chinks appear, their covering of pitch clean washed away, and give passage to the deadly tide. Behold, the rain falls in sheets from the bursting clouds; and you would think that the whole heavens were falling down into the sea and that the swollen sea was leaping up into the regions of the sky. The sails are soaked with rain, and with the waters from the sky the ocean's floods are mingled. No stars gleam in the sky and the black night is murky with its own and the tempest's gloom. Still flashing fires cleave the shadows and give light, and the waves gleam red beneath the lightning's glare. Now also the flood comes pouring within the vessel's hollow hull; and as a soldier, more eager than his fellows, when he has often essayed to scale a beleaguered city's walls, at last succeeds and, fired with the passion for praise, leaps over the wall and stands one man amid a thousand; so, when the waves nine times have battered at the lofty sides, the tenth wave, leaping with a mightier heave, comes on, nor does it cease its attack upon the weary ship until over the ramparts of the conquered barque it leaps within. So now a part of the sea still tries to invade the ship and part is already within its hold. All are in terrified confusion, just as a city is confused when some from without seek to undermine its walls and some hold the walls within. Skill fails and courage fails; and as many separate deaths seem rushing on and bursting through as are the advancing waves. One cannot restrain his tears; another is struck dumb; still another cries they are fortunate whom burial rites await; one calls on the gods in prayer and lifts unavailing arms to the unseen heavens, begging for help; one thinks upon his brothers and his sire, one on his home and children, and each on that which he has left behind. But Ceyx thinks on Alcyone: upon the lips of Ceyx there is no one but Alcyone; and, though he longs for her alone, yet he rejoices that she is far away. How he would love to see his native shores again and turn his last gaze upon his home. But where he is he knows not; for the sea boils in such whirling pools and the shadows of the pitchy clouds hide all the sky and double the darkness of the night. The mast is broken by a whirling rush of wind; the rudder, too, is broken. One last wave, like a victor rejoicing in his spoils, heaves itself high and looks down upon the other waves; and, as if one should tear from their foundations Athos and Pindus and hurl them bodily into the open sea, so fell this wave headlong, and with its overwhelming weight plunged the ship down to the very bottom; and with the ship the great part of the sailors perished, sucked down in the eddying flood, nevermore to see the light of day. But some still clung to broken pieces of the vessel. Ceyx himself, with the hand that was wont to hold the sceptre, clung to a fragment of the wreck, and called upon his father-in-law and on his father, alas! in vain. But most of all is the name of Alcyone on the swimmer's lips. He remembers her and names her again and again. He prays that the waves may bear his body into her sight and that in death he may be entombed by her dear hands. While he can keep afloat, as often as the waves allow him to open his mouth he calls the name of his Alcyone, far away, and murmurs it even as the waves close over his lips. See, a dark billow of waters breaks over the surrounding floods and buries him deep beneath the seething waves. Dim and unrecognizable was Lucifer that dawn; and since he might not leave his station in the skies, he wrapped his face in thick clouds.

Meanwhile the daughter of Aeolus, in ignorance of this great disaster, counts off the nights; now hastens on to weave the robes which he is to put on, and now those which she herself will wear when he comes back, and pictures to herself the home-coming which can never be. She dutifully burns incense to all the gods; but most of all she worships at Juno's shrine, praying for the man who is no more, that her husband may be kept safe from harm, that he may return once more, loving no other woman more than her. And only this prayer of all her prayers could be granted her.

But the goddess could no longer endure these entreaties for the dead. And that she might free her altar from the touch of the hands of mourning, she said: "Iris, most faithful messenger of mine, go quickly to the drowsy house of Sleep, and bid him send to Alcyone a vision in dead Ceyx' form to tell her the truth about his fate." She spoke; and Iris put on her cloak of a thousand hues and, trailing across the sky in a rainbow curve, she sought the cloud-concealed palace of the king of sleep.

Near the land of the Cimmerians there is a deep recess within a hollow mountain, the home and chamber of sluggish Sleep.[2] Phoebus can never enter there with his rising, noontide, or setting rays. Clouds of vapour breathe forth from the earth, and dusky twilight shadows. There no wakeful, crested cock with his loud crowing summons the dawn; no watch-dog breaks the deep silence with his baying, or goose, more watchful than the dog. There is no sound of wild beast or of cattle, of branches rustling in the breeze, no clamorous tongues of men. There mute silence dwells. But from the bottom of the cave there flows the stream of Lethe, whose waves, gently murmuring over the gravelly bed, invite to slumber. Before the cavern's entrance abundant poppies bloom, and countless herbs, from whose juices dewy night distils sleep and spreads its influence over the darkened lands. There is no door in all the house, so that some turning hinge should not creak; no guardian on the threshold. But in the cavern's central space there is a high couch of ebony, downy-soft, black-hued, spread with a dusky coverlet. There lies the god himself, his limbs relaxed in languorous repose. Around him on all sides lie empty dream-shapes, mimicking many forms, many as ears of grain in harvest-time, as leaves upon the trees, as sands cast on the shore.

When the maiden entered there and with her hands brushed aside the dream-shapes that blocked her way, the awesome house was lit up with the gleaming of her garments. Then the god, scarce lifting his eyelids heavy with the weight of sleep, sinking back repeatedly and knocking his breast with his nodding chin, at last shook himself free of himself and, resting on an elbow, asked her (for he recognized her) why she came. And she replied: "O Sleep, you, the rest of all things, Sleep, mildest of the gods, balm of the soul, who puts care to flight, soothes our bodies worn with hard ministries, and prepares them for toil again! Fashion a shape that shall seem a true form, and bid it go in semblance of the king to Alcyone in Trachin, famed for Hercules. There let it show her the picture of the wreck. This Juno bids." When she had done her task Iris departed, for she could no longer endure the power of sleep, and when she felt the drowsiness stealing upon her frame she fled away and retraced her course along the arch over which she had lately passed.

But the father rouses Morpheus from the throng of his thousand sons, a cunning imitator of the human form. No other is more skilled than he in representing the gait, the features, and the speech of men; the clothing also and the accustomed words of each he represents. His office is with men alone: another takes the form of beast or bird or the long serpent. Him the gods call Icelos, but mortals name him Phobetor. A third is Phantasos, versed in different arts. He puts on deceptive shapes of earth, rocks, water, trees, all lifeless things. These shapes show themselves by night to kings and chieftains, the rest haunt the throng of common folk. These the old sleep-god passes by, and chooses out of all the brethren Morpheus alone to do the bidding of Iris, Thaumas' daughter. This done, once more in soft drowsiness he droops his head and settles it down upon his high couch.

But Morpheus flits away through the darkness on noiseless wings and quickly comes to the Haemonian city. There, putting off his wings, he takes the face and form of Ceyx, wan like the dead, and stands naked before the couch of the hapless wife. His beard is wet, and water drips from his sodden hair. Then with streaming eyes he bends over her couch and says: "Do you recognize your Ceyx, O most wretched wife? or is my face changed in death? Look on me! You will know me then and find in place of husband your husband's shade. No help, Alcyone, have your prayers brought to me: I am dead. Cherish no longer your vain hope of me. For stormy Auster caught my ship on the Aegean sea and, tossing her in his fierce blasts, wrecked her there. My lips, calling vainly upon your name, drank in the waves. And this tale no uncertain messenger brings to you, nor do you hear it in the words of vague report; but I myself, wrecked as you see me, tell you of my fate. Get you up, then, and weep for me; put on your mourning garments and let me not go unlamented to the cheerless land of shades." These words spoke Morpheus, and that, too, in a voice she might well believe her husband's; he seemed also to weep real tears, and had the very gesture of her Ceyx' hands. Alcyone groaned, shed tears, and in sleep seeking his arms and to clasp his body, held only air in her embrace. She cried aloud: "Wait for me! Where do you hasten? I will go with you." Aroused by her own voice and by the image of her husband, she started wide awake. And first she looked around to see if he was there whom but now she had seen. For her attendants, startled by her cries, had brought a lamp into her chamber. When she did not find him anywhere, she smote her cheeks, tore off her garment from her breast and beat her breasts themselves. She stayed not to loose her hair, but rent it, and to her nurse, who asked what was her cause of grief, she cried: "Alcyone is no more, no more; she has died together with her Ceyx. Away with consoling words! He's shipwrecked, dead! I saw him and I knew him, and I stretched out my hands to him as he vanished, eager to hold him back. It was but a shade, and yet it was my husband's true shade, clearly seen. To be sure, he did not have his wonted features, nor did his face light as it used to do. But wan and naked, with hair still dripping, oh, woe is me, I saw him. See there, on that very spot, he himself stood, piteous"—and she strove to see if any footprints still remained. "This, this it was which with fore-boding mind I feared, and I begged you not to leave me and sail away. But surely I should have wished, since you were going to your death, that you had taken me as well. How well had it been for me to go with you; for in that case neither should I have spent any of my life apart from you, nor should we have been separated in our death. But now far from myself I have perished; far from myself also I am tossed about upon the waves, and without me the sea holds me. My heart would be more cruel to me than the sea itself if I should strive still to live on and struggle to survive my sorrow. But I shall neither struggle nor shall I leave you, my poor husband. Now at least I shall come to be your companion; and if not the entombed urn, at least the lettered stone shall join us; if not your bones with mine, still shall I touch you, name with name." Grief checked further speech, wailing took place of words, and groans drawn from her stricken heart.

Morning had come. She went forth from her house to the seashore and sadly sought that spot again from which she had watched him sail. And while she lingered there and while she was saying: "Here he loosed his cable, on this beach he kissed me as he was departing"; while she was thus recalling the incidents and the place and gazing seaward, away out upon the streaming waters she saw something like a corpse. At first she was not sure what it was; but after the waves had washed it a little nearer, although it was still some distance off, yet it clearly was a corpse. She did not know whose it was; yet, because it was a shipwrecked man, she was moved by the omen and, as if she would weep for the unknown dead, she cried: "Alas for you, poor man, whoever you are, and alas for your wife, if wife you have!" Meanwhile the body had been driven nearer by the waves, and the more she regarded it the less and still less could she contain herself. Ah! and now it had come close to land, now she could see clearly what it was. It was her husband! "It is he!" she shrieked and, tearing her cheeks, her hair, her garments all at once, she stretched out her trembling hands to Ceyx, crying: "Thus, O dearest husband, is it thus, poor soul, you come back to me?" Near by the water was a mole built which broke the first onslaught of the waters, and took the force of the rushing waves. To it she ran and leaped into the sea; it was a wonder that she could; she flew and, fluttering through the yielding air on sudden wings, she skimmed the surface of the water, a wretched bird. And as she flew, her croaking mouth, with long slender beak, uttered sounds like one in grief and full of complaint. But when she reached the silent, lifeless body, she embraced the dear limbs with her new-found wings and strove vainly to kiss the cold lips with her rough bill. Whether Ceyx felt this, or whether he but seemed to lift his face by the motion of the waves, men were in doubt. But he did feel it. And at last, through the pity of the gods, both changed to birds. Though thus they suffered the same fate, still even thus their love remained, nor were their conjugal bonds loosened because of their feathered shape. Still do they mate and rear their young; and for seven peaceful days in the winter season Alcyone broods upon her nest floating upon the surface of the waters.* At such a time the waves of the sea are still; for Aeolus guards his winds and forbids them to go abroad and for his grandsons' sake gives peace upon the sea.

Seeing these birds flying in loving harmony over the broad waters, some old man spoke in praise of their affection kept unbroken to the end. Then one near by, or perhaps the same speaker, pointing to a long-necked diver, said: "That bird also, which you see skimming along over the water and trailing his slender legs, is of royal birth, and his ancestors, if you wish in unbroken line to come down to him himself, were Ilus and Assaracus, Ganymede, whom Jove stole away, old Laomedon and Priam, who came by fate on Troy's last days.† He there was the brother of Hector; and had he not met

---

*Ovid is describing the habits of the kingfisher as perceived by observers of the time.
†The figures mentioned are kings of Troy, also called Ilium after Ilus, its first monarch.

his strange fate in early manhood, perhaps he would have a name no
less renowned than Hector's. While the daughter of Dymas bore
the one, the other, Aesacus, is said to have been born in secret be-
neath the shades of Ida by Alexiroë, daughter of the horned
Granicus.[3] He hated towns and, far from glittering palace halls,
dwelt on remote mountain-sides and in lowly country places, and
rarely sought the company of the men of Ilium. Still his heart was
not boorish nor averse to love, and often he pursued through all the
woody glades Hesperia, daughter of Cebren, whom he beheld dry-
ing her flowing hair in the sun upon her father's bank. The nymph
fled at sight of him as the frightened hind flees the tawny wolf, or
as the wild duck, surprised far from her forsaken pool, flees from the
hawk. But the Trojan hero followed her, swift on the wings of love
as she was swift on the wings of fear. Behold, a serpent, hiding in
the grass, pierced her foot with his curved fangs as she fled along,
and left his poison in her veins. Her flight stopped with life. Beside
himself, her lover embraced the lifeless form and cried: 'Oh, I repent
me, I repent that I followed you! But I had no fear of this, nor was
it worth so much to me to win you. We have destroyed you, poor
maid, two of us: the wound was given you by the serpent, by me was
given the cause! I am more guilty than he. But by my death will
I send death's consolation to you.' So saying, from a lofty cliff, where
the hoarse waves had eaten it out below, he hurled himself down
into the sea. But Tethys, pitying his case, received him gently as he
fell, covered him with feathers as he floated on the waters, and so
denied him the privilege of the death he sought. The lover was
wroth that he was forced to live against his will and that his spirit
was thwarted as it desired to leave its wretched seat. And when he
had gained on his shoulders his new-sprung wings, he flew aloft and
once more hurled his body down to the sea; but his light plumage
broke his fall. In wild rage Aesacus dived deep down below the
water and tried endlessly to find the way to death. His passion made
him lean; his legs between the joints are long, his long neck is still
long, his head is far from his body. He still loves the sea and has his
name because he dives beneath it."*

---

*The word *mergo*, meaning "to dive," also referred to a certain seabird.

BOOK XII

FATHER PRIAM, NOT KNOWING that Aesacus was still alive in feathered form, mourned for his son. At an empty tomb also, inscribed with the lost one's name, Hector with his brothers had offered sacrifices in honor of the dead. Paris was not present at the sad rite, Paris, who a little later brought a long-continued war upon his country with his stolen wife. A thousand ships and the whole Pelasgian race, banded together, pursued him, nor would vengeance have been postponed had stormy winds not made the sea impassable, and had the land of Boeotia not kept the ships, though ready to set sail, at fish-haunted Aulis. When here, after their country's fashion, they had prepared to sacrifice to Jove, and just as the ancient altar was glowing with the lighted fires, the Greeks saw a dark-green serpent crawling up a plane-tree which stood near the place where they had begun their sacrifices. There was a nest with eight young birds in the top of the tree, and these, together with the mother, who was flying around her doomed nestlings, the serpent seized and swallowed in his greedy maw. They all looked on in amazement. But Thestorides, the augur, who saw clearly the meaning of the portent, said: "We shall conquer. Rejoice, O Greeks, Troy shall fall, but our task will be of long duration"; and he interpreted the nine birds as nine years of war. Meanwhile the serpent, just as he was, coiled round the green branches of the tree, was changed to stone, and the stone kept the form of the climbing serpent.

But Nereus continued to be boisterous on the Aonian waters, and refused to transport the war. And there were some who held that Neptune was sparing because he had built its walls. But not so the son of Thestor. For he was neither ignorant of the truth nor did he withhold it, that the wrath of the virgin goddess must be appeased with a virgin's blood. After consideration for the public weal had overcome affection, and the father had been vanquished by the king, and just as midst the weeping attendants Iphigenia was standing before the altar ready to shed her innocent blood, the goddess was moved to pity and spread a cloud before their eyes; and there, while the sacred rites went on, midst the confusion of the sacrifice and the cries of suppliants, she is said to have substituted a hind for the maiden of Mycenae. When therefore, as was fitting, Diana had been appeased by the sacrifice of blood, when Phoebe's and the ocean's wrath had subsided together, the thousand ships found the winds blowing astern and, after suffering many adventures, they reached the shores of Phrygia.

There is a place in the middle of the world, between land and sea and sky, the meeting-point of the three-fold universe. From this place, whatever is, however far away, is seen, and every word penetrates to these hollow ears. Rumour dwells here, having chosen her house upon a high mountain-top; and she gave the house countless entrances, a thousand apertures, but with no doors to close them. Night and day the house stands open. It is built all of echoing brass. The whole place resounds with confused noises, repeats all words and doubles what it hears. There is no quiet, no silence anywhere within. And yet there is no loud clamour, but only the subdued murmur of voices, like the murmur of the waves of the sea if you listen afar off, or like the last rumblings of thunder when Jove has made the dark clouds crash together. Crowds fill the hall, shifting throngs come and go, and everywhere wander thousands of rumours, falsehoods mingled with the truth, and confused reports flit about. Some of these fill their idle ears with talk, and others go and tell elsewhere what they have heard; while the story grows in size, and each new teller makes contribution to what he has heard. Here is Credulity, here is heedless Error, unfounded Joy and panic Fear; here sudden Sedition and unauthentic Whisperings. Rumour herself beholds all that is done in heaven, on sea and land, and searches throughout the world for news.

Now she had spread the tidings that the Greek fleet was approaching full of brave soldiery; and so not unlooked for did the invading army come. The Trojans were ready to prevent the enemy's landing and to protect their shores. You first fell, Protesilaüs, before Hector's deadly spear. Those early battles proved costly to the Greeks and they soon learned Hector's warlike mettle by the slaughter that he dealt. And the Phrygians learned too, at no slight cost of blood, how mighty was the Grecian hand. And now the Sigean shores grew red; now Neptune's son, Cygnus, had given a thousand men to death; now was Achilles pressing on in his chariot and laying low whole ranks with the stroke of his spear that grew on Pelion; and, as he sought through the battle's press either Cygnus or Hector, he met with Cygnus. (Hector's fate had been postponed until the tenth year.) Then Achilles, shouting to his horses whose snowy necks were straining at the yoke, drove his chariot full at the enemy and, brandishing his spear with his strong arm, cried: "Whoever you are, O youth, have it for solace of your death that you were slain by Achilles of Thessaly." So spoke Aeacides. His heavy spear followed on the word; but, although there was no swerving in the well-aimed spear, the flying weapon struck with its sharp point without effect, and only bruised his breast as by a blunt stroke. Then Cygnus said: "O son of Thetis, for rumour has already made you known to me, why do you marvel that I am unscathed?" for he was amazed. "Neither this helmet which you behold, yellow, with its horse-hair crest, nor yet this hollow shield which burdens my left arm is intended for a protection; it's ornament that is sought from them. Mars, too, for this cause, wears his armor. Remove the protection of this covering: still shall I escape unharmed. It is something to be the son, not of Nereus' daughter, but of him who rules both Nereus and his daughters and the whole sea besides." He spoke and hurled against Aeacides his spear, destined only to stick in the curving shield. Through brass and through nine layers of bull's hide it tore its way, but stopped upon the tenth. Shaking the weapon off, the hero again hurled a quivering spear with his strong hand. Again his foeman's body was unwounded and unharmed; nor did a third spear avail to injure Cygnus, though he offered his body quite unprotected. Achilles raged at this just like a bull in the broad arena when with his deadly horns he rushes on the scarlet cloak, the object of his wrath, and finds it ever eluding his fierce attack. He examined the spear to see if the iron point had not been dislodged. It was still on the wooden shaft. "Is my hand then so weak," he said, "and has the strength, which it once had, ebbed away in this case alone? For surely I had strength enough when I as leader of the attack overthrew Lyrnesus' walls, or when I caused Tenedos and Thebes, the city of Eetion, to flow with their own blood, when the

Caïcus ran red with the slaughter of its neighbouring tribes, and when Telephus twice felt the strength of my spear.* On this field also, with so many slain, heaps of whose corpses upon the shore I have both made and see, my right hand has been mighty and still is mighty." He spoke and, as if he distrusted his former prowess, he hurled the spear full at Menoetes, one of the Lycian commons, and smote clean through his breastplate and his breast beneath. As his dying victim fell clanging down head first upon the solid earth, Achilles plucked out the spear from the hot wound and cried: "This is the hand, this the spear with which I have just conquered. I likewise shall use it on this foeman, and may the outcome be the same on him, I pray." So saying, he hurled again at Cygnus, and the ashen spear went straight and struck, unshunned, with a thud upon the left shoulder, off which it rebounded as from a wall or from a solid cliff. Yet where the spear struck, Achilles saw Cygnus marked with blood, and rejoiced, but vainly: there was no wound; it was Menoetes' blood! Then truly in headlong rage he leaped down from his lofty chariot and, seeking his invulnerable foe in close conflict with his gleaming sword, he saw both shield and helmet pierced through, but on the unyielding body his sword was even blunted. The hero could brook no more, but with shield and sword-hilt again and again he beat upon the face and hollow temples of his uncovered foe. As one gives way the other presses on, buffets and rushes him, gives him no pause to recover from the shock. Fear gets hold on Cygnus; dark shadows float before his eyes, and as he steps backward a stone lying on the plain blocks his way. As he lies with bent body pressed back upon this, Achilles whirls him with mighty force and dashes him to the earth. Then, pressing with buckler and hard knees upon his breast, he unlaces his helmet-thongs. With these applied beneath his chin he chokes his throat and cuts off the passage of his breath. He prepares to strip his conquered foe: he sees the armor empty; for the god has changed the body into the white bird whose name he lately bore.

This struggle, this battle, brought a truce of many days, and each side laid its weapons down and rested. And while a watchful guard was patrolling the Phrygian walls and a watchful guard patrolled the

*Achilles refers to city-states he sacked during the Trojan War's long stalemate.

trenches of the Greeks, there came a festal day when Cygnus' conqueror, Achilles, was sacrificing to Pallas with blood of a slain heifer. When now the entrails had been placed upon the blazing altars and the odour which gods love had ascended to the skies, the holy beings received their share and the rest was set upon the tables. The chiefs reclined upon the couches and ate their fill of the roasted flesh while they relieved their cares and quenched their thirst with wine. Nor were they entertained by sound of cithern, nor by the voice of song, nor by the long flute of boxwood pierced with many holes; but they drew out the night in talk, and valor was the theme of their conversation. Of battles was their talk, the enemy's and their own, and it was joy to tell over and over again in turn the perils they had encountered and endured. For of what else should Achilles speak, or of what else should others speak in great Achilles' presence? Especially did the talk turn on Achilles' last victory and Cygnus' overthrow. It seemed a marvel to them all that a youth should have a body which no spear could penetrate, invulnerable, which blunted the sword's edge. Aeacides himself* and the Greeks were wondering at this, when Nestor said: "In this your generation there has been one only, Cygnus, who could scorn the sword, whom no stroke could pierce; but I myself long ago saw one who could bear a thousand strokes with body unharmed, Thessalian Caeneus: Caeneus of Thessaly, I say, who once dwelt on Mount Othrys, famed for his mighty deeds; and to enhance the marvel of him, he had been born a woman."† All who heard were struck with wonder at this marvel and begged him to tell the tale. Among the rest Achilles said: "Tell on, old man, eloquent wisdom of our age, for all of us alike desire to hear, who was this Caeneus, why was he changed in sex, in what campaign did you know him and fighting against whom; by whom he was conquered if he was conquered by anyone." Then said the old man: "Though time has blurred my memory, though many things which I saw in my young years have quite gone from me, still can I remember much; nor is there anything, midst so many deeds of war and peace, that clings more firmly in my memory than this. And, if long-extended age could

---

*Aeacides means "descendant of Aeacus"—that is, Achilles.
†Caeneus also appears at the Calydonian boar hunt (book VIII).

have made anyone an observer of many deeds, I have lived for two centuries and now am living in my third.

"Famous for beauty was Elatus' daughter, Caenis, most lovely of all the maids of Thessaly, both throughout the neighbouring cities and your own (for she was of your city, Achilles), and she was the longed-for hope of many suitors. Peleus, too, perhaps, would have tried to win her; but he had either already wed your mother or she was promised to him. And Caenis would not consent to any marriage; but, so report had it, while walking along a lonely shore she was ravished by the god of the sea. When Neptune had tasted the joys of his new love, he said: 'Make now your prayers without fear of refusal. Choose what you most desire.' This, also, was a part of the same report. Then Caenis said: 'The wrong that you have done me calls for a mighty prayer, the prayer that I may never again be able to suffer so. Grant me that I be not woman: so grant all my prayers.' She spoke the last words with a deeper tone which could well seem to be uttered by a man. And so it was; for already the god of the deep ocean had assented to her prayer, and had granted her besides that she should be proof against any wounds and should never fall before any sword. Atracides went away rejoicing in his gift, spent his years in manly exercises, and ranged the fields of Thessaly.

"Bold Ixion's son had wed Hippodame and had invited the cloud-born centaurs to recline at the tables, set in order in a well-shaded grotto.[1] The Thessalian chiefs were there and I myself was there. The palace, in festal array, resounded with the noisy throng. Behold, they were singing the nuptial song, the great hall smoked with the fires, and in came the maiden escorted by a throng of matrons and young wives, herself of surpassing beauty. We congratulated Pirithoüs upon his bride, an act which all but undid the good omen of the wedding. For your heart, Eurytus, wildest of the wild centaurs, was inflamed as well by the sight of the maiden as with wine, and it was swayed by drunken passion redoubled by lust. Straightway the tables were overturned and the banquet in an uproar, and the bride was caught by her hair and dragged violently away. Eurytus caught up Hippodame, and others, each took one for himself according as he fancied or as he could, and the scene looked like the sacking of a town. The whole house resounded with the women's shrieks. Quickly we all sprang up and Theseus first cried out: 'What madness, Eurytus, drives you to this, that while I still live you dare provoke Pirithoüs and, not knowing what you do, attack two men in one?' The great-souled hero, that he might justify his threat, thrust aside the opposing centaurs and rescued the ravished maid from their mad hands. The other made no reply, for with words he could not defend such deeds; but with unruly hands he rushed upon the avenger and beat upon his face and noble breast. There chanced to stand near by an antique mixing-vat, rough with high-wrought figures; this, Theseus, rising to his fullest height, himself caught up and hurled full into the other's face. He, spouting forth gouts of blood along with brains and wine from wound and mouth alike, stumbled backward upon the reeking ground. His dual-formed brothers, inflamed with passion at his death, cried all with one accord, 'To arms! to arms!' vying with one another. Wine gave them courage, and in the first onslaught wine-cups and brittle flasks went flying through the air, and deep rounded basins, utensils once meant for use of feasting, but now for war and slaughter.

"First Amycus, Ophion's son, scrupled not to rob the inner sanctuary of its gifts, and first snatched from the shrine a chandelier thick hung with glittering lamps. This, lifted on high, as when one strives to break a bull's white neck with sacrificial axe, he dashed full at the head of Celadon, one of the Lapithae, crushing his face past recognition. His eyes leaped from their sockets, the bones of his face were shattered, and his nose driven back and fastened in his throat. But Pelates of Pella, wrenching off the leg of a table of maple-wood, hurled Amycus to the ground, his chin driven into his breast; and, as he spat forth dark blood and teeth commingled, his enemy with a second blow dispatched him to the shades of Tartara.

"Then Gryneus, gazing with wild eyes upon the smoking altar near which he stood, cried out, 'Why not use this?' and, catching up the huge altar, fire and all, he hurled it amid a throng of Lapithae and crushed down two, Broteas and Orios. Now Orios' mother was Mycale, who, men said, had by her incantations oft-times drawn down the horns of the moon, despite her struggles. 'You shall not escape unscathed, if I may but lay hand upon a weapon.' So cried Exadius, and found for weapon the antlers of a stag hung on a tall pine-tree as a votive offering. Gryneus' eyes were pierced by the double branching horns and his eyeballs gouged out. One of these stuck to the horn and the other rolled down upon his beard and hung there in a mass of clotted blood.

"Then Rhoetus caught up a blazing brand of plum-wood from the altar and, whirling it on the right, smashed through Charaxus' temples covered with yellow hair. The hair, caught by the greedy flames, burned fiercely, like a dry field of grain, and the blood scorching in the wound gave forth a horrid sizzling sound; such as a bar of iron, glowing red in the fire, gives when the smith takes it out in his bent pincers and plunges it into a tub of water; it sizzles and hisses as it is thrust into the tepid pool. The wounded man shook off the greedy fire from his shaggy locks, then tore up from the ground and heaved upon his shoulders a threshold-stone, a weight for a team of oxen. But its very weight prevented him from hurling it to reach his enemy. The massive stone, however, did reach Charaxus' friend, Cometes, who stood a little nearer, and crushed him to the ground. At this Rhoetus could not contain his joy and said: 'So, I pray, may the rest of the throng on your side be brave!' and he redoubled his attack with the half-burned brand, and with heavy blows thrice and again he broke through the joinings of his skull until the bones sank down into his fluid brains.

"The victor next turned against Euagrus, Corythus, and Dryas. When one of these, young Corythus, whose first downy beard was just covering his cheeks, fell forward, Euagrus cried: 'What glory do you get from slaying a mere boy?' Rhoetus gave him no chance to say more, but fiercely thrust the red, flaming brand into the man's mouth while still open in speech, and through his mouth clear down into his breast. You also, savage Dryas, he pursued, whirling the brand about his head; but his attack upon you did not have the same result. As he came on, rejoicing in his successive killings, with a charred stake you thrust him through where neck and shoulder join. Rhoetus groaned aloud, with a mighty effort wrenched the stake out from the hard bone, and then fled, reeking with his own blood. Orneus also fled and Lycabas and Medon, wounded in his right shoulder, and Thaumas and Pisenor; and Mermeros, who but lately had surpassed all in speed of foot, now fared more slowly because of the wound he had received; Pholus also fled and Melaneus and Abas, hunter of the boar, and Asbolus, the augur, who had in vain attempted to dissuade his friends from battle. He said to Nessus, who also fled with him in fear of wounds: 'Do not you flee; you will be reserved for the bow of Hercules.' But Eurynomus and Lycidas, Areos and Imbreus did not escape death; for all these the right hand of Dryas slew as they fought fronting him. In front you, also, Crenaeus, received your wound, although you had turned in flight; for, as you looked back, you received a heavy javelin between the eyes where nose and forehead join.

"Midst all this uproar Aphidas lay, buried in endless sleep which filled all his veins, unawakened, still holding his cup full of mixed wine in his sluggish hand and stretched at full length upon an Ossaean bear's shaggy skin. Him, all in vain striking no blow, Phorbas spied at a distance and, fitting his fingers in the thong of his javelin, cried out: 'Mingle your wine with the Styx and drink it there.' Straightway he hurled his javelin at the youth, and the iron-tipped ash was driven through his neck as he chanced to lie with head thrown back. He was not conscious of death, and from his filling throat out upon the couch and into the very wine-cup the dark blood flowed.

"I saw Petraeus striving to tear from the earth an acorn-laden oak. While he held this in both his arms, bending it this way and that, and just as he was wrenching forth the loosened trunk, Pirithoüs hurled a spear right through his ribs and pinned his writhing body to the hard oak. They say that Lycus fell by the might of Pirithoüs; by the might of Pirithoüs, Chromis. But Dictys and Helops gave greater fame to the conqueror than either of these. Helops was thrust through by a javelin which passed through his temples and, hurled from the right, pierced to his left ear. Dictys, while fleeing in desperate haste from Ixion's son who pressed him hard, stumbled on the edge of a steep precipice and, falling head-long, crashed into a huge ash-tree's top with all his weight and impaled his body on the broken spikes.

"Aphareus, at hand to avenge him, heaved to throw a rock torn from the mountain-side; but, even as he heaved, the son of Aegeus caught him with an oaken club and broke the great bones of his elbow-joint. Having no time nor care to inflict further injury on his maimed body, he sprang on tall Bienor's back, who never before had carried any but himself; and, pressing his knees into the centaur's

sides and with his left hand clutching his flowing locks, he crushed
face and mouth, screaming out threatenings, and hard temples with
his knotty club. With the club he slew Nedymnus and Lycopes,
famed for the javelin throw, Hippasos, his breast covered by his
flowing beard, and Ripheus, who overtopped the trees in height;
Thereus as well, who used to catch bears upon the Thessalian moun-
tains and carry them home alive and struggling. Demoleon could no
longer brook Theseus' unchecked success. He had been wrenching
away with all his might at an old pine, trying to tear it up, trunk and
all; failing in this, he broke it off and hurled it at his foe. But
Theseus, seeing the weapon coming, withdrew beyond its range, for
so had Pallas directed him; at least that is what he himself would
have us understand. But the tree-trunk did not fall without effect,
for it shore off tall Crantor's breast and left shoulder from the neck.
He had been your father's armor-bearer, Achilles, whom Amyntor,
king of the Dolopians, when overcome in war had given to Aeacides
as a faithful pledge of peace. When Peleus at some space away saw
him so horribly dismembered, he cried: 'At least receive a funeral of-
fering, Crantor, dearest of youths.' So saying, with his sturdy arm
and with all his might of soul as well, he hurled his ashen spear at
Demoleon; and this burst through his framework of ribs and hung
there quivering in the bones. The centaur wrenched out the wooden
shaft with his hands, leaving the head. This, also, he with much
trouble sought to reach; but the head stuck fast within his lungs. His
very anguish gave him frantic courage: wounded as he was, he
reared up against his foe and beat the hero down with his hoofs. But
Peleus received the blows on helm and resounding shield and, while
protecting himself, he held his own weapon ready. With this he
thrust the centaur through the shoulder, with one blow piercing his
two breasts. Before this encounter Peleus had already slain
Phlegraeos and Hyles, hurling from a distance, and, in close con-
flict, Iphinoüs and Clanis. To these he now added Dorylas, who
wore a cap of wolf's hide on his head and, in place of deadly spear,
a notable pair of curving bull's horns, reeking red with blood.

  "To him (for my courage gave me strength) I cried: 'See now how
little your horns avail against my spear'; and I hurled the spear.
Since he could not dodge this, he threw up his right hand to pro-
tect his forehead from the wound. And there his hand was pinned

against his forehead. A mighty shout arose, but Peleus, for he was near him, while the centaur stood pinned and helpless with that sore wound, smote him with his sword full in the belly. He leaped fiercely forward, trailing his entrails on the ground; and as he trailed he trod upon them and burst them as he trod, tangled his legs in them, and fell with empty belly to the earth.

"But your beauty, Cyllarus, did not save you from death in that great fight, if indeed we grant beauty to your tribe. His beard was just in its first growth, a golden beard, and golden locks fell down upon his shoulders. He had a pleasing sprightliness of face; and his neck, shoulders, breast, and hands, and all his human parts you would praise as equal to an artist's perfect work. His equine part, too, was without blemish, no way less perfect than his human part. Give him but neck and head, and he will be worthy of Castor's use: so shaped for the seat his back, so bold stood out the muscles on his deep chest. All blacker than pitch he was; yet his tail was white; his legs also were snowy white. Many females of his own kind sought him, but Hylonome alone had won him, than whom there was no other centaur-maid more comely in all the forest depths. She, by her coaxing ways, by loving and confessing love, alone possessed Cyllarus; and by her toilet, too, so far as such a thing was possible to such a form; for now she smoothed her long locks with a comb, now twined rosemary, now violets or roses in her hair, and some-times she wore white lilies. Twice each day she bathed her face in the brook that fell down from a wooded height by Pagasa, and twice dipped her body in the stream. Nor would she wear on shoulder or left side anything but becoming garments, skins of well-chosen beasts. They both felt equal love. Together they would wander on the mountain-sides, together rest within the caves. On this occasion also they had come together to the palace of the Lapithae, and were waging fierce battle side by side. Thrown from an unknown hand, a javelin came from the left and pierced you, Cyllarus, below where the chest rises to the neck. The heart, though but slightly wounded, grew cold and the whole body also after the weapon had been drawn out. Straightway Hylonome embraced the dying body, fondled the wound with her hand and, placing her lips upon his lips, strove to hold from its passing the dying breath. But when she saw that he was dead, with some words which the surrounding uproar prevented me from hearing, she threw herself upon the spear which had pierced Cyllarus and fell in a dying embrace upon her lover.

"Still there stands clear before my eyes one who had with knotted thongs bound together six lion-hides, Phaeocomes, thus protecting both man and horse. Hurling a log which two yokes of cattle could scarce move, he struck Tectaphos, the son of Olenus, a crushing blow upon the head. The broad dome of his head was shattered, and through his mouth, through hollow nostrils, eyes, and ears oozed the soft brains, as when curdled milk drips through oaken withes, or a thick liquid mass trickles through a coarse sieve weighted down, and is squeezed out through the crowded apertures. But I, even as he made ready to spoil his fallen victim—your father can testify to this—thrust my sword deep into the spoiler's groin. Chthonius also and Teleboas fell by my sword. The one had carried a forked stick as weapon; the other had a spear, and with this spear he gave me a wound—you see the mark!—the old scar is still visible. Those were the days when I should have been sent to capture Pergama; then with my arms I could have checked, if not surpassed, the arms of Hector. But at that time Hector was either not yet born or was but a little boy; and now old age has sapped my strength. What need to tell you how Periphas overcame the double-formed Pyraethus? Why tell of Ampyx, who with a pointless shaft thrust through the opposing front of the four-footed Echeclus? Macareus hurled a crow-bar at the breast of Pelethronian Erigdupus and laid him low. And I remember also how a hunting spear, thrown by the hand of Nessus, was buried in the groin of Cymelus. Nor would you have believed that Mopsus, the son of Ampycus, was only a seer telling what was to come; for by Mopsus' weapon the two formed Hodites fell, striving in vain to speak, for his tongue had been pinned to his chin and his chin to his throat.

"Caeneus had already put five to death: Styphelus and Bromus, Antimachus and Elymus and Pyracmos, armed with a battle-axe. I do not remember their wounds, but their number and names I marked well. Then forth rushed one, armed with the spoils of Emathian Halesus whom he had slain, Latreus, of enormous bulk of limb and body. His years were midway between youth and age, but his strength was youthful. Upon his temples his hair was turning grey. Conspicuous for his shield and sword and Macedonian lance, and facing either host in turn, he clashed his arms and rode round in a circle, insolently pouring out many boasts on the empty air: 'You too, Caenis, shall I brook? For woman shall you always be to me, Caenis shall you be. Does not your birth remind you, do you not remember for what act you were rewarded, at what price you gained this false appearance of a man? Heed well what you were born or what you have endured. Go then, take distaff and wool-basket and twist the spun thread with practised thumb; but leave wars to men.' As he thus boasted, Caeneus, hurling his spear, plowed up the centaur's side stretched in the act of running, just where man and horse were joined. Mad with the pain, the other smote the Phylleian youth full in the naked face with his long lance; but this leaped back again like a hailstone from a roof, or a pebble from a hollow drum. Then he closed up and strove to thrust his sword in his unyielding side. The sword found no place of entrance. 'But you shall not escape! with the sword's edge I'll slay you, though its point be blunt,' the centaur cried; then turned his sword edge-wise and reached with his long right arm for his foeman's loins; the blow resounded on the flesh as if on stricken marble, and the blade, striking the hardened skin, broke into pieces. When long enough he had stood unharmed before his amazed enemy, Caeneus exclaimed: 'Come now, let me try your body with my blade!' and clear to the hilt he drove his deadly sword in the other's side, and there in his vitals twisted and turned the buried weapon, inflicting wound within wound. Now, quite beside themselves, the double monsters rushed on with huge uproar, and all together against that single foe they aimed and drove their weapons. The spears fell blunted, and Caeneus, the son of Elatus, still stood, for all their strokes, unwounded and unstained. The strange sight struck them speechless. Then Monychus exclaimed: 'Oh, what a shame is this! We, a whole people, are defied by one, and he scarcely a man. And yet he is the man, while we, with our weak attempts, are what he was before. Of what advantage are our monster-forms? What our two-fold strength? What avails it that a double nature has united in our bodies the strongest living things? We are not sons of any goddess nor Ixion's sons, I think.* For he was high-souled enough to aspire to be

---

*Evidently, this centaur claims Juno herself as parent; see endnote 1 to book XII.

great Juno's mate, while we are conquered by an enemy but half-man! Come then, let us heap stones and tree-trunks on him, mountains at a time! let's crush his stubborn life out with forests for our missiles! Let forests smother his throat, and for wounds let weight suffice.' He spoke and, chancing on a tree-trunk overthrown by mad Auster's might, he hurled it at his sturdy foe. The others followed him; and in short time Othrys was stripped of trees and Pelion had lost his shade. Buried beneath that huge mound, Caeneus heaved against the weight of trees and bore up the oaken mass upon his sturdy shoulders. But indeed, as the burden mounted over lips and head, he could get no air to breathe. Gasping for breath, at times he strove in vain to lift his head into the air and to throw off the heaped-up forest; at times he moved, just as if lofty Ida, which we see there, should tremble with an earthquake. His end is doubtful. Some said that his body was thrust down by the weight of woods to the Tartarean pit; but the son of Ampycus denied this. For from the middle of the pile he saw a bird with golden wings fly up into the limpid air. I saw it too, then for the first time and the last. As Mopsus watched him circling round his camp in easy flight and heard the loud clangour of his wings, he followed him both with soul and eyes and cried: 'All hail, Caeneus, glory of the Lapithaean race, once most mighty hero, now sole bird of your kind!' This story was believed because of him who told it. Then grief increased our wrath and we were indignant that one man should be overwhelmed by so many foes. Nor did we cease to ply sword on behalf of our mad grief till half our foes were slain and flight and darkness saved all the rest."

As Pylian Nestor told this tale of strife betwixt the Lapithae and half-human Centaurs, Tlepolemus could not restrain his resentment that Alcides had been passed by without a word, and said: "Old sir, it's strange that you have forgotten to speak in praise of Hercules; for surely my father used often to tell me of the cloud-born creatures he had overcome." And sternly the Pylian answered him: "Why do you force me to remember wrongs, to reopen a grief that was buried by the lapse of years, and to rehearse the injuries that make me hate your father? He has done deeds beyond belief, Heaven knows! and filled the earth with well-earned praise, which I would gladly deny him if I could. But neither Deïphobus nor Polydamas nor even

Hector* do we praise; for who cares to praise his enemy? That sire
of yours once laid low Messene's walls, brought undeserved de-
struction upon Elis and Pylos, and devastated my own home with
fire and sword. To say nothing of the others whom he slew, there
were twelve of us sons of Neleus, a noble band of youths; and all
twelve, except for me alone, fell by Hercules' might. That others
could be conquered must be borne; but strange was the death of
Periclymenus; for to him Neptune, father of Neleus, had given
power to assume any form he pleased and to put it off again at will.
When now he had vainly changed to each of his forms in turn, he
took the form of the bird which carries the thunderbolts in his
hooked talons, a bird most dear to the king of the gods. With all his
might of wings, of curved beak and hooked claws, he had torn the
hero's face. Then the Tirynthian aimed his too unerring bow at him
as he bore his body high into the clouds and hung poised there, and
smote him where wing joins side. The wound was not severe; but
the sinews severed by the wound failed of their office and refused
motion and power of flight. Down to the earth he fell, his weakened
wings no longer catching the air; and the arrow, where it had lightly
pierced the wing, pressed by the weight of the body in which it
hung, was driven clear through the upper breast from the left side
into the throat. And now, O fairest leader of the Rhodian fleet, what
cause have I, think you, to sing the praises of your Hercules? Yet for
my brothers I seek no other vengeance than to ignore his mighty
deeds. Between me and you there is unbroken amity."

When Nestor with sweet speech had told this tale, at the con-
clusion of the old man's words the wine-cup went around once more
and they rose from the couches. The remainder of the night was
given to sleep.

But the god who rules the waters of the sea with his trident was
still filled with a father's grief for his son whose body he had
changed into the bird of Phaëthon. And, hating the murderous
Achilles, he indulged his unforgetting wrath excessively. And now
for almost ten years the war had been prolonged, when he thus ad-
dressed Sminthean Apollo of the unshorn locks: "O, by far the best

---

*Three Trojan heroes, Hector greatest among them.

beloved of my brother's sons, you who with me (though vainly) built the walls of Troy, do you not groan at sight of these battlements so soon to fall? Do you not grieve that so many thousands have been slain in defending these walls? Not to name them all, does not Hector's image come before you, dragged around his own Pergama? But Achilles, fierce and more cruel than war itself, still lives, the destroyer of our handiwork. Let him but come within my reach. I'll make him feel what I can do with my three-forked spear. But since it is not granted me to meet my enemy face to face, you ought to bring him to sudden death by your unseen arrow!" The Delian nodded assent and, indulging equally his own and his uncle's desire, wrapped in a cloud came to the Trojan lines. There midst the bloody strife of heroes he saw Paris taking infrequent shots at the nameless crowd. Revealing his divinity, he said: "Why do you waste your arrows in killing common folk? If you would serve your people, aim at Aeacides and avenge your slaughtered brothers!" He spoke and, pointing where Pelides was working havoc on the Trojans with his spear, he turned the bow in his direction and guided the well-aimed shaft with his death-dealing hand. This was the first cause for joy which old Priam had since Hector's death. So then, Achilles, you, the conqueror of the mightiest, you are yourself overcome by the cowardly ravisher of a Grecian's wife! But if you had been fated to fall by a woman's battle-stroke, how gladly would you have fallen by the Amazon's double axe!

And now that terror of the Phrygians, that ornament and bulwark of the Pelasgian name, Aeacides, the invincible captain of the war, was burned. One and the same god armed him and consumed him too. Now he is but dust; and of Achilles, once so great, there remains a pitiful handful, hardly enough to fill an urn. But his glory lives, enough to fill the whole round world. This is the true measure of the man; and in this the son of Peleus is still his real self, and does not know empty Tartara. His very shield, that you might know to whom it once belonged, still wages war, and for his arms arms are taken up. Neither Tydides nor Ajax, Oileus' son, dares to claim them, nor the lesser Atrides, nor the greater in prowess and in age,[*]

---

*The lesser Atrides (son of Atreus) is Menelaus; the greater Atrides is Agamemnon.

nor other chieftains. Only the son of Telamon and Laërtes' son were bold enough to claim so great a prize. To escape the hateful burden of a choice between them, Tantalides bade the Grecian captains assemble in the midst of the camp, and he referred to all the decision of the strife.

BOOK XIII

THE CHIEFS TOOK THEIR seats, while the commons stood in a ring about them. Then up rose Ajax, lord of the sevenfold shield. With uncontrolled indignation he let his lowering gaze rest awhile on the Sigean shores and on the fleet; then, pointing to these, "By Jupiter!" he cried, "in the presence of these ships I plead my cause, and my competitor is—Ulysses! But he did not hesitate to give way before Hector's torches, which I withstood, indeed, which I drove away from this fleet. It is safer, then, to fight with lying words than with hands. But I am not prompt to speak, as he is not to act; and I am as much his master in the fierce conflict of the battle-line as he is mine in talk. As for my deeds, O Greeks, I do not think I need rehearse them to you, for you have seen them. Let Ulysses tell of his, done without witness, done with the night alone to see them! I own that it is a mighty prize I strive for; but such a rival takes away the honor of it. It is no honor for Ajax to have gained a prize, however great, to which Ulysses has aspired. Already he has gained reward enough in this contest because, when conquered, he still can say he strove with me.

"And even if my valor were in doubt, I should still be his superior in birth; for Telamon was my father, who in company with valiant Hercules took the walls of Troy and with the Pagasaean ship sailed to Colchis.* His father was Aeacus, who is passing judgment in that silent world where Sisyphus Aeolides strains to his heavy stone; and most high Jupiter acknowledges Aeacus as his son. Thus Ajax is the third remove from Jove. But let this descent be of no avail to my cause, O Greeks, if I do not share it with the great Achilles. He was my cousin; a cousin's arms I seek. Why do you, the

---

*The journey of Jason and the Argonauts.

son of Sisyphus, exactly like him in his tricks and fraud, seek to associate the Aeacidae with the name of an alien family?

"Is it because I first came to arms with no detective that arms are denied me? And shall he appear the better man who came last to arms and by feigned madness shirked the war, till one more shrewd than he, but not to his own advantage, the son of Nauplius, uncovered this timid fellow's trick and dragged him forth to the arms that he shunned? Shall he take the best because he wanted to take none? And shall I go unhonored, denied my cousin's gifts, just because I was the first to front the danger?

"And oh, that his madness either had been real, or had never been detected, and that this criminal had never come with us against the Phrygians! Then, son of Poeas, Lemnos would not possess you, set off there to our sin and shame, you who, they say, hidden in forest lairs, move the very rocks with your groans and call down curses on Laërtes' son which he has richly merited, and which, if there are any gods, you do not call down in vain. And now he, who took oath with us for this same war, alas! one of our chieftains, who fell heir to Alcides' shafts, now, broken with disease and hunger, is clothed and fed by the birds, and in pursuit of birds uses those arrows which fate intended for Troy! But yet he lives at least, because he did not keep on with Ulysses. Ill-fated Palamedes, too, would prefer to have been left behind. He would be living still, or at least would have died without dishonor, whom that fellow there, all too mindful of the unfortunate exposure of his madness, charged with betraying the Greek cause, and in proof of his false charge showed the gold which he had already hidden there.[1] So then, either by exile or by death he has been drawing off the Grecian strength. So does Ulysses fight, so must he be feared!

"Though he should surpass even trusty Nestor in his eloquence, he will never make me believe that his desertion of Nestor was other than a crime. For when he, slow from his horse's wound and spent with extreme age, appealed to Ulysses, he was deserted by his friend. And that I am not making up this tale Tydides knows full well, for he repeatedly called upon him by name and chided his timid friend for flight. But the gods regard the affairs of men with righteous eyes. Behold he is in need of aid who rendered none; and as he left another, so was he fated to be left. He had established his own precedent. He cried aloud upon his friends. I came and saw him trembling, pale with fear, shrinking from impending death. I thrust forward my massive shield and covered him where he lay, and I saved his worthless life—small praise in that. If you persist in this contention let us go back to that spot; bring back the enemy, your wound and your accustomed fear; hide behind my shield and contend with me beneath it. But after I rescued him, he, who because of his wounds had had no strength to stand, now fled away not hindered by his wounds at all!

"Here is Hector, and he brings the gods with him into battle; and where he rushes on, not only you are terrified, Ulysses, but brave men also; so much terror does he inspire. Him, rejoicing in the success of his bloody slaughter, I laid low upon the ground with a huge stone which I threw; and when he challenged one to meet him, I alone bore the brunt of his attack. You prayed, O Greeks, that the lot might fall to me, and your prayers were heard. If you ask the outcome of the battle, at least I was not overcome by him. Behold, the Trojans bring sword and fire and Jove against the Greek ships. Where now is the eloquent Ulysses? But I with my own breast stood bulwark for the thousand ships, the hope of your return. Grant me these arms for all those ships.

"But if I may speak truth, the arms claim greater honor than do I; they share my glory, and the arms seek Ajax, not Ajax the arms. Let the Ithacan compare with these deeds his Rhesus and unwarlike Dolon, his Helenus, Priam's son, taken captive, and the stolen Palladium: nothing done in the light of day, nothing apart from Diomede.* If you do give that armor for so cheap deserts, divide it and let the larger share in them be Diomede's.

"But why give them to the Ithacan, who always does things stealthily, always unarmed, relying upon tricks to catch the enemy off his guard? The very glint of the helmet gleaming with bright gold will betray his snares and discover him as he hides. But neither will the Dulichian's head beneath the helmet of Achilles be able to bear so great a weight, nor can the spear-shaft, cut on Pelion, be otherwise than burdensome and heavy to his unwarlike arm. The shield also, a moulded picture of the vast universe, will not become his timid hand, the left one, made for stealing. Why do you seek a prize, you shameless

---

*All incidents found in the *Iliad*.

fellow, that will overtax your strength; a prize which, if by some mistake the Greeks should give it to you, will be reason for the foe to spoil, not fear you? And flight, in which alone you surpass all others, most timid as you are, will prove but slow for you if you carry such a weight. Consider also that that shield of yours, so rarely used in battle, is quite uninjured; while mine, pierced in a thousand places by the thrusts of spears, needs a fresh shield to take its place.

"Finally, what need of words? Let us be seen in action! Let the brave hero's arms be sent into the enemy's midst; bid them be recovered, and to their rescuer present the rescued arms."

The son of Telamon finished, and the applause of the crowd followed his closing words. At length Laërtes' heroic son stood up and, holding his eyes for a little on the ground, he raised them to the chiefs and broke silence with the words for which they waited; nor was grace of manner lacking to his eloquent speech.

"If my prayers and yours had availed, O Greeks, there would be no question as to the victor in this great strife, and you, Achilles, would still have your own armor, and we should still have you. But since the unjust fates have denied him to me and you" (and with his hand he made as if to wipe tears from his eyes), "who would better receive the great Achilles' arms than he through whom the Greeks received the great Achilles? Only let it not be to this fellow's profit that he seems to be, as indeed he is, slow of wit; and let it not be, O Greeks, to my hurt that I have always used my wit for your advantage. And let this eloquence of mine, if I have any, which now speaks for its owner, but often for you as well, incur no enmity, and let each man make the most of his own powers.

"For as to race and ancestry and the deeds that others than ourselves have done, I call those in no true sense our own. But the truth is, since Ajax claims to be great-grandson of Jove, Jove is the founder of my race as well, and I am just as many steps removed from him. For Laërtes is my father, Arcesius, his, and he, the son of Jupiter; nor in this line is there any exiled criminal.* I have also on my mother's side another claim to noble birth, Cyllenius. Through both my parents have I divine descent. But, neither because through my mother I am more nobly born, nor because my father is guiltless

---

*Ajax's uncle, Peleus, murdered his other uncle, Phocus (see book XI).

of his brother's blood, do I seek the armor that lies there. Weigh the cause on its deserts alone. Only count it not any desert of Ajax that Telamon and Peleus were brothers, and let not strains of blood, but the honor of manhood be considered in the award. Or, if you seek for next of kin and lawful heir, Peleus is Achilles' father, Pyrrhus his son. What room is there for Ajax? Bear the armor away to Phthia or to Scyrus. And Teucer is no less Achilles' cousin than he. Yet does he seek the arms, and if he did seek would he gain them? So then, since it is a sheer strife of deeds, I have done more deeds than I can well enumerate. Still I will tell them in their order.

"Achilles' Nereid mother, foreseeing her son's destruction, had disguised him, and the trick of the clothing that he wore deceived them all, Ajax among the rest. But I placed among women's wares some arms such as would attract a man. The hero still wore girl's clothing when, as he laid hands on shield and spear, I said to him: 'O son of Thetis, Pergama, doomed to perish, is keeping herself for you! Why do you delay the fall of mighty Troy?' And I laid my hand on him and sent the brave fellow forth to do brave deeds. So then, all that he did is mine. It was I who conquered the warring Telephus with my spear and healed him, vanquished and begging aid. That Thebes fell is my deed; credit Lesbos to me, to me Tenedos, Chryse and Cilla, cities of Apollo, and Scyrus too. Consider that by my hand the walls of Lyrnesus were battered to the ground. And, not to mention others, it was I, indeed, who gave the man who could destroy the warlike Hector. Through me illustrious Hector lies low!* These arms I seek in return for those by which Achilles was discovered. Arms I gave the living; after his death I ask them back.

"When the sorrow of one man came to all the Greeks, and a thousand ships were gathered at Euboean Aulis, there were no winds, though they waited for them long, or they blew contrary to the fleet. Then a cruel oracle bade Agamemnon sacrifice his innocent daughter to pitiless Diana. This the father refused to do and was angry at the gods themselves, having a father's feelings though he was a king. It was I that turned the kind father-heart to a consideration of the public weal; I indeed (I confess it, and may Atrides pardon as I confess) had a difficult cause to plead, and that,

---

*Ulysses thus takes credit for all of Achilles' feats of arms.

too, before a partial judge; still the people's good, his brother, and
the chief place of command assigned to him, all moved upon him to
balance praise with blood. Then I was sent to the mother, who was
not to be exhorted, but deceived by craft. But if the son of Telamon
had gone to her, our sails would even now be destitute of their winds.

"I was sent also as a bold ambassador to Ilium's stronghold and
visited and entered the senate-house of lofty Troy. It was still full of
heroes. Undaunted, I pleaded the cause which united Greece had
entrusted to me, I denounced Paris, demanded the return of Helen
and the booty, and I prevailed on Priam and Antenor who sided with
Priam. But Paris and his brothers and his companions in the robbery
scarce restrained their impious hands from me (you know that,
Menelaüs).[2] That was the first day of my dangers shared with you.

"It would take a long time to tell the things I accomplished for
your good both with thought and deed during the long-drawn war.
After the first battles the enemy kept himself for a long time within
his city's walls and there was no chance for open conflict. At last in
the tenth year we fought. What were you doing in the meantime,
you whose only knowledge is of battles? Of what service were you
then? If you ask what I was doing, I laid snares for the enemy, I sur-
rounded the fortifications with a trench, I encouraged our allies so
that they might bear patiently the tedium of the long war, I advised
as to how we should be fed and armed, I was sent on missions where
circumstance demanded.

"Behold, at Jove's command, being deceived by a vision of the
night, the king bids us give up the burden of the war we have under-
taken. He can defend his order by quoting the source of it. Now let
Ajax prevent this movement; let him demand that Pergama be de-
stroyed and, what he can do, let him fight! Why does he not stay
those who are starting home? Why does he not take arms and give
something for the straggling mob to rally round? This was not too
much for one who never speaks except in boasting. But what of the
fact that he himself fled also? I saw you, and I was ashamed to see,
when you turned your back and were for spreading your dishonored
sails. Instantly I cried: 'What are you doing? What madness, my
friends, is driving you to abandon Troy, which is already captured?
What are you taking home after ten years of war except disgrace?'
With such and other words, to which my very grief had made me

eloquent, I turned them from their intended flight and led them back. Atrides assembled the allies still perturbed and fearful; and even then the son of Telamon did not dare utter a single syllable. But Thersites dared, indeed, and chid the kings with words, unruly fellow, but, thanks to me, not without punishment! I arose and urged my faint-hearted comrades against the enemy, and by my words I aroused again their courage. From that time on, whatever brave deed my rival here can claim to have accomplished belongs to me who brought him back from flight.

"Finally, who of the Greeks praises you or seeks your company? But Diomede shares his deeds with me, approves me, and is ever confident with Ulysses at his side. Surely, it is something, alone out of the many thousand Greeks, to be picked out by Diomede! And it was not the casting of lots that bade me go. Still, spurning all perils of night and of the enemy, I went forth and slew Phrygian Dolon, who was on the same perilous errand with ourselves. And yet I did not slay him till I had forced him to tell all he knew and had learned what treacherous Troy was planning. I had found out all and had no further cause for spying, and I could now go back with the praise which I had striven for; but not content with this, I turned to Rhesus' tents and in his very camp I slew the captain and his comrades too. And so, victorious and with my prayers accomplished, I went on my way in my captured chariot in manner of a joyful triumph.* Now refuse his arms to me, whose horses my enemy had demanded as the price of his night's work, and let Ajax be the kinder! Why should I mention the Lycian Sarpedon's ranks which my sword cut to pieces? I laid low in bloody slaughter Coeranos, the son of Iphitus, Alastor and Chromius, Alcander, Halius, Noëmon, Prytanis, slew Thoön and Chersidamas, Charopes, Ennomos, driven by the pitiless fates; and others less renowned fell by my hand beneath their city's walls. I, too, have wounds, my comrades, noble for the very place of them. And trust no empty words of mine for that. See here!" and he threw open his garment with his hand; "here is my breast which has ever suffered for your cause! But the son of Telamon in all these years has lost no blood in his friends' behalf and his body can show no wound at all.

---

*A triumph was a formal procession celebrating a victorious general.

"And what matters it if he says that he stood up in arms for the Greek fleet against the Trojans and the power of Jove? I grant he did; for it is not my way maliciously to belittle the good that he has done. But let not him alone claim the honor that belongs to all, and let him give some credit to you also. It was the son of Actor, safe beneath the semblance of Achilles, who drove off the Trojans from the fleet, which else had burned together with its defender. He thinks that he alone dared to stand up against Hector's spear, ignoring the king, the chieftains, and myself, he but the ninth in proffered service and by the lot's grace preferred to us. But what was the outcome of your battle, bravest of men? Hector retired without a wound.

"Ah me, how grievous is the memory of that time when Achilles fell, the bulwark of the Greeks! And yet neither tears nor grief nor fear kept me from lifting up his body from the ground. On these shoulders, yes, on these very shoulders, I bore Achilles' body, armor and all, arms which now also I seek to bear. I have strength enough to bear their ponderous weight and I have a mind that can appreciate the honor you would do me. Was it for this, forsooth, that the hero's mother, goddess of the sea, was ambitious for her son, that those heavenly gifts, the work of heavenly art, should clothe a rough and stupid soldier? For he knows nothing of the relief-work of the shield: the sea, the lands, the deep starry heavens, the Pleiades, the Hyades, Arctos forbidden the sea, the scattered cities, and Orion's gleaming sword. He asks for armor which he cannot appreciate.

"What of his chiding me with trying to shun the hardships of the war and of coming late when the struggle had begun? Does he not know that he is reviling the great Achilles also? If it is a crime to have pretended, we both pretended. If delay is culpable, I was the earlier of the two. A loving wife detained me; a loving mother detained Achilles. Our first time was given to them, the rest to you. I do not fear a charge, even if I cannot answer it, which I share with so great a hero. Yet he was discovered by Ulysses' wit; but not by Ajax' wit, Ulysses.

"And let us not wonder that he pours out against me the insults of his stupid tongue; for he vents on you also shameful words. Was it base for me to have accused Palamedes on a false charge, and honorable for you to have condemned him? But neither was the son of Nauplius able to defend a crime so great, so clearly proved, nor did you merely hear the charge against him: you saw the proof, as it lay clearly revealed by the golden bribe.

"Nor should I be blamed because Vulcanian Lemnos holds the son of Poeas. Defend your own deed, for you consented to it. But I will not deny that I advised that he withdraw from the hardships of the war and the journey to it, and seek to soothe his terrible anguish by a time of rest. He took the advice—and lives! And not only was this advice given in good faith, but it was fortunate as well; though it is enough that it was given in good faith. Now, since our seers say that he is necessary for the fall of Pergama, do not entrust the task to me! Telamon's son will better go, and by his eloquence he will calm the hero, mad with pain and rage, or else by some shrewd trick will bring him to us. No, Simoïs will flow backward, Ida stand without foliage, and Greece send aid to Troy before the craft of stupid Ajax would avail the Greeks in case I should cease to work for your advantage. Though you have a deadly hatred, O harsh Philoctetes, for the allied Greeks and the king and me myself; though you heap endless curses on my head and long in your misery to have me in your power, to drink my blood, and pray that, as I was given a chance at you, so you may have a chance at me; still would I go to you and strive to bring you back with me. And I should get possession of your arrows (should Fortune favor me), just as I got possession of the Dardanian seer, whom I made captive; just as I discovered the oracles of the gods and the fates of Troy; just as I stole away from the midst of the enemy the enshrined image of Phrygian Minerva.[3] And does Ajax compare himself to me? The fact is, the fates declared that we could not capture Troy without this sacred statue. Where now is the brave Ajax? Where are those big words of the mighty hero? Why do you fear in such a crisis? Why does Ulysses dare to go out beyond the sentinels, commit himself to the darkness and, through the midst of cruel swords, enter not only the walls of Troy but even the citadel's top, steal the goddess from her shrine and bear her captured image through the enemy? Had I not done this, in vain would the son of Telamon have worn on his left arm the sevenfold bulls'-hide shield. On that night I gained the victory over Troy; at that moment did I conquer Pergama when I made it possible to conquer her.

"Cease by your looks and mutterings to remind us that Tydides was my partner. He has his share of praise. You, too, when you held your shield in defence of the allied fleet, were not alone. You had a throng of partners; I, but one. And if Diomede did not know that a fighter is of less value than a thinker, and that the prize was not due merely to a right hand, however dauntless, he himself also would be seeking it; so would the lesser Ajax, warlike Eurypylus and the son of illustrious Andraemon, and no less so Idomeneus and his fellow-countryman, Meriones; yes, Menelaüs, too, would seek the prize. But all these men, though stout of hand, fully my equals on the battlefield, have yielded to my superior intelligence. Your good right arm is useful in the battle; but when it comes to thinking you need my guidance. You have force without intelligence; while mine is the care for to-morrow. You are a good fighter; but it is I who help Atrides select the time of fighting. Your value is in your body only; mine, in mind. And, as much as he who directs the ship surpasses him who only rows it, as much as the general excels the common soldier, so much greater am I than you. For in these bodies of ours the heart is of more value than the hand; all our real living is in that.

"But do you, O princes, award the prize to your faithful guardian. In return for the many years which I have spent in anxious care, grant me this honor as the reward of all my services. And now my task is at an end; I have removed the obstructing fates and, by making it possible to take tall Pergama, I have taken her. Now, by our united hopes, by the Trojan walls doomed soon to fall, by the gods of which but lately I deprived the foe, by whatever else remains still to be done with wisdom, if still some bold and hazardous deed must be attempted, if you think anything still is lacking to the fate of Troy, I beg you remember me! Or, if you do not give the arms to me, give them to her!" and he pointed to the fateful statue of Minerva.

The company of chiefs was moved, and their decision proved the power of eloquence: to the eloquent man were given the brave man's arms. Then he who had so often all alone withstood great Hector, so often sword and fire and Jove, could not withstand one passion; and resentment conquered the unconquered hero. Then, snatching out his sword, he cried: "But this at least is mine; or does Ulysses claim this also for himself? This I must employ against myself; and the sword which has often reeked with Phrygian blood will now reek with its master's, lest any man but Ajax ever conquer Ajax." He spoke and deep in his breast, which had not until then suffered any wound, where the way was open for the blow, he plunged his fatal sword. No hand was strong enough to draw away the deep-driven blade; the blood itself drove it out. The ensanguined ground produced from the green sod a purple flower, which in old time had sprung from Hyacinthus' blood.* The petals are inscribed with letters, serving alike for hero and for boy: this one a name, and that, a cry of woe.

To the land of Queen Hypsipyle and the illustrious Thoas, once infamous for its murdered men of olden time, victorious Ulysses now set sail to bring back the Tirynthian arrows.[4] After he had brought these to the Greeks, and their master with them, the final blow was at last given to the long-drawn war. Troy fell and Priam with it. The poor wife of Priam after all else lost her human form and with strange barking affrighted the alien air where the long Hellespont narrows to a strait. Ilium was in flames, nor had its fires yet died down, and Jove's altar had drunk up the scanty blood of aged Priam. The priestess of Apollo, dragged by the hair, was stretching to the heavens her unavailing hands. The Trojan women, embracing the images of their country's gods while still they might and crowding their burning temples, the victorious Greeks dragged off, an enviable booty. And Astyanax was hurled down from that tower where he was wont often to sit and watch his father whom his mother pointed out fighting for honor and safeguarding his ancestral realm. And now the North-wind called them on their way and the sails flapped loud, swelled by the favoring breeze. The mariner gives command to sail. "O Troy, farewell! we are forced away," the Trojan women cry; they kiss their land, and turn their backs upon their smoking homes. The last to go on board, a pitiable sight, was Hecuba, discovered midst the sepulchres of her sons. There, as she clung to their tombs, striving to give her farewell kisses to their bones, the hands of the Dulichian dragged her away. Yet she rescued Hector's ashes only, and bore the rescued dust with her in her bosom. And on Hector's tomb she left locks of her hoary hair, a meagre offering, her hair and tears.

Opposite to Phrygia where Troy stood, there lies a land where dwelt the Bistones. There was the luxurious court of Polymestor, to

---

*As described in book X.

whom your father, Polydorus, secretly commended you for care, sending you far from Phrygia's strife; a prudent plan, if he had not sent with you a great store of treasure, the prize of crime, a temptation to a greedy soul. When the Phrygian fortunes waned, the impious Thracian king took his sword and thrust it into his young charge's throat; and just as if a murder could be disposed of with the victim's body, he threw the corpse from a cliff into the waves below.

On this Thracian coast Atrides had moored his fleet until the sea should quiet down and the winds be more favorable. Here on a sudden, up from the wide-gaping earth, Achilles sprang, large as he was in life. He had a threatening manner and a look as on that day when with his hostile sword he fiercely challenged Agamemnon. "And are you, then, departing, O Greeks," he cried, "forgetful of me? And have your thanks for my services been buried with me? It shall not be! And, that my tomb may not lack its fitting honor, let Polyxena be sacrificed and so appease Achilles' shade." He spoke, and the allied Greeks obeyed the pitiless ghost. Torn from her mother's arms, of whom she was nearly the only comfort left, the brave, ill-fated maid, with more than woman's courage, was led to the fatal mound and there was sacrificed upon the cruel tomb. Self-possessed she was, even when she had been placed before the fatal altar and knew the grim rites were preparing for her; and when she saw Neoptolemus* standing, sword in hand, with his eyes fixed upon her, she exclaimed: "Spill at last my noble blood, for I am ready; or plunge your sword deep in my throat or breast!" (and she bared her throat and breast. Polyxena, be sure, would not desire to live in slavery!) "Not by such a rite as this will you appease any god! Only I would that my mother may know nothing of my death. My mother prevents and destroys my joy of death. And yet she should not deprecate my death, but rather her own life. Only do you, that I may go free to the Stygian spirits, stand back, if my request is just, and let no rude hand of man touch my virgin body. More acceptable to him, whoever he is, whom by my sacrifice you are seeking to appease, will my free blood be. But if my last words move any of you (it is the daughter of King Priam and not a captive maid who asks it), restore my body to my mother without ransom; and let her pay

---

*The son of Achilles.

in tears and not in gold for the sad privilege of sepulture. She did pay in gold also when she could." She spoke, and the throng could not restrain their tears, though she restrained her own. Then did the priest, himself also weeping and remorseful, with deep-driven weapon pierce her proffered breast. She, sinking down to earth with fainting knees, kept her look of dauntless courage to the end. And even then, as she was falling, she took care to cover her body and to guard the honor of her modesty.

The Trojan women take up her body and count one by one the lamented Priamidae, and all the woes which this one house has suffered. You, royal maid, they weep, and you, who but yesterday were called queen-consort and queen-mother, you, once the embodiment of proud Asia, but now suffering hard lot even for a captive, one whom victorious Ulysses would not desire, except that she had given birth to Hector. A lord for his mother Hector scarcely found! She, embracing the lifeless body of that brave spirit, gives to it also the tears which she has shed so often for country, sons and husband. She pours her tears into her daughter's wound, covers her face with kisses, and beats the breasts that have endured so many blows. Then sweeping her white hair in the clotted blood and tearing her breast, this and much more she cried: "O child, your mother's last cause for grief—for what else is left me—my child, low you lie, and I see your wound, my wound. Behold, that I might lose none of my children without violence, you also have your wound. But you, because you were a woman, I thought safe from the sword; even though a woman, you have fallen by the sword; and that same Achilles, who has bereft Troy and me, who has destroyed so many of your brothers, has destroyed you also. But when he fell by Paris' and by Phoebus' arrows, 'Surely,' I said, 'now is Achilles to be feared no more.' But even now I was still to fear him. His very ashes, though he is dead and buried, are savage against our race; even in the tomb we have felt him for our enemy; for Achilles have I been fruitful! Great Troy lies low, and by a woeful issue the public calamity was ended; yet it was ended; for me alone Pergama still survives; my woes still run their course. But late on the pinnacle of fame, strong in my many sons, my daughters, and my husband, now, exiled, penniless, torn from the tombs of my loved ones, I am dragged away as prize for Penelope. And as I sit spinning my allotted task of wool, she will point me out to the dames of Ithaca and say: 'This woman is Hector's noble mother, this is Priam's queen.' And now after so many have been lost, you, who alone were left to console your mother's grief, you have been sacrificed upon our foeman's tomb. Yes, I have but borne a victim for my enemy. And to what end do I, unfeeling wretch, live on? Why do I linger? To what end, O wrinkled age, do you keep me here? To what end, O cruel gods, but that I still may see fresh funerals, do you prolong an old woman's life? Who would suppose that Priam could be happy when Pergama was overthrown? Happy is he in death. He does not see you, my daughter, lying murdered here; he left his life and kingdom, both at once. But I suppose, O royal maiden, you shall be dowered with funeral rites and your body buried in your ancestral tomb! Such is no longer the fortune of our house. Your funeral gifts shall be your mother's tears; your burial, the sand of an alien shore! We have lost all; but still there's something left, some reason why for a brief span I may endure to live: his mother's dearest, now her only child, once youngest of my sons, my Polydorus, sent to these shores to the Thracian king. But why do I delay, meanwhile, to wash my daughter's cruel wounds with water, her face bespattered with her blood?"

She spoke and with tottering steps of age went to the shore, tearing her grey hair as she went. "Give me an urn, O Trojan women," the wretched creature said, intending to dip up some water from the sea. And there she saw the body of Polydorus, cast up upon the shore, covered with gaping wounds made by Thracian spears. The Trojan women shrieked at the sight; but she was dumb with grief; her very grief engulfed her powers of speech, her rising tears. Like a hard rock, immovable she stood, now held her gaze fixed upon the ground, and at times lifted her awful face to the heavens; now she gazed upon the features of her son as he lay there in death, now on his wounds, but mostly on his wounds, arming herself and heaping up her rage. When now her rage blazed out, as if she still were queen, she fixed on vengeance and was wholly absorbed in the punishment her imagination pictured. And as a lioness rages when her suckling cub has been stolen from her, and follows the tracks of her enemy, though she does not see him, so Hecuba, wrath mingling with her grief, regardless of her years but not her deadly purpose, went straight to Polymestor, who wrought the heartless murder, and sought an audience with him, pretending that she wished to show him a store of gold which she had hoarded for her son and now would give him. The Thracian was deceived and, led by his habitual lust for gain, he came to the hiding-place. Then craftily, with smooth speech he said: "Come, Hecuba, make haste, give me the treasure for your son! I swear by the gods of heaven, all shall be his, what you give now and what you have given before." She grimly eyed him as he spoke and swore his lying oath. Then did her rising wrath boil over, and, calling the captive women to the attack, she seized upon him, dug her fingers into his lying eyes and gouged his eyeballs from their sockets—so mighty did wrath make her. Then she plunged in her hands and, stained with his guilty blood, she plucked out, not his eyes, for they were gone, but the places of his eyes. The Thracians, incensed by their king's disaster, began to set upon the Trojan with shafts and stones. But she, with hoarse growls, bit at the stones they threw and, though her jaws were set for words, barked when she tried to speak. The place still remains and takes its name from this incident, where she, long remembering her ancient ills, still howled mournfully across the Sithonian plains. Her sad fortune touched the Trojans and her Grecian foes and all the gods as well; yes, all, for even Juno, sister and wife of Jove, declared that Hecuba had not deserved such an end.

But Aurora, though she had lent her aid to the Trojan arms, had no time to lament the ruin and the fall of Troy and Hecuba. A nearer care, grief for her own son, harassed her, the loss of Memnon, whom she, his bright mother, had seen dead by Achilles' spear on the Phrygian plain. She saw and those bright hues by which the morning skies flush rosy red grew dull, and the heavens were overcast with clouds. And when his corpse was laid upon the funeral pyre his mother could not look upon it, but, with streaming hair, just as she was, she disdained not to throw herself at the knees of mighty Jove and with many tears to pray: "Though I am least of all whom the golden heaven upholds (for in all the world but few and scattered temples rise to me), still as a goddess I come. I ask not that you give me shrines and sacred days and altars to flame with sacrificial fires. And yet, should you consider what service I, though but a woman, render you, when each new dawn I guard the borders of the night, then you would deem that I should have some reward.

But that is not my care nor is that Aurora's errand, to demand honors which she may have earned. Bereft of my Memnon I come, who bore brave arms (though all in vain) in his uncle's service, and in his early years has fallen by Achilles' warlike hand (for so you willed it). Grant then, I beg, some honor to him as solace for his death, O most high ruler of the gods, and soothe a mother's wounded heart." Jove nodded his consent, when Memnon's lofty pyre, wrapped in high-leaping flames, crumbled to earth, and the day was darkened by the thick black smoke, as when rivers send forth the fogs they have begotten, beneath whose pall the sunlight cannot come. Dark ashes whirled aloft and there, packed and condensed, they seemed to take on form, drew heat and vitality from the fire. (Its own lightness gave it wings.) At first, it was like a bird; but soon, a real bird, it flew about on whirring pinions. And along with it were countless sisters winging their noisy flight; and all were sprung from the same source. Thrice round the pyre they flew and thrice their united clamour rose into the air. At the fourth flight the flock divided and in two warring bands the fierce contestants fought together, plying beak and hooked talons in their rage, wearying wing and breast in the struggle. At last these shapes kin to the buried ashes fell down as funeral offerings and remembered that they were sprung from that brave hero. The author of their being gave his name to the new-sprung birds, and they were called Memnonides from him; and still, when the sun has completed the circuit of his twelve signs, they fight and die again in customary ceremony for their dead father. And so others wept while the daughter of Dymas bayed; but Aurora was all absorbed in her own grief; and even to this day she weeps pious tears and bedews the whole world with them.

And yet the fates did not permit Troy's hopes to perish with her walls. The heroic son of Cytherea bore away upon his shoulders her sacred images and, another sacred thing, his father, a venerable burden. Of all his great possessions, the pious hero chose that portion, and his son, Ascanius. Then with his fleet of refugees he set sail from Antandros, left behind the sinful homes of Thrace and the land dripping with Polydorus' blood, and, with favoring winds and tides assisting, reached with his friends the city of Apollo. Him Anius, who ruled over men as king and served Phoebus as his priest, received in the temple and his home. He showed his city, the

new-erected shrines and the two sacred trees beneath which Latona
had once brought forth her children.* There they burned incense in
the flames, poured out wine upon the incense and, according to the
customary rite, they slaughtered cattle and burned their entrails in
the altar-fire; then sought the palace-hall and, reclining on the high
couches, they partook of Ceres' bounty and the wine of Bacchus.
Then pious Anchises said: "O chosen priest of Phoebus, am I mis-
taken, or did you have, when first I saw your city, a son and four
daughters as I recall?" And Anius, shaking his head bound with
snowy fillets, sadly replied: "No, mightiest of heroes, you are not
mistaken; you did see me the father of five children, whom now,
such is the shifting nature of men's fates, you see nearly bereft. For
of what help to me is my absent son, whom the land of Andros,
named from him, holds in place of his father; for he rules the land
as king. The Delian gave him the power of augury; but to my
daughters Bacchus gave other gifts, greater than they could pray or
hope to gain. For at my daughters' touch all things were turned to
corn and wine and the oil of grey-green Minerva, and there was rich
profit in them. When Agamemnon, ravager of Troy, learned this
(that you may know that we also have felt some share of your de-
structive storm), using armed force, he dragged my unwilling
daughters from their father's arms, and bade them feed the Grecian
army with their heavenly gift. They escaped, each as she could. Two
sought Euboea; two fled to their brother's Andros. Armed bands
pursued and threatened war unless they were surrendered. Fear con-
quered brotherly affection, and he gave up to punishment the per-
sons of his kindred. And you could forgive the timid brother; for
Aeneas was not here to succour Andros, nor Hector, through whom
you held your own for ten years. And now they were preparing fet-
ters for the captives' arms, when they, stretching their still free arms
to heaven, cried: 'O father Bacchus, help!' And he who gave their
gift did bring them aid—if you call it aid, in some strange sort to
lose their human form. For never did I know, nor can I now de-
scribe, how they lost it. But the outcome of my sad mishap I do
know: covered with plumage, they were changed to snow-white
doves, your consort's birds."

---

*Latona was the mother of Apollo and Diana.

With such and other themes they filled up the feast, then left the banquet board and retired to rest; and on the morrow they rose and sought the oracle of Phoebus. He bade them seek their ancient mother and kindred shores. On their departure the king went forth with them and gave them parting gifts: a sceptre to Anchises, a robe and quiver to his grandson, and a goblet to Aeneas which Ismenian Therses, a guest, had once brought to the king from the Aonian coast. Therses had sent him the cup, but it was the handiwork of Hylean Alcon, who had engraved upon it a long pictured story. There was a city, on which you could discern seven gates. These served to name it and tell you what it was. Before the city funeral rites were seen, with sepulchres and blazing funeral pyres; and women with dishevelled hair and naked breasts, proclaiming grief. Nymphs also seemed to weep and bewail their dried-up springs. The trees stood bare and leafless; goats nibbled in the parched and stony fields. See, in the Theban streets he represents Orion's daughters, one dealing a wound not apt for maiden's hands to her bared throat, the other dealing clumsy wounds with her weaving-shuttle, both falling as victims in the people's stead; then borne in funeral pomp through the town and burned to ashes midst the mourning throngs.[5] Then, that their race may not perish with them, from their virgin ashes spring two youths, whom fame has named Coroni. These join in the solemn rites due to their mother's dust. Such was the story told in figures gleaming on the antique bronze. Round the goblet's top, rough-carved, golden acanthus ran. The Trojans make presents in return of no less worth: an incense-casket for the priest, a libation-saucer and a crown, gleaming with gems and gold.

Then, remembering that the Teucrians sprang from Teucer's stock, they sailed away to Crete. Here, unable to endure for long the ills which Jove inflicted, they abandoned Crete with its hundred cities and set out with eager spirit for the Ausonian shores. The wintry seas raged and tossed the heroic band; and, when they came to the treacherous harbour of the Strophades, Aëllo, the harpy, frightened them. And now Dulichium's anchorage, Ithaca and Samos, the homes of Neritos, the false Ulysses' kingdom—past all these they sailed. Ambracia next, once object of heaven's strife, they saw, and the image of the judge once changed to stone—Ambracia, now famed for Actian Apollo's sake; Dodona's land, with its speaking oaks; Chaonia's sheltered bay, where the sons of King Molossus on new-grown wings escaped impious fires.

Next they sought the land of the Phaeacians, set with fertile orchards, and landed at Buthrotos in Epirus with its mimic Troy, a city ruled by the Phrygian seer. There having learned all that awaited them from the friendly prophecies of Helenus, Priam's son, they came to Sicily.* This land runs out into the sea in three capes. Of these, Pachynos faces to the rainy south, Lilybaeon feels the soft western breeze, and Peloros looks to the northern Bears, who never go beneath the sea. Here the Teucri came and with oars and favoring tides the fleet reached the sandy beach of Zancle as darkness fell. Scylla infests the right-hand coast, unresting Charybdis the left. The one sucks down and vomits forth again the ships she has caught; the other's uncanny waist is girt with ravening dogs. She has a virgin's face and, if all the tales of poets are not false, she was herself once a virgin. Many suitors sought her; but she scorned them all and, taking refuge with the sea-nymphs (for the sea-nymphs loved her well), she would tell them of the disappointed wooing of her lovers. There once Galatea, while she let the maiden comb her hair, first sighing deeply, thus addressed her: "You truly, maiden, are wooed by a gentle race of men, and you can repulse them without fear, even as you do. But I, whose father is Nereus and whose mother the sea-hued Doris, who am safe also in a throng of sisters, I was not allowed to shun the Cyclops' love without grievous consequence." Tears checked her further speech. When the maid with her white fingers had dried the goddess' tears and had consoled her, she said: "Tell me, O dearest one, and do not conceal the cause of your woe, for I am faithful to you." And the Nereid answered Crataeis' daughter in these words: "Acis was son of Faunus and a Symaethian nymph, great joy to his father and his mother, but greater joy to me; for he loved me with whole-hearted love. Beautiful he was, and at sixteen years a downy beard had marked his youthful cheeks. Him did I love, but the Cyclops loved me with endless wooing. Nor, if you should ask me, could I tell which was stronger in me, my hate of Cyclops or my love of Acis; for both were in equal measure. O mother Venus, how mighty is your sway!

---

*The preceding passage presents a concentrated version of much of the *Aeneid*.

Behold, that savage creature, whom the very woods shudder to look upon, whom no stranger has ever seen except to his own hurt, who despises great Olympus and its gods, he feels the power of love and burns with mighty desire, forgetful of his flocks and of his caves. And now, Polyphemus, you become careful of your appearance, now anxious to please; now with a rake you comb your shaggy locks, and now it is your pleasure to cut your rough beard with a reaping-hook, gazing at your rude features in some clear pool and composing their expression. Your love of slaughter falls away, your fierce nature and your quenchless thirst for blood; and ships come and go in safety. Meanwhile Telemus had come to Sicilian Aetna, Telemus, the son of Eurymus, whom no bird had deceived; and he said to grim Polyphemus: 'That one eye, which you have in the middle of your forehead, Ulysses will take from you.'* He mocked and answered: 'O most stupid seer, you are wrong; another has already taken it.' Thus did he scoff at the man who vainly sought to warn him, and stalked with huge, heavy tread along the shore, or returned, weary, to his shady cave. A wedge-shaped promontory with long, sharp point juts out into the sea, both sides washed by the waves. Here the fierce Cyclops climbed and sat down on the cliff's central point, and his woolly sheep, all unheeded, followed him. Then, laying at his feet the pine-trunk which served him for a staff, fit for a vessel's mast, he took his pipe made of a hundred reeds. All the mountains felt the sound of his rustic pipings; the waves felt it too. I, hiding beneath a rock and resting in my Acis' arms, at a great distance heard the words he sang and well remember them:

" 'O Galatea, whiter than snowy privet-leaves, more blooming than the meadows, surpassing the alder in your tall slenderness, more sparkling than crystal, more frolicsome than a tender kid, smoother than shells worn by the lapping waves, more welcome than the winter's sun and summer's shade, more goodly than orchard-fruit, fairer than the tall plane-tree, more shining-clear than ice, sweeter than ripened grapes, softer than swan's down and curdled milk, and, if only you would not flee from me, more beauteous than a well-watered garden.

---

*See book IX of the *Odyssey*; birds were commonly regarded as omens.

" 'Yet you, the same Galatea, are more obstinate than an untamed heifer, harder than aged oak, falser than water, tougher than willow-twigs and white briony-vines, more immovable than these rocks, more boisterous than a stream, vainer than a praised peacock, more cruel than fire, sharper than thorns, more savage than a she-bear with young, deafer than the sea, more pitiless than a trodden snake, and, what I would most of all that I could take from you, swifter not only than the stag driven before the baying hounds, but also than the winds and the fleeting breeze! But, if only you knew me well, you would regret that you have fled from me; you would yourself condemn your coy delays and seek to hold me. I have a whole mountain-side for my possessions, deep caves in the living rock, where neither the sun is felt in his midsummer heat, nor the winter's cold. I have apples weighing down their branches, grapes yellow as gold on the trailing vines, and purple grapes as well. Both these and those I am keeping for your use. With your own hand you shall gather the luscious strawberries that grow within the woody shade, cherries in autumn-time and plums, both juicy and purple-black and the large yellow kind, yellow as new wax. Chestnuts also shall be yours and the fruit of the arbute-tree, if you will take me for your husband; and every tree shall yield to your desire.

" 'And all this flock is mine. Many besides are wandering in the valleys, many are in the woods, still others are safe within their cavern-folds. No, should you chance to ask, I could not tell you how many in all I have. It's a poor man's business to count his flocks. And you need not believe my praises of them; here you can see for yourself how they can hardly walk for their distended udders. And I have, coming on, lambs in my warm folds and kids, too, of equal age, in other folds. There's always a plenty of snow-white milk. Some of it is kept for drinking, and some the rennet hardens into curds.

" 'And you shall have no easily gotten pets or common presents, such as does and hares and goats, or a pair of doves, or a nest taken from the cliff. I found on the mountain-top two cubs of a shaggy bear for you to play with, so much alike that you can scarcely tell them apart. I found them and I said: "I'll keep these for my mistress!"

" 'And now, Galatea, do but raise your glistening head from the blue sea. Now come and don't despise my gifts. Surely I know myself; lately I saw my reflection in a clear pool, and I liked my features when I saw them. Just look, how big I am! Jupiter himself up there in the sky has no bigger body; for you are always talking of some Jove or other as ruling there. A wealth of hair overhangs my manly face and it shades my shoulders like a grove. And don't think it ugly that my whole body is covered with thick, bristling hair. A tree is ugly without its leaves and a horse is ugly if a thick mane does not clothe his sorrel neck; feathers clothe the birds, and their own wool is becoming to sheep; so a beard and shaggy hair on his body well become a man. True, I have but one eye in the middle of my forehead, but it is as big as a good-sized shield. And what of that? Doesn't the great sun see everything here on earth from his heavens? And the sun has but one eye.

" 'Furthermore, my father is king over your own waters; and him I am giving to you for father-in-law. Only pity me and listen to my humble prayer; for I bow to you alone; I, who scorn Jove and his heaven and his all-piercing thunderbolt, I fear you alone, O Nereid; your anger is more deadly than the lightning-flash. And I could better bear your scorning if you fled from all your suitors. But why, though you reject Cyclops, do you love Acis, and why do you prefer Acis to my arms? And yet he may please himself and please you too, Galatea; but oh, I wish he didn't please you. But only let me have a chance at him! Then he'll find that I am as strong as I am big. I'll tear his vitals out alive, I'll rend him limb from limb and scatter the pieces over your waves—so may he mate with you! For oh, I burn, and my hot passion, stirred to frenzy, rages more fiercely within me; I seem to carry Aetna let down into my breast with all his violence. And you, Galatea, do not care at all.'

"Such vain complaints he uttered, and rose up (I saw it all), just as a bull which, furious when the cow has been taken from him, cannot stand still, but wanders through the woods and familiar pasture-lands. Then the fierce giant spied me and Acis, neither knowing nor fearing such a fate, and he cried: 'I see you, and I'll make that union of your loves the last.' His voice was big and terrible as a furious Cyclops' voice should be. Aetna trembled with the din of it. But I, in panic fright, dived into the near-by sea. My Symaethian hero had already turned to run, and cried: 'Oh, help me, Galatea, I pray; help me, my parents, and take me, doomed now to perish, to your kingdom.' Cyclops ran after him and hurled a piece wrenched from the mountain-side; and, though that merest corner of the mass reached Acis, still it was enough to bury him altogether. But I (the only thing that fate allowed to me) caused Acis to assume his ancestral powers. Crimson blood came trickling from beneath the mass; then in a little while its ruddy color began to fade away and it became the color of a stream swollen by the early rains, and it cleared entirely in a little while. Then the mass that had been thrown cracked wide open and a tall, green reed sprang up through the crack, and the hollow opening in the rock resounded with leaping waters, and, wonderful! suddenly a youth stood forth waist-deep from the water, his new-sprung horns wreathed with bending rushes. The youth, except that he was larger and his face of dark sea-blue, was Acis. But even so he still was Acis, changed to a river-god; and his waters kept their former name."

When Galatea had finished her story, the group of Nereids broke up and went swimming away on the peaceful waves. But Scylla, not daring to trust herself to the outer deep, returned to the shore, and there either wandered all unrobed along the thirsty sands or, when she was wearied, she would seek out some deep sequestered pool and there refresh her limbs in its safe waters. Behold Glaucus, sounding with his shell upon the sea, a new-come dweller in the deep waters; for his form had been but lately changed near Anthedon in Euboea. He saw the maid and straightway burned with love, and said whatever things he thought might stay her flight. Nevertheless, she fled him and, her speed increased by fear, she came to the top of a mountain which stood near the shore. It was a huge mountain facing the sea, rising into one massive peak, its shady top reaching far out over the water. Here Scylla stayed her flight and, protected by her position, not knowing whether he was a monster or a god, looked in wonder at his color, his hair which covered his shoulders and his back, and at his groins merging into a twisted fish-form. He saw her and, leaning on a mass of rock which lay at hand, he said: "Maiden, I am no monster or wild creature; I am a sea-god; and neither Proteus nor Triton nor Palaemon, son of Athamas, has greater power over the deeps than I.[6] I was mortal once, but even then devoted to the sea, and there my life was spent. Now I would draw in the nets full of fish, and now, sitting on some projecting rock, I would ply rod and line. There is a shore fringed by verdant meadows, one side of which is hemmed in by the waves and the other by herbage, which neither horned cattle have ever disturbed in grazing nor have the peaceful sheep nor hairy she-goats cropped it. No busy bee ever gathered flowers from there and bore them off; no festal wreaths for the head were ever gathered there, no hands with sickles ever mowed its grasses. I was the first to seat me on that turf, drying my dripping lines and spreading out upon the bank to count them the fish that I had caught, which either chance had brought to my nets or their own guilelessness had fixed upon my hooks. It sounds like an idle tale; but what advantage have I in deceiving you? My catch, after nibbling at the grass, began to stir, then to turn over and to move about on land as in the sea. And while I paused in wonder they all slipped down into their native waters, abandoning their new master and the shore. I stood a long time in amaze and doubt, seeking the cause of this. Had some god done it, or was it the grasses' juice? 'And yet what herb could have such potency?' I said, and plucking some of the herbage with my hands, I chewed what I had plucked. Scarce had I swallowed the strange juices when suddenly I felt my heart trembling within me, and my whole being yearned with desire for another element. Unable long to stand against it, I cried aloud: 'Farewell, O Earth, to which I shall nevermore return!' and I plunged into the sea. The sea-divinities received me, deeming me worthy of a place with them, and called on Oceanus and Tethys to purge my mortal nature all away. And then they purged me, first with a magic song nine times repeated to wash all evil from me, and next they bade me bathe my body in a hundred streams. Straightway the rivers that flow from every side poured all their waters upon my head. So far I can recall and tell you what befell me; so far can I remember. But of the rest my mind retains no knowledge. When my senses came back to me I was far different from what I was but lately in all my body, nor was my mind the same. Then for the first time I beheld this beard of dark green hue, these locks which sweep on the long waves, these huge shoulders and bluish arms, these legs which twist and vanish in a finny fish. And yet, what boots this form, what, that I pleased the sea-divinities, what profits it to be a god, if you are not moved by these things?" As he thus spoke and would have spoken more, Scylla fled from the god, and he, stung to mad rage by his repulse, betook him to the wondrous court of Circe, daughter of the Sun.[7]

BOOK XIV

AND NOW AETNA, HEAPED upon the giant's head, and the fields of the Cyclops, which knew nothing of the harrow or the plow, which owed no debt to yoked cattle, all these the Euboean haunter of the swelling waves had left behind; he had left Zancle also, and the walls of Rhegium which lay opposite, and the shipwrecking strait which, confined by double shores, hems in the Ausonian and Sicilian land. Then, swimming along with mighty strength through the Tyrrhene sea, Glaucus came to the herb-clad hills and the courts of Circe, daughter of the Sun, full of phantom beasts. When he beheld her, and a welcome had been given and received, he thus addressed the goddess: "O goddess, pity a god, I pray you! for you alone, if I but seem worthy of it, can help this love of mine. What magic potency herbs have, O Titaness, no one knows better than myself, for I was changed by them. That the cause of my mad passion may be known to you, on the Italian coast, opposite Messene's walls, I saw Scylla. I am ashamed to tell of the promises and prayers, the coaxing words I used, all scornfully rejected. But do you, if there is any power in charms, sing a charm with your sacred lips; or, if herbs are more effectual, use the tried strength of efficacious herbs. And I do not pray that you cure me or heal me of these wounds, nor end my love; let her but bear her part of this burning heat." But Circe (for no one has a heart more susceptible to such flames than she, whether the cause of this is in herself, or whether Venus, offended by her father's tattling,* made her so) replied: "Much better would you follow one whose strong desire and prayer was even as your own, whose heart burned with an equal flame. You were worthy on your own part to be wooed, and could be, of a truth; and, if

---

*Helios revealed the affair between Venus and Mars to Venus' husband, Vulcan.

you give some hope, I tell you truly you shall indeed be wooed. That you may believe this, and have some faith in your own power to charm, lo, I, goddess though I be, though the daughter of the shining Sun, though I have such magic powers in song and herb, I pray that I may be yours. Scorn her who scorns, and requite her love who loves you; and so in one act repay us both." But to her prayer Glaucus replied: "Sooner shall foliage grow on the sea, and sooner shall sea-weeds spring up on the mountain-tops, than shall my love change while Scylla lives." The goddess was enraged; and, since she could not harm the god himself (and would not because of her love for him), she turned her wrath upon the girl who was preferred to her. In hurt anger at the refusal of her love, she straightway bruised together uncanny herbs with juices of dreadful power, singing while she mixed them Hecate's own charms. Then, donning an azure cloak, she took her way from her palace through the throng of beasts that fawned upon her as she passed, and made for Rhegium, lying opposite Zancle's rocky coast. She fared along the seething waters, on which she trod as on the solid ground, skimming dry-shod along the surface of the sea. There was a little pool, curving into a deep bow, a peaceful place where Scylla loved to come. There would she betake her from the heat of sea and sky, when the sun at his strongest was in mid-heaven, and from his zenith had drawn the shadows to their shortest compass. This pool, before the maiden's coming, the goddess befouls and tinctures with her baleful poisons. When these had been poured out she sprinkles liquors brewed from noxious roots, and a charm, dark with its maze of uncanny words, thrice nine times she murmurs over with lips well skilled in magic. Then Scylla comes and wades waist-deep into the water; when all at once she sees her loins disfigured with barking monster-shapes. And at the first, not believing that these are parts of her own body, she flees in fear and tries to drive away the boisterous, barking things. But what she flees she takes along with her; and, feeling for her thighs, her legs, her feet, she finds in place of these only gaping dogs'-heads, such as a Cerberus might have. She stands on ravening dogs, and her docked loins and her belly are enclosed in a circle of beastly forms.

Glaucus, her lover, wept at the sight and fled the embrace of Circe, who had used too cruelly her potent herbs. But Scylla remained fixed in her place and, when first a chance was given her to vent her hate on Circe, she robbed Ulysses of his companions. She also would have wrecked the Trojan ships had she not before their coming been changed into a rock which stands there to this day. The rock also is the sailors' dread.

When the Trojan vessels had successfully passed this monster and greedy Charybdis too, and when they had almost reached the Ausonian shore, the wind bore them to the Libyan coast. There the Sidonian queen* received Aeneas hospitably in heart and home, doomed ill to endure her Phrygian lord's departure. On a pyre, built under pretence of sacred rites, she fell upon his sword; and so, herself disappointed, she disappointed all. Leaving once more the new city built on the sandy shore, Aeneas returned to the land of Eryx and friendly Acestes, and there he made sacrifice and paid due honors to his father's tomb. Then he cast off the ships which Iris, Juno's messenger, had almost burned, and soon had sailed past the kingdom of Hippotades, past the lands smoking with hot sulphur fumes, and the rocky haunt of the Sirens, daughters of Acheloüs. And now, his vessel having lost her pilot, he coasts along Inarime and Prochyte and Pithecusae, situate on a barren hill, called from the name of its inhabitants.† For the father of the gods, hating the tricks and lies of the Cercopians and the crimes committed by that treacherous race, once changed the men to ugly animals in such a way that they might be unlike human shape and yet seem like them. He shortened their limbs, blunted and turned back their noses, and furrowed their faces with deep wrinkles as of age. Then he sent them, clothed complete in yellow hair, to dwell in these abodes. But first he took from them the power of speech, the use of tongues born for vile perjuries, leaving them only the utterance of complaint in hoarse, grating tones.

When he had passed these by and left the walled city of Parthenope upon the right, he came upon the left to the mound-tomb of the tuneful son of Aeolus‡ and the marshy shores of Cumae, and, entering the grotto of the long-lived sibyl, prayed that

---

*Dido; her tragic love for Aeneas is the central episode of the *Aeneid*.

†Again, a compressed report of incidents from the *Aeneid*.

‡Misenus, Aeneas' herald, needed burial before the hero could enter the Underworld.

he might pass down through Avernus' realm and see his father's
shade. The sibyl held her eyes long fixed upon the earth, then lifted
them at last and, full of mad inspiration from her god, replied:
"Great things do you ask, you man of mighty deeds, whose hand, by
sword, whose piety, by fire, has been well tried. But have no fear,
Trojan; you shall have your wish, and with my guidance you shall see
the dwellings of Elysium and the latest kingdom of the universe;
and you shall see your dear father's shade. There is no way denied to
virtue." She spoke and showed him, deep in Avernal Juno's forest, a
bough gleaming with gold, and bade him pluck it from its trunk.
Aeneas obeyed; then saw grim Orcus'* possessions, and his own an-
cestral shades, and the aged spirit of the great-souled Anchises. He
learned also the laws of those places, and what perils he himself
must undergo in new wars. As he retraced his weary steps along the
upward way he beguiled the toil with discourse with his Cumaean
guide; and as he fared along the dismal road in the dim dusk he said:
"Whether you are a goddess in very truth, or a maid most pleasing
to the gods, to me you shall always seem divine, and I shall confess
that I owe my life to you, through whose will I have approached the
world of death, have seen and have escaped in safety from that
world. And for these services, when I have returned to the upper re-
gions, I will erect a temple to you and there burn incense in your
honor." The sibyl regarded him and, sighing deeply, said: "I am no
goddess, nor is any mortal worthy of the honor of the sacred in-
cense. But, so you do not mistake in ignorance, eternal, endless life
was offered me, had my virgin modesty consented to Phoebus' love.
While he still hoped for this and sought to break my will with gifts,
he said: 'Choose what you will, maiden of Cumae, and you shall
have your choice.' Pointing to a heap of sand, I made the foolish
prayer that I might have as many years of life as there were sand-
grains in the pile; but I forgot to ask that those years might be per-
petually young. He granted me the years, and promised endless
youth as well, if I would yield to love. I spurned Phoebus' gift and
am still unwedded. But now my joyous springtime of life has fled
and with tottering step weak old age is coming on, which for long
I must endure. Even now you see me after seven centuries of life,

*Another name for Pluto or Underworld; it approximately means "a tight place."

and, ere my years equal the number of the sands, I still must behold
three hundred harvest-times, three hundred vintages. The time will
come when length of days will shrivel me from my full form to but
a tiny thing, and my limbs, consumed by age, will shrink to a
feather's weight. Then will I seem never to have been loved, never
to have pleased the god. Phoebus himself, perhaps, will either gaze
unknowing on me or will deny that he ever loved me. Even to such
changes shall I come. Though shrunk past recognition of the eye, still
by my voice shall I be known, for the fates will leave me my voice."

While thus along the hollow way the sibyl told her story, out of
the Stygian world they emerged near the Euboean city. Making due
sacrifices here, Trojan Aeneas next landed on a shore which did not
yet bear his nurse's name. Here also Neritian Macareus, a comrade
of all-suffering Ulysses, had stayed behind after the long weariness
of his wanderings. He recognizes Achaemenides, whom they had
left long since abandoned midst the rocks of Aetna. Amazed thus
suddenly to find him still alive, he says: "What chance, what god has
saved you, Achaemenides? Why does a Greek sail in a Trojan ship?
What land does your vessel seek?" And to his questions
Achaemenides, no longer roughly clad, his garments no longer
pinned with thorns, but his own man once more, replied: "May
I look on Polyphemus yet again, and those wide jaws of his, drip-
ping with human gore, if I prefer my home and Ithaca to this ship,
if I revere Aeneas less than my own father. Nor can I ever pay my
debt of gratitude, though I should give my all. That I speak and
breathe and see the heavens and the constellations of the sun, for
this can I cease to thank him, and be mindful of him? It's due to him
that my life did not fall into the Cyclops' jaws, and though even now
I should leave the light of life, I should be buried in a tomb, but
surely not in that monster's maw. What were my feelings then (ex-
cept that fear took away all sense and feeling) when, left behind,
I saw you making for the open sea? I longed to call out to you, but
I feared to betray myself to the enemy. Even your vessel Ulysses' cry
almost wrecked. I saw when Cyclops tore up a huge rock from the
mountain-side and hurled it far out to sea. I saw him again throw-
ing great stones with his gigantic arms as from a catapult, and
I feared in case the waves or the wind should sink the ship, forgetting
that I was not in her. But when you escaped by flight from certain

death, he, groaning the while, went prowling all over Aetna, groping through the woods with his hands, and blindly dashing against the rocks. Then would he stretch out his bleeding arms to the sea and curse the whole Greek race, and say: 'Oh, that some chance would but bring Ulysses back to me, or some one of his friends, against whom my rage might vent itself, whose vitals I might devour, whose living body I might tear asunder with my hands, whose gore might flood my throat, and whose mangled limbs might quiver between my teeth! How nothing at all, or how slight a thing would the loss of my sight appear!' This and much more in fury. Pale horror filled me as I looked upon his face still smeared with blood, and his cruel hands, his sightless eye, his limbs and his beard, matted with human gore. Death was before my eyes, but that was the least of all my troubles. I kept always thinking: now he'll catch me, now he'll make my flesh part of his; and the picture stuck in my mind of that time when I saw him catch up two of my friends at once and dash them thrice and again upon the ground; and when, crouching like a shaggy lion over them, he filled his greedy maw with their vitals and their flesh, their bones full of white marrow, and their limbs still warm with life. A quaking terror seized me and I stood pale with horror as I watched him now chewing, now ejecting his bloody feast, now disgorging his horrid food mingled with wine. Such fate I pictured as in store for wretched me. For many days I kept myself in hiding, trembling at every sound, fearing death and yet longing to die, keeping off starvation with acorns and grass and leaves, alone, helpless and hopeless, abandoned to suffering and death. And then, after a long time, far in the distance I saw this ship, and I begged them by my gestures to save me, I rushed down to the shore and I touched their hearts: a Trojan ship received a Greek! Now do you also tell of your adventures, best of comrades, what your leader suffered and the company which put to sea with you."

Then Macareus told how Aeolus ruled over the Tuscan waters, Aeolus, son of Hippotes, confining the winds in prison. These winds, enclosed in a bag of bull's hide, the Dulichian captain had received, a memorable gift. Nine days they had sailed along with a good stern breeze and had sighted the land they sought; but when the tenth morning dawned, Ulysses' comrades were overcome by envy and by lust of booty; thinking that gold was in the bag, they untied the strings that held the winds. These blew the vessel back again over the waves they had just crossed, and she re-entered the harbour of the Aeolian tyrant. "After that," he said, "we came to the ancient city of Laestrygonian Lamus. Antiphates was ruling in that land. I was sent to him with two companions. One comrade and myself by flight barely reached a place of safety; but the third of us stained with his blood the Laestrygonians' impious mouths. Antiphates pursued us as we fled and urged his band after us. They came on in a mob, hurling stones and heavy timbers, and they sank our men and sank our ships. One of them, however, in which I and Ulysses himself sailed, escaped. Grieving for our lost companions and with many lamentations, we finally reached that land which you see at some distance over there. (And, trust my word, I found it was best to see it at a distance.) And you, most righteous Trojan, son of Venus (for now that the war is over, you are no longer to be counted foe, Aeneas), I warn you, keep away from Circe's shores! We also, having moored our vessel on the beach, and remembering Antiphates and the cruel Cyclops, refused to go further, but were chosen by lot to explore the unknown island. The lot sent me and the trusty Polites, Eurylochus also and Elpenor, too much given to wine, and eighteen others to Circe's city. When we arrived and stood within her courts, a thousand wolves and she-bears and li-onesses in a mixed throng rushed on us, filling us with terror. But there was no need to fear them; not one of them was to give us a single scratch upon our bodies. Why, they even wagged their tails in show of kindness, and fawned upon us as they followed us along, until attendant maidens took us in charge and led us through the marble halls to their mistress' presence. She sat in a beautiful retreat on her throne of state, clad in a gleaming purple robe, with a golden veil above. Her attendants were Nereids and nymphs, who card no fleece and spin no woollen threads with nimble fingers; their only task, to sort out plants, to select from a jumbled mass and place in separate baskets flowers and herbs of various colors. She herself oversees the work they do; she herself knows what is the value of each leaf, what ingredients mix well together, takes note and checks the weight of the herbs. When she saw us and when welcome had been given and received, she smiled upon us and seemed to promise us the friendship we desired. At once she bade her maidens spread a feast of parched barley-bread, of honey, strong wine, and curdled milk; and in this sweet drink, where they might lie unnoticed, she slyly squeezed some of her baleful juices. We took the cup which was offered by her divine hand. As soon as we had thirstily drained the cup with parched lips, the cruel goddess touched the tops of our heads with her magic wand; and then (I am ashamed to tell, yet will I tell) I began to grow rough with bristles, and I could speak no longer, but in place of words came only hoarse, grunting sounds, and I began to bend forward with face turned entirely to the earth. I felt my mouth hardening into a long snout, my neck swelling in brawny folds, and with my hands, with which but now I had lifted the goblet to my lips, I made tracks upon the ground. And then I was shut up in a pen with others who had suffered the same change (so great was the power of her magic drugs!). We saw that only Eurylochus was without the pig form; for only he had refused to take the cup. If he had not refused it, I should even now be one of the bristly herd, and Ulysses would never have been informed by him of our great calamity, and come to Circe to avenge us. Peace-bringing Cyllenius had given him a white flower which the gods call moly. It grows up from a black root. Safe with this and the directions which the god had given him, Ulysses entered Circe's palace and, when he was invited to drink of the fatal bowl, he struck aside the wand with which she was attempting to stroke his hair, and threatened the quaking queen with his drawn sword. Then faith was pledged and right hands given and, being accepted as her husband, he demanded as a wedding gift the bodies of his friends. We were sprinkled with the more wholesome juices of some mysterious herb, our heads received the stroke of her reversed rod, and words were uttered over us which counteracted the words said before. And as she sang, more and still more raised from the ground we stood erect, our bristles fell away, our feet lost their cloven hoofs, our shoulders came back to us, and our arms resumed their former shape. Weeping, we embraced him, weeping too, and clung to our chieftain's neck; and the first words we uttered were of gratitude to him. We tarried in that country for a year, and in so long a time many were the things I saw with my own eyes and many were the tales I heard. Here is one of the many which one of the four attendants appointed for such offices as have been mentioned told me privately. For, while Circe was dallying alone with our leader, this nymph pointed out to me a snow-white marble statue of a young man with a woodpecker on his head. The statue was set in a sacred fane and attracted attention for its many wreaths. When in my curiosity I asked who it was and why he was worshipped in that holy place and why he had the bird upon his head, she told me this story: 'Listen, Macareus, and learn from this how strong is my mistress' magic. And do you give diligent heed to what I say.

" 'Picus, the son of Saturn, was once the king of the Ausonian country and was very fond of horses fit for war. The hero's form was as you see it. And, though you should look upon his living beauty, still would you approve the true in comparison with his mimic form. His spirit was equal to his body. He could not yet have seen, as the years went by, four quinquennial contests at Grecian Elis; but already had he attracted to his beauty all the dryads sprung from the hills of Latium; the nymphs of the fountains pined for him, and the naiads who dwell in the Albula, beneath Numicus' stream and Anio's, short-coursing Almo, headlong Nar, and Farfar's shady waters; and those who haunt the wooded pool of Taurian Diana and the neighbouring lakes. But, spurning all these, he loved one nymph alone, whom once on the Palatine Venilia is said to have borne to two-headed Janus.[1] This maid, when she had ripened into marriageable years, was given to Laurentian Picus, preferred above all suitors. Rare was her beauty, but rarer still her gift of song, from which came her name, Canens. She used to move woods and rocks, soften wild beasts, stop the long rivers with her singing, and stay the wandering birds. Once, while she was singing her songs with her maidenly voice, Picus had sallied forth from home into the Laurentian fields to hunt the native boar. He bestrode a prancing courser, carrying in his left hand a brace of spears and wearing a purple mantle caught with a brooch of gold. The daughter of the Sun also had come to those selfsame woods and, to gather fresh herbs on the fertile hills, she had left the fields called Circaean from her name. As soon as she saw the youth from her leafy hiding-place she was struck with wonder. The herbs which she had gathered fell from her hands and burning fire seemed to creep through her whole frame. As soon as she could master her passion and collect her thoughts she was on the point of confessing her desire; but his swift-speeding horse and his thronging retinue prevented her approach to him. "You shall not escape me so," she cried, "not though the wind itself should bear you off, if I know myself, if my herbs' magic power has not wholly vanished, and if my charms have not failed." She spoke and fashioned an unsubstantial image of a boar and bade it rush across the trail before the prince's eyes and seem to take cover in a grove thick with fallen trees, where the woods were dense, places where a horse could not penetrate. The thing was done, and straightway Picus, all unconscious of the trick, made after his shadowy prey and, swiftly dismounting from his foaming steed, followed the empty lure on foot and went blindly groping in the forest depths. She seized upon this answer to her prayer and fell to muttering incantations, worshipping her weird gods with a weird charm with which it was her wont to obscure the white moon's features, and hide her father's face behind misty clouds. Now also by her magic song the heavens are darkened, and thick fogs spring up from the ground, while the retainers wander in the dim trails far from their king's defence. Having secured a fitting place and time, she says: "Oh, by those eyes which have enthralled my own, and by that beauty, fairest of youths, which has made even me, a goddess, suppliant to you, look with favor on my passion and accept the Sun, who beholds all things, as your father-in-law; and do not cruelly reject Circe, the Titaness." But he fiercely repelled her and her prayers, and said: "Whoever you are, I am not for you. Another has taken and holds my love in keeping, and I pray that she may keep it through all coming time. Nor will I violate my plighted troth by any other love so long as the fates shall preserve to me my Canens, Janus' daughter." Having tried oft-repeated prayers in vain, the Titaness exclaimed: "But you shall not go scathless, nor shall your Canens ever have you more; and you shall learn by experience not only what any woman, loving and scorned, can do, but what the woman, Circe, loving and scorned, can do!" Then twice she turned her to the west and twice to the east; thrice she touched the youth with her wand and thrice she sang her charms. He turned in flight, but was amazed to find himself running more swiftly than his wont, and saw wings spring out upon his body. Enraged at his sudden change to a strange bird in his Latian woods, he pecked at the rough oak-trees with his hard beak and wrathfully inflicted wounds on their long branches. His wings took the color of his bright red mantle, and what had been a brooch of gold stuck through his robe was changed to feathers, and his neck was circled with a golden-yellow band; and nothing of his former self remained to Picus except his name.

" 'Meanwhile his companions, calling often and vainly for Picus throughout the countryside and finding him nowhere, came upon Circe (for now she had cleared the air and had permitted the clouds to be dispelled by wind and sun), charged her flatly with her crime, demanded back their king with threats of force, and were preparing to attack her with their deadly spears. But she sprinkled upon them her baleful drugs and poisonous juices, summoning to her aid Night and the gods of Night from Erebus and Chaos,[2] and calling on Hecate in long-drawn, wailing cries. The woods, wonderful to say, leaped from their place, the ground rumbled, the neighbouring trees turned white, and the herbage where her poisons fell was stained with clots of blood. The stones also seemed to voice hoarse bellow-ings; the baying of dogs was heard, the ground was foul with dark, crawling things, and the thin shades of the silent dead seemed to be flitting about. The astounded crowd quaked at the monstrous sights and sounds; but she touched the frightened, wondering faces with her magic wand, and at the touch horrid, beast-like forms of many shapes came upon the youths, and none kept his proper form.

" 'Now the setting sun had bathed the Tartessian shores, and vainly had Canens watched for her lord's return with eyes and heart. Her slaves and her people scattered through all the woods, bearing torches in hope to meet him. Nor was the nymph content to weep, to tear her hair and beat her breasts; (all these she did, indeed) and, rushing forth, she wandered madly through the Latian fields. Six nights and as many returning dawns beheld her wandering, sleep-less and fasting, over hills, through valleys, wherever chance di-rected. The Tiber was the last to see her, spent with grief and travel-toil, laying her body down upon his far-stretching bank. There, with tears, in weak, faint tones, she poured out her mourn-ful words attuned to grief; just as sometimes, in dying, the swan sings a last funeral-song. Finally, worn to a shade by woe, her very marrow changed to water, she melted away and gradually vanished into thin air. Still her story has been kept in remembrance by the place which ancient muses fitly called Canens from the name of the nymph.'

"Many such things I heard and saw during a long year. At length, grown sluggish and slow through inactivity, we were ordered to go again upon the sea and spread our sails. The Titaness had told us of the dubious pathways of the sea, their vast extent, and all the desperate perils yet to come. I own I was afraid to face them and, having reached this shore, I stayed behind."

Macareus had finished his story; and Aeneas' nurse, buried in a marble urn, had a brief epitaph carved on her tomb:

HERE ME, CAIETA, SNATCHED FROM GRECIAN FLAMES,
MY PIOUS SON CONSUMED WITH FITTING FIRE.

Loosing their cables from the grass-grown shore, they kept far out from the treacherous island, the home of the ill-famed goddess, and headed for the wooded coast where shady Tiber pours forth his yellow, silt-laden waters into the sea. There did Aeneas win the daughter and the throne of Latinus, Faunus' son; but not without a struggle. War with a fierce race is waged, and Turnus fights madly for his promised bride. All Etruria rushes to battle-shock with Latium, and with long and anxious struggle hard victory is sought. Both sides augment their strength by outside aid; and many defend the Rutuli and many the Trojan camp. Aeneas had not gone in vain to Evander's home, but Venulus had vainly sought the city of the exiled Diomede. He had founded a large city within Iapygian Daunus' realm, and was ruling the fields granted to him as a marriage portion.[3] But when Venulus had done Turnus' bidding and asked for aid, the Aetolian hero pleaded his lack of resources as his excuse, saying that he was not willing to expose himself or his father-in-law's people to the risk of battle, nor did he have men of his own nation whom he might equip for war. "And, that you may not think my excuses false, although the very mention of my woes renews my bitter grief, still will I endure the telling of them. After high Ilium had been burned and Pergama had glutted the furious passions of the Greeks; and after the Narycian hero from a virgin goddess for a violated virgin had brought on us all the punishment which he alone deserved, we Greeks were scattered and, blown by winds over the angry waters, we suffered lightning blasts, thick darkness, storms, the rage of sky and sea and Caphereus, the climax of our disasters. Not to delay you by telling our sad mishaps in order, Greece at that time could have moved even Priam's tears. Well-armed Minerva's care, however, saved me from the waves; but again I was driven forth from my native Argos, for fostering Venus, still mindful of the old wound I had given her,* now exacted the penalty. So great toils did I endure on the high seas and so great toils of war on land that often did I call those blessed of heaven whom the storm, which all had suffered, and cruel Caphereus drowned beneath the waves; and I wished that I, too, had been one of them.

"And now my companions, having endured the uttermost in war and sea, became disheartened and begged me to make an end of wandering. But Acmon, who was naturally hot-headed and who was at times especially intractable because of our sufferings, exclaimed: 'What is there left, men, for your long-suffering to refuse to bear? What is there left for Venus to do further, supposing she wishes it? For, so long as we fear worse fortunes, we lie open to wounds; but when the worst possible lot has fallen, then is fear beneath our feet and the utmost misfortune can bring us no further care. Though she herself should hear and, as indeed she does, should hate all men less than she hates Diomede, still do we all scorn her hatred; and the power to do so is our chief defence.' With such insulting words did Pleuronian Acmon rouse Venus and revive her former anger. But few approved his words. We, the greater number of his friends, upbraided Acmon; and when he would have replied, his voice and throat together grew thin; his hair was changed to feathers, and feathers clothed a new-formed neck and breast and back. His arms acquired large pinion-feathers and his elbows curved into nimble wings; his toes were replaced by webbed feet and his face grew stiff and horny, ending in a sharp-pointed beak. Lycus viewed him in wonder, so also Idas, Rhexenor and Nycteus and Abas too; and, while they wondered, they became of the same form. The greater number flew up in a flock and circled round the rowers with flapping wings. If you ask of what sort were these questionable birds, while they were not swans, they were very like snowy swans. And now, as son-in-law of Iapygian Daunus, I have

---

*The incident appears in book 5 of the *Iliad*.

hard work to hold this settlement and this parched countryside with but a pitiful remnant of my friends."

So spoke the grandson of Oeneus. And Venulus departed from the Calydonian realm, passing the Peucetian bay and the regions of Messapia. Here he saw a cavern, dark with forest shades and hidden by a growth of waving reeds. The half-goat Pan now claims the place, but at one time the nymphs dwelt there. An Apulian shepherd of that region caused them to run away in terror, filling them at first with sudden fear. But soon, when their courage returned and they saw with scorn who was pursuing them, they returned to their choral dancing again with nimble feet. Still did the shepherd mock them, imitating their dance with his clownish steps, adding to this boorish insults and vulgar words. Nor did he cease speaking until the rising wood covered his mouth. For now he is a tree. You could tell its kind from the savor of its fruit; for the wild olive bears the traces of his tongue in its bitter berries. The sharpness of his words has passed to them.

When the ambassadors returned with the news that Aetolian help had been refused them, the Rutuli without that help went on with the war they had begun; and much blood was spilled on both sides. But lo, Turnus brought devouring torches against the pine fabric of the ships, and what the waves had spared feared the flames. And now Mulciber was burning the pitchy, resinous mass and other rich food for flames, and was spreading even to the tall masts and sails, while the cross-banks of the curving hulls were smoking; when the holy mother of the gods, mindful that these pines were felled on Ida's top, filled the air with the harsh beat of brazen cymbals and the shrill music of the boxwood flute.[4] Then, borne by her tamed lions through the yielding air, she cried: "Vainly, O Turnus, with impious hand you hurl those brands. For I shall rescue the burning ships, nor with my consent shall the greedy flames devour what was once part and parcel of my sacred woods." While yet the goddess spoke it thundered and, following the thunder, a heavy shower of rain began to fall, mingled with leaping hail, and the winds, Astraean brothers, wrought wild confusion in the air and on the waves, swollen by the sudden rush of waters, and mingled in the fray. The all-fostering mother, with the help of one of these, broke the hempen fastenings of the Phrygian ships and, forcing them head down, plunged them beneath the water. Straightway the wood softened and turned to flesh, the ships' curved prows changed to heads, the oars to toes and swimming legs; what had been body before remained as body and the deep-laid keel was changed into a spine; cordage became soft hair, and sail-yards, arms; the sea-green color was unchanged. And now, as water-nymphs, with maiden glee they sport in the waters which they feared before. Though born on the rough mountain-tops, they now throng the yielding waves and no trace of their first state troubles them. And yet, remembering the many perils they have often suffered on the deep, they often place helping hands beneath storm-tossed barques, except such as carried Greeks. Remembering still the Phrygian calamity, they hated the Pelasgian race and they rejoiced to see the broken timbers of Ulysses' ship, rejoiced to see the vessel of Alcinoüs grow stiff and its wood turn to stone.

After the fleet had been changed to living water-nymphs, there was hope that the Rutuli, in awe of the portent, would desist from war. But the war went on and both sides had their gods to aid them, and, what is as good as gods, they had courage too. And now neither a kingdom given in dowry, nor the sceptre of a father-in-law, nor you, Lavinian maiden, did they seek, but only victory, and they kept on warring through sheer shame of giving up. At length Venus saw her son's arms victorious and Turnus fell. Ardea fell, counted a powerful city in Turnus' lifetime. But after the outlander's sword destroyed it and warm ashes hid its ruins, from the confused mass a bird flew forth of a kind never seen before, and beat the ashes with its flapping wings. Its sound, its meagre look, its deathly paleness, all things which become a captured city, yes, even the city's name remained in the bird; and Ardea's self is beaten in lamentation by its wings.

Now had Aeneas' courageous soul moved all the gods and even Juno to lay aside their ancient anger, and, since the fortunes of the budding Iülus were well established, the heroic son of Cytherea was ripe for heaven. Venus had approached the heavenly gods and, throwing her arms around her father's neck, had said: "O father, who has never at any time been harsh to me, now be most kind, I pray. To my Aeneas, who is your grandson and of our blood, grant him, O most excellent, some divinity, however small I care not, if only you grant any. It is enough once to have looked upon the unlovely kingdom, once to have crossed the Stygian stream." The gods all gave assent; nor did the queen-consort keep an unyielding face, but peacefully consented. Then Father Jove declared: "You are both worthy of this heavenly gift, both you who pray and he for whom you pray. Have then, my daughter, what you desire." He spoke, and Venus, rejoicing, gave her father thanks. Then, borne aloft through the yielding air by her harnessed doves, she came to the Laurentian coast, where the river Numicius, winding through beds of sheltering reeds, pours its fresh waters into the neighbouring sea. She bade the river-god wash away from Aeneas all his mortal part and carry it down in his silent stream into the ocean depths. The horned god obeyed Venus' command and in his waters cleansed and washed quite away whatever was mortal in Aeneas. His best part remained to him. His mother sprinkled his body and anointed it with divine perfume, touched his lips with ambrosia and sweet nectar mixed, and so made him a god, whom the Roman populace styled Indiges and honored with temple and with sacrifice.*

Next, under Ascanius' sway, the state was of double name, Alban and Latin. Silvius succeeded him; his son, Latinus, took a name inherited with the ancient sceptre. Illustrious Alba succeeded Latinus; Epytus next, and after him Capetus and Capys, but Capys first. Tiberinus received the kingdom after them, and he, drowned in the waters of the Tuscan stream, gave his name to that river. His sons were Remulus and warlike Acrota. Remulus, the elder, perished by a thunderbolt while striving to imitate the thunder. Acrota, less daring than his brother, resigned the sceptre to brave Aventinus. He lies buried on the same hill where he had reigned and has given his name to the hill. And now Proca held dominion over the Palatine race.

Pomona flourished under this king: there was no other Latian wood-nymph more skilled in garden-culture than she nor more zealous in the care of fruitful trees, which explains her name. She cared nothing for woods and rivers, but only for the fields and branches laden with delicious fruits. She carried no javelin in her hand, but the curved pruning-hook with which now she repressed the too luxuriant growth and cut back the branches spreading out on every side, and now, making an incision in the bark, would

---

*Aeneas was worshipped near the Nemicus river under the name Jupiter Indiges.

engraft a twig and give juices to an adopted bough. Nor would she permit them to suffer thirst, but watered the twisted fibres of the thirsty roots with her trickling streams. This was her love; this was her chief desire; nor did she have any care for Venus; yet, fearing some clownish violence, she shut herself up within her orchard and so guarded herself against all approach of man. What did not the Satyrs, a young dancing band, do to win her, and the Pans, their horns encircled with wreaths of pine, and Silvanus, always more youthful than his years, and that god who warns off evil-doers with his sickle or his ugly shape?* But, indeed, Vertumnus surpassed them all in love; yet he was no more fortunate than they. Oh, how often in the garb of a rough reaper did he bring her a basket of bar-ley-ears! And he was the perfect image of a reaper, too. Often he would come with his temples wreathed with fresh hay, and could easily seem to have been turning the new-mown grass. Again he would appear carrying an ox-goad in his clumsy hand, so that you would swear that he had but now unyoked his weary cattle. He would be a leaf-gatherer and vine-pruner with hook in hand; he would come along with a ladder on his shoulder and you would think him about to gather apples. He would be a soldier with a sword, or a fisherman with a rod. In fact, by means of his many dis-guises, he obtained frequent admission to her presence and had much joy in looking on her beauty. He also put on a wig of grey hair, bound his temples with a gaudy head-cloth, and, leaning on a staff, came in the disguise of an old woman, entered the well-kept garden and, after admiring the fruit, said: "But you are far more beautiful," and he kissed her several times as no real old woman ever would have done. The bent old creature sat down on the grass, gazing at the branches bending beneath the weight of autumn fruits. There was a shapely elm-tree opposite, covered with gleaming bunches of grapes. After he had looked approvingly at this awhile, together with its vine companion, he said: "But if that tree stood there un-mated to the vine, it would have no value except for its leaves alone; and this vine, which clings to and rests safely on the elm, if it were not thus wedded, it would lie languishing, flat upon the ground. But you are not touched by the vine's example and you shun wedlock

---

*The sickle-wielder is the fertility god Priapus, also a protector of property.

and do not desire to be joined to another. And I would that you did desire it! Then would you have more suitors than ever Helen had, or she for whom the Lapithae took arms, or the wife of the timid, not the bold, Ulysses. And even as it is, though you shun them and turn in contempt from their wooing, a thousand men desire you, and half-gods and gods and all the divinities that haunt the Alban hills. But if you will be wise, and consent to a good match and will listen to an old woman like me, who love you more than all the rest, yes, more than you would believe, reject all common offers and choose Vertumnus as the consort of your couch. You have me also as guaranty for him; for he is not better known to himself than he is to me. He does not wander idly throughout the world, but he dwells in the wide spaces here at hand; nor, as most of your suitors do, does he fall in love at sight with every girl he meets. You will be his first love and his last, and to you alone he will devote his life. Consider also that he is young, blest with a native charm, can readily assume whatever form he will, and what you bid him, though without stint you bid, he will perform. Moreover your tastes are similar, and the fruit which you so cherish he is the first to have and with joyful hands he lays hold upon your gifts. But neither the fruit of your trees, nor the sweet, succulent herbs which your garden bears, nor anything at all does he desire but you alone. Pity him who loves you so, and believe that he himself in very presence through my lips is begging for what he wants. And have a thought for the avenging gods and the Idalian goddess who detests the hard of heart, and the unforgetting wrath of Nemesis! And that you may the more fear these (for my long life has brought me knowledge of many things), I will tell you a story that is well known all over Cyprus, by which you may learn to be easily persuaded and to be soft of heart.

"Iphis, a youth of humble birth, had chanced to see Anaxarete, a proud princess of old Teucer's line. He saw her, and at once felt the fire of love through all his frame. Long did he fight against it; but when he found he could not overcome his passion by the power of reason, he came as a suppliant to her door. Now he confessed his unhappy love to her nurse and begged her by her fond hopes for her dear foster-child not to be hard towards him; now, coaxing each one of her many servants, he earnestly begged her to do him a kindly turn; often he gave them coaxing messages on tablets to bear to her; at times he would hang garlands of flowers upon her door, wet with his tears, and lay his soft body down upon her hard threshold, complaining bitterly of her unfeeling bars. But she, more savage than the waves that rise at the setting of the Kids, harder than iron tempered in Noric fire, or living rock, which still holds firmly to its native bed, spurns him and mocks at him. And to her heartless deeds she adds insolent, haughty words, and utterly deprives her lover of hope itself. Unable to bear further the torment of his long agony, before her door Iphis cries these words as his last message to her: 'You win, Anaxarete, and no more need you be annoyed on my account. Celebrate your glad triumph, sing songs of victory, set a gleaming wreath of laurel on your head! For you have won, and I die gladly. Come then, rejoice, you of the iron heart! Surely you will be forced to admit that there is some feature of my love in which I am pleasing to you, and you will confess my merit. But remember that my love for you ended only with my life and that I must suffer the loss of two lights at once. And 'twill be no mere rumour that comes to announce my death to you; I shall myself be there, be well assured, and that, too, in visible presence, that you may feast your cruel eyes upon my lifeless body. But if, O gods, you see the things we mortals do, remember me (nothing further can my tongue hold out to pray) and have my story told long ages from now; and what time you have taken from my life give to my fame.' He spoke, and raising his tearful eyes and pale arms to the door-posts that he had often decorated with his floral wreaths, he fastened a rope to the topmost beam, saying the while: 'Does this garland please you, cruel and wicked girl?' Then he thrust his head into the noose, even in that act turning his face towards her, and then, poor fellow, hung there, a lifeless weight with broken neck. The door was struck by the convulsive motion of his feet; it seemed to give out a sound suggesting many fearful things and, being thrown open, showed what had happened there. The servants cried out in horror and took him down, but all in vain. Then (for his father was dead) they bore him to his mother's house. She took him in her arms and embraced her son's cold limbs. And after she had said the words which wretched parents say, and done the things which wretched mothers do, through the midst of the city she led his tearful funeral, and bore the pale corpse on a bier to the funeral pyre. Anaxarete's house chanced to be near the street where the mournful procession was passing, and the sound of mourning came to the ears of the hard-hearted girl, whom already an avenging god was driving on. Yet, moved by the sound, she said: 'Let us go see this tearful funeral.' And she went into her high dwelling with its wide-open windows. Scarce had she gained a good look at Iphis, lying there upon the bier, when her eyes stiffened at the sight and the warm blood fled from her pale body. She tried to step back from the window, but she stuck fast in her place. She tried to turn her face away, but this also she could not do; and gradually that stony nature took possession of her body which had been in her heart all along. And that you may not think this story false, Salamis still keeps a marble statue, the image of the princess. It has a temple in honor of the Gazing Venus also.[5] Have thought of these things, I pray you, and put away, dear nymph, your stubborn scorn; yield to your lover. So may no late spring frost ever nip your budding fruit, and may no rude winds scatter them in their flower."

When the god in the form of age had thus pleaded his cause in vain, he returned to his youthful form, put off the old woman's trappings, and stood revealed to the maiden as when the sun's most beaming face has conquered the opposing clouds and shines out with nothing to dim his radiance. He was all ready to force her will, but no force was necessary; and the nymph, smitten by the beauty of the god, felt an answering passion.

Next false Amulius by force of arms rules the Ausonian state; but old Numitor by the aid of his grandson gains the kingdom he has lost, and the walls of the City are founded on the shepherd's festal day.[6] Tatius and the Sabine fathers wage their war, and Tarpeia, having betrayed the passage to the citadel, gives up her life as forfeit beneath the arms heaped on her. Then the men of Cures, like silent wolves, with hushed voices steal on the Romans buried in slumber, and try the gates which Ilia's son has fastened with strong bars. But Saturnian Juno herself unfastened one of these, opening the gate on noiseless hinges. Venus alone perceived that the gate's bars had fallen, and would have closed it; but it is never permitted to gods to undo the acts of gods. Now the Ausonian water-nymphs held a spot near Janus' fane, where a cold spring bubbled forth. Venus asked aid of these, nor did the nymphs refuse the goddess her just request, but opened up their fountain's streaming veins. Up to that time the pass of Janus was still open, nor had the water ever blocked the way. Now they placed yellow sulphur beneath their living spring and heated the hollow veins with burning pitch. By these and other means the reeking steam filled the fountain through and through, and you waters, which dared but now to vie with Alpine cold, did not yield in heat to fire itself! The two gate-posts smoked with the hot fumes; and the gate, which had been opened (but now in vain) to the hardy Sabines, was made impassable by the new fountain, until the Roman soldiery could arm themselves. Then Romulus took the offensive, and soon the Roman plain was strewn with the Sabine dead and with its own as well, and the impious swords mingled the blood of son-in-law with blood of father-in-law. At last it was their will to end the war in peace, and not strive with the sword to the bitter end; and it was agreed that Tatius should share the throne.

Tatius had fallen and now, Romulus, you were meting equal laws to both the tribes, when Mars put off his gleaming helmet and thus addressed the father of gods and men: "The time is come, O father, since the Roman state stands firm on strong foundations and no longer hangs on one man's strength alone, to grant the reward which was promised to me and to your worthy grandson, to take him from earth and set him in the heavens. Once to me, in full council of the gods (for I treasured up your gracious words in my retentive mind, and now recall them to you), you declared: 'One shall there be whom you shall bear up to the azure blue of heaven.' Now let the full meaning of your words be ratified." The omnipotent Father nodded his assent; then, hiding all the sky with his dark clouds, he filled the earth with thunder and lightning. Gradivus knew this for the assured sign of the translation which had been promised him; and, leaning on his spear, dauntless he mounted his chariot drawn by steeds straining beneath the bloody yoke, and swung the loud-resounding lash. Gliding downward through the air, he halted on the summit of the wooded Palatine. There, as Ilia's son was giving kindly judgment to his citizens, he caught him up from earth. His mortal part dissolved into thin air, as a leaden bullet hurled by a broad sling is wont to melt away in the mid-heavens. And now a fair form clothes him, worthier of the high couches of the gods, such form as has Quirinus, clad in the sacred robe.

His wife was mourning him as lost, when regal Juno bade Iris go down to Hersilia on her arching way with these directions for the widowed queen: "O queen, bright glory both of Latium and of the Sabine race, most worthy once to have been the consort of so great a man, and now of divine Quirinus, cease your laments and, if you would indeed behold your husband, come with me to that grove which stands green on Quirinus' hill, shading the temple of the king of Rome." Iris obeyed and, gliding to earth along her rainbow arch, accosted Hersilia in the words which had been given her. She, scarce lifting her eyes and with modest look, replied: "O goddess (for I may not tell who you are, and yet it's plain you are a goddess), lead, oh, lead me on, and show me my husband's face. If only the fates grant me but once to see him, then shall I say I have gained heaven indeed." Straightway she fared along with Thaumas' daughter to the hill of Romulus. There a star from high heaven came gliding down to earth, and Hersilia, her hair bursting into flame from its light, goes up together with the star into thin air. Her with dear, familiar hands Rome's founder receives, and changes her mortal body and her old-time name. He calls her Hora, and now as goddess is she joined once more to her Quirinus.[7]

BOOK XV

MEANWHILE IT IS A question who can sustain the burden of so
great a task, who can succeed so great a king. Then Fame as a faith-
ful herald selects illustrious Numa for the throne. He, not content
with knowing the usages of the Sabine race, conceives larger plans
in his generous soul, and seeks to know what is Nature's general law.
His great fondness for this pursuit caused him to leave his native
Cures and take his way to the city which once gave hospitality to
Hercules. There, when he asked who was the founder of this
Grecian city on Italian soil,[1] one of the old inhabitants of the place,
well versed in its ancient lore, thus answered him: "It is said that the
son of Jove, returning from the Ocean enriched with the herds of
Spain, came by good fortune to the borders of Lacinium, and there,
while his cattle grazed upon the tender grass, he entered the home
and beneath the friendly roof of the great Croton and refreshed
himself by quiet rest from his long toil. And as he took his leave he
said: 'Here, ages from now, shall stand the city of your descendants.'
And the words proved true. For there was a certain Myscelus, son
of Alemon of Argos, the man of all that generation most beloved of
heaven. Standing over him as he lay buried in deep slumber, the
club-bearer thus addressed him: 'Up and away from your native
land; go, seek out the rocky channel of the distant Aesar'; and he
threatened him with many fearful things should he not obey. Then
did his slumber and the presence of the god withdraw together. The
son of Alemon arose and silently recalled the vision which was still
vivid in his memory. Long was he in great stress of doubt: the god
bade him depart, his country's laws prohibited his departure. The
punishment of death was appointed to the man who should desire
to change his fatherland. The bright Sun had hidden his shining
face beneath the sea, and thick Night had raised her starry face from
the waters, when the same god seemed to stand before him, to give

the same commands, and to threaten worse and heavier penalties if he should not obey. He was sore afraid. And as soon as he made ready to move his household belongings to a new abode, the rumour got abroad in the town, and he was tried as a breaker of the laws. When the case for the prosecution had been closed and the charge was clearly proved without need of witnesses, the wretched culprit, raising his face and hands to heaven, cried out: 'O you to whom your twelve great labours gave a claim to heaven, help me, I pray! for you are responsible for my sin.' It was the custom in ancient times to use white and black pebbles, the black for condemning prisoners and the white for freeing them from the charge. At this time also the fatal vote was taken in this way; and every pebble that was dropped into the pitiless urn was black! But when the urn was turned and the pebbles poured out for counting, the color of them all was changed from black to white; and so, by the will of Hercules, the vote was made favorable, and Alemon's son was freed. He first gave thanks to his patron, Amphitryon's son, and soon with favoring winds was sailing over the Ionian sea. He passed by Salentine Neretum, and Sybaris and Spartan Tarentum, the bay of Siris, Crimisa, and the Iapygian coast; and scarcely had he passed the lands which border on that coast when he found the destined mouth of Aesar's stream, and near by this a mound of earth which guarded the consecrated bones of Croton. There in that land, as the god had bidden him, he laid his city's walls and named it from him who had been buried there." Such was the ancient tale, confirmed by established fame, both of the place and the founding of the city on Italian soil.

There was a man here, a Samian by birth, but he had fled forth from Samos and its rulers, and through hatred of tyranny was living in voluntary exile.[2] He, though the gods were far away in the heavenly regions, still approached them with his thought, and what Nature denied to his mortal vision he feasted on with his mind's eye. And when he had surveyed all things by reason and wakeful diligence, he would give out to the public ear the things worthy of their learning and would teach the crowds, which listened in wondering silence to his words, the beginnings of the great universe, the causes of things and what their nature is: what God is, from where come the snows, what is the origin of lightning, whether it is Jupiter or the winds that thunder from the riven clouds, what causes the earth to quake, by what law the stars perform their courses, and whatever else is hidden from men's knowledge. He was the first to decry the placing of animal food upon our tables. His lips, learned indeed but not believed in this, he was the first to open in such words as these:

"O mortals, do not pollute your bodies with a food so impious! You have the fruits of the earth, you have apples, bending down the branches with their weight, and grapes swelling to ripeness on the vines; you have also delicious herbs and vegetables which can be mellowed and softened by the help of fire. Nor are you without milk or honey, fragrant with the bloom of thyme. The earth, prodigal of her wealth, supplies you her kindly sustenance and offers you food without bloodshed and slaughter. Flesh is the wild beasts', with which they appease their hunger, and yet not all, since the horse, the sheep, and cattle live on grass; but those whose nature is savage and untamed, Armenian tigers, raging lions, bears and wolves, all these delight in bloody food. Oh, how criminal it is for flesh to be stored away in flesh, for one greedy body to grow fat with food gained from another, for one live creature to go on living through the destruction of another living thing! And so in the midst of the wealth of food which Earth, the best of mothers, has produced, it is your pleasure to chew the piteous flesh of slaughtered animals with your savage teeth, and thus to repeat the Cyclops' horrid manners! And you cannot, without destroying other life, appease the cravings of your greedy and insatiable maw!

"But that pristine age, which we have named the golden age, was blessed with the fruit of the trees and the herbs which the ground sends forth, nor did men defile their lips with blood. Then birds plied their wings in safety through the heaven, and the hare loitered all unafraid in the tilled fields, nor did its own guilelessness hang the fish upon the hook. All things were free from treacherous snares, fearing no guile and full of peace. But after someone, an ill exemplar, whoever he was, envied the food of lions, and thrust down flesh as food into his greedy stomach, he opened the way for crime. It may be that, in the first place, with the killing of wild beasts the blade was warmed and stained with blood. This would have been justified, and we admit that creatures which menace our own lives may be killed without impiety. But, while they might be killed, they should never have been eaten.

"Further impiety grew out of that, and it is thought that the sow was first condemned to death as a sacrificial victim because with her broad snout she had rooted up the planted seeds and cut off the season's promised crop. The goat is said to have been slain at the avenging altars because he had browsed the grape-vines. These two suffered because of their own offences! But, you sheep, what did you ever do to merit death, a peaceful flock, born for man's service, who bring us sweet milk to drink in your full udders, who give us your wool for soft clothing, and who help more by your life than by your death? What have the oxen done, those faithful, guileless beasts, harmless and simple, born to a life of toil? Truly inconsiderate he and not worthy of the gift of grain who could take off the curved plow's heavy weight and in the next moment slay his husbandman; who with his axe could smite that neck which was worn with toil for him, by whose help he had so often renewed the stubborn soil and planted so many crops. Nor is it enough that we commit such infamy: they made the gods themselves partners of their crime and they affected to believe that the heavenly ones took pleasure in the blood of the toiling bullock! A victim without blemish and of perfect form (for beauty proves his curse), marked off with fillets and with gilded horns, is set before the altar, hears the priest's prayer, not knowing what it means, watches the barley-meal sprinkled between his horns, barley which he himself laboured to produce, and then, smitten to his death, he stains with his blood the knife which he has perhaps already seen reflected in the clear pool. Straightway they tear his entrails from his living breast, view them with care, and seek to find revealed in them the purposes of heaven. From this (so great is man's lust for forbidden food!) do you dare thus to feed, O race of mortals! I pray you, do not do it, but turn your minds to these my words of warning, and when you take the flesh of slaughtered cattle in your mouths, know and realize that you are devouring your own fellow-labourers.

"Now, since a god inspires my lips, I will dutifully follow the inspiring god; I'll open Delphi and the heavens themselves and unlock the oracles of the sublime mind. Great matters, never traced out by the minds of former men, things that have long been hidden, I will sing. It is a delight to take one's way along the starry firmament and, leaving the earth and its dull regions behind, to ride on the clouds, to take stand on stout Atlas' shoulders and see far below men wandering aimlessly, devoid of reason, anxious and in fear of the hereafter, thus to exhort them and unroll the book of fate!

"O race of men, stunned with the chilling fear of death, why do you dread the Styx, the shades and empty names, the stuff that poets manufacture, and their fabled sufferings of a world that never was? As for your bodies, whether the burning pyre or long lapse of time with its wasting power shall have consumed them, be sure they cannot suffer any ills. Our souls are deathless, and ever, when they have left their former seat, do they live in new abodes and dwell in the bodies that have received them. I myself (for I well remember it) at the time of the Trojan war was Euphorbus, son of Panthoüs, in whose breast once hung the heavy spear of Menelaüs.* Recently, in Juno's temple in Argos, Abas' city, I recognized the shield which I once wore on my left arm! All things are changing; nothing dies. The spirit wanders, comes now here, now there, and occupies whatever frame it pleases. From beasts it passes into human bodies, and from our bodies into beasts, but never perishes. And, as the pliant wax is stamped with new designs, does not remain as it was before nor keep the same form long, but is still the selfsame wax, so do I teach that the soul is ever the same, though it passes into everchanging bodies. Therefore, in case your piety be overcome by appetite, I warn you as a seer, do not drive out by impious slaughter what may be kindred souls, and let not life be fed on life.

"And since I am embarked on the boundless sea and have spread my full sails to the winds, there is nothing in all the world that keeps its form. All things are in a state of flux, and everything is brought into being with a changing nature. Time itself flows on in constant motion, just like a river. For neither the river nor the swift hour can stop its course; but, as wave is pushed on by wave, and as each wave as it comes is both pressed on and itself presses the wave in front, so time both flees and follows and is ever new. For that which once existed is no more, and that which was not has come to be; and so the whole round of motion is gone through again.

"You see how the spent nights speed on to dawn, and how the sun's bright rays succeed the darkness of the night. Nor have the

---

*An accurate detail from book 17 of the *Iliad*.

heavens the same appearance when all things, wearied with toil, lie
at rest at midnight and when bright Lucifer comes out on his snowy
steed; there is still another aspect when Pallantias, herald of the
morning, stains the sky bright for Phoebus' coming. The god's
round shield itself is red in the morning when it rises from beneath
the earth and is red when it is hidden beneath the earth again; but
in its zenith it is white, because there the air is of purer substance
and it is far removed from the debasing presence of the earth. Nor
has Diana, goddess of the night, the same phase always. She is less
to-day than she will be to-morrow if she is waxing, but greater if she
is waning.

"Then again, do you not see the year assuming four aspects, in
imitation of our own lifetime? For in early spring it is tender and full
of fresh life, just like a little child; at that time the herbage is bright,
swelling with life, but as yet without strength and solidity, and fills
the farmers with joyful expectation. Then all things are in bloom
and the fertile fields run riot with their bright-colored flowers; but
as yet there is no strength in the green foliage. After spring has
passed, the year, grown more sturdy, passes into summer and be-
comes like a strong young man. For there is no hardier time than
this, none more abounding in rich, warm life. Then autumn comes,
with its first flush of youth gone, but ripe and mellow, midway in
time between youth and age, with sprinkled grey showing on the
temples. And then comes aged winter, with faltering step and shiv-
ering, its locks all gone or hoary.

"Our own bodies also go through a ceaseless round of change,
nor what we have been or are to-day shall we be to-morrow. There
was a time when we lay in our first mother's womb, mere seeds and
hopes of men. Then Nature wrought with her cunning hands,
willed not that our bodies should lie cramped in our strained
mother's body, and from our home sent us forth into the free air.
Thus brought forth into the light, the infant lay without strength;
but soon it lifted itself up on all fours after the manner of the beasts;
then gradually in a wabbling, weak-kneed fashion it stood erect,
supported by some convenient prop. Thereafter, strong and fleet, it
passed over the span of youth; and when the years of middle life also
have been spent, it glides along the downhill path of declining age.
This undermines and pulls down the strength of former years; and

Milon, grown old, weeps when he looks at those arms, which once
had been like the arms of Hercules with their firm mass of muscles,
and sees them now hanging weak and flabby. Helen also weeps
when she sees her aged wrinkles in the looking-glass, and tearfully
asks herself why she should twice have been a lover's prey. O Time,
you, the great devourer, and you, envious Age, together you destroy
all things; and slowly gnawing with your teeth, you finally consume
all things in lingering death!

"And even those things which we call elements do not persist.
What changes they undergo, listen and I will tell you. In the eter-
nal universe there are four elemental substances. Two of these, earth
and water, are heavy and of their own weight sink down to lower
levels. And two, air and fire, purer still than air, are without weight
and, if unopposed, fly to the upper realms. These elements, al-
though far separate in position, nevertheless are all derived each
from the other, and each into other falls back again. The element of
earth, set free, is rarefied into liquid water, and, thinned still further,
the water changes into wind and air. Then losing weight again, this
air, already very thin, leaps up to fire, the highest place of all. Then
they come back again in reversed order; for fire, condensed, passes
into thick air, then into water; and water, packed together, solidifies
into earth.

"Nothing retains its own form; but Nature, the great renewer,
ever makes up forms from other forms. Be sure there's nothing per-
ishes in the whole universe; it does but vary and renew its form.
What we call birth is but a beginning to be other than what one was
before; and death is but cessation of a former state. Though, per-
haps, things may shift from there to here and here to there, still do
all things in their sum total remain unchanged.

"Nothing, I feel sure, lasts long under the same appearance. Thus
the ages have come from gold to iron; thus often has the condition
of places changed. I have myself seen what once was solid land
changed into sea; and again I have seen land made from the sea.
Sea-shells have been seen lying far from the ocean, and an ancient
anchor has been found on a mountain-top. What once was a level
plain, down-flowing waters have made into a valley; and hills by the
force of floods have been washed into sea. What was once marsh is
now a parched stretch of dry sand, and what once was dry and

thirsty now is a marshy pool. Here Nature sends forth fresh fountains, there seals them up; and rivers, stirred by some inward quakings of the earth, leap forth or, dried up, sink out of sight. So, when Lycus is swallowed up by the yawning earth, he emerges far away and springs forth again with different appearance. So Erasinus is now engulfed and now, gliding along in a hidden stream, reappears as a lordly river in the Argolic fields. And they say that the Mysus, ashamed of his source and former banks, now flows in another region as Caïcus. The Amenanus now flows full over the Sicilian sands, and at times, its sources quenched, is dry. The Anigrus was once wholesome to drink, but now it pours down waters which you would not wish to taste since there (unless all credence is to be denied to bards) the twiformed centaurs bathed their wounds which the arrows of club-bearing Hercules had dealt. Further, is not the Hypanis, sprung from the Scythian mountains, which once was fresh and sweet, now spoiled with brackish water?

"Antissa and Pharos and Phoenician Tyre were once surrounded by the waters of the sea; but now not one of them is an island. The old inhabitants of that region used to say that Leucas was once a part of the mainland; but now the waves wash clear around it. Zancle also is said to have been a part of Italy until the sea washed away their common boundary and thrust back the land by the intervening water.* If you seek for Helice and Buris, once cities of Achaia, you will find them beneath the waves; and the sailors still show you the sloping cities with their buried walls. Near Troezen, ruled by Pittheus, there is a hill, high and treeless, which once was a perfectly level plain, but now a hill; for (horrible to relate) the wild forces of the winds, shut up in dark regions underground, seeking an outlet for their flowing and striving vainly to obtain a freer, space, since there was no chink in all their prison through which their breath could go, puffed out and stretched the ground, just as when one inflates a bladder with his breath, or the skin of a horned goat. That swelling in the ground remained, has still the appearance of a high hill, and has hardened as the years went by.

"Though many instances that I have heard of and known suggest themselves to me, I shall tell but a few more. Why, does not even

---

*All geographically correct observations.

water give and receive strange forms? Your stream, horned Ammon, at midday is cold, but warm in the morning and at eventide; and they say that the Athamanians set wood on fire by pouring water on it when the moon has reached her last point of waning. The Cicones have a river whose waters, if drunk, turn the vitals into stone, make marble of everything they touch. Crathis and Sybaris, a stream not far from our own region, make hair like amber and gold; and, what is still more wonderful, there are streams whose waters have power to change not only the body, but the mind as well. Who has not heard of the ill-famed waves of Salmacis and of the Aethiopian lakes? Whoever drinks of these waters either goes raving mad or falls into a strange, deep lethargy. Whoever slakes his thirst from Clitor's spring shuns the wine-cup and abstemiously enjoys pure water only; whether there is a power in the water which counteracts the heating wine, or whether, as the natives say, Amythaon's son, after he had freed the frenzied daughters of Proetus of madness by his magic songs and herbs, threw into those waters his mind-purifying herbs, and the hate of wine remained in the spring. The Lyncestian river produces an effect the opposite of this; for if one drinks, e'en moderately, of its waters, he staggers in his walk just as if he had drunk undiluted wine. There is a place in Arcadia which the ancients called Pheneus, mistrusted for its uncertain waters. Shun them by night, for, drunk by night, they are injurious; but in the daytime they may be drunk without harm. So lakes and streams have now these, now those effects. There was a time when Ortygia floated on the waves, but now she stands firm. The Argo feared the Symplegades, which at that time clashed together with high-flung spray; but now they stand immovable and resist the winds. And Aetna, which now glows hot with her sulphurous furnaces, will not always be on fire, neither was it always full of fire as now. For if the earth is of the nature of an animal, living and having many breathing-holes which exhale flames, she can change her breathing-places and, as often as she shakes herself, can close up these and open other holes; or if swift winds are penned up in deep caverns and drive rocks against rocks and substance containing the seeds of flame, and this catches fire from the friction of the stones, still the caves will become cool again when the winds have spent their force; or if it is pitchy substances that cause the fire, and yellow sulphur, burning with scarce-seen flames, surely, when the earth shall no longer furnish food and rich sustenance for the fire, and its strength after long ages has been exhausted, and greedy Nature shall feel lack of her own nourishment, then she will not endure that hunger and, being deserted, will desert her fires.

"There is a story of certain men in Hyperborean Pallene who gain a covering of light feathers for their bodies after they have nine times plunged in Minerva's pool. I do not vouch for it, but the Scythian women also are said to sprinkle their bodies with certain magic juices and produce the same effect.

"Still, if credence is to be given to things that have actually been tested, do you not see that, whenever dead bodies by lapse of time or by the liquefying power of heat have become thoroughly putrid, tiny animals are bred in them? Bury the carcasses of choice bulls in a ditch after they have been offered in sacrifice (it is a well-known experiment), and from the putrid entrails everywhere will spring flower-culling bees which, after the fashion of their progenitors, frequent the country fields, are fond of work, and toil in hope of their reward. A horse, which is a warlike animal, buried in the ground will produce hornets. If you cut off the hollow claws of a sea-crab and bury the rest in the ground, from the buried part a scorpion will come forth threatening with his hooked tail. And worms that weave their white cocoons on the leaves of trees (a fact well known to country-folk) change into funereal butterflies.

"Slimy mud contains seeds that produce green frogs, without legs at first, but soon it gives them legs adapted to swimming, and, that these may be fitted for taking long leaps also, the hind-legs are longer than the fore. A cub that a she-bear has just brought forth is not a cub, but a scarce-living lump of flesh; but the mother licks it into shape, and in this way gives it as much of a form as she has herself. Do you not see how the larvae of the honey-bearing bees, which the hexagonal waxen cell protects, are born mere memberless bodies and later put on feet and wings? Juno's bird, which wears starry spots on its tail, and the weapon-bearing bird of Jove, and Cytherea's doves, and the whole family of birds—who would believe, who did not know the facts, that these could be born from the inside of an egg? There are some who think that when the backbone of a man has decomposed in the narrow tomb the spinal marrow is changed into a snake.

"Now all these things get their life's beginning from some other creature; but there is one bird which itself renews and reproduces its own being. The Assyrians call it the phoenix. It does not live on seeds and green things, but on the gum of frankincense and the juices of amomum. This bird, forsooth, when it has completed five centuries of life, builds for itself a nest in the topmost branches of a waving palm-tree, using his talons and his clean beak; and when he has covered this over with cassia-bark and light spikes of nard, broken cinnamon and yellow myrrh, he takes his place upon it and so ends his life amid the odours. And from his father's body, so they say, a little phoenix springs up which is destined to attain the same length of years. When age has given him strength, and he is able to carry burdens, he relieves the tall palm's branches of the heavy nest, piously bears his own cradle and his father's tomb through the thin air, until, having reached the city of the Sun, he lays the nest down before the sacred doors of the Sun's temple.

"But if there is anything to wonder at in such novelties as these, we might wonder that the hyena changes her nature and that a creature which was but now a female and mated with a male is now a male herself. That little animal, also, which gets its nourishment from wind and air immediately takes the color of whatever thing it rests upon. Conquered India gave to cluster-crowned Bacchus some lynxes as a present, whose watery secretions, as they say, change into stones and harden in contact with the air. So also coral hardens at the first touch of air, whereas it was a soft plant beneath the water.

"The day will come to an end and Phoebus will bathe his panting horses in the deep waters of the sea before I tell of all the things which have assumed new forms. So we see times changing, and some nations putting on new strength and others falling into weakness. So was Troy great in wealth and men, and for ten years was able to give so freely of her blood; but now, humbled to earth, she has nothing to show but ancient ruins, no wealth but ancestral tombs. Sparta was at one time a famous city; great Mycenae flourished, and Cecrops' and Amphion's citadels.[3] Sparta is now a worthless countryside, proud Mycenae has fallen; and what is the Thebes of Oedipus except a name? What is left of Pandion's Athens but a name? And now fame has it that Dardanian Rome is rising, and laying deep and strong foundations by the stream of Tiber sprung from the

Apennines. She therefore is changing her form by growth, and some day shall be the capital of the boundless world! So, they tell us, seers and fate-revealing oracles are declaring. And, as I myself remember, when Troy was tottering to her fall, Helenus, the son of Priam, said to Aeneas, who was weeping and doubtful of his fate: 'O son of Venus, if you keep well in mind my soul's prophetic visions, while you live Troy shall not wholly perish! Fire and sword shall give way before you. You shall go forth and with you shall you catch up and bear away your Pergama, until you shall find a foreign land, kinder to Troy and you than your own country. I see even now a city destined to the descendants of the Phrygians, than which none greater is or shall be, or has been in past ages. Other princes through the long centuries shall make her powerful, but a prince sprung from Iülus' blood shall make her mistress of the world. When earth shall have had her share of him, the celestial regions shall enjoy him and heaven shall be his goal.' These things I well remember that Helenus prophesied to Aeneas as he bore with him his guardian gods, and I rejoice that my kindred walls are rising and that the Greeks conquered to the profit of the Phrygians.

"But, not to wander too far out of my course, my steeds forgetting meanwhile to speed towards the goal, the heavens and whatever is beneath the heavens change their forms, the earth and all that is within it. We also change, who are a part of creation, since we are not bodies only but also winged souls, and since we can enter wild-beast forms and be lodged in the bodies of cattle. We should permit bodies which may possibly have sheltered the souls of our parents or brothers or those joined to us by some other bond, or of men at least, to be uninjured and respected, and not load our stomachs as with a Thyestean banquet![4] What an evil habit he is forming, how surely is he impiously preparing to shed human blood, who cuts a calf's throat with the knife and listens all unmoved to its piteous cries! Or who can slay a kid which cries just like a little child, or feed on a bird to which he himself has just given food! How much does such a deed as that fall short of actual murder? What is the end of such a course? Let the bull plow and let him owe his death to length of days; let the sheep arm you against the rough north wind; let the she-goats give full udders to the milking. Have done with nets and traps, snares and deceptive arts. Catch not the bird with the limed twig; no longer mock the deer with fear-compelling feathers, nor conceal the barbed hook beneath fair-seeming food. Kill creatures that work you harm, but even in the case of these let killing suffice. Make not their flesh your food, but seek a more harmless nourishment."

They say that Numa, with mind filled with these and other teachings, returned to his own land and, being urged thereto, assumed the guidance of the Latin state. He, blessed with a nymph for wife, blessed with the Muses' guidance, taught holy rites and trained a fierce, warlike people in the arts of peace. When he, now ripe in years, laid down his sceptre and his life, the Latin mothers, the commons, and the fathers all mourned for the departed Numa. For his wife fled from the city and hid herself away in the dense forests of the Arician vale, and by her groans and lamentations she disturbed the worship of Orestean Diana. Oh, how often the nymphs of wood and lake urged her to desist and spoke words of consolation! How often to the weeping nymph the heroic son of Theseus said: "Have done with tears, for yours is not the only lot to be lamented. Think upon others who have borne equal losses; then will you bear your own more gently. And I would that I had no experience of my own with which to comfort you in your grief! But even mine can comfort you.

"You may have heard some mention of Hippolytus, how he met his death through the easy credence of his father and the wiles of his accursed stepmother. You will be amazed and I shall scarce prove my statement, but nevertheless I myself am he. Pasiphaë's daughter once, when she had tried in vain to tempt me to defile my father's couch, perverting truth, charged me with having done what she herself wished me to do (was it through fear of discovery or offence at her repulse?), and, guiltless though I was, my father drove me from the city and cursed me as I went with a deadly curse. Banished from home, I was making for Troezen, Pittheus' city, in my chariot, and now was coursing along the beach of the Corinthian bay, when the sea rose up and a huge mound of water seemed to swell and grow to mountain size, to give forth bellowings, and to be cleft at its highest point. Then the waves burst and a horned bull was cast forth, and, raised from the sea breast-high into the yielding air, he spouted out great quantities of water from his nostrils and wide mouth. The hearts of my companions quaked with fear; but my own soul was unterrified, filled with sad thoughts of exile. Then suddenly my spirited horses faced towards the sea and, with ears pricked forward, quaked and trembled with fear at the monstrous shape; then dashed with the chariot at headlong speed over the steep, rocky way. I vainly strove to check them with the reins, flecked with white foam, and, leaning backward, strained at the tough thongs. Still would the horses' mad strength not have surpassed my own had a wheel, striking its hub against a projecting stock, not been broken and wrenched off from the axle. I was thrown from my car, and while the reins held my legs fast, you might see my living flesh dragged along, my sinews held on the sharp stake, my limbs partly drawn on and in part caught fast and left behind, and my bones broken with a loud, snapping sound. My spent spirit was at last breathed out and there was no part of my body which you could recognize, but it all was one great wound. Now can you, dare you, nymph, compare your loss with my disaster? Further, I saw the rayless world of death and bathed my torn body in the waves of Phlegethon. And there should I still be had Apollo's son* by his potent remedies not given me back my life. And when I had regained it by the help of strong juices and medicinal aid, though it was against the will of Dis, then Cynthia threw a thick cloud around me, so that I would not be seen and stir up envy of my gift of life. And, that I might be safe and able to be seen without fear of punishment, she gave me the look of age and left me no features that could be recognized. She debated long whether to give me Crete or Delos for my home. But, deciding against Crete and Delos, she placed me here and bade me lay aside the name which could remind me of my horses, and said: 'You who were Hippolytus shall now be Virbius.'† From that time I have dwelt within this grove and, one of the lesser deities, I hide beneath my mistress' deity and am accepted as her follower."

But Egeria's loss could not be assuaged by the woes of others, and, lying prostrate at a mountain's base, she melted away in tears; until Phoebus' sister, in pity of her faithful sorrow, made of her body a cool spring and of her slender limbs unfailing streams.

---

*Aesculapius; Ovid describes his birth and boyhood in book II.
†Originally a minor native deity, later assimilated into the worship of Hippolytus.

This strange event struck the nymphs with wonder; and the son of the Amazon was no less amazed than was the Tyrrhene plowman when he saw in his fields a clod, big with fate, first moving of its own accord, and with no one touching it, then taking on the form of man and losing its earthy shape, and finally opening its new-made mouth to speak things that were to be. The natives called him Tages, who first taught the Etruscan race how to read the future. And no less amazed than was Romulus when he saw his spear-shaft, which had once grown on the Palatine hill, suddenly putting forth leaves, and standing, not with iron point driven in the earth, but with new-grown roots; and now it was not a spear at all, but a tough-fibred tree, giving unexpected shade to those who gazed on it in wonder; or than was Cipus when in a clear stream he saw horns springing from his head. For he saw them and, thinking that he was deceived by the reflection, lifting his hands again and again to his forehead, he touched what he saw; nor did he fight against the portent, blaming his own eyes, but, as a victor coming from his con-quered foe, he lifted his hands and eyes to the heavens and cried: "O gods, whatever is portended by this monstrous thing, if it be for-tunate, let the good fortune befall my country and the people of Quirinus;* but if it threaten ill, may the ill be mine." Then, making an altar of green turf, he appeased the gods with a fragrant burnt-offering, made a libation of wine, and consulted the quivering en-trails of the slaughtered victims as to what they might mean for him. When the Etruscan seer inspected these he saw the signs of great enterprises there, but not yet clearly visible. But when he raised his keen eyes from the sheep's entrails to the horns of Cipus, he cried: "All hail, O king! for to you, to you, Cipus, and to your horns shall this place and Latium's citadels bow down. Only delay not and make speed to enter the open gates! Such is fate's com-mand; for, received within the city, you shall be king and wield the sceptre in safe and endless sway." He started back and, keeping his gaze stubbornly turned from the city's walls, he said: "Far, oh, far from me may the gods keep such a fate. Better far it is that I should spend my days exiled from home than that the Capitol should see me king." He spoke and straightway called a joint assembly of the

---

*That is, of Romulus; thus, Romans.

people and the reverend senate. But first he hid his horns with a wreath of peaceful laurel; then, standing on a mound raised by the brave soldiery and praying to the ancient gods according to the rite, he said: "There is one here who will be king unless you drive him from your city. Who he is, not by his name but by a sign I will disclose to you: he wears horns upon his brow! The augur declares that if once he enters Rome he will reduce you to the rank of slaves. He might have forced his way through your gates, for they stand open; but I withstood him, though no one is more closely bound to him than I. Do you, Quirites, keep him from your city, or, if he deserves it, bind him with heavy fetters, or end your fear of the fated tyrant by his death!" At this such a murmur arose among the people as comes from the thick pine-grove when the boisterous wind whistles through them, or as the waves of the sea makes heard from afar. But, midst the confused words of the murmuring throng, one cry rose clear: "Who is the man?" They looked at each other's forehead, and sought to find the horns that had been spoken of. Then Cipus spoke again and said: "Him whom you seek you have"; and removing the wreath from his head, while the people sought to stay him, he showed to them his temples marked with the two horns. All cast down their eyes and groaned aloud, and (who could believe it?) reluctantly looked upon that deservedly illustrious head. Then, not suffering him further to stand dishonored, they replaced upon his head the festal wreath. But the senate, since you might not come within the walls, gave you, Cipus, as a gift of honor, as much land as you could enclose with a yoke of oxen and a plow from dawn till close of day. And the horns in all their wondrous beauty they engraved upon the bronze pillars of the gates, there to remain through all the ages.

Reveal to me now, O Muses, you ever-helpful divinities of bards (for you know, nor has far-stretching time dimmed your memory), from what place did the island bathed by the deep Tiber bring Coronis' son* and set him midst the deities of Rome.

In olden time a deadly pestilence had corrupted Latium's air, and men's bodies lay wasting and pale with a ghastly disease. When, weary with caring for the dead, men saw that their human efforts

---

*In other words, Aesculapius.

were as nothing, and that the healers' arts were of no avail, they sought the aid of heaven, and, coming to Delphi, situate in the earth's central spot, the sacred oracle of Phoebus, they begged that the god would vouchsafe with his health-bringing lots to succour them in their wretchedness and end the woes of their great city. Then did the shrine and the laurel-tree and the quiver which the god himself bears quake together, and the tripod from the inmost shrine gave forth these words and stirred their hearts trembling with fear: "What you seek from this place you should have sought, O Roman, from a nearer place. And even now seek from that nearer place. Nor have you any need of Apollo to abate your troubles, but of Apollo's son. Go with kindly auspices and call on my son." When the senate, rich in wisdom, heard the commands of the god they sought in what city the son of Phoebus dwelt, and sent an embassy by ship to seek out the coast of Epidaurus. When the embassy had beached their curved keel upon that shore, they betook them to the council of the Grecian elders and prayed that they would give the god who with his present deity might end the deadly woes of the Ausonian race; for thus the oracle distinctly bade. The elders disagreed and sat with varying minds. Some thought that aid should not be refused; but the many advised to keep their god and not let go the source of their own wealth nor deliver up their deity. And while they sat in doubt the dusk of evening dispelled the lingering day and the darkness spread its shadows over the world. Then did the health-giving god seem in your dreams to stand before your couch, O Roman, even as he is wont to appear in his own temple, holding his rustic staff in his left hand and with his right stroking his flowing beard, and with calm utterance to speak these words: "Fear not! I shall come and leave my shrine. Only look upon this serpent which twines about my staff, and fix it on your sight that you may know it. I shall change myself to this, but shall be larger and shall seem as great as celestial bodies should be when they change." Straightway the god vanished as he spoke, and with the voice and the god sleep vanished too, and the kindly day dawned as sleep fled. The next morning had put the gleaming stars to flight when the chiefs, still uncertain what to do, assembled at the sump-tuous temple of the sought-for god and begged him by heavenly tokens to reveal where he himself wished to abide. Scarce had they ceased to speak when the golden god, in the form of a serpent with high crest, uttered hissing warnings of his presence, and at his coming the statue, altars, doors, the marble pavement and gilded roof, all rocked. Then, raised breast-high in the temple's midst, he stood and gazed about with eyes flashing fire. The terrified multitude quaked with fear; but the priest, with his sacred locks bound with a white fillet, recognized the divinity and cried: "The god! behold the god! Think holy thoughts and stand in reverent silence, all of you who are in this presence. And, O you, most beautiful, let this vision of you be expedient for us and bless this people who worship at your shrine." All in the divine presence worshipped the god as they were bid, repeating the priest's words after him, and the Romans, too, performed their pious devotions with heart and lips. The god nodded graciously to them and, moving his crest, assured them of his favor and with darting tongue gave forth repeated hisses. Then he glided down the polished steps and with backward gaze looked fixedly upon the ancient altars which he was about to leave, and saluted his well-known home and the shrine where he had dwelt so long. And then the huge serpent wound his way along the ground covered with scattered flowers, bending and coiling as he went, and proceeded through the city's midst to the harbour guarded by a curving embankment. Here he halted and, seeming with kindly expression to dismiss his throng of pious followers, he took his place within the Ausonian ship. It felt the burden of the deity and the keel was forced deep down by the god's weight. The Romans were filled with joy and, after sacrificing a bull upon the beach, they wreathed their ship with flowers and cast loose from the shore. A gentle breeze bore the vessel on, while the god, rising on high and reclining heavily with his neck resting upon the ship's curving stern, gazed down upon the azure waters. With fair winds he sailed through the Ionian sea and on the sixth morning he reached Italy, sailed past the shores of Lacinium, famed for Juno's temple, past Scylaceum, left Iapygia behind, and, avoiding the Amphrisian rocks upon the left and the Cocinthian crags upon the right, skirted Romethium and Caulon and Narycia; then passed the Sicilian sea and Pelorus' narrow strait, sailed by the home of Hippotades, past the copper mines of Temesa, and headed for Leucosia and mild Paestum's rose-gardens. Next he skirted Capreae, Minerva's promontory, and the hills of Surrentum rich in vines; and then sailed to Herculaneum and Stabiae and Parthenope, for soft pleasure founded, and from there to the temple of the Cumaean Sibyl. Next the hot pools were reached, and Liternum, thick grown with mastic-bearing trees, and the Volturnus, sweeping along vast quantities of sand beneath its whirling waters; Sinuessa, with its thronging flocks of snow-white doves; unwholesome Minturnae and the place named for her whose foster-son entombed her there; the home of Antiphates, marsh-encompassed Trachas, Circe's land also, and Antium with its hard-packed shore. When to this place the sailors turned their ship with sails full spread (for the sea was rough) the god unfolded his coils and, gliding on with many a sinuous curve and mighty fold, entered his father's temple set on the tawny strand. When the sea had calmed again, the Epidaurian god left his paternal altars and, having enjoyed the hospitality of his kindred deity, furrowed the sandy shore as he dragged his rasping scales along and, climbing up the rudder, reposed his head on the vessel's lofty stern, until he came to Castrum, the sacred seats of Lavinium and the Tiber's mouth. Here the whole mass of the populace came thronging to meet him from every side, matrons and fathers and the maids who tend your fires, O Trojan Vesta,[5] and they saluted the god with joyful cries. And where the swift ship floated up the stream incense burned with a crackling sound on altars built in regular order on both the banks, the air was heavy with sweet perfumes, and the smitten victim warmed the sacrificial knife with his blood. And now the ship had entered Rome, the capital of the world. The serpent raised himself aloft and, resting his head upon the mast's top, moved it from side to side, viewing the places fit for his abode. The river, flowing around, separates at this point into two parts, forming the place called the Island; on each side it stretches out two equal arms with the land between. On this spot the serpent-son of Phoebus disembarked from the Latian ship and, resuming his heavenly form, put an end to the people's woes and came to them as health-bringer to their city.

Now he came to our shrines as a god from a foreign land; but Caesar is god in his own city. Him, illustrious in war and peace, not so much his wars triumphantly achieved, his civic deeds accomplished, and his glory quickly won, changed to a new heavenly body,

a flaming star; but still more his offspring deified him. For there is
no work among all Caesar's achievements greater than this, that he
became the father of this our Emperor. Is it indeed a greater thing
to have subdued the sea-girt Britons, to have led his victorious fleet
up the seven-mouthed stream of the papyrus-bearing Nile, to have
added the rebellious Numidians, Libyan Juba, and Pontus, swelling
with threats of the mighty name of Mithridates, to the sway of the
people of Quirinus,* to have celebrated some triumphs and to have
earned many more—than to have begotten so great a man? With
him as ruler of the world, you have indeed, O heavenly ones, show-
ered rich blessings upon the human race! So then, that his son
might not be born of mortal seed, Caesar must needs be made a
god. When the golden mother of Aeneas saw this, and saw also that
dire destruction was being plotted against her high-priest and that
an armed conspiracy was forming, she paled with fear and cried to
all the gods as she met them in turn: "Behold what a crushing
weight of plots is prepared against me, and with what snares that life
is sought which alone remains to me from Dardanian Iülus. Shall
I alone for ever be harassed by well-founded cares, since now the
Calydonian spear of Diomede wounds me and now the falling walls
of ill-defended Troy overwhelm me, since I see my son driven by
long wanderings, tossed on the sea, entering the abodes of the silent
shades and waging war with Turnus, or, if we speak plain truth, with
Juno rather? But why do I now recall the ancient sufferings of my
race? This present fear of mine does not permit me to remember
former woes. Look! do you not see that impious daggers are being
whetted? Ward them off, I pray, prevent this crime and let not
Vesta's fires be extinguished by her high-priest's blood!"

The anxious goddess cried these complaints throughout the sky,
but all in vain. The gods were moved indeed; and although they
were not able to break the iron decrees of the ancient sisters, still
they gave no uncertain portents of the woe that was at hand. They
say that the clashing of arms amid the dark storm-clouds and fear-
inspiring trumpets and horns heard in the sky forewarned men of
the crime; also the darkened face of the sun shone with lurid
light upon the troubled lands. Often firebrands were seen to flash

---

*A litany of the military conquests of Julius Caesar.

amid the stars; often drops of blood fell down from the clouds; the morning-star was of dusky hue and his face was blotched with dark red spots, and Luna's chariot was stained with blood. In a thousand places the Stygian owl gave forth his mournful warnings; in a thousand places ivory statues dripped tears, and in the sacred groves wailing notes and threatening words were heard. No victim sufficed for expiation; the liver warned that portentous struggles were at hand and its lobe was found cleft amid the entrails. In the market-place and around men's houses and the temples of the gods dogs howled by night, the shades of the silent dead walked abroad and the city was shaken with earthquakes. Yet even so, the warnings of the gods were unable to check the plots of men and the advancing fates. Naked swords were brought into the sacred curia; for no place in the whole city would do for this crime, this dreadful deed of blood, but only that. Then indeed did Cytherea smite on her breast with both her hands and strive to hide her Caesar in a cloud in which of old Paris had been rescued from the murderous Atrides and in which Aeneas had escaped the sword of Diomede. Then thus the Father spoke: "Do you, by your sole power, my daughter, think to move the changeless fates? You yourself may enter the abode of the three sisters. You shall there behold the records of all that happens on tablets of brass and solid iron, a massive structure, tablets which fear neither the crashings of the sky, nor the lightning's fearful power, nor any destructive shocks which may befall, being eternal and secure. There you shall find engraved on everlasting adamant your descendant's fates. I have myself read these and marked them well in mind; and these will I relate, that you may no longer be ignorant of that which is to come. This son of yours, goddess of Cythera, for whom you grieve, has fulfilled his allotted time, and his years are finished which he owed to earth. That as a god he may enter heaven and have his place in temples on the earth, you shall accomplish, you and his son. He as successor to the name shall bear alone the burden placed on him, and, as the most valiant avenger of his father's murder, he shall have us as ally for his wars. Under his command the conquered walls of leaguered Mutina shall sue for peace; Pharsalia shall feel his power; Emathian Philippi shall reek again with blood; and he of the great name shall be overcome on Sicilian waters. A Roman general's Egyptian mistress, who did not well to rely upon the union, shall fall before him, and in vain shall she have threatened that our Capitol shall bow to her Canopus.[6] But why should I recall barbaric lands to you and nations lying on either ocean-shore? No, whatsoever habitable land the earth contains shall be his, and the sea also shall come beneath his sway!

"When peace has been bestowed upon all lands he shall turn his mind to the rights of citizens, and as a most righteous jurist promote the laws. By his own good example shall he direct the ways of men, and, looking forward to future time and coming generations, he shall bid the son, born of his chaste wife, to bear his name and the burden of his cares; and not till after he as an old man shall have equalled Nestor's years shall he attain the heavenly seats and his related stars. Meanwhile you catch up this soul from the slain body and make him a star in order that ever it may be the divine Julius who looks forth upon our Capitol and Forum from his lofty temple."

Scarce had he spoken when fostering Venus took her place within the senate-house, unseen of all, caught up the passing soul of her Caesar from his body, and not suffering it to vanish into air, she bore it towards the stars of heaven. And as she bore it she felt it glow and burn, and released it from her bosom. Higher than the moon it mounted up and, leaving behind it a fiery train, gleamed as a star. And now, beholding the good deeds of his son, he confesses that they are greater than his own, and rejoices to be surpassed by him. And, though the son forbids that his own deeds be set above his father's, still fame, unfettered and obedient to no one's will, exalts him spite of his desire, and in this one thing opposes his commands. So does the great Atreus yield in honor to his son, Agamemnon; so does Theseus rival Aegeus, and Achilles, Peleus; finally, to quote an instance worthy of them both, is Saturn less than Jove. Jupiter controls the heights of heaven and the kingdoms of the triformed universe; but the earth is under Augustus' sway. Each is both sire and ruler. O gods, I pray you, comrades of Aeneas, before whom both fire and sword gave way, and you native gods of Italy, and you, Quirinus, father of our city, and Gradivus, invincible Quirinus' sire, and Vesta, who has always held a sacred place amid Caesar's household gods, and you, Apollo, linked in worship with our Caesar's Vesta, and Jupiter, whose temple sits high on Tarpeia's rock, and all of you other gods to whom it is fitting for the bard to make appeal: let that day be far distant and later than our own time when Augustus, abandoning the world he rules, shall mount to heaven and there, removed from our presence, listen to our prayers!

And now my work is done, which neither the wrath of Jove, nor fire, nor sword, nor the gnawing tooth of time shall ever be able to undo. When it will, let that day come which has no power but over this mortal frame, and end the span of my uncertain years. Still in my better part I shall be borne immortal far beyond the stars and I shall have an undying name. Wherever Rome's power extends over the conquered world, I shall have mention on men's lips, and, if the prophecies of bards have any truth, through all the ages shall I live in fame.

ENDNOTES

Book I

1. (p. 3) *for you yourselves have wrought the changes:* Many contemporary scholars believe the manuscript should not read *nam vos mutastis et illas* ("for you yourselves have wrought the changes") but *nam vos mutastis et illa* ("for you have changed them [my undertakings] too"), thus meaning that the gods prodded Ovid to switch genres from his characteristic elegy to epic. If Ovid does credit (or blame) the gods for his change of poetic direction, it is at least half-jocularly.

2. (p. 4) *the liquid, weightless ether:* Not the gas once used in anesthesia, this "ether" was an invisible, ambient substance formerly thought to fill even the reaches of interstellar space; indeed, the idea that light was produced by waves traveling through the ether was not finally abandoned until Einstein's Theory of Relativity offered a superior alternative.

3. (p. 5) *After Saturn had been banished to the dark land of death, and the world was under the sway of Jove:* In Hesiod's *Theogony*, Cronus swallowed his children to forestall a prophecy that one would overthrow him. But Rhea (Roman Ops) slipped him a stone in place of Zeus (Jupiter); reared secretly, he returned to overthrow his father and free his siblings from Cronus' belly. The Roman Saturn, though a loose equivalent of Cronus, may have had Etruscan origins and remained popular as patron god of the Saturnalia, the holiday that is the predecessor of Christmas.

4. (p. 8) *"his equally unworthy household gods":* Every Roman household contained images of *lares* and *penates*, minor deities honored, with small offerings from every meal, for protecting the home.

5. (p. 9) *to destroy the human race beneath the waves and to send down rain from every quarter of the sky:* While Ovid's source is Greek, the tale of divine wrath loosing a worldwide inundation originates before Genesis, the earliest written version being found on eighteenth-century B.C.E. tablets carved in Sumerian—then already a dead language, indicating that the story itself dates back much further. Recent speculation connecting this fabled flood with the formation of the Black Sea, however, ignores numerous differences between the stories and the historical evidence.

6. (pp. 21–22) *she is worshipped as a goddess by the linen-robed throng. A son, Epaphus, was born to her . . . and throughout the cities dwelt in temples with his mother:* After the Greek and Roman conquests of Egypt (fourth and first centuries B.C.E., respectively), the ancient gods of that land (where linen was worn) became associated with Greco-Roman equivalents of more recent vintage. Isis, whose worship spread throughout the Mediterranean, and the bull-god Apis were accommodated to the Greco-Roman figures Io and Epaphus.

Book II

1. (p. 36) *the geese which one day were to save the Capitol with their watchful cries:* Early in the fourth century B.C.E., Rome was purportedly (or, in terms of Ovid's chronology, would be) warned of a night-time Gallic raid by the honking of the geese in Juno's temple. Geese are sensitive to disturbance and noisy when disturbed, and the watch-goose was a familiar figure of ancient times; one way Baucis and Philemon establish their pious hospitality is by offering to serve theirs to their guests (book VIII).

2. (p. 36) *"Once upon a time a child was born, named Erichthonius, a child without a mother":* Erichthonius, a legendary king of Athens, arose from the semen spilled on the ground in Vulcan's failed rape of Pallas Minerva (Greek Athena; hence, Athens); his name means "earth-born." Either half-serpentine or accompanied by snakes, Erichthonius is given to the three daughters of Cecrops, mythic first king of Athens; in most versions of the legend, two look into the chest, go mad, and hurl themselves from the Acropolis.

3. (p. 37) *"how Nyctimene outraged the sanctity of her father's bed? And, bird though she now is . . . tries to hide her shame in darkness, outcast by all from the whole radiant sky":* Nyctimene of Lesbos slept with her father, King Epopeus. Hiding herself in the woods, she was found by Minerva and changed into an owl, a bird that shuns daylight. See also the parallel tale of Myrrha and Cinyras in book X.

4. (p. 39) *half-divine son of Philyra:* Chiron was the child of Saturn and the nymph Phylira (daughter of Oceanus and Thethys); he would eventually choose to die rather than live in eternal agony after being accidentally struck by a poisoned arrow from the bow of Hercules (in some traditions, he cedes his immortality to Prometheus). Regarding Apollo's child, Aesculapius, see book XV (where he is identified only as the son of Apollo).

5. (p. 41) *the son of the Lemnian, without mother born:* The Lemnian is Vulcan (Hephaistus), who crashed on the island of Lemnos after Jupiter hurled him from Olympus for interfering in a quarrel between himself and Juno, Vulcan's mother; the island became a center of his worship. The child, of course, is Erichthonius.

Book IV

1. (p. 71) *Nor will I tell how once Sithon, the natural laws reversed, lived of changing sex, now woman and now man. . . . how Crocus and his beloved Smilax were*

changed into tiny flowers: Ovid appears to be having fun with his readers here, as none of these tales seem to have been very well known in ancient times; indeed, no other reference to Sithon has survived.

2. (p. 72) *"such has the moon, eclipsed, red under white, when brazen vessels clash vainly for her relief":* Causing a great din during a lunar eclipse was thought to help restore the moon and prevent evil spirits from occupying the darkness. That Ovid implies such rituals have no effect is one indication that he disbelieves in the literal occurrence of the far more astounding events his tales narrate.

3. (p. 75) *Here Tityos offered his vitals to be torn. . . . and the Belides, for daring to work destruction on their cousin-husbands, with unremitting toil seek again and again the waters, only to lose them:* Tityos attempted to rape Latona, the mother of Apollo and Diana; Tantalus evidently betrayed the laws of hospitality, though descriptions of his precise crime differ; Sisyphus had the temerity to chain Death on one occasion and outwit Pluto on another; Ixion both murdered his father-in-law and attempted to rape Juno; the fifty Belides (granddaughters of Belus, a descendant of Io and legendary king of Egypt) killed their husbands.

4. (p. 82) *the head of Medusa, daughter of Phorcys:* Phorcys and Ceto (root of "cetacean," the adjective based on the scientific name for the order comprising whales, porpoises, and dolphins), children of the primal gods Earth (Ge) and Sea (Pontus), bear six daughters: the three Gray Sisters, who share a single eye, and the three Gorgons (Medusa, Euryale, and Stheno). Perseus steals the Gray Sisters' eye, forcing them to reveal the location of the nymphs who give him the magic weapons he uses to kill Medusa.

5. (p. 83) *he smote her head clean from her neck, and from the blood of his mother swift-winged Pegasus and his brother sprang:* When killed by Perseus, Medusa is pregnant by the god Poseidon; from her blood springs not only the winged horse Pegasus, but the anthropomorphic Chrysaor ("he of the golden sword"), who later fathers the monstrous children Geryon and Echidna. By calling Chrysaor the "brother" of the flying equine Pegasus, Ovid suggests the humorous consequences of taking the myths too literally.

Book V

1. (pp. 90–91) *Victorious Perseus, together with his bride, now returns to his ancestral city; and . . . wars on Proetus. For Proetus had driven his brother out . . . and seized the stronghold of Acrisius:* As often, Ovid assumes his reader's familiarity with the basic myth, expanding instead on a tangential incident. Thus, after pages on the relatively minor fight in Phineus' palace, he dispenses with generations of conflict in a paragraph: Acrisius had denied that Perseus, the son of his daughter Danaë, was actually Jupiter's child and cast them adrift in a chest. The old King's feud with Proetus began in the womb.

2. (p. 91) *But you, O Polydectes, ruler of Little Seriphos, were not softened by the young man's valor. . . . And with the Medusa-face [Perseus] changed the features of the king to bloodless stone:* After being exiled by Acrisius, Perseus and his mother washed ashore on the small island of Seriphos. Polydectes, its king, sent Perseus on the seemingly impossible quest to obtain the Gorgon's head so that he might seduce Danaë without interference. Having disposed of Polydectes, Perseus conferred the throne upon the King's brother, Dictys, who had fished him from the sea and brought him up to manhood.

3. (p. 97) *"'Arethusa, Alpheus' daughter'":* Arethusa is "daughter" of the river of Olympia, Alpheus, only in the most metaphoric sense. Ovid tells his own version of the well-known ancient legend concerning the pursuit of Arethusa by Alpheus immediately after the Proserpine story concludes. "Alph, the sacred river" in Coleridge's "Kubla Khan" probably derives its name from Alpheus.

4. (p. 98) *"'Ascalaphus, whom Orphne, not the least famous of the Avernal nymphs, is said to have borne to her own Acheron within the dark groves of the lower-world'":* Acheron and Orphne are river-gods of the Underworld; even Plutonian rivers have their attendant deities. In Apollodorus (Greek; first or second century C.E.; see "For Further Reading") the mother is called Gorgyra, and Ceres (under her Greek name, Demeter) buries Ascalaphus under a stone that is later removed by Hercules during that hero's journey to the land of the dead; only then does Ceres transform Ascalaphus into an owl, a bird of the night.

Book VI

1. (p. 105) *She wrought Asterie, held by the struggling eagle; she wrought Leda, beneath the swan's wings:* It is unclear to what tale Ovid alludes when he mentions Asterie; other sources do mention a Titan, Asteria, who turned (or was turned) into a quail for spurning Jupiter's advances, but no eagle is mentioned. In the form of a swan, Jupiter rapes Leda, a union that produces Helen (of Troy), Clytemnestra, and Castor and Pollux, all of whom hatch from eggs.

2. (p. 106) *how, in a satyr's image hidden, Jove filled lovely Antiope with twin offspring; how he was Amphitryon when he cheated you, Alcmena; how in a golden shower he tricked Danaë; Aegina, as a flame; Mnemosyne, as a shepherd; Deo's daughter, as a spotted snake:* Antiope, one of the women Ulysses (Odysseus to the Greeks) sees in Hades (*Odyssey*, book XI), bore Jupiter the sons Amphion and Zethus, founders of Thebes. Alcmena bore Hercules; Danaë, Perseus. Aegina's son, Aeacus, became one of the three judges of the Underworld. Mnemosyne had the nine muses. With "Deo's daughter"—that is, Prosperpine, his own daughter by Ceres—Jupiter, according to some traditions, produced Zagreus (Bacchus), killed by the Titans and reborn through Semele.

3. (p. 106) *now as Enipeus you beget the Aloidae, as a ram deceivedst Bisaltis. The golden-haired mother of corn, most gentle, knew you as a horse; the snake-haired mother of the winged horse knew you as a winged bird; Melantho knew you as a*

dolphin: The Aloidae were the giants Ephialtes and Otas, who threatened Jupiter by stacking Ossa on Pelion (see book I). Bisaltis (also known as Theophane) bore the ram who produced the golden fleece; Ceres, "mother of corn," the horse Arion; Melantho the nymph Eirene, and Medusa, "snake-haired mother," the legendary king of Iberia, Chrysaor. Divine sex was seldom unproductive.

4. (p. 106) *Here is Phoebus like a countryman; and she shows how he wore now a hawk's feathers, now a lion's skin; how as a shepherd he tricked Macareus' daughter, Isse:* Of the episodes involving Phoebus (Apollo), only the story of his seduction of Isse (also known as Amphissa) survives; their offspring founded the royal line of the city of Isse in Locris.

5. (p. 106) *how Bacchus deceived Erigone with the false bunch of grapes; how Saturn in a horse's shape begot the centaur, Chiron:* Erigone's father, a shepherd given the secret of wine by Bacchus, was murdered by his colleagues after he had "poisoned" some of them by making them drunk. Led to the body by the family dog, Erigone hanged herself; the dog threw itself down a well. The love of the gods seldom benefits humans. See also endnote 4 to book II.

6. (p. 111) *the borders of Lycia, home of the Chimaera:* According to other sources, the Chimaera was a monster born from the union of the giant Typhoeus (see books III and V) and Echidna (the venomous "Hydra" of book IV—Echidna is also the mother of the Lernean Hydra that Hercules kills, and of Cerberus, called "the Echidnean dog" in book VII). The Chimaera combined the forms of lion, dragon, and goat. Bellerophon, the hero of some of the most ancient (and least well-preserved) Greek myths, killed the creature, whose name has come to mean an impossible being, a phantom or bogey.

7. (p. 113) *Argos and Sparta and Peloponnesian Mycenae; Calydon, which had not yet incurred Diana's wrath; fertile Orchomenos and Corinth, famed for works of bronze; warlike Messene, Patrae, and low-lying Cleonae; Nelean Pylos and Troezen, not yet ruled by Pittheus:* The cities Ovid names figure importantly in the Greek myths that concern the generations immediately before and during the Trojan War; by Ovid's own time, many were only memories or names.

8. (p. 117) *It was the time when the Thracian matrons were wont to celebrate the biennial festival of Bacchus:* Thrace was reputedly the first region of Greece to accept the worship of Dionysus. Like Pentheus of Thebes (see book III), King Lycurgus opposed the new god, but Dionysus avoided his traps, warned by Charops, the grandfather of Orpheus (Orphic and Dionysiac rituals were among the most important of the ancient world), whom he installed as king. Bacchantes—female worshippers of Bacchus—embodied the liberation of otherwise suppressed feminine power.

Book VII

1. (p. 122) *And now the Minyans were plowing the deep in their Thessalian ship. . . . they reached at last the swift waters of muddy Phasis:* Jason sailed to

Colchis on the Black Sea (for Greeks, the end of the earth) to obtain the Golden Fleece as required by the usurper Pelias and so reclaim his own father's throne. The gods deprived Phineus of sight and afflicted him with the harpies for his presumption in telling the future. Jason drove off the harpies so Phineus could eat; in return, he foretold the hero's proper course.

2. (p. 124) *She took her way to an ancient altar of Hecate, the daughter of Perse, hidden in the deep shades of a forest:* Hecate, patron of sorcery, daughter of the Titan Perse, was an underworld goddess of immense power; even Jupiter left her alone in her chosen realm. Associated with night and crossroads, she was often imagined as having three faces, perhaps representing underworld, earth, and air (or birth, life, and death). The idea of witchcraft held by Reformation clerics derives a great deal of its imagery from classical accounts of Hecate and Medea.

3. (p. 127) *"With your help when I have willed it, . . . I move the forests, I bid the mountains shake, the earth to rumble and the ghosts to come forth from their tombs":* This is perhaps Shakespeare's favorite passage from the *Metamorphoses*. Close echoes of it can be found in Owen Glendower's remark to Hotspur: "I can call spirits from the vasty deep," in *Henry IV, Part One* (act 3, scene 1); Prospero's description of his own sorcery, which begins "Ye elves of hills, brooks, standing lakes, and groves," in *The Tempest* (act 5, scene 1); and Calpurnia's report of the omens foretelling civil war (*Julius Caesar*, act 2, scene 2), which begins "Caesar, I never stood on ceremonies."

4. (pp. 131–132) *High up she sped over shady Pelion, the home of Chiron, over Othrys and the regions made famous by the adventure of old Cerambus. . . . upon the home of Eumelus, who lamented that his son now dwelt in air:* Most of the stories over whose locations Medea flies are obscure. Some have precedents: The Telchines were evidently magical smiths, though the idea they could kill with a look may be original to Ovid; the daughter of Alcidamas, Ctesylla, died in childbirth and was transformed into a dove; Apollo changed Botres, the son of Eumelus, into a bird after his father killed him for offending against the rites of sacrifice.

5. (p. 133) *Aegeus' rejoicing over his son's return was not unmixed with care. Minos . . . was seeking to avenge the death of his son Androgeos:* After winning all the events at the Panathenaic games, Androgeos was killed by the jealous losers. In some versions of the story, Aegeus himself challenges the Cretan prince to fight the great bull of Marathon, which kills him. As a result of the punitive expedition Minos consequently undertakes, Athens must send fourteen noble youth (seven boys, seven girls) every year (less often in some texts) as sacrifices to the minotaur.

6. (p. 137) *" 'O Jove, if it is not falsely said that you loved Aegina, daughter of Asopus, and if you, great father, are not ashamed to be our father, either give me back my people or consign me also to the tomb' ":* Jupiter in fact raped the nymph Aegina, daughter of Asopus, a minor river-god; Sisyphus was consigned to eternal punishment in Hades partly for revealing this act.

7. (p. 138) *Phocus, son of Aeacus, received them at the threshold; for Telamon and his brother were marshalling the men for war:* Ironically, Phocus himself would be slain by his half-brother Peleus, the father of Achilles (see book XI). Other sources blame this crime on Telamon, but Ovid characteristically chooses the tradition that more fully steeps the warrior-hero (here, Achilles) in blood.

Book VIII

1. (p. 147) *"She is a true mate for you who with unnatural passion deceived the savage bull by that shape of wood and bore a hybrid offspring in her womb":* Scylla refers to Pasiphae, the wife of Minos and daughter of the sun-god, Helios. In the most elaborate version of the story, Minos receives a bull from Neptune for sacrifice, but substitutes a less magnificent animal. In revenge, Neptune inspires Pasiphae with an uncontrollable desire for the bull. The craftsman Daedalus fashions a wooden cow from inside which she can couple with the beast; their child is the minotaur.

2. (p. 150) *Now the land of Aetna received the weary Daedalus, where King Cocalus took up arms in the suppliant's defence and was esteemed most kind:* Cocalus was king of the Sicilian city of Camicus. In some versions of the story, Minos discovers Daedalus by tricking Cocalus into providing him with a threaded seashell—only Daedalus could perform such a delicate engineering feat. Usually, Minos pursues his craftsman, only to die when his rival's daughters cunningly drown him in a seething bath. Ovid, however, seems to allude to open warfare between Crete and Camicus.

3. (p. 151) *the son of Oecleus, who had not yet been ruined by his wife:* Amphiaraus, the son of Oecleus, was a seer who joined Polynices' doomed attempt to wrest back control of his father Oedipus' city, Thebes, from his brother, Eteocles—an episode known as "The Seven Against Thebes," which became a favorite subject for classical writers. At the price of a bribe from Polynices, Eriphyle, wife of Amphiaraus, convinced her husband to accompany an expedition from which he knew none would return.

4. (p. 151) *Then at last Meleager and a picked band of youths assembled, fired with the love of glory: the twin sons of Leda, . . . and Atalanta of Tegea, the pride of the Arcadian woods:* The heroes in this list mainly date to a generation before the Trojan War—for example, Telamon is the father of Ajax, Peleus of Achilles, and Laertes ("the father-in-law of Penelope") of Ulysses. The sons of Leda (and Jupiter), however, are Castor and Pollux, who appeared at the same time as their sisters, Clytemnestra and Helen. The story of Caeneus is told fully in book XII.

5. (p. 157) *all but Gorge and great Alcmena's daughter-in-law:* Gorge subsequently married Andraemon; their son, Thoas, led the Aetolians in the Trojan War and was chosen as one of the soldiers who would spring from the belly of the Trojan horse. Alcmena's daughter-in-law was Deianira, the wife of Hercules.

6. (p. 160) *Next she placed on the board some olives, green and ripe, truthful Minerva's berries:* Legend has it that, in the time of Cecrops, the city of Athens was named for Athena (the Greek equivalent of Minerva) because she offered it as her gift the olive tree, which was judged of greater worth than the horse (or salt, in variant sources) introduced by Poseidon (to the Romans, Neptune). Thus, the olive was sacred to Athena/Minerva as the laurel was to Apollo.

Book IX

1. (p. 167) *" 'It was the task of my cradle days to conquer snakes; and though you should outdo all other serpents, Acheloüs, how small a part of that Lernaean monster would you, just one snake, be?' ":* While still an infant, Hercules strangled two enormous snakes sent by Juno to his cradle to cut short his life; she was jealous of the glorious fate foretold for yet another product of her husband's infidelities. Hercules later destroyed the Lernaean hydra as one of the twelve labors imposed upon him by King Eurystheus. Hercules served this tyrant because the Delphic oracle prophesied he would thereby win immortality.

2. (p. 169) *the son of Amphitryon:* Jupiter made love to Alcmena after having taken on the form of her husband, Amphitryon, while the latter was away. Puzzled by her indifference upon his return, he learned the truth from Tiresias and himself made love to Alcmena, who subsequently bore Hercules one night before his half-brother, Amphitryon's son Iphicles.

3. (p. 169) *enthralled by love of Iole:* While Ovid here makes it sound as if the love between Iole and Hercules might be mere rumor, other sources confirm an actual affair. Indeed, the reason Hercules ravages Pylos (book XII) is that Neleus refused to purify him after he killed Iole's brother in one of his recurrent fits of madness. When Nestor explains his enmity toward the great champion, he curiously omits any reference to Hercules' motives.

4. (pp. 170–171) *"Was it for this I slew Busiris. . . . And there are those who can believe that there are gods!":* Hercules gives an extremely compressed account of the twelve labors he undertook for King Eurystheus and other highlights of his long career; characteristically, Ovid avoids the tale of glorious triumph a fuller narration of Hercules' prime would produce. After the hero's death, Eurystheus continued to oppress Alcmena and Iole until defeated by a largely Athenian force in battle; Iolaus, the nephew of Hercules, killed his uncle's old nemesis.

5. (p. 172) *you, illustrious son of Jove, cut down the trees which grew on lofty Oeta, built a huge funeral pyre, and bade the son of Poeas, . . . destined once again to see the realm of Troy:* Hercules himself has sacked Troy; the city cannot fall to the later Greek coalition that seeks the return of Helen until Philoctetes, marooned by his compatriots after suffering a snake-bite that produced a wound unbearably foul to smell, has been retrieved so that Paris may be killed with the bow of Hercules.

6. (p. 174) *"as the girl strove to rise, she kept her there and changed her arms into the forelegs of an animal. . . . And still, as of yore, she makes our dwelling-place her*

home": The animal to which Alcmena refers is the weasel. As late as the twelfth
century C.E., bestiaries continued to record the belief that weasels were fertil-
ized through the ears and gave birth through the mouth—or perhaps, some
mused, it was the other way around.

7. (p. 175) *"Lotis, a nymph, while fleeing from Priapus' vile pursuit, had taken refuge
   in this shape, changed as to features but keeping still her name"*: Priapus was a fer-
   tility god whose cult statues invariably showed him sporting an enormous erec-
   tion; the medical condition "priapasm" is named for him. By Ovid's time, he
   was often ridiculed, Roman men priding themselves on sexual continence. In
   the *Fasti*, Ovid relates how Priapus approaches the sleeping Lotis in his usual
   state of excitation, but the bray of Silenus' donkey wakes her, and she flees her
   encumbered pursuer.

8. (p. 176) *"Thebes is even now embroiled in civil strife, Capaneus shall be invincible
   but by the hand of Jove himself; the two brothers shall die by mutual wounds"*:
   Themis gives the continuation of the "Seven Against Thebes" story (see end-
   note 3 to book VIII): Capaneus, one of the seven, almost penetrates the walls
   of Thebes but blasphemes and is struck dead by Jupiter; the two brothers who
   kill each other are Eteocles and Polynices.

9. (p. 176) *"he shall be hounded by the Furies and by his mother's ghost until his wife
   shall ask of him the fatal golden necklace and the sword of Phegeus shall have drained
   his kinsman's blood. . . . and shall in an act change beardless boys to men"*: Alcmaeon
   kills his mother, Eriphyle, for betraying Amphiaraus ("the prophet-king"; see
   endnote 3 to book VIII); pursued by Furies for kin-slaying (as Orestes would
   be), he delivers the necklace of Harmonia with which his mother had been
   bribed to the daughter of King Phegeus, but a plague forces his departure.
   Eventually, he is purified by the river-god Acheloüs and marries his daughter
   Callirhoë, but he is killed by Phegeus' sons for having deserted their sister.

10. (p. 176) *Pallantis lamented her husband's hoary age; mild Ceres bewailed Iasion's
    whitening locks; Mulciber demanded renewed life for Erichthonius, and Venus, too,
    with care for the future, stipulated that old Anchises' years should be restored:* These
    are several instances of gods with aging human lovers or children: Pallantis
    ("daughter of Pallas") is Aurora, whose human lover, Tithonus, obtains eternal
    life but not eternal youth, shrinking in time to the chirp of a cricket;
    Erichthonius is the son of Mulciber, better known as Vulcan, god of the forge
    (see endnote 2 to book II); the child of Venus and Anchises was Aeneas, who
    escaped the wreck of Troy to found Rome.

11. (p. 183) *the dog Anubis, sacred Bubastis, dappled Apis, and the god who enjoins
    silence with his finger on his lips; there also were the sacred rattles, and Osiris, cease-
    less object of his worshippers' desire, and the Egyptian serpent swelling with sleep-
    producing venom:* Greco-Romans assimilated Io to the Egyptian god Isis, who
    searched for and reassembled the pieces of her brother/lover Osiris so that he
    could be resurrected after his murder by Set. The dog/jackal-headed Anubis
    superintended burials and conducted the dead to the throne of his father,

Osiris; Bubastis, a cat-headed goddess, was also known as Bastet. The snake-god
Apep contributed to creation in Egyptian myth. Regarding Apis, see endnote 6
to book I.

Book X

1. (p. 189) *since Attis, dear to Cybele, exchanged for this his human form and stiffened
   in its trunk:* Born directly from Earth, Cybele is originally hermaphroditic, but
   losing her phallus leaves her purely female. Attis is born from a blossom of the
   tree into which the phallus grows; Cybele, smitten by his beauty, drives him
   mad when he spurns her. Attis castrates himself and dies, but Jupiter allows a
   penitent Cybele to make his body incorruptible. Greco-Romans identified
   Cybele with Rhea, mother of Jupiter and the Olympian gods.
2. (p. 192) *"Also the time will come when a most valiant hero shall be linked with this
   flower, and by the same markings shall he be known'":* The markings on the petals
   of the hyacinth resemble the letters "AI," which may stand either for the sound
   of Apollo's mournful wail or the name Ajax (spelled "Aiax" in Latin, "Aias" in
   Greek). See book XIII for the story of how the name of Ajax comes to be
   inscribed on the flower.

Book XI

1. (p. 216) *But still the fates did not suffer the banished Peleus to continue in this land.
   The wandering exile went on to Magnesia, and there, at the hands of the
   Haemonian king, Acastus, he gained full absolution from his bloodguiltiness:*
   Acastus, the son of Medea's victim, Pelias (book VII), drove Jason from Ioclus
   and became king. After he cleansed Peleus, the story continues in other
   sources, his wife fell in love with the hero; when Peleus refused her, she
   charged him with attempting her seduction. Refusing to kill a man he had pu-
   rified, Acastus stranded Peleus weaponless in hostile centaur country, but
   Chiron, the most civil centaur, rescued him.
2. (p. 221) *Near the land of the Cimmerians there is a deep recess within a hollow
   mountain, the home and chamber of sluggish Sleep:* The Cimmerians were a leg-
   endary people living either beyond the Atlantic in the uttermost West or north
   of the Black Sea. The entrance to the land of the dead was located in
   Cimmeria; Ulysses follows the directions of Circe to reach this land, where he
   learns the course of his homeward journey from the shade of Tiresias (*Odyssey*,
   book 11).
3. (p. 225) *"While the daughter of Dymas bore the one, the other, Aesacus, is said to
   have been born in secret beneath the shades of Ida by Alexiroë, daughter of the
   horned Granicus":* Aesacus was thus the grandson of the river-god Granicus,
   while Hector's grandfather was the human king Dymas; the daughters of both
   wed Priam, but Hecuba was his primary mate. Aesacus was a seer best known

for prophesying that the infant Paris would one day cause Troy's ruin; the child was subsequently left in the open to die, but rescued and raised by the usual kindly shepherd.

Book XII

1. (p. 231) *"Bold Ixion's son had wed Hippodame and had invited the cloud-born centaurs to recline at the tables, set in order in a well-shaded grotto":* Ixion, the father of the fully human (if rather undomesticated) Pirithoüs, also gave rise to the centaurs. The story is that Ixion desired Juno; Jupiter deceived him by fashioning a cloud into her shape. The cloud either produced the centaurs directly or else gave birth to the monstrous but anthropomorphic Centaurus, who in turn fathered the centaurs upon the mares of Mount Pelion. Lapiths and centaurs are thus virtual cousins.

Book XIII

1. (p. 244) *"He would be living still, . . . showed the gold which he had already hidden there":* To avoid the war, Ulysses feigned madness by yoking an ox and a donkey to the same plow and sowing his fields with salt. Palamedes, legendary inventor of the Greek alphabet, exposed Ulysses' chicanery by placing his infant son, Telemachus, in the path of the blade; by swerving around the child, Ulysses confirmed his sanity. Most traditions agree that Ulysses falsified charges to destroy Palamedes, but disagree on the method he used.

2. (p. 248) *"I denounced Paris, demanded the return of Helen and the booty, and I prevailed on Priam and Antenor who sided with Priam. But Paris and his brothers and his companions in the robbery scarce restrained their impious hands from me (you know that, Menelaüs)":* As an ambassador to the court of Priam, Ulysses convinced Priam and Antenor, Hecuba's brother, to return Helen and so avoid the war; however, the multitudinous sons of Priam would not agree. Antenor in particular was credited with foiling a plot to kill the Greek ambassadors; consequently allowed to leave Troy unscathed at the end of the war, he founded the Italian city of Padua (in Latin, Patavium).

3. (p. 251) *"just as I stole away from the midst of the enemy the enshrined image of Phrygian Minerva":* This escapade, like the retrieval of Philoctetes, involved yet another prophecy that needed to be fulfilled before Troy could fall; as revealed by the seer Helenus, whom Ulysses captured, the citadel would stand until the statue of Pallas Minerva departed from her temple. Ulysses managed to steal it.

4. (p. 253) *To the land of Queen Hypsipyle and the illustrious Thoas . . . victorious Ulysses now set sail to bring back the Tirynthian arrows:* The arrows belonged to the hero of Tiryns, Hercules, who bequeathed them to Philoctetes. Thoas ruled Lemnos, whose women were cursed by Venus for neglecting her worship; she

made them repugnant to their husbands (in some traditions, by a stink like Philoctetes'). When the men slept with captive women from Thrace instead, their wives killed them (excepting Thoas); the island was repopulated following an extended stay by the Argonauts.

5. (p. 260) *Orion's daughters, one dealing a wound not apt for maiden's hands to her bared throat, the other dealing clumsy wounds with her weaving-shuttle, both falling as victims in the people's stead; then borne in funeral pomp through the town and burned to ashes midst the mourning throngs:* In order to lift a pestilence that had fallen upon Thebes, the daughters of Orion, Metioche and Menippe, killed themselves in accordance with an oracle that indicated the sacrifice of two virgins would heal the city. They were subsequently transformed into comets. Indeed, book XIII repeatedly suggests that war itself inevitably sacrifices both women themselves and feminine values.

6. (p. 265) *"Maiden, I am no monster or wild creature; I am a sea-god; and neither Proteus nor Triton nor Palaemon, son of Athamas, has greater power over the deeps than I":* This is a tale from book IV: Offended by the care Ino, daughter of Cadmus, provided her nephew, Bacchus, Juno drove Ino's husband, Athamas, mad. After killing one son (Learchus), Athamas chased Ino and their other child, Melicertes, over a cliff. So manifestly unjust was this outcome that the gods transformed Ino into Leucothoe and her son into Palaemon as they fell; both lived on as divinities of the ocean.

7. (p. 266) *Scylla fled from the god, and he, stung to mad rage by his repulse, betook him to the wondrous court of Circe, daughter of the Sun:* Circe's father was the sun-god Helios. Most traditions also identify Aeëtes of Colchis as Circe's brother (occasionally, he, rather than Helios, appears as her father), thus making her the aunt of Medea and so relating the two most prominent sorceresses of classical tradition. The most famous episode involving Circe appears in the *Odyssey* (book 10).

Book XIV

1. (p. 275) *" 'he loved one nymph alone, whom once on the Palatine Venilia is said to have borne to two-headed Janus' ":* Venilia was a nymph; Janus, a native Roman god of great antiquity. Associated with crossroads and beginnings, the two- or four-faced Janus saw both ahead and behind at once. The month of January is named for him.

2. (p. 277) *" 'she sprinkled upon them her baleful drugs and poisonous juices, summoning to her aid Night and the gods of Night from Erebus and Chaos' ":* According to Hesiod's *Theogony*, Chaos was the chasm or void that preceded all creation: from it sprang the five original, eternal beings: Ge (earth), Tartarus (the Underworld), Eros (desire), Erebus (the subterranean shadows of Tartarus), and Night. Circe thus calls upon the first dark forces of the universe, prompted by the equally ancient Eros.

3. (p. 278) *Aeneas had not gone in vain to Evander's home, but Venulus had vainly sought the city of the exiled Diomede. He had founded a large city within Iapygian Daunus' realm, and was ruling the fields granted to him as a marriage portion:* Diomede, companion of Ulysses in the Trojan War, fled his native Argos to escape the plots of his adulterous wife, Aegialia, who had turned the Argives against him. She was influenced, in Ovid's version of the story, by Venus, whom Diomede had wounded at Troy, but other sources blame the son of Palamedes (see endnote 1 to book XIII). Settling in Italy, Diomede married the daughter of Daunus and founded a royal line.

4. (p. 280) *when the holy mother of the gods, mindful that these pines were felled on Ida's top, filled the air with the harsh beat of brazen cymbals and the shrill music of the boxwood flute:* Worship of Cybele, the "mother of the gods," originated in Asia Minor; thus, she intervenes to save ships built from the timber of Mount Ida, the sacred mountain of Troy.

5. (p. 286) *"It has a temple in honor of the Gazing Venus also":* The title perhaps recalls the pre-Hellenic character of Venus, a fairly minor deity of fortune in the Latin world before it felt the considerable influence of Greece. Between the third century B.C.E. and Ovid, Venus absorbed the identity of the Greek Aphrodite, goddess of desire, a being whose worship extends back through the Canaanite (Phoenician) goddess Astarte and the Babylonian Ishtar to the Sumerian Inanna at the start of written records.

6. (p. 286) *Next false Amulius by force of arms rules the Ausonian state; but old Numitor by the aid of his grandson gains the kingdom he has lost, and the walls of the City are founded on the shepherd's festal day:* The festival in question was the springtime Palilia; no one can account for its association with Rome's foundation. After Numitor's brother, Amulius, usurped his throne, the rightful king's daughter gave birth to twin boys by Mars. Amulius left them in the wild to die, but a she-wolf raised them and, as Romulus and Remus, they restored their grandfather to power. Rome, of course, is named for Romulus. (In order to reconcile conflicting accounts of the origin of Rome, Aeneas was credited with founding the Roman state, and Romulus the enclosed city itself.)

7. (p. 288) *Her with dear, familiar hands Rome's founder receives, and changes her mortal body and her old-time name. He calls her Hora, and now as goddess is she joined once more to her Quirinus:* Quirinus, originally a figure from Sabine mythology, is the name given Romulus after his deification, though it also assimilates him to Mars (some authorities explained that the deified Romulus was the peacetime identity of the god of war). In any case, Hersilia, wife of Romulus/Quirinus joins him in the heavens as the goddess Hora.

Book XV

1. (p. 289) *this Grecian city on Italian soil:* So heavily Greek was the population of southern Italy in classical times that the area was known as Magna

Graecia—greater Greece. Indeed, a significant minority of the region continued to speak Greek until the nineteenth-century unification of Italy.

2. (p. 290) *There was a man here, a Samian by birth, but he had fled forth from Samos and its rulers, and through hatred of tyranny was living in voluntary exile:* The Samian is Pythagoras (sixth century B.C.E.), the philosopher from the island of Samos who founded an academy in the Italian city of Crotona. While it is impossible to differentiate the teachings of Pythagoras from the work of later disciples, his philosophy (for which he was much better known in ancient times than the mathematical discoveries attributed to him) evidently proclaimed the unity beneath the multiplicity of appearance.

3. (p. 299) *"Sparta was at one time a famous city; great Mycenae flourished, and Cecrops' and Amphion's citadels":* A famous instance of Ovid's play with time frames; while these cities (Cecrops' citadel is Athens and Amphion's is Thebes) had diminished or been destroyed by Ovid's own time, when Pythagoras lived Athens and Sparta, at least, had yet to attain the pinnacle of their power.

4. (p. 300) *"not load our stomachs as with a Thyestean banquet!":* Not that Thyestes had much dietary choice; he was unknowingly served the flesh of his own sons by Atreus, his brother, as part of a struggle for control over the throne of Mycenae.

5. (p. 307) *O Trojan Vesta:* Vesta, equivalent to the Greek Hestia, was the goddess of the hearth; the Vestal Virgins maintained her sacred fire, the symbolic hearthside of the whole Roman people. In exchange for maintaining perpetual virginity, the Vestals received unusual privileges for women in classical times. They were all the daughters, in fact, of noble families.

6. (pp. 309–310) *"A Roman general's Egyptian mistress . . . shall fall before him, and in vain shall she have threatened that our Capitol shall bow to her Canopus":* Ovid provides here a brief account of the defeat of the Roman general Mark Antony and his "Egyptian mistress," Cleopatra (actually of Greek descent), by the troops of Octavian, later to be known as Augustus. The decisive naval battle, Actium, took place in 31 B.C.E.; it ensured that the capital would not move from Rome to the Egyptian city of Canopus, but also made rich Egypt the private property of Augustus.

AN ATLAS OF
THE *METAMORPHOSES*:
INDEX AND MAPS

INDEX OF PLACES

The maps for this edition of the *Metamorphoses* are drawn from Samuel Butler's *Atlas of Antient Geography* (1851), which, by reason of its intelligent selection of detail, features exceptionally clear and readable images of the Roman Mediterranean. The maps render place names in their Latin forms, so readers should be aware of slight variations in spelling from Miller's translation—for example, the text's "Thessaly" appears on the map as "Thessalia." Many place names also appear in the text primarily as adjectives; again, it should be easy to perceive the noun from which the modifier is derived—for example, that "Boeotian" comes from "Boeotia." Whenever an adjective form involves more than the addition of a letter or letters to the noun, it is listed parenthetically following the noun form. In any case, this index does not attempt to reproduce every place name in Ovid's epic; merely to identify the principal settings of the tales.

MAPS

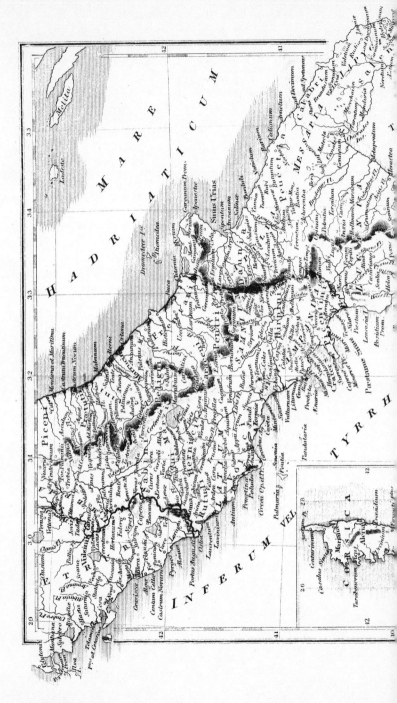

MAP 1   Southern Italy.

ITALIÆ ANTIQVÆ
PARS MERIDIONALIS.

Roman Miles

MARE IONIVM

SINVS

MARE

SARDINIA

SICILIA

Published by Lea & Blanchard Philad.ª

Longitude East 3 from Ferro.

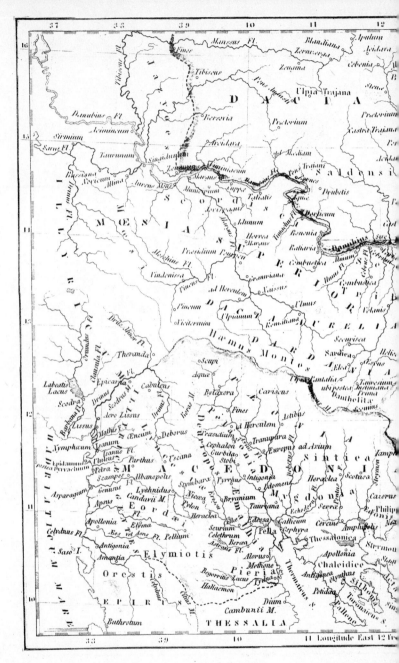

MAP 2 Macedonia, Moesia, Thracia, and Dacia.

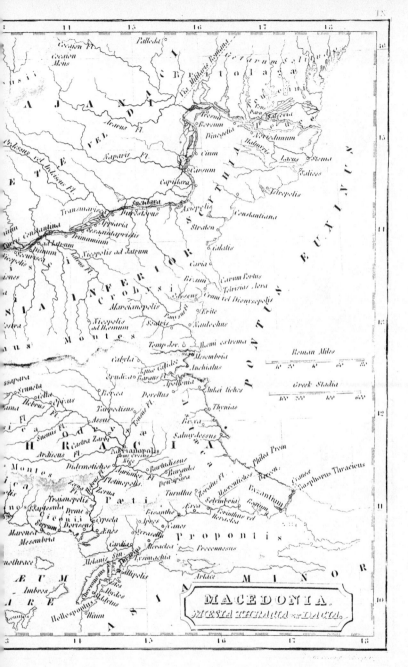

MACEDONIA,
MŒSIA THRACIA et DACIA

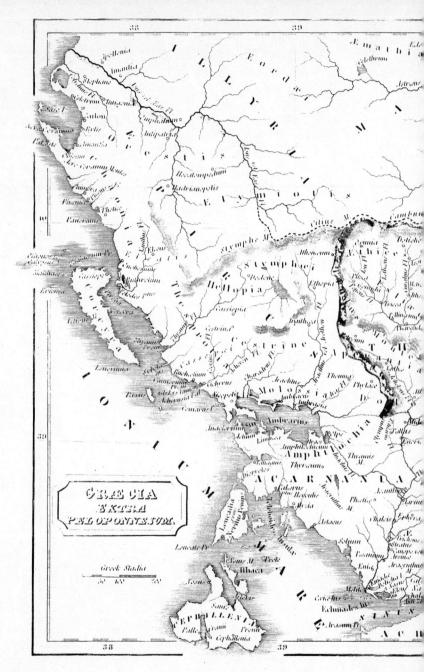

MAP 3   Northern Greece.

MAP 4   Southern Greece.

PELOPONNESUS ET GRÆCIA
MERIDIONALIS.

Greek Stadia
25 50   100   200   300

ard Philad.ᵃ

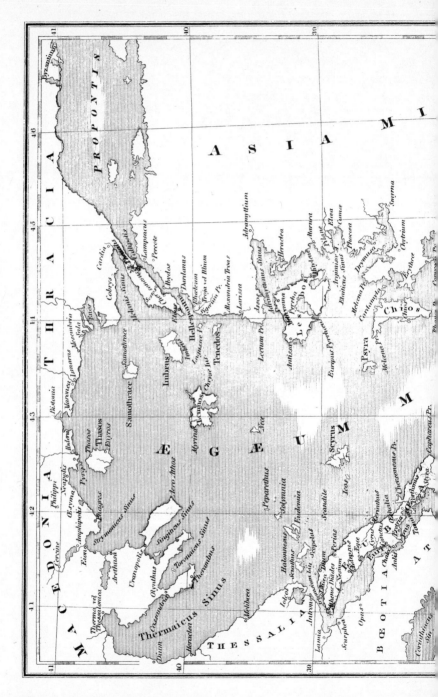

MAP 5   Islands of the Aegean Sea.

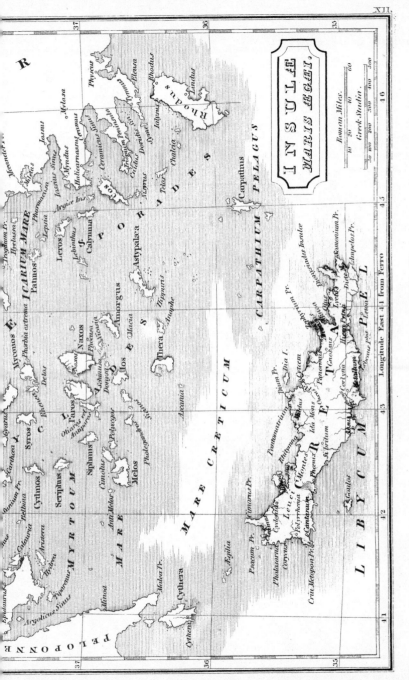

INSULÆ
MARIS ÆGÆI.

Roman Miles.
10   20   60
Greek Stadia.
100   200   300
30 100 200 400 300

PELOPONNE

MARE MYRTOUM

MARE CRETICUM

CARPATHIUM PELAGUS

SPORADES

ICARIUM MARE

Rhodus

Lindus

Carpathus

LIBYCUM PELAGUS

CRETE

Longitude East 44 from Ferro

Published by Lea & Blanchard Philad.a

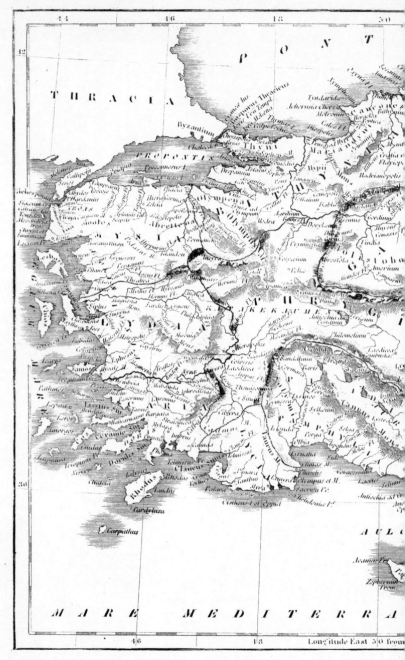

MAP 6 Asia Minor.

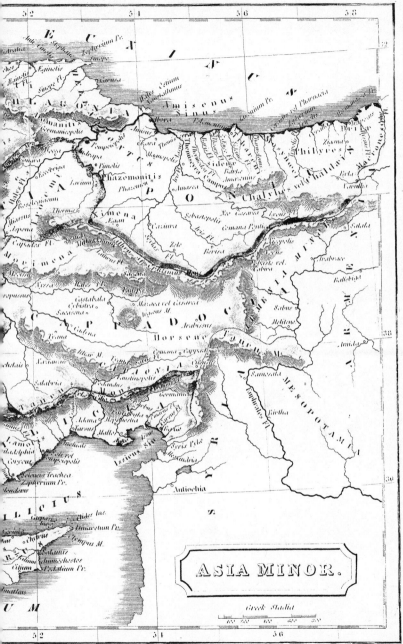

ASIA MINOR.

Greek Stadia

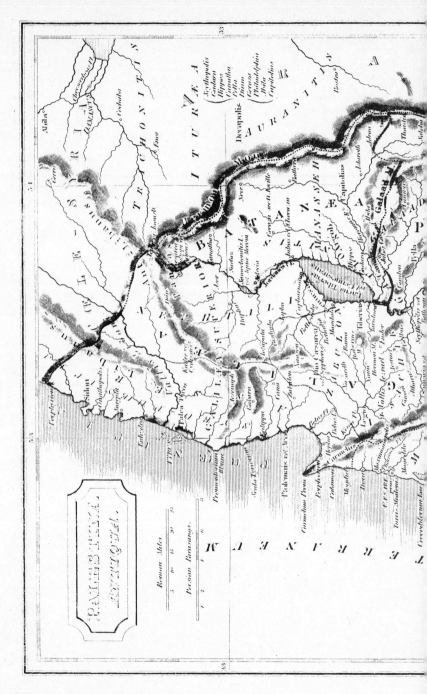

MAP 7   Ancient Palestine.

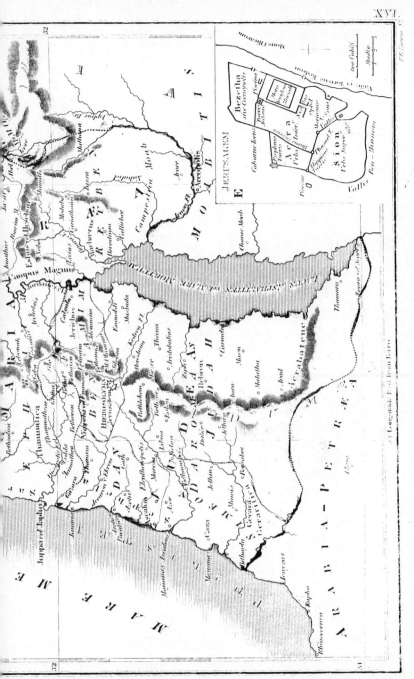

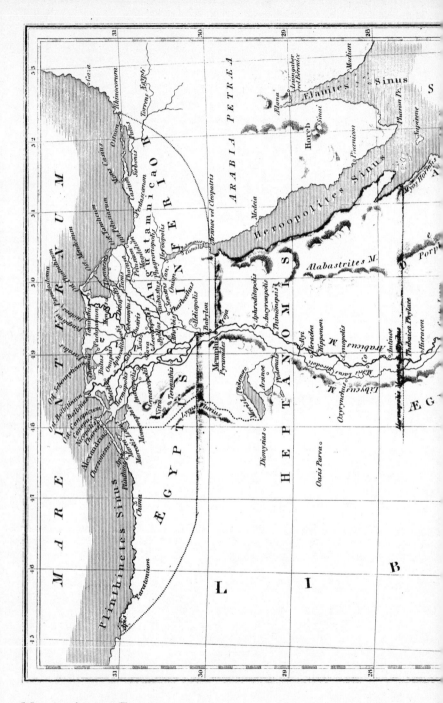

MAP 8   Ancient Egypt.

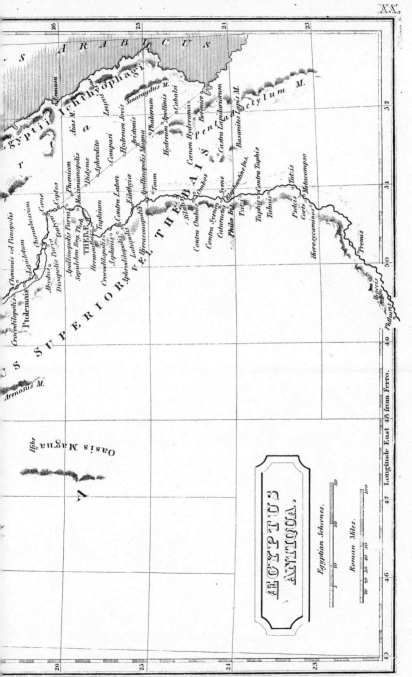

ÆGYPTUS ANTIQUA.

Egyptian Schœnes.

Roman Miles.

Published by Lea & Blanchard Philada.

XX

Longitude East 48 from Ferro.

Although Ovid did not create the classical myths, he recorded and popularized them, and he introduced thematic and literary innovations that increased their complexity. The established versions of many of these myths stem directly from Ovid's *Metamorphoses*, and the fact that they continue to pervade our cultural consciousness is a testament to Ovid's poetic skill and persuasiveness. It was Ovid who originated the concept of Pygmalion as the sculptor of his beloved statue of Aphrodite rather than simply an admirer of it. And it was Ovid who first linked the thematically related stories of Narcissus and Echo. Additionally, Ovid saved stories such as the tale of the lovers Pyramus and Thisbe from extinction. The classical myths, as popularized by Ovid, are some of the most deeply ingrained and enduring stories in Western culture.

The Early Days

After several early successes and some renown, the author ended his life in ignominy, exiled by Augustus to Tomis, a remote port on the Black Sea, where he died in 18 C.E. Nevertheless, writers and critics of the first century continued to read and comment upon his works—philosopher and playwright Seneca (4 B.C.E.–65 C.E.) drew material from Ovid, as did the epigrammatist Martial (c.40–103 C.E.). After Constantine, the emperor of Rome, converted to Christianity in about 312 C.E., Ovid's popularity declined further due to his pagan, and therefore immoral, subject matter. It wasn't until 700 years after Constantine's conversion that Ovid reappeared in world literature in any significant way, though he was never completely neglected: Sixth-century grammarian Lactantius Placidus created prose summaries of the *Metamorphoses*, possibly for use in schools; and in the late eighth and early ninth centuries the reading of Ovid was advocated by Theodolphus, bishop of Orleans, a member of Charlemagne's royal court and a patron of education.

During the Middle Ages Ovid achieved a glorious rebirth, becoming Europe's most popular Latin poet. The twelfth and thirteenth centuries are now known as the *aetas Ovidiana*, or Age of Ovid, and interest in the poet burgeoned as early as the eleventh century. Elaborate interpretations of his writings appeared; some of these added morals to the stories of the *Metamorphoses* or related them to Christian myth, most likely to provide moral meaning to works once deemed depraved. The *Metamorphoses* was taught in schools, widely copied by writers throughout Europe, and translated into French, German, and other languages. Some poets of this time even falsely attributed their own works, derived from the *Metamorphoses*, to Ovid himself.

Dante and the Italian Renaissance

The earliest major writer to show the influence of Ovid was Italy's great poet Dante Alighieri, author of the Christian allegory *La Divina commedia* (*The Divine Comedy*; c.1310–1314). In this epic work, the poet Virgil leads Dante through different stages of the afterlife: Hell (*Inferno*), Purgatory (*Purgatorio*), and Paradise (*Paradiso*). In the course of his journey, Dante meets Ovid, who has been consecrated as one of the virtuous pagans allowed to reside in Limbo, alongside Homer and Horace. The *Metamorphoses* was Dante's primary source for the classical myths, and all three parts of *The Divine Comedy* are laden with references to Ovid's text.

The Italian poet Petrarch (1304–1374) was another student of Ovid and classical antiquity. His influential sonnet sequences are devoted to the beautiful Laura and liken her to the mythological figures of Daphne (when describing her elegance and beauty) and Medusa (when indicating the power of her censure). In an early ode, Petrarch describes undergoing a transformation akin to those in the *Metamorphoses* when Laura slights him. Completing the triumvirate of great Italian writers of the fourteenth century is Giovanni Boccaccio (1313–1375), best known for the *Decameron*, a mosaic of 100 stories that mimics the structure of the *Metamorphoses*. Boccaccio was intensely interested in Ovid during his youth; his allegorical work *Amorosa Visione* retells the story of Pyramus and Thisbe, among others from the *Metamorphoses*, and mentions Ovid by name.

England: The Middle Ages and the Elizabethan Era

England's great medieval poet Geoffrey Chaucer (c.1343–1400) profited perhaps more than any other writer from exposure to Ovid. His very first poem is a retelling of the mythical tale of Ceyx and Alcyone recounted in the *Metamorphoses*. In *The House of Fame*, Chaucer dedicates a pillar to "Venus clerk, Ovyde, / That hath y-sowen wonder wyde / The grete god of Loves name." *Troilus and Criseyde* uses Ovid for details of Trojan society, and tales from Ovid appear in *The Parliament of Fowls* and *Legend of Good Women*. Chaucer's masterwork, *The Canterbury Tales*, tells the story of a motley group of travelers making a pilgrimage to Canterbury. Like the *Metamorphoses*, the work is structured as an assemblage of stories, and the *Metamorphoses* seems to have been in Chaucer's mind throughout its composition; Ovid's influence manifests most clearly in the Prologue and in the tales of the Manciple, the Knight, and the Wife of Bath.

Ovid's preeminence surged in England during the age of Queen Elizabeth I, aided especially by an immensely popular English translation of the *Metamorphoses* by Arthur Golding in 1567. The poet Edmund Spenser, a classicist, knew Ovid's works well and frequently invokes the poet in his allegory *The Faerie Queene* (1590–1596). In this epic poem, Spenser glorifies Queen Elizabeth through the stories of twelve knights, each representing a different virtue.

Shakespeare and Milton

William Shakespeare (1564–1616) based his first published poem, *Venus and Adonis*, on an Ovidian tale, and Ovid remained Shakespeare's primary source for classical mythology throughout his career. Lines adapted from both Ovid's original Latin and the flowing Golding translation of the *Metamorphoses* appear in nearly all of Shakespeare's plays, most of which explicitly refer to the *Metamorphoses* or its author. Shakespeare's most Ovidian work is probably *A Midsummer Night's Dream* (c.1595), which is also his most popular comedy. Set in a forest full of fairies and magic, it is a celebration of mischief and courtship that concludes with a production of the play *Pyramus and Thisbe*. Other examples of Shakespeare's indebtedness to the *Metamorphoses* are found in the violent *Titus Andronicus* (c.1593), likely Shakespeare's earliest tragedy, which takes some of its plot from the myth of Philomela; *The Winter's Tale* (c.1610), which includes the *Metamorphoses*'s Autolycus in its cast of characters and uses the Pygmalion story for the reanimation of Hermione; and *The Tempest* (c.1611), Shakespeare's final play, which draws explicitly from Ovid's version of the Medea story for Prospero's speech, in which he bids farewell to magic.

At age fourteen, the great English author John Milton (1608–1674) composed more than 1,400 lines in Latin summarizing Ovid's poem in blank pages of his copy of the *Metamorphoses*. Milton gracefully adapted Ovid's mythological subject matter in his early works "L'Allegro" and "Il Penseroso" (both c.1632) and *Comus* (1634). Milton's assistants during the time of his blindness attest that the author consulted Ovid frequently while composing the great Christian myths *Paradise Lost* (1667) and *Paradise Regained* (1671), notably for descriptions of Chaos, Creation, and the Flood.

The Renaissance

In England and on the Continent, the Renaissance marked the last period of Ovid's primacy in literature. The *Metamorphoses* continued to be taught in schools, and men of letters continued to respect the work through the eighteenth and nineteenth centuries, although its direct influence on great works of literature had waned. In the last years of the seventeenth century, England's one-time poet laureate John Dryden (1631–1700) translated the twelfth book of the *Metamorphoses*. This began a trend among the great poets of the day: A composite translation of the *Metamorphoses* collected by Samuel Garth appeared in 1717 with renderings by Dryden, Garth, Joseph Addison, Alexander Pope, and other prominent writers. Moreover, Pope alludes to Ovid in *Windsor Forest* (1713) and the *Dunciad* (1728), while *Gulliver's Travels* author Jonathan Swift adapted book VIII of the *Metamorphoses* in his poem "Baucis and Philemon" (1709). In the late eighteenth century, Ovid was a favorite of William Blake, author of *Songs of Innocence* (1789) and *Songs of Experience* (1794).

The Nineteenth Century

Among nineteenth-century writers, Ovid's influence is most notable in the works of Germany's Johann Wolfgang von Goethe; Goethe studied Ovid extensively and borrowed from him for his poetic drama *Faust* (1808, 1832), the second part of which features the characters Philemon and Baucis. English poet Percy Bysshe Shelley (1792–1822) carried Ovid's works with him during his travels in Italy. Ovid's influence can also be seen in the works of other English romantics, including George Gordon, Lord Byron (1788–1824), John Keats (1795–1821), Alfred, Lord Tennyson (1809–1892), Robert Browning (1812–1889), and Algernon Charles Swinburne (1837–1909). Scottish novelist Sir Walter Scott, author of *Ivanhoe*, drew from Ovid for his later works *The Pirate* (1821) and *Woodstock* (1826). In America, Nathaniel Hawthorne, author of *The Scarlet Letter*, retold stories from the *Metamorphoses* in his *Tanglewood Tales for Girls and Boys* (1853).

The most influential retelling of Ovid in the nineteenth century occurred in *Bulfinch's Mythology*, a collection of three books (*The Age of Fable*, 1855; *The Age of Chivalry*, 1858; and *Legends of Charlemagne*, 1863) by American author Thomas Bulfinch. The works vividly recount the most fascinating and timeless Greek, Roman, Scandinavian, Celtic, and Eastern stories in stirring and readable English prose. In Bulfinch's own words, the *Metamorphoses* provided "most of our stories of Grecian and Roman mythology." Bulfinch's renderings were extremely popular in their own day and remain so today.

Kafka, Modernism, and Beyond

In 1915 an innovative short work with explicit eponymous ties to Ovid's masterpiece was published to instant acclaim: "The Metamorphosis" ("Die Verwandlung" in the original German), the signature story by Austrian writer Franz Kafka. The nightmarish tale begins with one of the most famous opening lines in all of literature: "As Gregor Samsa awoke from unsettling dreams one morning, he found himself transformed in his bed into a monstrous vermin." Kafka's story delineates with grim realism the despair Gregor, who had been a traveling salesman in his human life, feels when he can no longer support his parents and sister. Now a gigantic insect, Gregor cannot leave the house; he spends much of his time scuttling up the walls of his prison-like room and hiding under his bed. During the lonely days leading up to his death, Gregor is ostracized by his family and even physically attacked by his father. Kafka's haunting parable of alienation and transformation has itself become an inspiration for generations of writers. Colombian author of magical realism Gabriel García Márquez wrote, "When I read the [first] line I thought to myself I didn't know anyone was allowed to write things like that. If I had known, I would have started writing a long time ago. So I immediately started writing short stories."

Ovid also served as inspiration for several key figures in the modernism movement. T. S. Eliot's *The Waste Land* (1922), perhaps the most seminal poem of the twentieth century, has as its main character Tiresias, the blind seer of Thebes, who morphs from man to woman and back again—echoing Ovid's overarching themes of change and the melding of diffuse elements. In his footnotes to *The Waste Land*, Eliot cites Tiresias's appearance in book III of the *Metamorphoses*; he also writes, "What Tiresias *sees*, in fact, is the substance of the poem." More Ovidian in style than *The Waste Land*, Eliot's poem "The Death of St. Narcissus," an unpublished early fragment that bore on the creation of the later work, retells the familiar story of Narcissus from the *Metamorphoses*. Finally, the first book published by the Ovid Press, a short-lived venture by literary man John Rodker, was Eliot's *Ara vos prec* (1920), published in America as *Poems*.

American poet Ezra Pound, who edited *The Waste Land*, called Arthur Golding's 1567 translation of the *Metamorphoses* "the most beautiful book in the language (my opinion and I suspect it was Shakespeare's)." Ovidian subjects figure in many of Pound's *Cantos*, which appeared in several volumes between 1925 and 1970 (canto 2 is one good example). Metamorphosis is also a main theme of English novelist Virginia Woolf's *Orlando* (1928), a fantasy-biography in which the title character changes from man to woman and ages a mere thirty-six years over four centuries.

Irish author James Joyce is another modernist influenced by Ovid and interested in the theme of transformation. The main character of Joyce's novel *A Portrait of the Artist as a Young Man* (1916), Stephen Dedalus, takes his name from Ovid's story of Daedalus and Icarus, and the novel's epigraph, *Et ignotas animum dimittit in artes* ("And he abandoned his mind to obscure arts"), comes from book VIII of the *Metamorphoses*. Stephen Dedalus reappears in Joyce's *Ulysses* (1922), a complex work fashioned after Homer's *Odyssey*.

Almost two decades later, the "Anna Livia Plurabelle" section of *Finnegans Wake* (1939) transforms two gossipy washerwomen into "yonder elm" and "yonder stone"; the novel's main character, Humphrey Chimpden Earwicker (HCE), morphs into the biblical Adam, Humpty Dumpty, Henrik Ibsen's Master Builder, Jesus Christ, King Arthur, and the Duke of Wellington.

In 1914 Joyce's fellow Dubliner George Bernard Shaw premiered his play *Pygmalion*, the title of which derives from a myth in Ovid's collection. The play recounts how Henry Higgins, a professor of phonetics, transforms a Cockney girl named Eliza Doolittle into a respectable woman by teaching her to speak properly. *Pygmalion* itself metamorphosed into the Broadway musical *My Fair Lady* (1956), written by Alan Jay Lerner and Frederick Loewe, and the 1964 film of the same name directed by George Cukor.

The close of the twentieth century saw a healthy handful of Ovid-inspired works. In particular, Michael Hofmann and James Lasdun commissioned sixty poems by high-profile contemporary writers for their volume *After Ovid: New Metamorphoses* (1994). The collection features poems by Ted Hughes ("Creation / Four Ages / Flood" and three others), Jorie Graham ("Flood"), Kenneth Koch ("Io"), Tom Paulin ("Cadmus and the Dragon"), Robert Pinsky ("Creation According to Ovid"), Seamus Heaney ("Orpheus and Eurydice"; "Death of Orpheus"), and several other prominent writers. Hughes, the former poet laureate of England, continued exploring the *Metamorphoses* in his *Tales from Ovid* (1997), a highly acclaimed free translation of twenty-four of Ovid's stories.

Writer-director Mary Zimmerman's hit play *Metamorphoses* ran for a year on Broadway beginning in March 2002, winning Zimmerman a Tony for Best Direction and garnering nominations for Best Play and Best Scenic Design. The play uses a small cast of actors who play multiple roles to enact several of Ovid's stories. Noting that water is a symbol for change in nearly every culture, Zimmerman's innovative script calls for a swimming pool in the center of the stage, which is utilized by actors throughout the performance. *Time* magazine called her sensitive, simple, and ultimately arresting adaptation "the theater event of the year."

American author Jeffrey Eugenides credits Ovid as a main inspiration for his Pulitzer Prize–winning novel *Middlesex* (2002), which describes the transformation of a woman—Detroit-born Calliope (Cal) Stephanides—into a man at age fourteen. The comic mock epic traces Cal's family history back to nineteenth-century Asia Minor, infusing the book's historical accounts, its shifting views on gender and medicine, and its compelling personal narrative into a tale that is both elegant and riveting.

COMMENTS & QUESTIONS

In this section, we aim to provide the reader with an array of perspectives on the text, as well as questions that challenge those perspectives. The commentary has been culled from sources as diverse as reviews contemporaneous with the work, letters written by the author, literary criticism of later generations, and appreciations written throughout the work's history. Following the commentary, a series of questions seeks to filter Ovid's Metamorphoses *through a variety of points of view and bring about a richer understanding of this enduring work.*

Comments

SENECA THE ELDER
Ovid rarely declaimed *controversiae* [disputes], and only ones involving portrayal of character. He preferred *suasoriae* [persuasion], finding all argumentation tiresome. He used language by no means over-freely except in his poetry, where he was well aware of his faults—and enjoyed them.

—translated by M. Winterbottom,
from *Controversiae* (1974)

QUINTILLIAN
Ovid has a lack of seriousness even when he writes epic and is unduly enamoured of his own gifts, but portions of his work merit our praise.

—translated by H. E. Butler, from
The Institutio Oratoria of Quintillian (1922)

JOHN DRYDEN
If the imitation of nature be the business of a poet, I know no author who can justly be compared with [Ovid], especially in the descriptions of the passions. And to prove this, I shall need no other judges than

the generality of his readers: for all passions being inborn with us, we are almost equally judges when we are concerned in the representation of them. Now I will appeal to any man who has read this poet, whether he finds not the natural emotion of the same passion in himself which the poet describes in his feigned persons? His thoughts, which are the pictures and results of those passions, are generally such as naturally arise from those disorderly motions of our spirits. Yet, not to speak too partially in his behalf, I will confess that the copiousness of his wit was such that he often writ too pointedly for his subject, and made his persons speak more eloquently than the violence of their passion would admit: so that he is frequently witty out of season; leaving the imitation of nature, and the cooler dictates of his judgment, for the false applause of fancy. Yet he seems to have found out this imperfection in his riper age; for why else should he complain that his *Metamorphosis* was left unfinished? Nothing, sure, can be added to the wit of that poem, or of the rest; but many things ought to have been retrenched, which I suppose would have been the business of his age, if his misfortunes had not come too fast upon him. But take him uncorrected as he is transmitted to us, and it must be acknowledged, in spite of his Dutch friends the commentators, even of Julius Scaliger himself, that Seneca's censure will stand good against him:

nescivit quod bene cessit relinquere:

he never knew how to give over when he had done well; but, continually varying the same sense an hundred ways, and taking up in another place what he had more than enough inculcated before, he sometimes cloys his readers instead of satisfying them; and gives occasion to his translators, who dare not cover him, to blush at the nakedness of their father. This, then, is the allay of Ovid's writings, which is sufficiently recompensed by his other excellencies: nay, this very fault is not without its beauties: for the most severe censor cannot but be pleased with the prodigality of his wit, though at the same time he could have wished that the master of it had been a better manager. Everything which he does becomes him, and if sometimes he appears too gay, yet there is a secret gracefulness of youth which accompanies his writings, though the staidness and sobriety of age be wanting.

—from his preface to *Ovid's Epistles* (1680)

EZRA POUND

Ovid—urbane, sceptical, a Roman of the city—writes, not in a florid prose, but in a verse which has the clarity of French scientific prose.

"Convenit esse deos et ergo esse credemus."

"It is convenient to have Gods, and therefore we believe they exist."; and with all pretence of scientific accuracy he ushers in his gods, demigods, monsters and transformations. His mind, trained to the system of empire, demands the definite. The sceptical age hungers after the definite, after something it can pretend to believe. The marvellous thing is made plausible, the gods are humanized, their annals are written as if copied from a parish register; their heroes might have been acquaintances of the author's father.

In Crete, in the reign of Minos, to take a definite instance, Daedalus is constructing the first monoplane, and "the boy Icarus laughing, snatches at the feathers which are fluttering in the stray breeze, pokes soft the yellow wax with his thumb, and with his play hinders the wonderful work of his father."

A few lines further on Ovid writes in witness of Daedalus' skill as a mechanic, that observing the backbone of a fish, he had invented the first saw: it might be the incident of Newton and the apple. On the whole there is nothing that need excite our incredulity. The inventor of the saw invents an aeroplane. There is an accident to his son, who disregards his father's flying instructions, and a final jeer from an old rival, Perdix, who has simplified the process of aviation by getting himself changed into a bird. It is told so simply, one hardly remembers to be surprised that Perdix should have become a partridge; or at most one feels that the accurate Naso has made some slight error in quoting well-established authority, and that we have no strict warrant for assuming that this particular partridge was Daedalus' cousin Perdix.

—from *The Spirit of Romance* (1910)

GILBERT MURRAY

Ovid is one towards whom the present generation has resolutely turned its blind spot. If he were archaic, or uncouth, or earnest, or nobly striving after ideals he cannot reach; if he were even difficult or eccentric, so as to make some claim upon us; we should doubtless be attracted to him and read him with our imaginations alert.

But he does his work too well, he asks no indulgence; he is neat and swift and witty and does not need our help; consequently we have no use for him. I suspect we are wrong. "My work is done," he writes at the end of the *Metamorphoses*. . . . He was a poet utterly in love with poetry: not perhaps with the soul of poetry—to be in love with souls is a feeble and somewhat morbid condition—but with the real face and voice and body and clothes and accessories of poetry. He loved the actual technique of the verse, but of that later. He loved most the whole world of mimesis which he made. We hear that he was apprenticed to the law, but wrote verses instead of speeches. He married wives and they ran away or died and he married others. He had a daughter and adored her, and taught her verses. He was always in love and never with anyone in particular. He strikes one as having been rather innocent and almost entirely useless in this dull world which he had not made and for which he was not responsible, while he moved triumphant and effective through his own inexhaustible realm of legend. He came somehow under the displeasure of the government, and by a peculiar piece of cruelty was sent with all his helpless sweetness and sensuousness and none of the gifts of a colonist, to live in exile in that dreadful region

> Where slow Maeotis crawls, and scarcely flows
> The frozen Tanais through a waste of snows.

Where, like an anodyne for a gnawing pain, he tried to forget himself in verses and yet more verses, until he died.

What a world it is that he has created in the *Metamorphoses*! It draws its denizens from all the boundless resources of Greek mythology, a world of live forests and mountains and rivers, in which every plant and flower has a story, and nearly always a love story; where the moon is indeed not a moon but an orbèd maiden, and the Sunrise weeps because she is still young and her belovèd is old; and the stars are human souls; and the Sun sees human virgins in the depths of forests and almost swoons at their beauty and pursues them; and other virgins, who feel in the same way about him, commit great sins from jealousy and then fling themselves on the ground in grief and fix their eyes on him, weeping and weeping till they waste away and turn into flowers; and all the youths and maidens are indescribably beautiful and adventurous and passionate, though not well brought up, and, I fear, somewhat lacking in the first elements of self-control; and they all fall in love with each other, or, failing that, with fountains or stars or trees; and are always met by enormous obstacles, and are liable to commit crimes and cause tragedies, but always forgive each other, or else die. A world of wonderful children where nobody is really cross or wicked except the grown-ups; Juno, for instance, and people's parents, and of course a certain number of Furies and Witches. I think among all the poets who take rank merely as storytellers and creators of mimic worlds, Ovid still stands supreme. His criticism of life is very slight; it is the criticism passed by a child, playing alone and peopling the summer evening with delightful shapes, upon the stupid nurse who drags it off to bed. And that too is a criticism that deserves attention.

—from *Essays and Addresses* (1921)

Questions

1. Aside from the omnipresent theme of transformation, do you see an idea or argument or value that organizes the great variety of incidents and characters in the *Metamorphoses*?

2. It has recently been argued that ancient Greco-Roman religion as revealed in stories of gods and semi-divinities constitutes a religion more tough-minded and true to the disorder, tragedy, absurdity, and madness of human existence than the existing established religions. Do Ovid's stories support this argument? Do his stories seem more true to life than those of Christianity, Judaism, or Islam?

3. Is there any one of the stories in the *Metamorphoses* that strikes you especially as a parable of something recurrent in human life? If so, which one?

4. Can the *Metamorphoses* be read as a series of satires of today's attitudes, institutions, and practices? If so, what is it that they are saying?

Roman Culture and Society during Ovid's Lifetime

Adkins, Lesley, and Adkins, Roy A. *Handbook to Life in Ancient Rome*. New York and Oxford: Oxford University Press, 1994. Although sometimes prone to over-generalization, this is a lucid and complete guide to virtually every facet of Roman life, including both what was common to nearly every era of Roman history and what was specific to each period, including the Augustan.

Galinsky, Karl. *Augustan Culture: An Interpretive Introduction*. Princeton, NJ: Princeton University Press, 1996. This analytical survey of all areas of Roman culture in the time of Augustus presents an argument on the nature of Augustan culture as well as a descriptive account. Illuminating and stimulating for a scholarly audience, it is written in such a fashion that the nonexpert should also be able to follow it with relative ease.

Shelton, Jo-Ann. *As the Romans Did: A Sourcebook in Roman Social History*. Second edition. New York and Oxford: Oxford University Press, 1998. This extremely useful collection of documents reveals Roman attitudes toward the whole range of social phenomena, from family and entertainment to government and religion. While the texts come from all periods of Roman history, many especially illuminate the Augustan era.

Ovid and the Metamorphoses

Hardie, Philip, ed. *The Cambridge Companion to Ovid*. Cambridge: Cambridge University Press, 2002. This is unquestionably the best general critical volume on Ovid available—challenging and fascinating for the nonexpert, indispensable to serious undergraduate study of Ovid, and extremely valuable for leading the graduate student of the classics to fuller treatments of its myriad topics. Short, suggestive essays by the leading specialists in each field cover twenty different aspects of Ovid studies, many dealing largely or entirely with the *Metamorphoses*. The book also provides extensive bibliographies detailing both the history of Ovid criticism and the state of contemporary opinion.

Knox, Peter E. *Ovid's* Metamorphoses *and the Traditions of Augustan Poetry.* Cambridge: Cambridge Philological Society, 1986. This is an erudite discussion of the manner in which Ovid responds to his poetic forebears, though it can be rather hard going for the inexperienced reader (Latin quotations, for instance, are left untranslated).

McClure, Laura K., ed. *Sexuality and Gender in the Classical World.* Oxford and Malden, MA: Blackwell, 2002. This volume is valuable not only for its section on Roman women but for reprinting P. K. Joplin's essay "The Voice of the Shuttle Is Ours," a brilliant analysis of the Ovidian version of the story of Philomel that has become one of the foundational pillars of feminist theory.

Solodow, Joseph B. *The World of Ovid's* Metamorphoses. Chapel Hill: University of North Carolina Press, 1988. A somewhat difficult march for one unacquainted with the world of classical poetry, this work nevertheless presents a lucid and largely jargon-free interpretation of the epic's critique of traditional ideas of structure and order.

Tissol, Garth. *The Face of Nature: Wit, Narrative, and Cosmic Origins in Ovid's* Metamorphoses. Princeton, NJ: Princeton University Press, 1997. This discussion of the epic examines the manner in which the style of Ovid's poem reflects its overriding theme of transformation.

Wheeler, Stephen M. *A Discourse of Wonders: Audience and Performance in Ovid's* Metamorphoses. Philadelphia: University of Pennsylvania Press, 1999. This book focuses on the character of the poem as a fictitious oral performance—that is, a work that embeds the reactions of its ostensible audience into the work itself, as if it was listening to rather than reading the poem. Indebted to reader-response theory, it shows both the strengths and limitations associated with that school of criticism.

The Ancient Context: Analogs and Sources of the Metamorphoses

Apollodorus. *The Library of Greek Mythology*. Translated by Robin Hard. Oxford World's Classics. Oxford and New York: Oxford University Press, 1997. This handbook of the most familiar versions of the ancient myths was compiled in the first or second century C.E. and is narrated in a very plain, unadorned fashion. The contrast to Ovid's mode (and the many differences in detail between the two authors' versions of the tales themselves) is very illuminating.

Apuleius. *The Golden Ass*. Translated by E. J. Kenney. London and New York: Penguin, 1998. In the ancient world, this work of the second century C.E. was also known as the *Metamorphoses*; it offers a different approach to the epic of transformation than Ovid's.

Cicero. *The Nature of the Gods*. Translated by P. G. Walsh. Oxford World's Classics. New York: Oxford University Press, 1998. This is a first-century C.E. encapsulation of the attitudes an educated Roman might hold toward the nature of divinity and the validity of myths as historical accounts.

Hesiod. *The Theogony*. Translated by M. L. West. Oxford World's Classics. Oxford and New York: Oxford University Press, 1988. (Also includes *Works and Days*). Roughly contemporary with Homer (eighth century B.C.E.), Hesiod represents the earliest account of the origin and nature of the Greek Pantheon, and this work remained influential for many centuries. Explicitly misogynistic, it also offers the clearest impression of the nature of anti-female prejudices in the ancient world.

Lucretius. *On the Nature of Things*. Translated by R. E. Latham. London and New York: Penguin Books, 1994. From the first century

B.C.E., this rationalist's approach to epic offers a scientific examination of the question of origins, transformation, and history.

Virgil. *Aeneid*. Translated by Robert Fitzgerald. New York: Vintage, 1990. Commissioned by Augustus, this account of the voyage of Aeneas to found Rome appeared late in the first century B.C.E. and virtually defined the epic for Ovid's generation. The *Metamorphoses* carries on an almost continual dialogue with Virgil's poem.